DRESSED
for a Kill

BRIAN BIANCO

DRESSED FOR A KILL

This book is a work of fiction. The characters, names, incidents, dialogue and plot are the products of the author's imagination or are used fictitiously. Any resemblance to actual persons or events is purely coincidental.

ISBN – 978-0-9877420-1-8

Chapter 1

Maria Zimmerman sat on top of the stairs and stared blindly at the space in front of her. The suitcases were already waiting by the front door, which was partially open, waiting for the driver to come and take them. She was anxious to leave so she could get to Boston, which was three hours away, where she would board her flight to another city and vanish forever. It was the final link in her desperate attempt to disconnect herself from Eastbrook and a life that no longer existed. Maria refocused her eyes and checked her watch. She told herself to be patient. *He'll be here like he promised—just be patient.* Maria dabbed at her eyes and then drifted back to her dream while she waited for Jacob.

Just after one thirty in the afternoon, the black taxi slowed in the heavy rain and turned into the long driveway with the white picket fence. The driver slipped the vehicle into park and applied the brake, but before getting out, the driver paused and stared longingly at the house and then shook his head in disbelief. It had only been months, but for Jacob it was still hard to imagine how one family could be wiped from the face of the earth in such an incredibly short period of time. Since the time of the first incident, it was still hard to fathom how one family could be gutted like a fish and then the good parts thrown away as if they were of little value to anyone. Jacob could only imagine what it must feel like to have lost everything in the blink of an eye, but from all appearances, Maria had come out of it still intact, a survivor to anyone who saw her. To those who knew her, there was no doubt that the effects of what had happened to her family would last a lifetime, especially for Maria. As for Jacob, he too was still coming to terms with the two senseless murders and how one family could have suffered as much as the Zimmerman's did.

Jacob finally exited the taxi and hurried along the pebbled concrete slabs that led to the front door. He stopped on the wooden landing and shook the rain from his coat before brushing his hand through his curly hair when he noticed the partially open door.

"Maria."

He rapped on the door before pushing it open.

"Maria."

His voiced echoed through the empty foyer and up the stairs with his eyes in pursuit.

Maria wanted to linger there where it was safe, but when Jacob's voice called out to her a second time, the dream shattered like falling glass. Suddenly Maria felt the chill of a blustery autumn just beyond the open door as Joseph and the sound of the lawnmower disappeared along with the patio and the beautifully filled rooms behind her. Rachel was no longer at the lake with her friends. The blue sky along with the sun was gone. So was the lawn with its neat rows of freshly cut grass. Maria quickly shuddered and then tugged at the sweater that was draped over her shoulders.

"Are you okay?" he asked, stepping inside.

Startled, Maria quickly dabbed her eyes with the soft tissue. "Yeah, I'm fine, Jacob" she said dolefully.

"I must have caught you napping," he said. "You look a little surprised to see me."

"No. I didn't forget," she said without smiling back. "I was just thinking about them—that's all."

"You mustn't think too much, Maria. It's not good at

a time like this. It's best to be thinking about something else. It may be autumn," said Jacob, looking back through the door, "but this is, excuse my cussing, one hell of an ugly day. I hope you got something better to wear than just that there sweater. It's pouring buckets out here."

"In the closet," she said, pointing through the railing to the door in the hall. "My umbrella's in there, too."

"Would you like me to get them for you?" he asked, moving towards the door down the hall.

"No. Its okay, Jacob," she said. She stood and quickly checked her watch. "I think we should get going. If you want to take my bags, I'll get my coat and meet you at the car."

Jacob took the hint and stepped back towards the open door.

"I'll just go and put these in the cab then. I'll wait for you out there." He nodded and smiled at her and then took the bags and disappeared through the door.

Jacob watched the house and the rain while he waited for Maria. He knew it was hard to let go, but Maria finally emerged from the house and sat up front after locking the door and slipping the key under the mat. She studied the house and the yard as Jacob gently backed out of the driveway. From appearances, the place certainly looked neglected. The grass had grown as tall as a crop of barley. The flowerbeds were cluttered with twigs and branches from the previous winter storms. Dead and fallen leaves were strewn everywhere. The trees needed pruning. No time, she told herself, which wasn't true. She just didn't care. The For Sale sign was from Patriot Realty, which sat just inside the white picket fence. It had been spiked into the lawn less than a week ago. They would start showing the house in a couple of days, after the crew they hired cleaned up the yard. "But not till I'm gone," she told them. "You can send me the bill."

Maria watched as the house slowly disappeared behind the curve in the road. Emotions were building again. Jacob could hear her choking back the tears. The pain was back. From the corner of his eyes he watched as she nimbly placed her hand across the scar that ran across her throat that the doctors had stitched with great efficiency—but it was still noticeable.

"Are you alright?" he asked.

"I've tried so hard, Jacob. I've lain awake at night because I can't sleep, trying to recount what happened, but I just can't remember," she said, talking to the window. "I need to remember, Jacob—for Rachel's sake."

"It'll be okay, Maria," he said, patting her hand. "Everything's going to be just fine. They'll find them. And when they do, you'll get your justice. But now's not the time. Let's talk about something else."

"I'm sorry, Jacob." She turned and looked at him. Her eyes were blurry, drowning helplessly in a sea of tears. "I just miss them so much."

"I know, Maria. So do I." Jacob looked for the house in the rearview mirror. "So do I."

Chapter 2

EIGHT YEARS LATER…

Being inside a courtroom was nothing new to either Lionel Holt or his sidekick toady, David Masalla. They had been in front of the courts before for lesser crimes of drunk and disorderly, auto theft, unlawful confinement, and assault causing bodily harm, to name just a few. At ages thirty-one respectively, they had spent the better part of their adult life wandering through the state prison system—a year at the work camp in St. Anthony, four years at Cottonwood, and then nine more at Orofino with a little time off for good behavior. It had been a natural progression with little to show in the way of rehabilitation. But now they were dealing with something far more grievous than anything before, something much more heinous than any local could have ever imagined would happen in their little town—the rape and murder of two teens.

Bail was denied. The residents of Tweeksbury were still reeling from the brutality. Hostility towards the pair was visibly noticeable on the streets of the small town. "For your own safety and that of the community, you will be confined to the state institution at Cottonwood until trial," stated the judge.

In the year they spent at Cottonwood, aside from their attorneys, they had little in the way of visitors. Masalla was an orphan with no family. If he was expecting anyone, nobody came. Holt's mother had left him for a better life with a different man in a different state, so no visit was expected. He hadn't seen her since he was twelve. The aunt who took him in abandoned him when he was convicted and sent to St. Anthony. Lionel Holt barely knew his wealthy father. Benjamin Holt had little time for a wife and son, and so he contributed greatly to his family's demise. His thriving global business had become too large and too important, and as the years went by, it took most, if not all of his time. Except for the odd phone call and the one visit at Orofino and the other while he was held at Cottonwood, Lionel had seen little of Benjamin Holt in nineteen years. He would not be there when the trial started.

The trial had taken just over three weeks to complete. Deliberations had started on Thursday. Four days and three hours into Monday morning and the verdicts were ready. Court was set to reconvene at two o'clock in the afternoon.

Holt and Masalla sat quietly at one end of a long, mahogany table, saying very little in the way of what was about to happen, while their two lawyers, brought in and paid for by Lionel's wealthy father, conversed with each other. Holt looked noticeably loose and relaxed, the chip on his shoulder hidden somewhere in that veneer of a personality that could change at the slightest provocation. His chair was pointed in the direction of the half-filled gallery. His arms were folded across his chest, his legs stretched outward as he watched them pour in. He was smiling smartly to himself. They had come to watch him and Masalla get theirs, to pay for what they had done, which only made him smile more.

Masalla looked visibly thin in a suit that was now one size too big because in the past two weeks he had eaten little. His slightly sunken eyes darted to the clock above the empty judge's bench, watching as the seconds slowly ticked away. He breathed deeply. His eyes then stared fearfully at the empty juror's box across the courtroom.

He bit his lip and tried to keep his knees from shaking. His white shirt stuck to his skinny torso like a second layer of skin. Beads of sweat glistened along his hairline. Edgy, he peered over his left shoulder towards the open doors. The flow of people and their shuffling feet echoing around him was pushing him into a near panic. Anxious, he carefully patted his buttoned-down collar just to make sure it was still tight. The deep scratch marks on his cheek and at the base of his neck, once prominent during his and Holt's arraignment, were now healed, revealing only a slight pinkish discoloration of the skin. He checked the clock for a second time and then quickly refocused his small eyes on the open doors. The thought grazed his consciousness that if he moved now, he could make it through the doors and maybe to freedom. He felt his muscles stiffen.

Holt's dark eyes had drifted from the gallery moments earlier, distracted by Masalla's erratic behavior. His constant twitching like a second grader who couldn't sit still had caught his attention. Holt turned his chair towards his partner and slapped Masalla lightly on the shoulder. David Masalla shuddered as if he was asleep and turned quickly towards his partner. Holt stared at him. He didn't look so good.

"What's your problem?" he asked. "You worried? Is that it?"

Masalla hesitated like he was in another world, trying to collect his thoughts. He then pulled his chair closer to Holt and spoke in a whisper. He didn't want anyone to hear.

"Yeah, I'm worried." His voice cracked. "The jury's been out too bloody long."

Feeling the effects of the heat, Masalla reached over and filled one of the paper cups with the jug that sat on the table and gulped the water viciously.

"If they were gonna find us not guilty, it should've only taken a couple of hours, not four fuckin' days," Masalla said in a hushed snarl. He held up four fingers that shook and thrust them towards Holt's face.

Holt pushed his hand away, waving him off as if this was nothing.

It was a masterful plan, a brilliant piece of work planned and implemented by the wild man himself. According to how Holt saw it, they would be back on the sidewalks before the day was out, and there was nothing anybody could do about it. With no fingerprints and nothing to tie them to the slaughter, this charade was nothing more than a waste of time. The only mistake had been when Michelle King fought back and scratched Masalla's face and neck, but Holt had taken care of that by slicing off her hands at the wrist and then ditching the knife and the body parts where nobody could find them. As far as he was concerned, this was a sure thing—a lock, for Christ's sake! *Just play it cool, and everything will be alright.*

Holt quietly tore into him.

"Jesus Christ. Look at yourself. Get a grip, will ya," Holt said in a low, controlled voice. "No jury is going to believe the prosecution's crap! They can't convict." His voice broke. "Nothing they've said even puts us there. We're..."

Masalla drank again, gulping quickly, spilling some on his shirt before cutting him off.

"Will you lower your voice!" Masalla said in an angry hiss, glancing quickly at those up front. "They're gonna hear ya."

Brian Lee, who heard the mild commotion, turned towards his clients. He gripped the back of Vandenberg's chair and motioned for both men to keep it down. Holt nodded at Lee with a smirk, like he gave a damn before turning back towards Masalla. Lee, expecting nothing less from his uncooperative client, glared at him and then went back to talking to his partner.

"You worry too much," fired Holt.

Masalla stared at him with a look of disbelief at what he was hearing, almost shrugging his shoulders before hanging his head. What the hell was he talking about? The prosecution had attacked Holt's plan with a vengeance. An eyewitness had testified that they were seen talking to the girls the day they went hiking up by the lake. Holt hadn't planned on that. Masalla was convinced the prosecution had swayed the jurors—at the very least to cause enough doubt and send them away for good, that is if they didn't decide to kill them first using a firing squad.

He wiped the sweat from his forehead, thinking the worst like he had so many times in the past year while he sat idle in his cell, waiting for the trial to begin. If he hadn't been such a follower, he wouldn't be in this mess, but it was too late for that. Masalla could feel the dryness in his mouth once again. He had a headache, and his heart was thumping hard in his chest. He felt a heavy push on his shoulder.

"Just relax, will ya. Everything's gonna be all right." Holt patted Masalla's knee. "In a couple of hours we're gonna to be walking outta here." He propped his chair on two legs and poked his thumbs into his pockets. "You'll see," he said with a healthy grin.

Masalla turned back and peered over his shoulder towards the doors. He pursed his lips together and thought of his chances if he bolted for the doors while they were still open. Maybe he could make it while he still had the courage.

Five blocks away on the top floor of the four-story Tweeksbury Hotel, Miles Fischer lay dead to the world. He was an investigative reporter for the *Chicago Tribune* who had slept little the night before because of the heat, and with the jury still out he decided to take a nap. He left instructions with the clerk downstairs to wake him as soon as he heard the jury had reached a verdict.

Suddenly the phone rang, waking him from his sleep. Miles fumbled wildly for the receiver and pressed it neatly to his ear. He listened for about ten seconds, and then abruptly slammed it down.

From the window he could see the Clearwater County Courthouse and the manicured green lawns that surrounded it. It sat on an elevated piece of land alongside the library with a coffee shop next door. The old courthouse was surrounded by parked cars as if it were under siege. People the size of ants were converging on the grounds from all corners. Fischer cursed the dumb-ass clerk for not waking him sooner and quickly headed for the door. Five minutes and six blocks later he was standing at the back of the long line, trying to catch his breath.

"How's the lineup today?" he asked the couple in front of him.

"Slower than usual," said the man in his midsixties. "It looks like the whole town closed up just to be here."

Miles shoved his hands in his pockets and took a look behind him. There were already ten others standing next to him, and more were coming.

"I guess it's going to be another packed house."

"Looks like it."

After ten minutes of on and off conversations with

those around him, Miles finally made it to the front of the line and through the open doors, past the armed guards that were there waiting with metal detectors.

Fischer had been there for the past three weeks, covering the trial of the brutal rape and murder of two teens found in the national park just outside of Tweeksbury. The girls were strung up by their feet and then left to hang there like bats. Their throats had been slashed. Every cavity had been filled with drain cleaner and then doused with bleach to destroy the evidence.

Miles quickly removed himself from the crowd just past the doors and found a half-empty bench in the back. A man in his fifties followed seconds later and sat next to him. Miles looked at him rather suspiciously. *What was this man thinking,* he thought. It had to be close to a hundred degrees in here.

He was dressed like a farmer. He wore a plaid shirt with long sleeves that was buttoned at the neck coupled with a pair of blue denim overalls and heavy boots. Miles shook his head in disbelief. Aside from a few portable fans in front and a couple of open windows overhead, there was nothing available to circulate the hot, dead air. The outdated courtroom had no air-conditioning.

A potato farmer instantly came to mind. Idaho was famous for its potatoes. Miles expected a greeting of sorts—possibly a nod, a how-do-you-do, maybe even a handshake. Farmers were known for being friendly, but not this farmer. Without so much as looking his way, the farmer quickly slid his hands under his heavily stained armpits and looked straight ahead in the direction of the defendants.

At just past two, the double doors began to close. Masalla watched from his seat as the two guards closed and then stood with their backs to the doors. Masalla's shoulders gave way as his chest quickly emptied. Suddenly he felt his stomach tighten. Any lingering thoughts of bolting from the courtroom had all but evaporated along with his false belief that somehow he would actually do it. It had been nothing more than deception, a wild dream because David Masalla had neither the fortitude, nor the courage to carry it through. David Masalla had always been a coward, a coward who now realized he wasn't going anywhere.

"All rise. This court is now in session. The Right Honorable Judge Reinhold presiding."

A tall, thin figure in a black robe with ghostly white hair suddenly appeared from nowhere and quietly took his seat. A gentle hush slowly permeated through the crowd as all eyes watched from the gallery and the adjoining walls. Reinhold, who was sixty-seven, studied them with a quiet nervousness. Against his better judgment, he had acquiesced to their wishes, allowing the citizens of Tweeksbury to pack the courthouse. From his elevated bench he could already see the uneasiness on their faces. Choosing to err on the side of caution, he had order two more guards be added for security in case all hell broke loose. Somewhat apprehensive, he slowly opened his court. He spoke loudly so he could be heard over the large fans that were positioned in the far corners on either side of where he now sat.

"Good afternoon, ladies and gentlemen. For those of you who are left standing, the court wishes to remind you that you are here at the invitation of this court, as are those of you who were lucky enough to find a seat," he said, staring down from the bench. "Because of the nature of these proceedings, I expect each and every one of you to conduct yourself accordingly and to act within the rules I put forth in the preceding days. Emotions are

14

running high, and because of the seriousness of this crime, I expect each and every one of you to remain in your seats. Or in your case," he added, looking to the back wall, "to remain where you are until the court has adjourned. Otherwise, I will be forced to clear my court." He paused for effect, allowing his threat to resonate through the courtroom. "I hope I have made myself clear." With nothing to add, Reinhold motioned for the bailiff to summon the jurors.

Twelve jurors entered from a side door leading into the small jury box. They were of mixed age and gender. Reinhold studied them carefully, waiting for them to settle in before addressing the foreman.

"Have you reached a verdict?"

"We have, Your Honor."

Reinhold quietly read what was written on the slip of paper before quietly handing it back to the bailiff, who handed it back to the foreman. He turned to the table where Holt and Masalla were seated.

"Will the defendants please rise and face the jury."

Fischer had researched both of their backgrounds and written lengthy articles on the lives of both men, but Holt's quick departure from his chair caught him completely off guard. He wondered if anyone else had noticed it. He squeezed forward and watched intently as Holt calmly clasped his hands in front of him. *Is that a smile? Jesus Christ! The son-of-a-bitch is looking forward to this.* He looked for Masalla as a small ripple moved through the courtroom. Reinhold would have scowled at them, but he was preoccupied. He stared intently in the direction of David Masalla, waiting on him.

The shorter David Masalla hadn't moved. He was glued to his seat, unable or unwilling to rise to his feet as requested. It seemed like minutes, but under the glaring eye of Reinhold—not to mention the prodding of his lawyers—Masalla finally pried himself loose. He stood like a man headed for the gallows. He was slightly bent at the knees and the waist. His shoulders were partially slumped. He rubbed his sweaty palms against his jacket and held the edges to keep his hands from shaking. Reinhold continued to glare at Masalla before finally turning to the foreman.

"Mr. Foreman, would you please read your verdict to the court?"

Masalla tensed up like a brick and quickly pinched his eyes shut and held his breath.

"We, the jury, find the defendant, David Masalla, not guilty on both counts of rape and murder in the first degree with respect to the two victims, Michelle King and Heather Burton."

Masalla, trembling noticeably, stumbled backward against his chair. The shock of the verdict had caused his muscles to go limp. Air exploded from his chest.

Behind him, moans and groans hastily trickled through the rows. Short, quick stares exchanged across the aisle way. Like sprouts, people began to pop randomly from their seats. Those standing along the back wall bristled openly with contempt. All hell was about to break loose.

George King, upset with the verdict, bolted recklessly from his seat in the third row behind the prosecution. He pushed rudely through the long legs and bent knees, keeping his eyes focused where Holt and Masalla stood. If he got that far, he intended to strangle Masalla in front of the judge. Damn the consequences!

From the doors, the guards strayed in the direction of the seated gallery. From the fifth row, two elderly couples opted to leave in the confusion rather than stay. To the right of Fischer, three more headed for the exit. To his left, he watched the potato farmer, who was sweating profusely, jump from his seat. He gripped the back of the bench and glared noticeably in the direction Holt and Masalla before making his way down the row, past Fischer, towards the aisle before heading for the doors.

Masalla, shocked back to life, caught a glimpse of the rogue bull coming his way before quickly cowering behind the taller Holt. From the perimeter, people pointed at the oncoming King. Fischer quickly jumped to his feet.

Reinhold was already standing. He glared at the chaos in front of him and clubbed the wooden block violently. "Order!"

The call went unheeded.

From the side wall, two deputies bolted and intercepted King before he could reach the defendants' table. With two hands, one pulled on King's outstretched hand like a one-armed bandit, sending him into a spin, and then locked his arm behind his back. The other quickly grabbed his left forearm and forced his right hand underneath his armpit, almost lifting him from the floor. In seconds they brought the larger King under control in the aisle way between the rows. Somewhat sympathetic to his plight, they gently ushered him through the double mahogany doors into one of the small rooms off the hall.

"Order in this courtroom!" The gavel exploded onto the wooden block.

Reinhold stood there and scowled at the chaos. His large blue eyes had already narrowed above his thick brows. He glared through his wire frames as the ruckus showed signs of receding. It was tempting to show them the power he had by finding them all in contempt, but instead, Reinhold waited on them. As their will crumbled, he slowly panned the room, looking for any idiot who had the guts to ignore him.

Masalla stood sheepishly but kept his cowardly eyes peeled to the floor. He stood in back of Holt this time, as if trying to hide in case the jury decided to change their minds.

"This despicable conduct will not be tolerated in my courtroom," yelled the judge, still wanting to let off a little steam. "Do I make myself clear? If there are any more outbursts, just the tiniest bit of an outbreak, I will clear my courtroom," he growled angrily. "Do you understand?"

The short lecture and intimidating stare droned on for what seemed like a full minute. Most, if not all, kept their eyes on the bench. Some nodded, thinking they would be spared if Reinhold decided to carry out his threat.

"Mr. Foreman, if you're ready."

The foreman nervously cleared his throat and then continued. "We, the jury, find the defendant, Lionel Holt, not guilty on both counts of rape and murder in the first degree with respect to the two victims, Michelle King and Heather Burton." With that said, the foreman quickly took his seat.

Judge Reinhold glanced over his shoulder toward the gallery. If they challenged him in the slightest, he would pounce on them.

Lionel Holt smiled crookedly and nodded his head slightly before turning back towards Masalla. He winked at him, uncaring about the gallery, out of view of the jury who had just set them free.

Reinhold turned to the jurors. "Is this the true will of the jury?"

In fractured unison they replied, "It is, Your Honor."

"Does the prosecution wish to solicit the individual

vote of the respective jurors?"

A dumbfounded Tom Fletcher stood and hesitated and then replied in a calm but stunned voice, "No, Your Honor." He took his seat.

Reinhold scribbled a couple of notes on his legal pad before swiveling his chair towards the jury. It was the same speech he had given a hundred times or more in the same dry tone. When he was finished thanking them, he looked over at the defendants.

"In accordance with the law of this state and the will of this court, you are hereby released. This case is closed. Court is adjourned." He cracked his gavel on the wooden block.

"All rise," shouted the bailiff.

The words mixed and echoed with that of the gavel and the people as they rose to their feet. On cue, Reinhold, disgruntled with what was probably his last court, turned his chair towards his chambers, grabbed the folder, and disappeared through the door.

The courtroom erupted again as soon as Reinhold left the room. The jurors were the first to leave. It took only seconds for the last one to reach the door and disappear. Fischer stayed seated, willing to wait in the hot air while he finished writing what had just taken place. Those on the bench next to him had already left. Half the benches in front were now empty. Behind him, he could hear their angry discussions as they waited in the crowd for their turn to exit for the cooler air outside. In the aisle way, some spectators stood and stared as the two men shook the hands of their big city attorneys before turning in disgust and making their way to the back. Holt, resonating with smug joy, hugged his friend, patting him on the back before escaping the smaller Masalla's embrace, pushing him away to where they were at arm's length.

"What did I tell you?" queried a cocky Holt. "I told you they couldn't convict us," he said, his voice sure of himself. "There was no way in hell. No way!" he stated in a loud, halting tone. "We're walking outta here."

Masalla pushed back the wet strands of black hair that stuck to his sticky forehead. A weak smile slid across his pale face.

"Yeah, just like you said."

Chapter 3

The Foxhole sat on the edge of Tweeksbury, the last building on a dead-end road. It had stood there for sixty-eight years, a converted warehouse, sharing a common dirt parking lot with the second of two local hardware stores. The faded brown exterior exhibited a single, double window to the left of the only steel door leading down wooden steps to a dirt curb, the sidewalk having ended at the hardware store some hundred feet away. It wasn't high-class, but neither was the clientele.

They sat at a small, circular table in the northwest corner. Behind them, signs of neon bristled with advertisements for Budweiser and Miller Lite along the back wall. They had been there since late afternoon, having waited since Monday for the heat to die down. They drank longnecks by the bushel and played pool on the tables just across from where they now sat, filling in the dead spots with obnoxious comments toward every female who dared walk by. For some reason, nobody challenged them. What friends they had had all but disappeared, evaporating into thin air from the time of their arrest to their surprising acquittal. They entered wearing the same cowboy boots and faded denim jeans as the ones they had worn on the day of their arrest and the last time they were seen at the Foxhole—such was the state of their bravado. The state would not appeal a case they could not win.

Holt butted his cigarette and slapped another fifty on the table. He whistled loudly to the front, standing unsteady in a haze of blue and gray smoke that hovered just above his head, motioning with his hand for another round for him and Masalla.

Minutes later, a waitress stood in the dim light to the

right of the two men, cradling her tray that carried two more beers and two Jack Daniel's shooters. Across the room, diagonally from her right, was the only side door that opened to a dirt parking lot. Two old, rustic pool tables sat quietly in between on the wooden floor. From the bare rafters hung twin, stained glass shades coated in a layer of thick dust. A broken-down shuffleboard rested along the south wall, next to the jukebox that played tunes from the sixties. Past the side door and beyond that was the protruding end of the bar where Jimbo, the owner, poured drinks and held lookout from the half-moon mirror he had nailed to the rafters just above the bar. Only three windows graced the architecture of the Foxhole: the one in the front and one on each side of the northwest corner where Holt and Masalla now sat alone. All were decorated with iron bars.

Outside, lightning flashed brilliantly, illuminating the small corner, followed by thunder soon after. Within seconds, rain started to spatter against the north side window. It was a welcome relief since it hadn't rained in over a month, but neither one noticed. They were too involved in celebrating their wrenching of the legal system and getting too drunk to care. Besides, something else now caught their eye. Two couples sitting nearby were just leaving. They had decided to give up their night out after Holt and Masalla started harassing their women. Rather than offer up some resistance, they headed for the door.

Tammy placed the drinks on the table and then took a step back.

"That'll be nine dollars and fifty cents."

Holt pulled the bill off the table and held it firmly, waiting for Tammy to come and get it. A smile slid across his face. Masalla sat to his left and drank his Bud and quietly watched his friend. They hunted as a pack. Holt led and Masalla followed. Routine.

"Now you're a pretty young thing," said Holt with a noticeable slur. "Are you new, or have I just been away for a while?" He looked at his friend and smiled, seemingly amused by his own wit. He took a large gulp from his longneck and stared at the long legs extending past the short leather skirt standing just to his right. Masalla snickered cruelly in the background.

At age twenty-five, she had been serving drinks for close to four years in rundown bars in small towns just like Tweeksbury. From Prineville to Oskaloosa, she had served every kind of barfly imaginable. She had heard every pickup line, come-on, and one-liner that was ever dreamt and conceived by every loudmouth bar jerk across five states, but Lionel Holt and his little friend were more than just a couple of bar jerks. They were also predators who preyed on women—killers who had gotten lucky and beaten the system. As wily a veteran of the bar scene as she was, the sight of Holt and Masalla sitting across from where she stood made her feel a little uneasy.

She moved closer to the table, cautious of the man in front of her and took hold of the note but said nothing when Holt didn't let go. Predators were something to be wary of. Getting into it with the likes of someone like Lionel Holt was not a good thing.

Masalla took this as his cue. He leaned on his good buddy with his right shoulder. "What time you get off, honey?" he asked. The coward dragged on his half-finished cigarette and then leaned on the table before blowing the gray smoke out in her direction, past Holt, up towards her face. He spoke in stops and starts, slurring his words. "We're kinda new in town, and well—we're looking for some fun 'til something better comes along."

He laughed bravely, his performance in court just days ago all but forgotten.

Tammy glared at him, trying to evade the smoke, but she said nothing in return. Along with Holt, she ignored him as if he didn't exist. With no acknowledgement, Masalla quietly wilted back into his seat.

Holt pulled on it a little tighter, calmly sipping his beer, waiting for a reaction. Masalla, still hurt, glared at her from his seat.

Tammy thought of walking away because this was just the kind of game jerks played. She could leave and stand next to Jimbo until they left. Forget the money. Let Jimbo handle it. Tammy pulled in a deep breath before expelling it from her lungs.

"Are you going to let go?"

"Yeah, sure, darlin'. Whatever ya say."

Holt took another gulp and then slowly released his grip. He pulled a lighter from his pocket and lit a cigarette. Tammy quickly placed the change on the edge of the table next to him.

"Thanks, darlin'."

Eager to leave, she reached in and quickly gathered the empty bottles and glasses. She turned from the table and headed for the bar.

"Now where ya sneaking off to? We haven't finished with ya yet."

Holt pulled awkwardly at the barmaid's short skirt with his right hand. She turned quickly, almost pulling him from his chair, which sent the bottles teetering. Two fell onto the wooden floor. She was lucky. They were still intact.

"Seems I put the scare into ya," he said with a short snicker. "You'll have to forgive me," he said, watching her pick them up. "I haven't been out of the house for a while." He looked over at his friend, and both of them began to laugh. She stood without so much as a word and went to leave.

"Now hold on there, sweetness. Aren't ya forgetting something?" Like it was contrived, Holt casually poured one of the Jack Daniel's over the table. "Ya don't expect us to drink from this here dirty table, do ya?"

Tammy momentarily froze and glared at him. Nervous, she looked to the bar, but Jimbo had his back to her.

"What's the matter, darlin'?"

Tammy could feel the tension in the pit in her stomach. She told herself to stay calm. *It's not worth a scene. Just wipe the table and leave.*

Leery, she moved back towards the table, between the two men but as far away from Holt as she could get before applying a damp cloth to the surface.

Masalla drank steadily from his chair, watching Holt maneuver, watching her large breasts gyrate with the sweeping motion of her hand. The way Holt could manipulate women always fascinated him, but then again, Masalla was almost an idiot.

"Yeah, darling," said Holt, watching her hips move. "No doubt you heard. We know how to show a girl a good time, if you know what I mean."

"Make that two girls," interrupted Masalla with a bulging grin.

Amused, the two drunks slapped each other, breaking into uncontrollable heavy laughter. By the side door, a young couple was already on their way out. They turned and looked back in their direction, and then quickly left.

"There," Tammy said in a rather irritated tone. "Are we happy now?"

"Not yet, darlin'." Holt smartly flicked the ashtray to

the edge of the table and smiled at her.

"Think ya can please the two of us?" he continued. He jerked his head towards his friend.

His harsh remarks were getting bolder, more brazen than before, which made the blonde hair on the back of her neck stand up. She froze for that split second where she thought of telling him off but her mounting fear of Holt stopped her so she begrudgingly did what she was asked. *Besides,* she thought. *It would only take a second and then she would be gone.*

She quickly reached in and hastily emptied the ashtray into a large can that sat on her tray.

Masalla, noticing the look on her face, was quick to join in.

"I'll bet you got a tight one," he said. Masalla rose from his seat and sniffed the air like a wolf. "Man, I can smell it from here. Smells yummy."

Tammy was used to the usual bar sniping, the crude remarks, but not this foul crap. Fed up, she carelessly flung the ashtray across the table to where it slid off the edge. Then, almost by instinct, she grabbed the cloth and threatened Masalla. Holt grinned from his chair.

"How would you like it if I stuffed this filthy rag into that dirty mouth of yours?"

Stunned, David Masalla quickly retreated. He sank into his seat and said nothing.

"That don't sound like a heck of a lot of fun there, darlin'," interrupted Holt. "But I sure know what I would like to put in yours."

Holt eased his body from the chair, weaving like stiffened gelatin before grabbing at his crotch. He laughed. David Masalla, feeling brave again, joined in.

Angry, Tammy grabbed her tray and left. In the background, she could hear the two men laughing out loud as she made her way to the front and the security of Jimbo.

Jimmy Mack was way ahead of her. From behind the bar he had heard the raunchy dialogue. He had watched them closely in the mirror above the bar. He now wandered over to the corner where Holt was still standing.

Jimbo leaned heavily on the table with both hands, causing it to creak. The grayish, white sleeves were rolled up to the elbows. His forearms were thick and muscular. His dull, salt-and-pepper ponytail clung to his back along his spine, between his two hulking shoulders. He stared at Holt with his one good eye and ignored Masalla. A patch made of black leather covered the empty eye socket.

"I think you boys have had enough," he said. "Why don't you finish up what you're drinking and head on home?"

Holt took a long sip of his beer and held his arms out to his sides like he had done nothing wrong. He then cooed like a pigeon. "What's the fuss, Jimbo? Can't a couple of guys have some fun?"

"Not here. Not tonight." Jimbo stayed leaning on the table, staring straight at Holt.

Holt turned from the cold stare and looked at Masalla.

"Well, I believe we've just bin cut off. Guess we'll just leave this fine fuckin' establishment and find ourselves some fun somewhere else," he stated, again slurring his words.

Jimbo slowly straightened up and stepped back from the table. Lightning struck again, only closer, slightly illuminating the three men.

Unconscious of the weather just beyond the window, Holt slowly pushed himself up from his chair, wavering gently from side to side before gingerly placing his cigarette in the ashtray. Conspicuously unstable, he slowly gulped what was left of his beer, dripping part of it on his half-open shirt. Masalla, for his part, did what he was told. He quickly picked up his beer, drained what was left with a single swallow, shot the whiskey into his mouth, and then butted out what was left of his cigarette. Content with the outcome, Jimbo headed back to his post behind the bar.

Holt grabbed his burning cigarette from the ashtray and staggered in a diagonal line toward the side door on the other side of the room, heading out to the dirt parking lot with Masalla weaving in pursuit, their cowboy boots scuffing hard against the wooden floor.

"Let's go get somethin' to eat," suggested Masalla, tugging at his pants.

The peanuts and bar food from earlier in the day had left him famished. The absence of food in his stomach always made him jittery to the point where he would shake. Though not visible, he was shaking now.

Holt reached for the handle but could not resist the pleasure of one last piece of one-way dialogue with the upset barmaid. Shouting from the doorway, he leaned on the door heavily and glared in her direction as she stood at the corner of the bar. Jimbo stood calmly on the other side, amongst the bottles and glasses, leaning his big frame on the counter next to her, his head tilted, watching in the half-moon mirror. Holt flashed his slanted smile, exposing his beige teeth.

"See ya, darling. See all of ya later."

Holt laughed loudly before flinging the metal door outward hard. The two predators then stumbled into the low light and onto the small platform outside.

The only light illuminating the stairs was a single bulb that was positioned just above the door, casting their shadows down three steps to the ground below. Holt, still laughing and ahead of Masalla, was the first to feel and react to the weather, which quickly darkened his mood. He cursed harshly.

"Fuckin' rain!"

Holt tugged at the collar of his plaid shirt to shield his skin from droplets that fell from the edge of the small overhang above the door. He dug deep into his right pocket, searching for his keys. The pelting rain had a slightly sobering effect on both men as they made their way down the stairs, towards Holt's pickup parked against the wall of the hardware store, opposite the doorway from which they had just come. Both men had trouble as they navigated their way towards the pickup, the mixture of booze and mud making it a slow trek. Masalla was the first to feel it.

He took what sounded like a hard gulp. He stopped with a startled jerk from the searing pain and hastily looked down at his muscle undershirt. Shock and terror quickly overcame him. His eyes grew wide to where they almost exploded. His jaw hung open, and he began to stammer. Feeling faint, he sucked in a quick, stuttering breath and then clutched at his chest. His hands were coated in blood. His muscles quickly stiffened. He looked up and stared ahead through the downpour, at the back of Holt. He tried to speak but almost choked. Within seconds his legs buckled and then collapsed beneath him, forcing him heavily to his knees. His muscles locked, and he gasped for air. He gurgled twice through the blood that was collecting in his throat and then fell dead onto his pale shadow.

Holt turned when a dead Masalla hit the soggy ground with a heavy splat. He stood frozen in a large puddle, the silt and water seeping into his white alligator boots. Holt's drunkenness started to wane, giving rise to a sobriety there was little time for. In a state of shock, dazed and confused from the alcohol, Holt's cigarette dropped from his gaping mouth. He was stunned, like some forest animal in a set of oncoming headlights before impact. It washed over him in an instant, clogging his head, pressurizing it to where it wanted to explode. His heart had already accelerated. He felt sick. He turned quickly towards his pickup, fumbling with the keys, his eyes bulging with terror. The alligators slipped as he peddled hard, searching for safety.

Like Masalla before him, he never saw or heard it either. The aluminum arrow pierced his soaked shirt, close to his heart, shredding muscle and ripping arteries. Blood spurted instantly like an open spigot. Out of control, his body jerked forward. He clutched at his chest where the arrow should have been. Blood filled his hands. He staggered two more steps and then toppled over. Seconds later, he lay still.

From the roof of the hardware store, the lone figure quickly admired the silhouettes of the two men lying in the slick mud, the empty crossbow limp at its side. Holt and Masalla lay dead in the faint light, pelted by the rain, caught between the L-shaped backdrop of the Foxhole and the red brick of the hardware store. Across the yard, the two sleek black arrows with their black and yellow fletching were stuck in the mud, close to the building the two men had just exited seconds ago. From the rooftop, it was better than anything imagined.

"*Necessitas non habet legem.*" Necessity has no law.

Content, the wings were quickly unlocked and folded. The crossbow was then hooked onto a leather strap, high on the inside of the dark trench coat alongside the four remaining arrows. The enigma then slipped over the side of the store and into the back alley and what was left of the night. It had been worth the wait.

Chapter 4

Friday morning. Fischer was on the West Coast and waiting for the elevator, working on an assignment that really wasn't his. Patrick Lynch, his editor, had caught him early on Thursday morning. He had been gazing out the window, drinking the only cup of coffee he allowed himself. There was the familiar tap on the glass and the "have you got a moment" comment, and when he turned around, there Pat was. There was to be a change of plans, which irked him. Mahaffey was not coming in. He was being rushed into the emergency room to have his appendix removed after it exploded in his gut. Mahaffey came within an hour of lying in a morgue, and the rest of the staff was spared from attending another funeral.

Thirty-two interviews in twenty-one major cities split between three reporters. This was the twenty-sixth interview on successful women in business, from the country's top CEOs to those who had started and maintained a healthy, successful business. It was a story that could not wait for a fit Mahaffey. "I've got no one else, Miles." It had taken seven unsuccessful calls over the previous six weeks before the eighth one paid off and the interview was confirmed. Mahaffey had told Pat and he told Miles that she sounded like a bitch. "Be careful and watch what you say," said Pat. Fischer had looked at him with a scowl. He had little interest in the movie business, never mind interviewing the owner of a company that did makeup artistry but Pat cut him off before he could tell him what he thought of the trifling assignment. "There are no options on this, Miles."

Fischer stood to the rear of the elevator and waited for the others to enter. The wet umbrella, which he had borrowed from the hotel clerk, sat in the corner to his right against the steel wall. He was headed for the sixteenth floor for the second time in four hours and a meeting with "the bitch." He had arrived just before ten thirty and was told by her receptionist that his subject was running late but was expected to be there at around two. Ms. Joffe mentioned something about a sudden vacation and the office having to close for three weeks. This was her first day back, so everything was behind schedule—of course. "It's to be expected," stated the calm voice. He was hardly listening after he heard the word "late." The receptionist asked if he could come back in the afternoon—if he wasn't too busy. He stared at Ms. Joffe, cursing the nowhere-to-be-seen Paletti under his breath. His time was valuable. Or maybe "the bitch" didn't care. Then he reminded himself, *It was to be expected.*

Miles thanked her and accepted the invitation to return. He had over three hours to kill. He milled about, browsing the curious, exclusive shops and brand-name stores before taking in lunch at one of the bars just three blocks from her office. A Mariners ball game played on the overhead screen while he ate a small steak and drank two Cokes. He strolled along the streets smoking cigarettes under his umbrella before pressing the button for the sixteenth floor a second time. Fischer followed the painted chair rail down the wide corridor before walking through the single glass door for Two-Faced Productions, Inc.

"So nice you could make it back," said Ms. Joffe.

Joffe wasn't much to look at. At sixty-three, her best years were behind her. Her skin was pale. Her small, brown eyes matched her small face. Age spots dotted her soft temples. Her hair deadened her appearance even more. It was a dull brown with thick gray streaks pulled tightly behind her head and knotted. She wore a white blouse with a long skirt.

"I expect her any minute. Would you like to wait in her office?"

It sounded like a good plan since it was the best he had done all day, aside from lunch. His first attempt never got him past Ms. Joffe.

"You can put your umbrella over there if you like." Joffe pointed to the brass umbrella stand just to the left of the door, next to the brass coat rack. It contained one, which meant Paletti was not even in the building yet.

"Make yourself comfortable." From the open door, she pointed to the chairs in front of Paletti's desk. It was almost three times the size of Ms. Joffe's, painted in equal parts of fresh fern and the color of a mushroom. The thick carpet was dark green. "She should be here any minute."

"Thanks."

Miles watched her small, stunted frame walk the short hall and then disappear to her right. So much for what he had in mind: a quick interview and a hasty departure. With time to waste and Joffe gone, he decided to cruise.

He stepped over to his left where a massive oak desk was just back of center from the rest of the room. Three full-length windows to the left brought in light from the outside. A shiny gold nameplate said this was the desk of Anita Paletti. He studied the framed lithographs of Hollywood movies that hung on the large wall behind the desk separated by a single door. Curious, he tried the door but found it locked. He moved to his right, close to the entrance. Two black pole lamps radiated light from opposite corners. A green leather sofa with a complementary coffee table sat in front. Behind the sofa was a table with a fake plant and two pictures. He quietly knelt on the sofa. One picture of vampires and dead souls had a plaque glued to its base. He picked it up and read the inscription. "Congratulations on a job well done." It was dated 1993.

"Can I get you a coffee or something?"

Jesus Christ! Joffe scared the hell out him. She was standing just inside the door.

Miles spun and locked his eyes on the small woman before nervously clearing his throat.

"No. No, thank you. I'm fine thanks." He quickly pulled himself from the sofa. "Any word yet on Mrs. Paletti?" Impatient, he looked at his watch hoping she would get the message. Joffe was stalling.

"She should be here any minute, and I must correct you. It's Ms. Paletti. No Mrs.," she said, shaking her finger.

Miles took the center seat and studied the pictures on the wall. Five minutes later, he checked his watch. It was just past two thirty.

"Hi. I'm Anita Paletti, and you must be Roger Mahaffey from the *Tribune*." She stood just behind him to his right and held out her right hand.

Christ! Not again.

His upper torso did a quick shiver like it had been dipped in ice water. The thick carpeting had completely muffled the sound of her steps, allowing her to sneak up on him. He stood quickly from his chair and turned as her scent came towards him.

"Good afternoon. I'm Miles Fischer from the *Tribune*. Roger couldn't make it."

"I'm sorry," she said with a soft smile. "I didn't mean to startle you."

They shook hands. She then left him there, turning back towards the door. She asked about his flight, and he replied it was good, meaning it was safe, as she hung her coat on a hanger and pinned it on the hook behind the door. He took his seat while she slid behind her desk. She looked a little tired for someone who had been on vacation.

"Could you excuse me for a moment?" She picked up the receiver and pressed a button. After issuing instructions to Ms. Joffe, Paletti put the receiver down, saying, "I hope it's nothing too serious that Mr. Mahaffey couldn't make it?"

He downplayed the appendicitis. If he was going to do the quick interview, he certainly didn't want to waltz with Paletti on the state of Mahaffey's health.

"Just a little appendicitis," he responded. "Nothing too serious."

If first impressions were an indication of a person's personality then Roger Mahaffey had her all wrong. She did not sound anything like a bitch, and she certainly did not look like one. Her eyes were large, chestnut in color, and she had lips that almost pouted. Her hair was jet black and cut short in a trendy style. Her frame was slender, athletic by all appearances.

"I'm sorry to hear that," she said with a note of sadness. "When you get back to Chicago, tell him I send my best wishes for a speedy recovery."

"I'll make sure I tell him."

"Now." She slapped her desk with both hands. She looked eager. "Sorry I'm late. I had some business that I had to attend to." She didn't mention the vacation. "I hope I didn't inconvenience you too much. I know we've had some difficulty arranging this interview, so I hope I haven't kept you waiting too long. Did Abigail offer you something to drink?"

"Abigail?"

"Yes. Ms. Joffe. My receptionist."

"Oh, yes. Yes, she did." He said this with a nervous chuckle. It broke the stiffness he felt for staring at her. The information Pat had given him said she was forty-three. She looked much younger—at least ten years younger. He immediately thought of a facelift. *Paletti must have spent her Caribbean vacation in the shade*, he thought. There was no hint of a tan. "Sorry. I didn't know her first name was Abigail."

"That's quite all right. Mr. Fischer, is it?"

"Yes, but you can call me Miles."

She opened the top drawer and removed two white pills from a small vial. "Forgive me. I'm just a little excited for some reason. When I get this way, I find it hard to concentrate on things. Sometimes I can't even remember what I did five minutes ago," she said with a short chuckle.

There was a tap on the door. Ms. Joffe placed a tall glass of clear water just short of the green blotter and then quietly disappeared back through the open door. Anita tossed back the pills and drank from the glass.

"Okay. Miles it is. And you can call me Anita. So, how do we get started?"

"Well, if you don't mind, I brought a tape recorder along." Miles reached into his pocket. "I don't know how familiar you are with giving interviews, but it's easier this way than scratching notes on a pad. This way, nothing gets missed."

Miles placed the small black machine with its mini tape on the edge of the green blotter and pressed the button prematurely.

"Good news?"

Silence

"Good news? You said you were excited. I assume

it's good news regarding your business, and since I'm here to report on a successful businesswoman..."

Paletti quickly leaned over and pressed the off button. "I didn't think good reporters assumed anything." Her tone was now cold and defensive, her voice almost gruff. Her eyes narrowed. "I thought reporters investigated before jumping to conclusions." She stared intently into a set of deep blue eyes. "Is that your style, Mr. Fischer?"

"No, not at all," said Miles rather defensively. He sensed a little of the "bitch" was present, making him slightly uncomfortable. *I guess Roger was right after all*, he said to himself.

Miles settled back in his chair, shrugging off the fact that he had made a rookie's mistake. He was bored with the assignment, not to mention the long wait, and in a hurry to leave.

Anita shifted her mood and smiled, and then turned the recorder back on, her tone melting as her hand slid from the tape recorder.

"That's good to hear, Miles."

"Can we start?"

She nodded, slipping a roguish smile over her lips.

Miles checked his watch and then leaned over and pushed the off button.

"Are we finished?" she asked.

He nodded. "Yes, unless you have something you want to add?"

"No. I think we covered everything. When will they be putting this to print?"

"I don't know exactly." Miles took the black recorder and slipped it back into his pocket. "I'll get somebody from the department to give you a call the day before it goes to print."

"That'll be fine." They shook hands across her desk. "Can I get Abigail to call you a cab?"

"If it's not a bother."

Anita escorted him to the front desk, where she instructed Joffe to call for a cab to take Miles back to his hotel. They shook hands and Anita left.

Miles waited outside, away from the doors leading into the building with the collar of his white shirt turned up, watching the heavy downpour spatter against the pavement. The temperature had dropped, and it felt cold out. Summer in the Northwest could be so unpredictable at times. Minutes later a taxi rolled to the curb.

"Where to?" the cabbie asked.

"Pacific Hotel."

Miles quickly folded the umbrella and then dropped into the backseat and closed the door. His flight was for seven. He would grab a bite to eat at the airport while he waited to board. He would neglect the papers. He would read about them Monday morning.

Chapter 5

Fischer exited the elevator on the fourth floor, alone, and headed for the national desk and Lynch's office. He pushed the door open and flipped the Paletti tape rather aggressively onto Pat's desk before heading in the other direction towards his office. It looked out onto the Chicago River and a parking lot with an obstructed view of the NBC Tower at Cityfront Center two blocks away.

He parked his briefcase and jacket on the first of two chairs and tossed the small paper sack along with the newspaper on his desk. He would read it later. Thirsty, he pulled the donut from the bag and exited back through the door, weaving through the rows of empty desks headed for the small lunchroom and his first and only cup of coffee.

Fischer blew into the Styrofoam cup, trying to cool it so he could at least drink it before noon as he headed for his office and, since it was still early, the newspaper sitting on his desk.

"Hey, kid. Come 'ere."

Fischer stopped and peered through the glass wall before backtracking towards the door. A shorter and much older Anthony Torricelli was sitting at his desk.

"You're up awfully early."

"You read the story in today's paper?" Torricelli asked. His accent was thick.

"No, I haven't had a chance yet. I had to get my coffee first." Miles held up the evidence so Big Tony could take notice.

Tony removed his large feet from the desk and leaned forward, pulling the unlit cigar from his mouth.

"I think it might be of interest to you, kid. It's about

those two guys who got off in that trial you just covered. It came over the wire on the weekend. It seems they got whacked by some person or persons unknown." Tony tossed the paper in front of him. "They used a crossbow on the sons-of-bitches."

Fischer quickly made his way past the doorway and took a seat in one of the two chairs. He released his cup of coffee to the cluttered surface of Tony's desk and quickly grabbed the paper as if he was looking for his own obituary.

"How do they know it was a crossbow?"

"Smaller arrows than your conventional type bow and arrow, I imagine," replied Tony sarcastically.

Anxious, Miles quickly thumbed through the pages.

"Page seven, bottom right," instructed Tony. He leaned back in his chair and patiently chewed on his stubby cigar.

Miles quickly turned to page seven and looked to the bottom right of the page as instructed. "When did this happen?"

"Thursday night or Friday morning. They don't exactly know. They were found early Friday morning, but the owner of the bar thought they left before midnight. Who knows? He doesn't check his watch."

"Who found them?"

"Some customers. Said they nearly drove over them." Tony waited a bit before leaning forward and pulling the cigar from his mouth. "Here's the best part, kid. Two clean shots right through their fucking hearts and out the other side. They found the arrows stuck in the mud, if you can believe it."

Tony waited for Fischer's reaction, but there was none. His eyes were still glued to the page.

"Can you imagine?" he continued. "An arrow right

through the fucking heart and clean through to the other side. Ouch! That's gotta hurt," he said with an ugly grin.

Fischer waved a hand towards Tony, basically telling him to shut up so he could finish reading. Tony leaned back in his chair and sipped his coffee, content to let him read before he continued with any more of his insight into their deaths.

"Well, what do ya think, kid?"

Fischer finished the last sentence before flipping the paper into the clutter that smothered Tony's desk. "I'm not surprised," he said rather flatly.

Tony leaned forward and yanked the cigar from his mouth. His eyes narrowed. "What the hell was that?"

"What?"

"That. What you just said."

"Well." He shrugged his shoulders. "What did you want me to say?"

"Shit, kid! From what I read of your stories, I thought you would have at least had something a little more poignant to say than that—something with a little more *gusto*. You know, a little more *sensazione*," he said, motioning with his hands. "You were there, were you not? You see the faces of those grieving parents, don't you?" Tony searched for just the right words before placing the cigar back in his mouth. "You need a bigger set of *cogliones*, kid. What you should have said was those bastards got what they fucking well deserved. You know, something along those lines. You may be a reporter, kid, but when you start to lose your *sensibilita*, its time ya found another profession."

"You didn't let me finish," interrupted Miles. He was almost serious before he decided to change the path of the conversation. "Tell me. How much of that stuff do you drink a day?"

42

Tony was taking a big gulp of his coffee and was unable to talk.

"You might want to cut it back. I think it's making you a little edgy. You know, how do you say it…?" he asked, quickly snapping his fingers. "Oh yeah. *Animato*," said Fischer with a smile, rather pleased with his Italian. "What I was going to say is it doesn't really shock me."

"Yeah. Well you should have seen the *espressione* on your face," replied Tony rather smugly.

Miles slouched back in his chair, trying to relax, almost burying himself. "Okay. I guess I was a little shocked at first," he said, trying to recover. "I just didn't think that somebody would actually do it. The people of that town hated those two for what they did. They destroyed two families, not to mention killing those two girls. The townspeople talked about it openly. Everybody knew and heard it. It was circulating around Tweeksbury like a brush fire."

"What did you hear?"

"That if they walked, it wouldn't be for long. People were talking about storming their cells and hanging them by their balls 'til their scrotums snapped. You know—Wild West stuff."

"That's *cogliones*, kid." His feet were back on his desk.

Miles ignored the correction.

"Anyway. The trial hadn't even started before they were talking about getting them. As far as they were concerned, they were guilty as hell. It seemed everybody in Tweeksbury thought so."

"Then how come they don't convict those two bastards? And how the hell do they allow the trial to be held in Tweeksbury in the first place? Is that not against our system of a fair trial?" said Tony with a scowl. "You know, an impartial jury."

Miles leaned forward and took his first sip of coffee.

"Judge Reinhold wouldn't allow it. He said that as long as there were twelve honest people in the county, then the trial would go ahead in the town nearest to where the rape and murders of the two girls took place. The defense tried to have it moved, but it was overruled. In hindsight, it worked in their favor."

Tony seized the opportunity to expound on his ideas of just how the judicial system should be overhauled for the betterment of all concerned. He removed his feet and quickly leaned forward, clearing away part of the rubble. He may need something to pound on.

"That's the trouble with this bloody country. We've got too many damn judges just like him sitting on the bench. This country and the whole damn judicial system will be a lot better off when these bastards start to retire or pass through to the next life. They can take the goddamned legislators with them, too, when they go. Then we can replace them with those who know how to make the law and uphold the law. A real judge would have been able to see through all that incest and inbreeding that spawns thinking like that," he said, pointing to his head. "He should have moved it," he said angrily. His nostrils flared, and his face became flushed, making his eyes stand out. Finished, he wiped the spit from his mouth.

"I don't think that was the reason for their acquittal," said Fischer, moving farther back in his chair. "I think it was based more on the evidence," stated Miles, who wasn't intimidated in the least by an irate senior editor who regularly ripped into those who held the power in this country. "The lawyers for Holt and Masalla were more effective in arguing their clients' case."

"Well, they may have won the case, but I believe somebody ended up biting them on the ass." He picked up the paper and stabbed at it with his finger. "It seems to me that the people of Clearwater County got the justice they couldn't get in a court of law in this damn country. The whole fuckin' place is going to the dogs, if ya ask me. It's all the fault of those damn ass-kissing liberals. They should put the whole damn bunch of them on a chain gang for a month. That would show them. Be the damned longest chain gang ya ever see."

"Yeah, Big Tony," replied Miles softly, nodding his head like he agreed, "that would show them."

Tony tossed the paper back on his desk. A stack of papers waffled like they would take flight before they relaxed. He leaned back in his chair, again with his feet up. His face was still flushed, but his voice was calmer. He folded his hands over his head and almost smiled.

"So tell me. Who do ya think would do something like this? Some crazy townsfolk?"

Miles had no intention of getting into a guessing game. He wanted to think about it first, after the shock wore off. He reached for his cup and proceeded to extract himself from his chair, the clutter, and Tony's office.

"I don't know. I haven't got a clue. But I'll bet you this," he said, standing behind the chair. "Whoever it is, they're probably heroes by now." He moved to the door and stopped just outside the doorway. "By the way, thanks for keeping me up to date on the story, and don't forget about what I said about you know what." Miles gestured with his cup.

"Yeah, no problem, kid."

Miles closed the door to his office and stood by the window and watched the street, letting the full impact sink in. He thought of the hundred faces he had seen in the courtroom and those he had talked to on the streets. Everything was off the record, of course. Nobody wanted to risk arrest for uttering a death threat or a possible felony charge of conspiracy to commit murder on a couple of lowlifes. King's rampage through the rows made him a logical choice. He sympathized with him, but was he really that stupid? He thought of Alex Burton, the father of the other girl who was raped, but Miles quickly shrugged him off. He didn't believe in capital punishment.

Fischer closed his eyes and rubbed his temples, contemplating the real shock. "Son of a bitch! A crossbow," he said, staring back out the window. "Big Tony was right," he said, smiling slightly. "That's gotta hurt."

Miles removed his jacket from the chair and hung it on the hanger behind the door and took his seat. He threw the empty sack into the trash can next to his desk. Through the open door, the decibels were climbing, higher now than when he left for Illinois Avenue for a cigarette and some fresh air so he could think after what Big Tony had told him. Half the desks were now occupied. Monitors were warming up with bright blue screens. Keyboards were being struck with the intensity of a Monday morning. People were flowing in from the elevators like it was Grand Central. He ignored all this and pulled out the sports section and scanned the headlines. His team, the White Sox, lost again. They had a real streak going. There was a tap on the glass.

"Morning, Miles. Got a minute?"

Patrick Lynch was an imposing figure, almost brutish looking. He was tall with a thick frame and a full head of white hair and deep blue eyes with lids that drooped at an angle.

"Morning, Pat. What's up?" He had an unpleasant look on his face.

Pat pulled at the chair cradling Miles's briefcase. "I take it this is yours," he remarked with an irritated look, scooping up the briefcase. He held it out in front of him.

Miles reached from behind his desk and retrieved the briefcase.

"You don't sound like you're in a particularly good mood. Bad weekend?"

Miles placed it on the credenza adjoining his desk, alongside the piles of papers and a desktop computer that sat to his right. Between the piles of paper and the three-tiered tray sat an eight-by-ten picture of him and his dog. A picture of him and his wife, taken while they were dating, lay covered with papers in the bottom drawer. It had been there since January. Nobody ever commented.

"No, not at all. Had a fine weekend," he said with no expression. He sat in the chair and crossed his legs. "Did you happen to read the story in this morning's edition?"

"Are you talking about what happened in Tweeksbury?"

"Yeah," replied Pat.

"Big Tony pointed it out to me."

"What did you think?"

"I was a little surprised, I guess."

Lynch wasted little time. He pulled his leg in tighter and stiffened his jaw. "I want someone back there today," he stated emphatically. "It's obvious to me, and I'm sure it is to you, that this story isn't over. I don't want to rely on the town yokels or the boys from AP on this," he stated with a scowl. He pointed to the paper on Miles's desk. "They already scooped us on this one. There's a possibility this may be bigger than the original trial, but before I make that decision, I wanted to get your opinion on it first. I know what you and Erin have gone through in the past. I wanted to get your feeling on this first."

"I don't think it would be a problem." He hesitated, thinking of the tremors she had been sending out.

"Are you sure? Maybe you want to talk it over with her first because of the difficulties she's going through." Lynch uncrossed his legs. "I know you're the most knowledgeable on this, but I can send Haskills in your place. That's not a problem, but we can't afford to stand around and wait on this. I want someone back there before the end of the day."

Miles's eyes lit up. He shook his head slightly and breathed hard through his nose. The mere suggestion of putting Haskills on the story, his story, had him mildly upset. He leaned over his desk.

"You gotta be kidding me," he stated. "Far be it for me to badmouth someone, but Haskills is an idiot. You saw what he did with the Wainwright interview."

Lynch checked his watch.

"If it was my decision, I'd choose someone else."

"Well, it's not your decision, Miles," replied Lynch with a scowl. "And besides, I don't have time for this. I have a whole department to run. What I want to know is if you're taking it or staying put."

Miles sank back in his chair. He stared back at Lynch for what seemed like a long moment and said, "No, it'll be fine. I said I was taking it, but Haskills. Shit!"

"By the way, how is she?"

The excitement of Haskills was gone, replaced with a twinge of unpleasantness. The image of her being pregnant and how it happened for the second time made him sick.

"She's fine," he said. "My sister is still there during

the week making sure she sticks to the regimen."

"That's good. I'm glad to hear she's coping okay." Pat crossed his thick arms and held them high against his chest. "So, you got any ideas?"

"It could have been anybody. Like I was telling Big Tony, everybody thought they were guilty." He thought for a moment. "King made that bold gesture in the courtroom, but somehow I don't think he's capable. He's as religious as hell." He chuckled. "From what I heard, he doesn't make a move without consulting God first. I think the man lives in divine fear. He may have threatened them, but that's only because of what he was going through. I don't think he reacted any differently than any other father would have. It would surprise me if he was—"

"Maybe we got another psychotic running loose. Another nut job like those two guys, Holt and what's his name?" Lynch shook his head slightly. "Amazing!" he said, before letting out some air. "Just what we need." He grabbed the side arms of the chair with his large hands. "A modern-day Robin Hood running loose, but instead of robbing people, he's killing them with his little bow and arrows. Makes you wonder what the hell this world is coming to."

"What intrigues me is the use of a crossbow. When was the last time anybody used a crossbow to kill someone in this country?"

It drew no response from Pat other than a blank stare. Both men looked at each other, trying to rethink the past.

"I guess there's no way they can be traced?" He sounded a little unsure of himself. He immediately wished he hadn't said it and did his best to ease from the conversation. "Anyway, it doesn't matter. I'm sure they wiped everything clean. I'll check it out when I get back there. By the way, when do you want me out of here?"

Lynch pushed himself from the chair. "As soon as possible. Get a hold of Sally and see what arrangements can be made. If there's a red-eye to Tweeksbury, I want you on it." He pushed his hands deep into his pockets and hunched his shoulders. He headed for the door.

"No airport. It'll have to be Boise."

"Okay. Boise."

Miles followed Lynch out and stopped just beyond the door. "What about the Croft investigation?"

Lynch replied in a witty tone as he walked away. It was loud so that those closest to Miles's office could hear him. "If you can't fit it in, put it on my desk before you leave. Maybe I'll get Haskills to look it over."

Miles smiled halfheartedly at the suggestion as he watched Lynch fade into the large newsroom before retreating into his office. He slowly gazed around the room with his hands on his hips, thinking of what he was going to tell his wife. He hadn't been totally truthful when he answered Pat's question. They had argued about his traveling, about his being away with her being pregnant and all. They had been arguing since Christmas after what she was told in the bathroom at the *Tribune* Christmas party even though Fischer knew nothing about it. Erin hadn't told him yet. She only argued the point from her perspective, keeping him in the dark. Looking perplexed, he tossed the gum in the trash can and headed across the newsroom floor for the small lunchroom in search of a Coke.

Chapter 6

Fischer was in front of his monitor, his nose stuck in the Avery Croft file, so little of what was happening outside his office actually registered. He had called Tweeksbury on three separate occasions, and on each occasion, Sheriff Knibbs was not available. Miles left his number just in case Knibbs had a spare moment and wanted to talk. It would take all of five minutes and, possibly, given the right information, save him a trip to a town he no longer wanted to visit. Sally was still making the arrangements. She said she would call when she had something. Veronica was somewhere in the newsroom, checking the archives.

Little of what he had read sunk in. He was thinking of Tweeksbury, another flight and a long drive into a small town that he had grown tired of. The people of Tweeksbury had been less than cooperative, forcing him to return. So had Holt and Masalla by being on the streets where they ran the risk of being hit. He could be gone another couple of days, starting tonight, which meant the possibility of another heated debate. Erin was pressing him to slack off a bit. She wanted him closer to home, closer to her. The baby was coming. It could be any day. The women of her family had a history of premature births. Why should she be any different, she said. He sensed something more at stake than just the possibility of a premature birth. Ever since Christmas, his work had become a subject of intense interest. His sister Barbara was there, handling the weekdays. His mother, who was now a widow, took the weekend shift and the weeknights, when he was on the road. Barbara, who lived close by, was a nurse who had taken a leave of absence to raise her two boys, who were almost teens. Who better than a nurse and a mother who had already raised three of her own?

Veronica slipped in quietly through the open door and quickly plunked the small stack of papers zipped off the Internet and the photocopier on his desk before leaving in a huff and without so much as a word. Fischer pulled his nose away from the monitor just long enough to watch her leave. He studied her long legs, her tight, compact butt with the nice wiggle, and her auburn hair that brushed her shoulders until she sat at her desk just beyond the glass wall. He had done this often. Sometimes he would sit there quietly and admire the behind view when she was walking away or the perfect curves when she was leaning over the low partition to talk to the girls next to her. She was a distraction but the kind of distraction that was tolerated and admired by every man from every vantage point in the office.

He pushed the button on the monitor, and instantly the screen went black. He sat and watched her perfect figure sitting in the small secretarial chair before heading in the direction of her desk.

"I couldn't help noticing," he said, pointing in the direction of his office. "Is something wrong?"

She stopped shuffling another stack of papers and turned towards him. Her bright emerald eyes were glowing. Miles stood to her right, leaning against the low partition with his arms folded.

"Miles, I'm not one to complain, but the 'Bitch Tank' gets on my damn nerves! One of these days I'm going to tell her off, and I don't care who hears me."

Laura, who sat two seats to Veronica's left, overheard the sharpness of her voice. She shot up from her chair. "You go, girl."

Laura was long and black. Her hair had grown out

from the short, cropped look of a couple of years ago. It was now long and braided.

Miles looked up at her and shook his head. He quickly gestured when Veronica wasn't looking. No point in inflaming her temper any more than it was.

"Thanks, Laura."

"Anytime."

"Laura, do you mind?"

"Yeah, yeah. Okay, Miles, but everyone knows she's a bitch." She quickly scooped up a file and headed towards them, shaking her head. "Nothing worse than seeing a grown man beg," she said, "unless, of course, you're getting something for it." Laura smiled devilishly and disappeared into one of the offices twenty feet away. Miles looked at her suspiciously.

"That's the last," Veronica stated adamantly. "I mean it. That's the last time that I do anything for her. I just can't stand the way she tries to boss me around," she said, clenching both fists. "Who does she think she is?" Veronica swung back to her desk. "Next time, I'm telling her off. And if I ever hear her say another thing behind my back about the way I dress, I swear I'm going to let her have it. That's it!"

Miles had heard the rare outbursts before, her use of cutting-edge pseudonyms. She had a bit of a temper. She got it from her father, she said, who got it from his Irish mother.

She had been with the *Tribune* for just over a year. She had a degree in political science and was studying for her master's at Loyola University at night. In two years, she would have her master's and then she would be out of here and into a career—hopefully with the State Department.

"Do you want to talk about it?" he asked warmly.

"We can go into my office if you like."

The phone rang for the third time before Laura, who had just left Ruchinski's office, heard it while walking back towards her desk.

"I hate to break this up, Miles," she said brushing by him, "but your phone is ringing."

Veronica traded smiles with Laura before following Miles into his office, carrying a white file folder. She sat in the chair in front of the small pile of letter-sized paper she had left there earlier and crossed her legs. Miles was already in his chair, the receiver pressed to his ear.

Sally was on the other end, telling him that his ticket would be waiting for him at the airport. Miles listened and then cupped his hand over the receiver. "She's got me on hold."

"I'm sorry you had to see that," said Veronica, sounding apologetic and pointing behind her. "It's not like me to lose control like that."

He smiled at her before pressing the receiver closer to his ear. It was a nine o'clock flight on a national carrier into St. Louis said Sally. He would have to switch carriers with two stopovers on a smaller airline before Boise. It was the best she could do on such short notice. There would be a car waiting for him at the airport. She also booked him a room at the Tweeksbury Hotel, the same hotel he had stayed at during the trial. He thanked her and hung up the phone.

Miles leaned back in his chair. "Pat wants me back in Tweeksbury by tonight."

Veronica tried to appear uninterested. She had been on vacation for the past week, he had been on the other side of the country for most of the previous three, and in those four weeks, she had seen very little of him.

"The flight is going to be longer than I thought.

There's no direct flight into Boise. Plus there are two stopovers on the way. That'll at least add another hour and a half. Then there's the three-hour drive. I won't get into Tweeksbury 'til about..." Miles quickly did the math, "four or five in the morning." He didn't appear all that happy. He paused for a moment, contemplating his hours ahead.

"How long will you be gone?" she asked.

"I don't know. A day, maybe two."

They stared at each other for what felt like a long moment before their eyes detached. He cleared his throat. "Is that from the archives?" He pointed to the file sitting in her lap.

Veronica placed a single sheet in front of him without so much as a word, preoccupied with what he had said, that he would be away, possibly for a day or two.

Miles leaned back in his chair and began to read the story about a student at Stanford studying to be a criminal lawyer. Born and raised in the Philippines, she had come to the United States in search of completing her education. Instead, she ended up dead, killed from the arrow of a crossbow on the grounds of the university in one of the parking lots that dotted the campus. It had happened at night, and there were no witnesses. There was the possible link that her death was attributed to her father's business with the U.S. government, but there were no details. It had happened in 1996. It was the story he and Pat could not remember.

He quickly leaned forward.

"I remember this now," he said. "It ran in all the major newspapers. It caused quite a stink in the State Department."

"I found this one," she said without bothering to wait. "It's about a white male who was accused of the rape and murder of a young teen. They found him in a back alley. The press said he may have been released on bail by mistake." Veronica passed him a copy.

"When did this happen?" Miles quickly grabbed the sheet and scanned the article.

"It happened back in..." Veronica's voice trailed off as she searched for the date on her copy. "In 1993, in a place called Whatley."

Suddenly the phone rang. Miles quickly picked it up, thinking it might be Knibbs, and placed it to his ear.

"Fischer here."

"I've got your sister on the line. It sounds urgent."

"Put her on."

"Erin took a tumble when she was getting up out of the tub," said the calm voice.

"Is she okay?" he asked. He stood quickly and stared into the newsroom.

"I don't know. The ambulance is outside, and they're taking her to the emergency room."

He immediately tensed up, causing his jaw to tighten. "Right now?"

"Yes, right now! But I think she's going to be okay. I think you should meet us there. I'm going to follow them in my car."

"Can I talk to her?"

"No, Miles. You can't talk to her," she said sternly. "They're putting her into the ambulance as we speak."

"What hospital?"

"St. James."

"Shit!" He was now in a mild panic.

"Erin's fallen getting out of the tub," he said, placing down the receiver.

"Is it bad?"

"I don't know," replied Miles, heading for his sport

jacket hanging behind the door. "I've got to go to the hospital. They're taking her there right now. I have to go."

He dashed past her and through the opening without saying good-bye or whether or not he'd be back.

"What about the file?"

"Shit!"

Miles stopped in his tracks and headed back to where Veronica was standing just outside his office door, taking little notice of the eyes that were now on him.

"Is this everything?"

"Yes, and be careful," she said. "I'm sure she'll be fine."

Miles gave an obligatory smile before making an about face and headed at full speed for the elevators, weaving and dodging through the rows and corridors, not to mention the people standing in his way. Veronica stood by the door and watched him leave.

Sally was about to come through the newsroom doors. She paused and held the door open, watching Miles steam towards her, papers swirling behind him. Seeing Miles flying pass the desks like an Olympic sprinter with papers cascading to the floor, she asked Miles the inevitable as he dashed by her and pushed the elevator button.

"Is she having the baby?"

"No. They've taken her to the hospital." He spoke in halting tones, trying to catch his breath. "She fell getting out of the bathtub. I can't talk right now. I've got to go to the hospital."

"What about the tickets?" she asked.

"Not now, Sally. Tell Lynch I've gone to the hospital. Tell him he'll have to get someone else."

Frantic, he repeatedly pushed the down button. He

paced the floor, waiting for at least one of the elevators to take him to the street. "Christ! Can't these things go any faster?" Fischer quickly checked his watch. He swore twice and disappeared through a side door leading to the stairs.

"Was that Miles I just saw leaving?" asked Lynch to nobody in particular. He stood just outside his office. He waited, his eyes searching. With no answer, he headed for Sally in reception.

"Was that Miles I just saw leaving in a hurry?" asked Pat.

"Yes. His wife's being rushed to the hospital. She fell getting out of the tub."

He leaned against the counter to her left and stared at the elevator doors, trying to figure out what to do about the story waiting in Tweeksbury. He quickly straightened up. His voice was curt.

"Sally, see if you can track down Haskills! I want to see him in my office right away. And tell him he's going to Tweeksbury!"

Chapter 7

The small city claimed it took less than thirty minutes to drive in either direction to Chicago Heights when the traffic wasn't too heavy. He had never done it in less than fifty in the year they had lived there, but that was always in rush hour traffic. Because this was an emergency, he managed to shave ten minutes off his best time. He drove like he owned the streets, running red lights when the risk wasn't too great, weaving in and out of afternoon freeway traffic like they were stationary pylons. His blue eyes watched closely in the rearview mirror for a cop, ready with an explanation as to why he was driving like such an ass. He would explain his predicament and hopefully escape with just a warning. Two speeding tickets along with numerous parking violations were already sitting in the top drawer of his desk. He didn't need any more.

The parking lot was a multilevel job on the east side of the medical complex just off of Fifteenth Street. He ignored it. Instead, the shiny black SUV screamed into the entrance of St. James Hospital used by emergency vehicles and quickly parked alongside one of its walls, closest to the entrance that was clearly marked with the words, EMERGENCY. He placed a cardboard printout with the words *Chicago Tribune* on the dash and quickly exited. Hopefully, it would keep the tow trucks away.

Miles thumped his cigarette to the asphalt next to an idle ambulance and yanked open one of the doors. He ran the length of the wide corridor, dodging those in front of him until he reached the small waiting area and the nurses' station. He saw Barbara sitting in one of the chairs, reading a magazine. He pushed his sunglasses to the top of his head and approached her.

"How is she?" he asked in a mild state of panic. He breathed heavily.

"We don't know yet," she replied calmly. "They took her upstairs for some tests." She checked her watch. It was almost three. "That was about an hour ago."

"Have you spoken to anybody?" he asked in a shaky voice from the restricted breathing.

"No. Not yet."

He glanced at the nurses' station and then back towards Barbara.

"How the hell did this happen? You were supposed to be looking after her."

"I don't know. We had a late lunch. When we finished, she went upstairs and took a bath because of the heat. I was in the kitchen cleaning up when I heard a loud thud come from upstairs. I rushed upstairs and found her on the floor, leaning against the tub. She said she slipped and fell stepping over the side of the tub. I noticed she was bleeding, so I called the emergency number and helped her into bed."

"Bleeding? What kind of bleeding?"

"She had some vaginal bleeding."

"Christ! That can't be good."

"I don't know, Miles. It's hard to say. I don't want to go jumping to conclusions and say the wrong thing. Why don't we just wait and see what the doctor has to say? There's a machine just around the corner. Why don't you get yourself a soda or something and try to relax. There's nothing we can do until the doctor finishes his diagnosis."

Fischer slowly stepped back. He removed his glasses and brushed his hair back. "What I could really use is a stiff drink."

"You can do that when you get home. For now, why don't you try the machine."

Miles searched through the change in his pocket and then, without saying anything, disappeared around the corner. Barbara went back to her seat and her magazine, looking at the pictures, ignoring the black print.

Miles pushed the coins through the slot and grabbed the can from the base of the machine. He bought a candy bar, too.

He sat in a chair across from his sister and took a bite of his chocolate bar. Barbara pointed to it.

"Those things are going to kill you, you know."

"Not if this doesn't get me first." He smiled smartly, holding up his Coke. He took another bite.

"You really should consider taking better care of yourself Miles."

"Yeah, I know, Sis. In due time, when things calm down, but not right now. I need as much sugar as I can get."

He took sip of his Coke. Barbara shook her head in disgust and went back to flipping pages.

Miles glanced toward the other end of the hall and carefully watched a nurse make her way back towards the waiting area. He immediately jumped to his feet and approached the counter, placing his hands, the can of Coke, and what was left of the chocolate bar on the counter. Barbara watched from her seat.

"I'm here to see my wife, Erin Fischer. She was brought in here about an hour ago."

She checked the roster. "The doctor is still with her."

"Doctor Faraday?" asked Miles.

"That's right. He should be finished shortly, and then we'll be able to let you know how she is."

"When can I see her?"

"As soon as the doctor is finished. He'll let us know."

Miles took the Coke and what remained of his

chocolate bar and returned to his seat.

"She said they would let us know."

Barbara nodded and flipped peacefully through a travel magazine.

Ten minutes later.

"Mr. Fischer."

Miles quickly approached the desk.

"Mr. Fischer, you can go up now. The doctor will be waiting for you."

"Thanks."

Miles quickly motioned for Barbara to follow him to the elevators. He led in a rush, passing an attendant who was pushing a mop and pail, headed in the other direction. Barbara followed behind. The elevator doors opened, and Miles and Barbara entered alone. He pushed the button and leaned against the wall, waiting for the doors to close.

"I hope to God this doesn't end up like the last time."

"I'm sure everything's going to be fine, Miles." She put her hand on his shoulder as they watched the doors close. They rode in silence to the floor for maternity.

Miles quickly slid his body between the doors, not bothering to wait for them to fully open. His sister waited and then followed him down the hallway, speaking as he pulled away. He was jogging now.

"Whatever you do, don't get in his face."

"How is she, Doc?" asked Miles, still some twenty feet away, but approaching rapidly.

Faraday stood next to the counter, writing on a clipboard. Behind the counter, nurses and support staff were busy with paperwork and checking schedules. He placed the clipboard back with the others that were held in elevated slots on the corner of the nurses' station. He patted Miles on the shoulder.

"She's going to be fine."

Barbara pulled in behind.

"Hey, Barbara. It's nice to see you again." Dr. Faraday reached over and hugged her, leaving Miles in a state of limbo.

"It's been a while."

He smiled warmly, exposing two rows of white teeth against his dark skin. A stethoscope was around his neck. The white smock was buttoned and covered his six-three frame to just below the knees. It was as white as his teeth and without a crease.

Barbara smiled back. "Twelve years."

"That long?"

"I'm afraid so."

He scratched his head, thinking of just where the years went. His hair was short and black, his temples slightly gray above the ears. "Wow. That's a long time. When were you thinking of coming back? We're always looking for good nurses."

"I haven't decided. I'm still in a state of mother-hood."

"That's a very noble profession." He chuckled. "They always need good nurses there, too." He chuckled again and remembered Miles standing behind him. "Excuse me, Barbara, but I've got a patient I have to attend to, and he's right over here." Faraday quickly turned and pointed his thick finger at Miles.

Miles had stewed quietly, waiting for the two of them to finish with their reunion. He barely managed a tight smile.

"How's the baby?"

"The fetus is fine, Miles." Faraday placed his large hand on his shoulder. "No need to worry. Both are doing just fine."

Miles took a deep breath and forced it from his lungs. "What about the bleeding?"

"It's just a slight hemorrhage outside of the womb. The baby's fine and so is Erin, but we're going to keep her here until she has the baby. Her hip and back are a little sore from the fall, but she'll be fine in a couple of days. We just want to be sure that everything remains on track."

"Can I see her?"

"I don't see why not."

Dr. Faraday led the way, talking with Barbara down the brightly lit hallway with Miles in tow. Faraday stopped just short of her room and held the door. Barbara stayed behind and talked with Dr. Faraday.

Miles made his way to the head of the bed. Erin was no more than five foot three with dark hair and blue eyes. She was stretched out on the bed, lying halfway between a horizontal and vertical line. A single white sheet covered her to her waist, or what was left of it. With no makeup, she looked tired.

He kissed her lightly on the lips. It was the same kind of kiss they had shared for the past year or so.

"How are you doing?" he asked.

Erin had followed him with her eyes the moment he entered the room. He was definitely handsome. *Any woman would love to have him*, she thought. Her girlfriends were all envious, or so she imagined. "How did you manage to nab him?" they had asked her on more than one occasion.

She hadn't given it much thought until now. She had been less than candid with him about getting pregnant the first time, but she didn't care. The relationship was in trouble. She had to do something or he might leave so she forgot to take the pill on purpose. It was a risk, sure, but it had been worth it—right? Just look at those eyes. Besides, where was the harm? They were married and happy, were they not? Isn't that what was important? And besides, that was all behind them. It was all in the past. They were less than a month away from being parents this time. This would make them even happier. After what she had been told at the Christmas party, this was surely enough to keep her away and him at home.

"Okay, I guess. I'm just a little sore," she replied in a soft tone.

Miles placed his hand on top of her large stomach. "How's the baby doing?"

"Don't you mean our baby?" she quickly corrected, smiling awkwardly like she was still seeking his approval.

His brow furrowed, narrowing his eyes.

"What did I say?" He had the inquisitive look of a child, like he had done something wrong.

"The baby," she stated rather reluctantly.

He patted her hand and smiled appropriately. "Sorry. I meant our baby."

She hesitated and stared at him as if judging his sincerity and then said, "She's fine."

Erin's insecurity was becoming more visible. She was in the habit of correcting everything he said. For Miles, it was becoming a life of eggshells under the constant strain of a relationship that was still in trouble and had been before Erin got pregnant and they tied the knot. Wanting to talk about something else, Miles quickly changed subjects.

"How come you took a bath? You always take a shower," he asked, taking a step back.

"It was so hot out; I thought a bath would be better than a shower. I just wanted to soak for a while and cool off. I guess it wasn't the best thing to do." Erin studied his ruffled appearance. "From the looks of it, you could use a shower yourself," she said, back with a better smile, pawing softly at the space between them.

"Yeah, I know. You couldn't guess I worked for the *Tribune*." Miles flipped the end of his tie.

"Can't say you do, but then again, we kind of put you through hell."

Miles ignored what she said. It was a moot point, a minefield that he did not wish to visit.

"Did Dr. Faraday mention anything to you about staying in the hospital until the baby is born?"

"Yes, but it's for the better, I guess." Her face showed her disappointment. "I'd rather be at home, but he knows what's best. At least it'll give Barbara a chance to be home with her kids. She's really been great. I'm sure they would rather have her at home instead of with their aunt." Erin cupped her hands around her large belly. "So how was your day before all of this?"

"Nothing spectacular except for Barbara's phone call."

"What about the rest of it?"

"Not much better than yours."

He turned and sat in the chair between the blinking monitors and the window. He took a deep breath.

"Lynch had me scheduled to go back to Tweeksbury tonight. There was another murder." He nervously tapped the side of his chair. "Seems the two guys who got off in the trial I covered got hit—with a crossbow, no less." He noticed her hard stare, forcing him to gaze out the window to his left. He paused long enough to take another breath and then turned back towards her. "I didn't know how I was going to tell you since I hadn't been home with you in three weeks. I guess in one way, this is a blessing." But he didn't feel that way at all. Erin being in the hospital was no blessing. Driving foolishly through afternoon traffic with a heart rate way above normal was no blessing, either. Assuming Haskills was on his way to Tweeksbury to cover his story was almost nauseating. "Now I don't have to go. I think he's going to send Haskills instead."

"Why would he do that? You told me he wasn't that good a reporter. I think you called him an idiot once."

Miles threw up his hands and did not elaborate. "It's Pat's call."

A momentary silence ensued. He did not want to get into the merits of whether Haskills was an "idiot" or not. He couldn't be bothered. Miles crossed his legs. He nervously tapped the side of his chair.

"I talked to Jack Morgan this morning," he said, changing the subject

"Oh, how is he?"

"He's fine. I think he's put on more weight, though. This morning he was trying to tell me how busy he is. I can't say that I bought it."

Neither one noticed the door open slowly.

"Is it okay to come in?" Barbara asked, tapping on the door.

Erin waved her hand to summon her into the room. "Yeah, we're finished with all the love stuff."

Miles nodded in agreement to his sister. He sighed quietly, almost wiping his brow. Her timing could not have been more perfect. They had run out of things to say. His sister could take over, leaving him free to do other things like watch the monitors.

"How are you feeling?" Barbara made her way to the side of Erin's bed, opposite her brother, and touched her hand.

"Fine. Just a little sore," answered Erin.

"I'm not going to stay," she stated, almost apologizing. "I just wanted to make sure you were okay. I was just talking with Dr. Faraday, and he told me everything was fine. I've got kids and a husband to feed. Job never stops, you know." She hesitated and then smiled. "Are you sure you still want to go through with this? They're a lot of work."

"I think it's a little late, don't you?" said Erin, holding her stomach.

Barbara made her way back towards the door. "I'll come and see you tomorrow to see how you're doing. Can I bring you anything?"

"Let's wait a day. By then I'm sure I'll need something better than their hospital food."

"Don't forget to let me know." Barbara opened and held the door. "I'll see you tomorrow then. See you, Miles." Barbara waved and then eased through the door.

"I guess I'll have to make arrangements for someone to look in on the dog while I'm at work since you and Barbara won't be around. I'll ask Mike next door. See if his kids can look in on him and maybe take him for a walk around the block. You know, give them a couple of bucks."

"You can give them a bit more, you know."

Again there was a quiet knock on the door. Dr. Faraday walked in and proceeded to the spot Barbara had recently vacated.

"How's my patient doing?" asked Dr. Faraday.

"I'm fine."

"Good, good." Dr. Faraday looked at this watch. "I'm going to book off now, Erin, so if you don't need me anymore today, I think I'll head back to my office and see how things are going over there. I'll come in and see you tomorrow morning, just to check up on you and see how you're doing."

"That'll be fine, Doctor. Thanks."

"Yeah, Doc. Thanks for all your help." Miles left his chair and shook his hand.

"No problem." Faraday pointed his finger at Erin, making one last remark. "I'll see you tomorrow, little mother."

They watched as he disappeared behind the door.

"So, can I get you anything?" Miles asked.

"No, I'm fine. Barbara packed me a suitcase while we were waiting for the ambulance, but you look like you want something." She smiled thinly, almost frowning. "You look like you want a cigarette."

"How you can tell?"

"I can always tell when something's bothering you. Let's just say we've been together long enough for me to know the signs. I do have a wife's intuition, you know."

Miles pointed at the door. "Do you mind?"

"No. Go ahead, but you really should quit. You're going to be a father, Miles. I want you here with us, not six feet under. You want to stick around, don't you?"

Miles stood at the foot of the bed and reached for his cigarettes, not giving the pointed remark a second thought.

"I'll be back in about ten minutes."

He gave her a short wave and disappeared through the door. He pushed the button and rode the elevator to the main floor and exited through the double doors from the emergency ward.

He stood to the left in a pocket of shade. Miles figured Lynch had sent the "idiot" in his place. He made a mental note to talk to Haskills when he got back in a day or so—unless, of course, things changed. In the meantime, he would stay with Erin until it was time to go home and check on the dog and have something to eat while he read through the information that Veronica had given him on his way out of the *Tribune* earlier in the day.

Chapter 8

He should have been sitting in the airport in St. Louis, headed for Boise and then Tweeksbury, piecing together the story on the sudden deaths of Lionel Holt and David Masalla. Instead, he was at home, suffering in the heat because there was little else to do. With Erin's sudden fall and the sudden events in Tweeksbury, everything was now on hold—including the investigation of Avery Croft. While driving Interstate 94, headed for the hospital, Fischer had reluctantly called his informant at the Illinois State Board of Education and cancelled their meeting set for four in Gateway Park. They would reschedule in a couple of days. Patrick Lynch had called and left a short message on the machine. Because of Erin, he was not expected in.

It was almost midnight, and he was still up after arriving home late. Dinner had consisted of a warm pizza and cold beer bought at one of the local pizza joints not far from their home. The shirt and tie along with the long pants had been discarded, replaced with a pair of loose-fitting shorts and no shirt because the house was like an oven and he needed to cool off. In the family room, the ceiling fan was on full but gave little in the way of comfort.

He had been at it for close to two hours, sifting through the file, scrutinizing every detail for a possible connection to what had happened in Tweeksbury. After all, who in their right mind used a crossbow to administer justice when a gun would do the trick? America led the free world when it came to the use of guns in the commission of a crime. AK47s, semiautomatic assault rifles, handguns of all types and sizes. You name it. Those and everything else were out there for the taking.

After sweating for most of those two hours, he finally gave in to the heat and peeled himself from the chair. He hastily pulled another beer from the fridge and called his dog before vacating the kitchen for what he hoped would be cooler air outside. He leaned against the railing and placed the beer on the ledge and lit a cigarette while Rocky went about his business down below.

According to Veronica and the archives of the *Tribune*, Tweeksbury was just the tip of the iceberg, the latest in a series of crimes where a crossbow was used in the commission of a crime that could be directly linked to another that involved sexual assault causing death. The white file folder, its contents now scattered across the kitchen table, held three others that spanned the last eight years, including the student at Stanford, starting in 1991. Veronica had separated and then organized the clippings in chronological order as to date, holding them together with the use of a paper clip. The thickness varied on each with the lead story of the brutal rape and murder of the victim under bold headlines on top, followed by stories on the initial investigations that led to nowhere. With no witnesses and little in the way of evidence, every investigation seemed to lead to a dead end until bodies starting showing up months later in places like Chester Junction and Whatley.

He had neatly tracked the particulars on a yellow legal pad, noting the names, dates, times, the particulars that were common to each case, including what had just happened in Tweeksbury, and then after careful consideration, narrowed the list down to three after Stanford was eliminated because of a single discrepancy. There had been no sexual assault.

Chester Junction and Whatley were places he had never heard of, not even Eastbrook, where the

Zimmerman family took the worst of it. In a span of four months, the family of three had been reduced to one, leaving Maria Zimmerman as the only survivor. Rachel, unlike her mother, had not survived the vicious sexual assault behind Grayson's gas station that for some reason closed early that night. The authorities, after interviewing those who had seen them last, concluded that what had started out as a friendly get-together with friends ended with the brutal sexual assault against the two women after their vehicle had stalled and coasted into the empty station. A passing motorist looking for air to inflate his tires had noticed the body of Maria Zimmerman near the front of the building. She had apparently crawled from the rear of the station, where they later found Rachel. It probably saved her life, the doctor said. Maria Zimmerman spent the next nine weeks in a private room where doctors healed her wounds and probed her psyche in the hope that she could remember. There were no pictures of either of the victims, either before or after. Five days after the assault, Rachel was buried in the local cemetery in front of family and friends. Maria Zimmerman did not attend.

The next two articles were somewhat interesting, leaving Miles rather perplexed. The first one was dated December 28, 1991, almost eight months after Rachel was killed. Two males in their early twenties were found dead some thirty miles away in a town called Chester Junction. Both were the victims of a crossbow. Two months later, a second article confirmed that the two victims, Earl Thornton and James Patrick, were the ones responsible for savagely raping Maria and Rachel Zimmerman before slitting their throats. Miles had stared at the article after reading it a second time, trying to figure out how that was possible. There were no witnesses to what happened behind the station.

The final article on the Zimmerman family was all too common where alcohol and speed were involved. Joseph Zimmerman had unexpectedly passed away, the victim of a drunk driver who failed to heed a red light. Veronica had included the article, linking the unfolding story of the demise of the Zimmerman family. It had happened just before Christmas. There were photos of the intersection and what was left of his '91 Chevy wrapped around a light pole and of the Ford pickup after it had flipped a half-dozen times before coming to rest farther down the street. Although alcohol was found in the pickup, speed was definitely a factor, according to the write up. There were no survivors, but that came as no surprise considering the circumstances. There was a small photo of Joseph in a business suit with a warm smile. He would be dearly missed, it was noted.

He found the story of the babysitter underneath the Zimmerman case. The story was plastered on the front page of the *Whatley Examiner*, a small local newspaper that, according to the header, only published twice a week. There was a small picture of the grieving parents and one of Tiffany Ambro, the young teen who was raped and then murdered by having her throat slit. She was only fifteen. The parents for whom she was babysitting found her slumped over the sofa after a night out. The town was in shock. "It's a sad day," said the mayor. Funeral services were set for Wednesday, June sixteenth.

The next article explained how she died. The intruder had impersonated a cop and then gained entry when he flashed his badge. The suspect was a twenty-four-year-old male, the only son of a wealthy family who, after he was arrested, was released on bail—a mistake, according to the judge, who had ties to the family. Miles cursed loudly, mumbling something about money and politics and how it was corrupting the system.

Three days later, Roger Wilcox was found in a back alley, slumped against a dumpster. He had been killed with an arrow from a crossbow. On the last page, Miles read about Tiffany Ambro's funeral. Roger Wilcox was not mentioned.

Unlike the others, there was nothing in the file on the original story associated with the *Tribune* or the AP until the death of Roger Wilcox. Curious, Fischer searched for it on a map that he had pulled from a drawer. Somehow, for whatever reason, the *Tribune* and the AP had missed the original story, which was odd considering it was just across state lines. He purposely put a large asterisk next to it.

Lynch could be right, he thought. What happened in Tweeksbury could be bigger than the original trial, but it was still too early to tell. He would have to wait and talk to Haskills first. If Haskills reported what he thought he might, then he would take it a step further. If he was wrong, he could monitor it from the sidelines while he and his informant attacked Avery Croft.

Chapter 9

He drank heavily when he was alone, which was most of the time. He also slept late because at the moment there was little to do and because of the heavy drinking, it took longer for the effects to wear off. When the phone rang, there was little in the way of movement. A leg twitched, but there was little life there. His brain was almost dead, and his body wanted to sleep. His large mass lay still on a wine-colored couch, dressed in a pair of boxers and a T-shirt, unable to move. It rang again and this time, his body jerked wildly. The sudden, violent twitch slowly woke him to the ill effects of a throbbing head. The third ring intensified the sharp ache between his temples. He felt the couch move with the rest of the room, so he quickly braced himself. His right hand dropped like a weighted anchor, his left hand strangling a cushion. When it rang again, he forced himself to sit up, causing his head to almost explode. By the fifth ring, he was on unsteady feet. He steadied himself against the couch and rubbed his hurting eyes. He wobbled slightly and then staggered half-blind towards the phone when it rang a sixth time. "Hold on, for Christ's sake!" He felt for the chair and then fell into it heavily. He lifted the receiver and placed it to his ear.

"Mr. Carboni?" asked the man on the other end of the line.

"Yeah, this is he," he growled. His voice was low, raspy, like he needed to clear his throat.

The caller had taken the chance he would be in. He had called him moments earlier at his home but got no answer. The apartment with its cheap furnishings was empty. Bruno hadn't been there for days, preferring instead to sleep in the office. Those who drank heavy usually fell into bed hard and slept late, so the caller had purposely called early. He cared little if he happened to wake him.

"I need you to investigate a matter of great importance," stated the dull voice at the other end.

Bruno's eyes were shut, and he yawned long. He was punch drunk from consuming too much, so much of what was said was not getting through.

"Do you read the newspaper, Mr. Carboni?" asked the caller.

His eyes were now open but saw little. The sunlight that came through the twisted blinds that hung in the window to his left caused his eyes to flicker. The tiny cutouts revealed what they could of large, brown eyes above his beefy nose. The long, thick black hair was everywhere, matted in sweat and lying in all directions. Bruno pulled at his face. Three days' growth against his rough palms sounded like sandpaper.

"Yeah, who doesn't?"

The caller's dull tone irritated the whiskey-induced pounding. It sounded deliberate. He found it annoying.

"Which paper do you read, Mr. Carboni?"

"Look, pal, I'm not interested."

"Don't be so hasty, Mr. Carboni. I can be of great help to you in your hour of need."

Dead silence.

"Which paper, Mr. Carboni?"

A lack of sleep and four-fifths of whiskey the night before made him irritable, dulling his senses to where he could not think straight. "I read a few—*Tribune* mostly." That was just in his tiny office. There was no way of recollecting what he drank at the bar just up the street the day before. He never kept count. "Is this a survey? Because if it is, I'm not interested."

"No, not at all, Mr. Carboni. I have a job for you, and I want you to take it," he droned on.

Three hours' sleep and a head that thumped unmercifully. He quickly checked his watch. "Do you know what time it is, pal?"

"I have a job for you, Mr. Carboni. Does it matter?"

He was in a nasty mood. "Yeah, it matters! Why don't you call back at a more decent time?"

"That won't be necessary. This shouldn't take long, Mr. Carboni."

"It may be shorter than you think, pal." Bruno yanked open the top drawer. "By the way," he asked abruptly, searching for something to take the sour taste from his mouth. "I didn't get your name."

"Have you ever heard of Tweeksbury, Mr. Carboni?"

There was a dead silence. Holt waited on the other end for Carboni to respond. Drunks needed time to sort through the fog that they constantly lived in. Carboni concentrated on finding something sweet.

"Mr. Carboni?"

"Yeah, hold on!"

"Take your time, Mr. Carboni."

Tweeksbury sounded vaguely familiar. He thought hard. "Yeah, I remember," he said halfheartedly, searching through the drawer. "I think it was in the paper a couple of weeks ago," barked Carboni. Bruno found a stick of gum and placed it on his thick tongue before pulling his chair closer to his desk, cradling the phone against his head. The constant questioning was starting to aggravate him, pushing him closer to the edge where he would flare up. He raised his tone and asked a second time, "Just who the hell are you?"

"I'm Mr. Benjamin Holt, Mr. Carboni. I'm the father of Lionel Holt, one of the two boys who were falsely accused in the deaths of those two girls."

Bruno could taste the mint as it refreshed his stale mouth. He chewed between sentences. "So why are you calling me? He got off."

"You obviously haven't read the newspapers since then, Mr. Carboni. My son is dead." He paused, and then his voice came back faint, almost cracking. Bruno thought he heard him choke. "He was found in the parking lot of a run-down bar, Mr. Carboni. Buried face down in mud." There was another pause, and then his voice came back, only stronger. "That's no way to die, Mr. Carboni. Wouldn't you agree?"

"So what you're saying is that he was murdered?"

"Precisely. And do you know what he was killed with, Mr. Carboni? An arrow from a crossbow. What do you think of that, Mr. Carboni?"

The answer never came. In his hour of need, he cared little about who killed some irritating stranger's son. He was more interested in parking his butt on the couch and sleeping until his hangover disappeared.

"I'm sorry to hear about the death of your son, Mr. Holt, but if you'll excuse my rudeness, I've got some unfinished business to attend to."

"Not so fast, Mr. Carboni. We haven't finished our conversation. I hear you're very good at what you do."

Bruno hesitated, letting the unexpected compliment massage his soft ego. His head still throbbed, but the cloud was lifting. It had been a while since he had heard anything positive about himself or what he did. He reached for a cigarette and lit it.

"Did I hear you right? Did you say an arrow?"

"That's right, Mr. Carboni, an arrow."

Bruno stared at the empty whisky bottle sitting on his desk. "And I take it you want me to investigate his murder?"

"That's right."

More curious than concerned, he asked, "When did this happen?"

"Early Friday morning, Mr. Carboni."

"Don't you think you should let the authorities investigate it first before you go around waking people up?" he said angrily. Bruno did not have the foggiest clue where Tweeksbury was, nor did he care. The compliment had already worn off. "It's only been three days."

"Mr. Carboni, do you know anything about small town life?"

Bruno twisted in his chair. The caller sounded like he was about to give a lecture. *Who the hell cares?* All this talk was intensifying the pain between his ears.

"Mr. Holt. Can I call you Ben?"

No answer.

"Look, Ben," said Bruno sternly. "I'd appreciate it if you would stop using my last name every time you feel you have something to say. It's irritating the hell out of me, and it's giving me a fucking headache. And, no," he shot back. "I was born and raised in the city! What the hell business is it of yours?" he asked tersely.

His shouting quickly produced a sharp pain that shot up the side of his head. He closed his eyes, which pinched his face. He slowly massaged his temples and waited for it to subside.

Again Holt ignored him.

"Nothing much ever gets done in a small town, especially in one like Tweeksbury, Mr. Carboni."

Benjamin Holt was used to getting things done his way, on his own terms. Over thirty years of success in the mining industry had come by way of producing results, by getting things done when they had to be done, by skirting the law if need be, not by waiting for protocol.

"I'm not interested in waiting for an inept small town posse to find the killers of my son, Mr. Carboni. I did not get to where I am today by waiting for things to happen. Do you understand, Mr. Carboni?"

This wasn't going well. His body ached, not to mention his head. Three hours' sleep. A stranger droning on about something he couldn't care less about. It was hard to think. He was an ex-cop who liked the occasional scrap, and Bruno wanted nothing more than to fight this little shit! Bare knuckles, if need be, and the little twerp at the other end was making it all the harder to resist. If he heard his last name one more time, he was going to tell the little fuck off.

"And just where are you, Ben?" he asked warmly, the pain having subsided somewhat. Alert, his eyes now came to life at the prospect that he may be close by.

"That's not important, Mr. Carboni. Are you with me?"

Bruno needed to think. He dragged hard on his cigarette. At present, he was an investigator with no current clients who needed work. The rent was coming due. The phone bill was in the top drawer, unpaid. And there was Martino to deal with. He wanted his money. His anger slacked off a bit as he thought about it. *Maybe it's better to listen first*, his brain told him. He could mull it over and then decide. If he didn't like it, he could tell him in his own terms what he could do with his offer and then go back to the couch. He ignored his impulse: to run his mouth, to tell the little shit to go fuck himself, and hang up the phone. He decided to listen.

"So, what are you suggesting?"

"I want you to find whoever killed my son." Benjamin Holt's voice was passionate. "I don't care what you have to do, but I want you to find who killed my boy."

It was the second time he heard Holt display any sign of emotion. He distinctly heard him choke back the words.

"I don't care what it takes. I want whoever did this to my son found." Holt pushed his plan forward. "I'm sending you a lump sum to get you started. I don't care what you have to do to find out who did this, but I want them found. Make no mistake about my resolve, Mr. Carboni. I want them found. Do I make myself clear, Mr. Carboni?"

Holt's assumption brought a swift and heated reply.

"Hold on there, pal," he stated loudly. "I never said I was taking your damn case. Nobody dictates to me. I decide what cases I'm going to investigate. You don't tell me. I tell you!"

It was tough talk from a guy with little money and no clients. Again he grabbed his head, not thinking. The pain was now in front, between his two soft lobes, and it hurt like hell.

"Oh, I think you will, Mr. Carboni. From what I've heard, you have quite an appetite. Do you like to gamble, Mr. Carboni?"

"What are you getting at, Ben?"

"Let's just say I know all about you and your little habit. You're deeply in debt, Mr. Carboni. From what I hear, a certain Mr. Martino is not one to be disappointed. You need a job, and I'm here to help you. Consider me a friend who wants to help someone out of a jam."

This little tidbit caught him off guard. He wondered what else he knew.

"Just who the hell have you been talking to?" questioned Bruno.

"That's not important, Mr. Carboni. What's important is that I'm offering you an opportunity, something that is very hard to come by at Carboni Investigations. Isn't that right, Mr. Carboni?"

"Where the hell do you—"

"Don't be too hasty, Mr. Carboni. You should think before you talk. Think of it this way. Think of this as a business partnership. You help me, I help you. You are in the business of making money, are you not Mr. Carboni?"

Bruno didn't answer. He was trying to collect his thoughts, but it was nearly impossible. Without thinking, angry about what he had been told, he blurted it out.

"I earn seven hundred dollars a day plus expenses!"

The request was inflated, but he cared little. He had an ego, and it needed to be soothed. Bullying came with a price. If it was too much, he had a couch waiting.

Holt came at him again.

"I believe twenty thousand should get you started."

Bruno didn't answer, crushing his cigarette in the ashtray instead. Holt was coming at him like a pit bull. He had to think. He was heavily in debt. There were no clients.

"Do we have a deal, Mr. Carboni?"

He was still thinking. Seven hundred dollars a day. At that burn rate, he could chew through the twenty thousand in less than three weeks. He could have asked for double and probably gotten away with it. There had been no haggling about the price, no counteroffer.

"How much did you say?"

"Twenty thousand. If you need more, it'll be there."

"And when did you say you were sending the money?"

"I'm writing the check as we speak. It'll be arriving at

your office sometime Tuesday. Let's say, around eleven." He paused and then said, "Nice to have you aboard, Mr. Carboni. Find me the killer before anyone else, and I'll see about your creditors. I take care of those who do as I ask, Mr. Carboni. Keep in touch."

Holt hung up the receiver, smiling, and exited the booth. He watched the street with its centuries-old buildings, inhaling the warm afternoon air of Lisbon's thriving Baikal district with its shoppers and tourists.

Carboni's money was sitting in a brown envelope in a safe at the headquarters of Holt International Inc., in Chicago, ready to be delivered only it wasn't a check. It was in notes—twenty one-thousand-dollar U.S. bills along with a letter addressed to "Mr. Bruno Carboni c/o Carboni Investigations." Holt had been pretty sure that Carboni would take the case. He was in trouble with the wrong crowd. He needed money, and fast, and the promise of paying his debts was just an added incentive. The smiling Benjamin Holt had gotten just what he wanted.

Holt checked his watch and then quickly stepped into the limo parked at the curb. There would be no record of his call.

Bruno leaned on the desk with both elbows and massaged his aching head. His brain throbbed, and the effort to think hurt like hell. The pit bull sounded as mysterious as the role he played in the life of his son, according to what he could recollect, which was very little. The image of Benjamin Holt was not a flattering one.

He tried vainly to place a face with a name from those who may have talked about his addiction to an outsider, probably one of the department heads who had it in for him and successfully gutted his career. His fraternizing with undesirables had cost him dearly in the days and months that followed. First his marriage and then over the years his children who no longer wanted anything to do with him, which he attributed to his ex, not to mention his career with the department. Seventeen years—ten with vice and seven with the white-collar crime division. All gone, flushed down the toilet. And so was his early pension.

He stared blankly at the empty bottle, trying to remember how he made it to the couch. One drink had led to two, which had led to three, which had led to who knows how many more. It was a binge like all the others. He rubbed his face with both hands, pulling on the deep creases on either side. His head still throbbed, and the couch was behind him. Tired and aching, he quickly spat out the gum and then pulled the receiver and slept until two.

Chapter 10

Just before eleven, the elevator doors opened, and Fischer stepped out onto the fourth floor with the file folder tucked under his arm. He was alone, and except for Sally, the lobby was empty.

"We weren't expecting you," said Sally from behind the counter, looking surprised. "Pat told me you wouldn't be in today."

"Sorry, Sally. Change of plans." He pushed his sunglasses above his eyes and approached the counter.

"Is Pat in?"

"He just stepped out. He should be back in about half an hour."

"I take it Haskills is in Tweeksbury?"

"He left yesterday afternoon. He wasn't too happy about it."

"He'll get over it," he said.

"How's Erin?" she asked.

"She's fine. They're going to keep her in the hospital until she delivers. Rocky and I have the place to ourselves for a while." He moved towards the doors. "I need you to do me a favor. If and when Haskills calls, make sure you tell him that I want to speak to him. It's important."

Miles excused himself and pushed past the set of glass doors that separated reception from the chaos of the newsroom. He had planned ahead of time to make it to his office before the deluge started. While driving from the hospital, he had decided it would be better to send a general e-mail. It was easier rather than spending the next twenty minutes repeating the same answers to the same questions from those who were deeply concerned about yesterday and the health of the Fischer family when a simple e-mail would do the trick. It was nothing personal. It was just easier.

He kept his head down as if this somehow made him invisible. He moved quickly between the rows, past the desks cluttered with stacks of paper and brightly lit monitors with people working the keyboards. He half-waved and nodded to those who caught him with his head up, but he kept moving, saying nothing. If there were any hurt feelings, he would explain it all later, but not now.

He slipped in quickly and shut the door. It was almost eleven, which meant it was almost eight in Tweeksbury. Sheriff Knibbs was about to make his appearance on the streets of Tweeksbury like some grand peacock. He hoped Haskills was up and hauling ass to greet him.

On his way in he had done a little research, stopping at a corner store after visiting Erin and buying a copy of the *Sunday-Times*, their competitor. He leafed through it while parked at the curb with the engine running and the air-conditioning blasting, sipping a Coke. Tweeksbury was not mentioned.

He grabbed the receiver and dialed 9 and then 0. He waited for the operator and then asked for the number of the Chester Junction police department.

He hung up the receiver after talking with the folks on Dearborn Street and stared at his blank computer screen. Suddenly the door opened.

"I did it!"

Veronica quickly parked her nice little butt in one of the chairs and crossed her legs.

He stared at her, surprised by her entry, and then asked, "Did what?"

"I did it. I told her off," she said from behind that smug little smile of hers.

"Sorry, Veronica, but can't this wait? I've got something really important—"

"This will only take a minute, Miles."

He stared at the phone and then slowly receded deeper into his chair, not quite sure if he could spare the time, but he relented. "Yeah, okay. I guess I can spare five minutes."

"You know I have to have my coffee first, right?" He nodded. "Well, I'm sitting in the lunchroom when she walks in, and without even saying good morning, she just starts barking out these orders about wanting me to do some work for her. I don't know what happened. I just lost it," she said before shrugging her shoulders.

"So what did you say?"

"I asked her where Charlotte was. She said that she was away. I said it wasn't my problem. I told her she'd have to find someone else. I told her that if she had a problem with it, she should speak with you or Tony. Then I called her a cow. I didn't think she heard me, but it seemed to do the trick."

"What do you mean?"

"She stormed out of the room, and I haven't seen her since. If I had known that, I would have called her a cow a long time ago." She chuckled and then suddenly her jaw stiffened. "You don't think I'm going to get into trouble over this, do you? I mean, you don't think I'll get fired, do you? I can't afford to lose this job."

"I doubt it. She doesn't carry that much weight around here. If Pat says anything to me, I'll just tell him how she's been badmouthing you around the office."

He suddenly winced, wishing he hadn't said what he said, but it was too late. Suddenly her eyes became enlarged. She moved to the edge of her seat.

"What do you mean, badmouthing me?"

This was going to be awkward. He moved forward and placed his elbows on the desk.

"Look, Veronica. It isn't anything you haven't already heard. I told you before that I told her I didn't like the way she went around and talked about people behind their backs."

"Did she say something to you? Because if she did, I'll go straighten her out right now."

He shook his head. "You don't want to do that."

"I don't?"

"No. It won't get you anywhere. Besides, she's going to be retiring in a couple of months. It's not worth it."

Veronica pursed her lips together, thinking about what Miles had said, before pulling in a deep, heavy breath and expelling it from her lungs. She stared at the ceiling.

"Is everything okay?"

She leveled her head.

"I guess I'm a little stressed from all the studying, too many late nights. I don't have much of a social life right now." She frowned. "I guess it's getting to me."

Miles glanced at his watch. It was past eleven thirty.

"Look, I don't need you right now, and it looks like Tony's out. Why don't you take a break? Go get yourself a coffee or something."

She pushed her hand through her hair. "I guess I'm letting Tang get to me. It's either her or my studies. Thanks." She smiled and was at the door. "God, I almost forgot." She turned. "Forgive me, Miles? How's Erin?"

"Everything's fine. I'll tell you about it later. Right now I've got something I have to do."

"Do you want anything?"

"No, I'm fine. You go ahead."

Built in the early nineteen hundreds, it was once part of the vibrant downtown core. Now the Lincoln Building (a name used liberally and often by patriotic Americans) sat quietly in a forgotten section of the downtown South Side, away from the life and energy of uptown called the Loop. The instructions were simple enough. Just drop the package off at the old Lincoln Building on Wabash Avenue and leave. Fifth floor, corner suite to your right, the instructions said. No signature required, so don't bother knocking. Just drop it off and leave.

He parked in the alley at precisely eleven o'clock as instructed and exited his truck, carrying a large brown manila envelope. He was a courier who worked for UPS who thought this was odd and who wasn't accustomed to this cloak and dagger stuff. The instructions, though explicit, were a little strange because no signature was required from the receiver, which was usually a mandatory prerequisite on the part of the sender in case they said it was not delivered. The extra hundred bucks in his pocket for delivering this package at this exact address at this precise hour said it was okay, so he didn't ask any questions.

He took the stairs because the elevator did not work. By the time he made it to the fourth floor, he was almost out of breath due to his excessive weight. He could hear his heavy footsteps echo through the empty hallways above and below as he climbed another flight of stairs to the fifth floor, making the open staircase and the halls sound eerily hollow. He quickly checked the suite number with the instructions. Heavy snoring could be heard from the other side. He hesitated and checked the number again to be sure and then quietly slipped the envelope under the door of Carboni Investigations, Ltd., and left. A hundred bucks—piece of cake.

Eleven forty-five in the morning, and still Haskills had not called. *He's probably still sleeping,* he thought, *instead of hauling ass.* Miles had punched the numbers to his cell three times and hung up three times, changing his mind at the last minute. He would give him another hour and then he would call, and this time he promised he wouldn't hang up.

After five minutes of waiting and doing nothing, he changed his mind and thought about calling and waking the idiot up. *It shouldn't take this long,* he thought. All he had to do was to be there at eight and ask a few simple questions to find out whether or not there were any suspects and if they were incarcerated and if not, then when. How hard was that? If it were up to him, he would have been out of bed before the sun peeked over the horizon with his ass parked on the steps until Knibbs showed up, and then he would have been in his face asking the kinds of questions that were waiting to be answered.

He tapped a pencil while he waited. The authorities in Whatley and Chester Junction had already confirmed what was not in the file. Each case was still cold, sitting and collecting dust in one of their filing cabinets with nothing else to report. He had called the FBI in three different states, starting with Massachusetts, on the chance that they were involved now that Holt and Masalla were dead. *If they suspect anything, anything at all, then for sure they will be involved,* he thought. He got nowhere with the first three and then for some reason got rerouted to South Dearborn Street. After waiting and being passed through numerous internal channels, he finally connected with Agent Abrams, whom he knew, but Abrams had little to say.

"I can't answer that. Yes. No comment. No comment. Look, I gotta go. I've got another call."

Click!

Damn, this was aggravating.

He rubbed his forehead and thought of the idiot. *Where the hell is he?* He was checking his watch a second time when suddenly the phone rang. It was Sally. Haskills was waiting on the other end.

"Put him through."

Chapter 11

Lynch's office was a corner suite with more space and more windows, and it had pictures of George Washington and Ulysses S. Grant hanging on the walls. Lynch was inside, sitting in his chair. The desk was cluttered with paperwork. Fischer, without speaking, tapped the door with a firm knock and then went inside.

"Miles."

"Morning, Pat." He parked his ass in one of the chairs, placing the folder in front of him.

"Sally told me you were in. I take it you got my message?"

"Yeah, I did, but there was nothing to do at home."

"I heard about Erin. I'm glad everything's okay. You know that I sent Haskills in your place?"

"Sally told me."

A man of few words, Lynch leaned back in his chair and clasped his hands behind his head.

"So, what's up?"

Miles moved to the edge of his chair, closer to the desk.

"After we talked yesterday about what happened in Tweeksbury, I decided to do a little research. I had Veronica search the archives to see what was there. I took it home and studied it last night." He tossed the file in front of Lynch. "There were two other crossbow killings prior to the one in Tweeksbury. One was in 1991 in Chester Junction involving two guys who were later implicated in the murder of a teen and the attempted murder of her mother in Eastbrook. The other one involved this guy Wilcox over in Whatley. He was out on temporary release after his family posted the bail bond— a couple of million, if my recollection is right. He was accused in the rape and murder of a teen who was babysitting for a young couple. He impersonated a cop to gain entry."

"How in the hell did he make bail?" Lynch leaned forward and took the file and began to leaf through it. "You don't just get bail for impersonating a cop."

"It was a mistake, according to the judge who signed the bond. He was a friend of the family. You know how it is with big money. They found her bent over the sofa when they returned home. Two days after he's out on bail, he's on the streets, a violation of his bond. The next morning someone finds him in a dark alleyway with an arrow through his chest."

"Sounds like the family picked the wrong friend to help their son," he said without looking up.

"I think there could be a connection between those places and Tweeksbury. I called the authorities in Chester Junction and Whatley when I came in this morning, and they confirmed that those cases are still sitting in their files, unsolved. I talked to Haskills just a minute ago, and there is nothing coming out of Tweeksbury, either. All they have in the way of evidence is the nylon rope that the killer used to get to the roof of the hardware store and the arrows used to kill Holt and Masalla, but nothing else to link the killer to their murders—no fingerprints, hair, none of this DNA stuff that's floating around, nothing."

"So what's the connection?" he asked, still reading.

"The use of a crossbow. How many killers use a crossbow to murder their victims? A gun would have been so much easier, don't you think?"

"It's unusual, I know," he said, still looking through the file, "but it doesn't necessarily mean they're connected. Did you consider that it might be a copycat?" He stopped reading and looked at Miles. "We've seen it before. Some local gets pissed off at these guys because he's a father with a daughter of his own, and after a few drinks he decides he's Dick Tracy and takes the law into his own hands. There's no shortage of loose cannons out there, you know."

"I don't think so."

"Why not?"

"Because there's no evidence to support it. If each murder was done by a different person, then there should have been some evidence left at one of the scenes that would lead to the person responsible—some hair possibly, a footprint, a cigarette butt maybe while they waited for their victim, even a tire track or something with a perfect image of their fingerprint. Killers can do stupid things, but in each instance there's not a thing that the authorities can utilize that would lead them to the persons responsible. If there were different killers involved, then it would have produced different results. Besides, it doesn't explain what happened in Eastbrook."

"What do you mean?"

"Nobody knew who attacked those women. There were no witnesses."

"What about the mother?" he asked.

"She doesn't remember a thing because of the beating she took."

Lynch placed the file on the desk.

"Doesn't help your story much, does it? What's the motive?"

"I don't know. Maybe it's like you said. Maybe it's a vigilante."

"If it's a vigilante, then it could be just about anybody."

"Could be, but I don't think so."

"Why not?"

"Because what happened in Tweeksbury and Whatley was after the fact."

"You mean the Zimmerman family?"

"Exactly," he said, moving deeper into his chair. "Up until then, there are no reported cases involving the use of a crossbow to take out someone who was involved in a rape and murder. I don't know how to explain it, but I have this strange feeling that everything originates from Eastbrook."

"We don't investigate a story based on feelings, Miles. We investigate based on facts."

"I know, but somebody had to have seen something. That's the only way to explain what happened. The question is who? That's why we have to investigate what happened in Eastbrook and Whatley. Don't you think it's strange that on three separate occasions a crossbow was used on the perpetrators? And not just on any crime, but ones involving the rape of minors, excluding the mother, of course, who were then murdered."

"I guess, but this is America, Miles. There's nothing strange about what goes on in this country. Hell, take a look around you."

"I know it sounds a little crazy."

"Sounds more like some wild goose chase," he said, leaving his desk for the window. "From what you've told me so far," he said, slipping his hands into his pockets, "you really don't have much to go on. Tell me, how can you write a story when you have no witnesses?"

"Christ, Pat." Miles was back to sitting on the edge of his chair. "Didn't you tell me in my office yesterday that you felt what happened to Holt and Masalla could be bigger than the original trial?"

"Yes, but not in the context of what you're thinking right now. What I meant was the killing of those two boys in the context of what it would do to the town if it was a local who killed Holt and what's-his-name. Maybe it is a vigilante, but now you want to expand it to two other cases that have been collecting mothballs for years. How are you going to get anyone to remember anything? Hell, I can barely remember what I did yesterday."

"You can't just blow it off."

"Don't be so sure."

"Then explain to me how Thornton and Patrick were killed months later if there were no witnesses? If the mother can't remember anything then somebody had to have witnessed the rape or at least part of it."

"I don't have to," he said angrily. "I'm not the one who wants to include cases that are year's old and collecting mothballs in someone's office. They're cold for a reason Miles. Whether we like it or not, cases go unsolved in this country every year and people get away with it. I don't like it anymore than you do but that's just the way it is."

The room went quiet. Miles crossed his legs and settled deeper into his chair. Both men were obviously entrenched in their beliefs, unwilling to budge or look at each other. Finally, one of them spoke.

"I called the FBI," Miles said rather quietly. "I think they may be involved after what happened in Tweeksbury. I had to make three different calls to three different cities before I finally got through to someone who knew something about these crossbow killings. In fact, I ended up talking to Abrams over on South Dearborn. I asked him if the FBI was involved in the cases in Chester Junction and Whatley. After a long pause, he replied that they had been. I asked him if it was ongoing, and he said he couldn't comment. I then asked him if they were involved in what just happened in

Tweeksbury, and again he wouldn't comment. Then he told me he had an incoming call he had to take, so that was the end of the conversation."

"Why is the Chicago office involved in this?"

"I asked him, but he wouldn't say. But the important point here is when he said they *had been*. They've obviously looked into it. If they suspect the same killer is responsible for what happened in Chester Junction and Whatley, that their suspect crossed state lines, then they're involved for sure. The way I see it, up until now they haven't been able find anything, so they've just let it sit, hoping that something would come up to move the investigation along. Now they have the killings of Holt and Masalla. I asked Haskills if he knew if the FBI was involved in Tweeksbury, but he said he didn't know. They may get involved in Tweeksbury if they think there's a connection."

"Possible."

"There's something else that I think is interesting. I noticed that what happened in Whatley wasn't carried by us until Wilcox was killed. Veronica copied the original story about the babysitter from the local paper, but there was nothing from the *Tribune* or the AP. Kind of odd, don't you think?"

"What are you getting at?"

"If the babysitter killing wasn't reported by us or the AP or the major networks or their affiliates at the time it happened, then maybe it was picked up by another newspaper somewhere in the country."

"I don't follow."

"Maybe that's how the killer knew about this Wilcox guy."

"I still don't follow, Miles."

"Whatley has no television or radio station. With no

services to transmit the news and a paper that only publishes two days a week, that would support the fact why the story never came to light in the major newspapers until three or four days later, after Wilcox was killed. If a local didn't do the killing, how did the killer know about the rape and murder of the babysitter? They had to read about it in another paper, but which one? The *Whatley Examiner* only publishes twice a week—Wednesdays and Saturdays. The murder of the babysitter happened on a Friday. Wilcox was arrested on Saturday night, so his name isn't in the paper. Sunday his family gets him out of jail by posting bail. That's a difference of almost four days before the next publication. Plus, I'm sure Wilcox's family tried to keep this quiet, considering their connections. Would you want your neighbors to know that your son was arrested for raping and killing an innocent babysitter? At least you would want to keep it as quiet as possible given your affluence in a place as small as Whatley. They probably paid somebody off. That would explain Wilcox getting his bond. Don't forget the judge was a friend of the family. It's happened before. The killing of Wilcox in Whatley is unsolved, so who did it if it wasn't a local? It would be pretty easy to track the whereabouts of twelve thousand people, don't you think, if any one of them did the killing? And how do you hide the fact if any of the townsfolk owned a crossbow? Everyone knows everyone else's business. It would be pretty hard to hide something like that. Somebody said something. The question is who said it and who did they say it to."

"That may be true Miles but don't you think the authorities have already figured that out?"

"I don't think so. They're not newspaper people. They don't think like we do. At least, I don't think they do. How are they going to figure out which newspaper carried what story? I doubt that they're even thinking along those lines, especially the locals. Hell, it's probably their first murder investigation. If the FBI is involved, all they know is that they've got two unsolved cases on their hands—end of story. Three, when you count what happened in Tweeksbury. I don't know about you, but I think it's a valid point about who may have carried the story."

Lynch moved back behind his desk.

"What makes you think that you can find the story with no witnesses? That's the one question that keeps nagging me." Lynch picked up the file and then released it back onto his desk. "Christ Miles! These happened six, eight years ago. How are you going to do that?"

"I'm not sure I can, but I think it's worth investigating, don't you?"

"I'm not totally convinced."

"Maybe you can answer this then. Why only these three murders using a crossbow? Why isn't this person taking to the highways and killing a rapist/murderer every time he reads about one in the newspaper?" Miles didn't wait for an answer. "This killer is smart. There's a reason why he's doing what he's doing, but he's not perfect. No killer is. He's going to make a mistake if he hasn't already. All we have to do is find the mistake, and when we do, we'll know who the killer is."

"I don't know, Miles. From everything you've said, I'm pretty sure the FBI and anybody else who is in on these cases would know all this. I don't know what you're going to find that isn't already out there."

"Except which newspaper beside the local journal carried the original on Wilcox," he stated unequivocally, leaning forward.

"Granted, but we don't know that yet."

"Not yet, but it shouldn't be a problem. People talk. People love to talk. Look, Pat. Somewhere out there somebody knows something or saw something or maybe both. Somewhere out there, there's a killer with a special skill. He's clean and neat and leaves no traces. He's doing society a favor by killing these rapists and murderers, but he's still a criminal. It's up to us to find out who it is and print the story."

Miles stayed perched at the edge of his chair and waited for the big man to make a decision. He had given him everything he had, laid it out as best he could. Frankly, the decision wasn't all that difficult, if it was up to him. Lynch sat quietly in his chair and stared at the file, saying nothing.

"Maybe you forgot, but I did you a favor the other day filling in for Mahaffey," he added, trying to sway his decision.

"Shit, Miles, don't pull that crap on me."

"Then say yes so I can get the hell out of here. We're a newspaper, for Christ's sake. We have an obligation to every citizen out there who believes in what we do. Maybe I haven't convinced you, but I'm telling you there's a connection."

Lynch stared at him with no expression, carefully considering his options.

"Okay, Miles," he finally said, tossing the file back in front of him. "I'm not totally convinced, but I'll give you a week. No more."

Miles stared at Lynch, not at all happy about the time constraint.

"Seven days?"

"That's right."

"I was thinking more of—"

"Don't push me, Miles. You've got a week. Take it or leave it."

Miles pursed his lips together, which narrowed his eyes. He hesitated, thinking, and then he said, "I guess I'll see you in seven days, then." Miles grabbed the folder and quickly headed for the door before Lynch could change his mind.

"Don't forget. One week, Miles, and then I want to see you back in my office."

Miles was already out the door.

"That's Tuesday, Miles," he said loudly.

He splashed his face with cold water from the sink next to the toilet, thinking about the money, all twenty thousand of it in one-thousand-dollar notes. In less than twenty-four hours, Benjamin Holt had become the biggest contributor in the short, unassuming existence of Carboni Investigations and currently its only source of revenue. *But who cares? These are good times, so enjoy it.* "Twenty thousand," he mumbled. He congratulated himself in the mirror and splashed his face again. At the moment he looked like hell. His eyes were still bloodshot after his long nap, with bags under each one, and he looked older than his age of fifty-one. There appeared to be more lines, too. Plus, there was an extra fifty pounds on his large frame that made him look bloated, mostly from the booze and the lousy food he ate, but at this moment he didn't care. He had twenty thousand, and there would be more if he needed it. It was the most money he had ever had in his life at any one time, so what he saw in the mirror did not bother him. In his alcohol-induced state, with little time to decipher what the caller had said, he thought Benjamin Holt was off his rocker. He had literally grabbed a figure out of thin air, and somehow it had worked. He was still in shock, but what the hell—it felt good and it would soon wear off when the money started to disappear. *So enjoy it,* he told himself. "Twenty thousand," he said, thinking how lucky he was to have Benjamin Holt literally fall into his lap. He had out-negotiated a man who made deals around the world worth millions. He had beaten him at his own game. *What a schmuck,* he thought, chuckling to himself.

Bruno dried his face with a paper towel and began to whistle, making his way back to his little office down the hall. The light melody carried easily in the empty hallway, wafting to the open staircase and to the floors above and below. Twenty thousand, and there was more where that came from. These, indeed, were good times.

It was just a matter of time before the writing on the letter that accompanied the twenty thousand would start to fade. Thanks to a special chemical in the paper, the ink would be gone in three to four days, erasing the name and signature of Benjamin Holt along with the purpose of sending the money, thus rendering the letter useless.

It was planned that way.

Chapter 12

It seemed like only yesterday he was out west, covering the trial in Tweeksbury. Now, four and a half weeks later, he was on the East Coast, driving towards Eastbrook. It was Thursday, day two with five days to go before he had to meet Lynch back in his office. He had driven to Whatley on Wednesday morning and then on to St. Louis for a brief stopover before catching an early morning flight to Boston.

His visit with Erin the night before had not gone well. Erin made a point of listing how many days he had been away in the past four weeks.

"I can't help that," he said.

"I hardly see you anymore," she replied back.

"There was nothing I could do," he told her.

Erin took it up a notch and questioned his commitment about having a baby. He shot back, telling her that it was her idea about starting a family and not his, and the argument was on. It could be heard all the way down the hall. He left a short time later, but not before he asked her why she married him in the first place if his job was such a problem when it wasn't before. There was no answer from Erin, just an icy stare. He reluctantly kissed her on the lips and told her he would be back in a couple of days, and then he left.

What he had told Lynch back in his office on Tuesday morning was only a hunch about whether or not the story from Whatley had been leaked to another newspaper. He had no name, no description, and no third party to lead him to the person responsible, if that's what actually happened. He had nothing.

Miles had first thought about walking into the office of the *Examiner* and asking whoever was behind the counter if they knew who might have passed on the information, but then he dismissed it as a stupid idea. Reporters were like lawyers. Besides being competitive, they were also secretive. They didn't divulge anything unless they had to. It would be almost impossible to explain what he was looking for without alerting them to the possibility that a serial vigilante may be behind what happened to Wilcox and the others. "What others?" they would ask. Without a name, any line of questioning would be too suspicious.

After going over all of his options and checking his hair in the mirror just above the visor, Miles decided on the next best thing. A barbershop was the hub of a small town, a microcosm where everybody spoke of the goings-on in their community. What better place than a barbershop?

Miles found the barbershop on the corner of Old Town Road and Oak and went inside. He took a seat by the front window, where two men were waiting their turn. They were somewhere in their fifties and talking loudly about hunting and possibly killing something in the fall. He sat next to them and casually flipped through a magazine, a dated *Field and Stream*. Less than an hour later, he was sitting in the chair, getting a trim and browsing through the local paper while the clippers buzzed around his ears.

"You must be new," Sam said. "I haven't seen you around here before. Where are you from?"

"Up north," replied Miles, without getting into the specifics. "I'm on my way to St. Louis."

Sam had been cutting hair for close to forty years. The hair was almost gray.

"So what do you do for a living?" he asked.

"I'm a writer."

"A writer, eh. What kind of things do you write about?"

"People mostly."

"Oh, you mean like those Hollywood magazines."

"No, not quite," Miles said, trying not to laugh. "Right now, I'm working on something a little different. I'm trying to put together a story on the Wilcox kid."

Sam stopped cutting and stared at him rather curiously.

"What do you want to do that for?"

"I'm kind of interested in who may have killed him."

"You're wasting your time," said Sam, who was back to cutting. "The police still don't know who it is. It sure as hell wasn't one of us."

Two older gentlemen waiting their turn looked at Miles in much the same manner as Sam did. They were roughly the same age, somewhere in their seventies.

Sam looked at him again, only suspiciously this time. "You're not here to stir up any kind of trouble, are you?"

"No, nothing like that. It's just that I heard a rumor that somebody may have tipped off another newspaper before it was printed in the *Examiner*."

"Who told you that?"

"They asked me to keep it confidential."

"It was probably Abe over at the gas station," whispered one of the men, looking at his friend. "He never could keep his mouth shut."

"Nah. It's probably Dalton who used to own the paint store," said the other one.

"Ah, you're wrong." He waved at him, brushing him off. "It was Abe, I tell you."

"You're full of beans. It was Dalton. He used to be a ham operator."

"So what? You think you have to be a ham operator

in order to know what's going on around here. It's Abe, I tell you."

"Don't listen to him," said the taller man. "He doesn't know what he's talking about."

Miles looked at him but didn't say anything, thinking this might lead somewhere.

"I do so."

"It's Dalton, I tell you. He's the one who owned a police scanner. He used to tell me stories about some of the things they used to do. Remember me telling you about the time the police drove that guy out of town who they caught drunk over by the co-op? Remember? They drove him a couple of miles out of town and then let him walk back to sober up. Remember? The wife kicked him out of the house for a while."

"Oh yeah. I forgot. What was his name?"

"Charlie something or other."

"Oh yeah, Charlie."

"Ah, you don't know him."

"I do so."

"Then what's his last name?"

"I don't know. I can't think of it right now."

"See. I told you that you didn't know him."

"Where's this Dalton fellow now?" Miles asked.

"He's dead. He died of MS a couple of years ago."

"I didn't know he owned a police scanner," interrupted the gentleman who couldn't remember who Charlie was.

"You probably don't remember that his nephew used to work for the *Examiner*, either."

"He did?"

"Did you forget to take your pill today?" He looked over at Miles and the barber. "Look who I'm asking."

"This nephew that you mentioned—does he happen

to still work for the newspaper?" Miles asked while the barber brushed him off.

"Nope. Left about six months before the Ambro girl was killed."

"Do you remember his name?" Miles asked while he paid the barber.

"Jim Rutherford."

"Don't listen to him." The man looked over at his buddy. "That's your nephew, stupid. Take your dam pill, will you? His name is Malcolm," he said, looking back at Miles. "Malcolm Whitehead."

"Do you happen to know where he went? What newspaper?"

The old guy shook his head. "Don't know. He never told anybody."

Miles streamed out of there with a smile on his face. On his way up Oak, Miles called the *Tribune* and asked Sally to put him through to Veronica. It was urgent, he said. Miles quickly explained what he was looking for and told her to check every newspaper, from the East Coast to the West Coast, north and south, beginning with the major carriers. She was to call him on his cell phone if she found anything; otherwise, he would catch up with her when he got back. Maybe Malcolm Whitehead and the newspaper he worked for had printed the story about the death of Tiffany Ambro.

Chapter 13

Miles passed a mobile amusement park next to a strip mall and a sign that said, "WELCOME TO FRIENDLY EASTBROOK." The road was spotted with trailer parks and houses set far back into the tall trees. Farther ahead he passed a gas station with a partially rusted chain-link fence that cordoned it off from everything else. A sign saying, "Grayson's Filling Station" hung on the siding over the door, and another said it was for sale.

He tossed the map on the seat next to him and turned down Pendleton, the main drag that ran through Eastbrook. It was lined with two-story shops that looked like they were built in the forties. There was metered parking and a liquor store on the corner. He crossed the intersection and then guided his rental into one of the stalls in front of the sheriff's office.

Miles quietly closed the door and walked to the counter. An officer sat at one of four desks with his feet up. He was on the phone and talking loudly. The young deputy glanced at him, said a few words, and then hung up the phone. He casually pushed his long, lanky frame from the chair and strode to the counter like he owned the place, but not before peeking through the blinds that covered the window. His right hand rested on the revolver that sat on his square hip. He didn't appear all that friendly.

"Can I help you?"

"Nice town you have here," Miles stated, wanting to appear friendly.

"We like it," Tucker said with a frown. "Anything I can do for you?"

"Yeah, I'm looking for some information."

"What kind of information?"

"I was interested in that gas station about," Miles pointed in the direction of the door, "three miles back."

"What about it?"

"Do you know if it's for sale?"

"Why—you interested?"

Behind him, the door opened, and a tall figure walked through. He closed the door and walked across the floor using his long strides, his shiny black boots scuffing slightly against what felt like an elastic floor as it bounced beneath his weight. He stared at Miles, who was leaning on the counter.

"Hey, Dan. Who have we got here?"

Miles studied the tall figure as he came towards him. He was at least six foot two with thick thighs and a bright, shiny buckle that hung around his protruding belly. Big, silvery sunglasses with black wire frames sat on his flat nose. The walrus-like mustache almost covered both his lips. There was no introduction.

"This guy is looking for some information on the old Grayson filling station. He says he's interested in buying it."

Appleby made his way past Fischer, pushing the button on the other side of the pint-size door that separated the public from the law before letting it close behind him. Tucker moved to his left, making room for his boss before eventually moving back behind his desk.

"You thinking of selling gas from that old station? Because if you are, you could end up like old Tom." Appleby leaned forward and dropped an envelope onto a shelf below the counter and then grasped the counter with both hands. He stood in front of Fischer like a giant oak.

"What do you mean?"

"Old Tom had that station for nearly twenty-three years. After what happened back in '91, he couldn't make a go of it no more. He did some refinancing to try and make it better, but it didn't pan out. About three years later, he plumb gave up. The bank ended up repossessing it after Tom quit."

Miles could see a faint image of himself in Appleby's polished sunglasses from the bright sun coming in from the windows. Appleby seemed friendlier than Tucker. Information seemed to be readily available.

"What incident are you talking about?" queried Miles, furrowing his brow.

"The Zimmerman rape and murder. Killed the daughter and almost killed the mother." Appleby tossed his patrol hat in the direction of his desk, exposing his bald head. "Since then, the place started going downhill. Even his best customers drove in the other direction to get gas. Before he knew it, he was out of business."

"That's kind of strange for a small town, isn't it? I mean, for people, regular customers to just give up on a business like that, especially if they were loyal to it."

"Yeah, you would think so, but it didn't quite happen that way. Poor Tom took sick for a while after the incident. He had nothing to do with it, but you couldn't tell him that. He blamed himself for what happened. According to Tom, it's not all that busy at night. Usually he would be open until midnight, but he decided to close early on account that he was taking the missus on a little vacation. Didn't think there would be any harm in closing early. A day later, said if it wasn't for him, the Zimmerman girl would still be alive. Needless to say, Tom and the missus never went on that vacation. They never made it out of the driveway before the phone rang with the bad news. He took it really hard. That's when the drinking started. He closed his business down for almost two months. He told me he didn't know if his

111

heart was in it—too many bad memories. In a way, I guess you could say he took the brunt of it." He paused, eyeing the stranger in front of him more closely before nodding and pursing his lips together. "You're not from around here, are you?"

"No, I'm from out of town, but yeah, I remember reading something about that, now that you mention it." Miles did his best to look uninterested. "So that's where it happened," he said nonchalantly. "This Tom—does he still live around here?"

"Nope. He died about two years ago. Wife moved away soon after. She lives with her daughter over in Springfield."

"I take it you," Miles panned his finger in their general direction, "were the two officers who were called to the scene?"

Appleby looked uneasy. "Yeah." He raised his right knee, propping his leg on the shelf below. "You still interested in buying it?" he asked, moving the conversation in another direction. "I know the realtor in this town. I can point you in the direction of his office, if you like." He moved towards his desk. "I've got one of his cards sitting right here on my desk. I keep them here just in case."

"Well, like I was telling your deputy over there," Miles pointed in the direction of where Tucker was now sitting. He was picking at his fingernails with a paper clip but listening intently. "I said I was interested in the property, but I never said I was interested in buying it." He chuckled nervously, noticing the glare of Appleby and the stare of Tucker.

Appleby smelled a rat. He raised his glasses to the middle of his shiny, bald head. He moved back towards Miles. Clasping his fingers, he bent them backwards, cracking all his knuckles, a sure sign of intimidation.

"Well, if you're not interested in buying it, then just why are you asking about it?"

"I was interested in the incident you just talked about. I was wondering if you knew where I could find Mrs. Zimmerman. I was interested in talking with her."

Appleby leaned on the counter and stared at Fischer.

"Why do you want to talk to her?" queried Appleby.

"Sorry, but it's confidential. You know, client privilege, that sort of thing," he said, motioning with his hands.

"What did you say you did for a living?" Appleby stepped towards the window and peeked out.

"I didn't."

"You wouldn't be a reporter, now would you?"

"No. Why do you ask?"

He moved towards his chair, glaring in Fischer's direction.

"Because we don't like them. They're bad for morale, and since you're driving a rented vehicle, we especially don't like out-of-town ones. Get my drift?"

"I would just like to talk to her. If you boys can help me out, that would be really appreciated."

"I don't think that would be a good idea—Miles, is it?" he asked sarcastically. He rested his size-fourteen boots on his desk and clasped his hands behind his head. "You see, she's been through enough, losing her daughter and all. She left Eastbrook some time ago. She's made a new life for herself—tried to put it all behind her." He paused. "Mr. Fischer, I think it's best if you let sleeping dogs lie, if you know what I mean."

"Look, I just want to talk to her. If you boys can tell me where she moved to, I'll be on my way."

"Why don't you tell us why you want to talk to her,

and maybe we can help you," he stated, staring intently.

"I would if I could, but like I told you, it's a personal matter."

"Seems like if it's a personal matter, then you don't need our help. Since you're not a reporter, maybe you're her lawyer or maybe her stockbroker, in which case you should know where to find her," he said, smiling. "Doesn't sound like you need our help at all. Ain't that right, Dan?"

"Sounds about right to me," he said, still tending to his nails.

Fischer paused and quietly exhaled a deep breath. He stared at the both of them in mild disbelief. He chuckled nervously.

"You're kidding me, right? I mean, you boys are putting me on? This is some kind of a joke, right?"

"I don't think so. Hey, Dan, you know where Mrs. Zimmerman moved to?" Appleby looked over at his seated deputy. Tucker was leaning back in his chair, still picking at his fingernails with a paper clip.

"Can't say I remember too well, myself." He stopped picking and stared at Miles. "That was such a long time ago."

Miles turned to Appleby. "So I take it you're not interested in helping me find out where she lives?"

Appleby and Tucker looked at each other. Appleby stared at Miles and curled his lip and then shook his head slowly.

"Doesn't seem like it."

Frustrated, Miles glared at both men and then quietly strode toward the door. He opened it and then turned towards them.

"Have you boys ever read that sign as you're driving into your little town of Eastbrook?" he asked sarcastically.

"Yeah, what about it?" spat Appleby.

"You may want to rethink that slogan you so proudly display coming into your little town."

He placed his sunglasses back over his eyes and left.

He found a gas station after getting directions to the Zimmerman place and pulled alongside one of the pumps.

"How would you like to fill it up?"

"Regular?"

"Yeah. Is your boss around?"

"Old man Jenkins is inside." He pointed in the direction of the garage.

Miles walked the short distance to the entrance of the white and blue garage. From inside he could hear the faint sound of a radio as he approached the two open bays. He removed his sunglasses, taking a second for his eyes to adjust to the change in light, and then he carefully walked into the darkened bay, stepping over the greasy car parts that were strewn along the wall adjoining the small office. He continued until he reached the back of the garage. A small man in striped overalls was standing in front of a large workbench. Behind him, an older model vehicle sat quietly with a portable light hanging from the opened hood. Above the old man, a rack of old tires sat on makeshift shelving, along with mufflers still attached to their tailpipes and the odd car door.

"Can I help you?" asked the white-haired gentleman.

Jenkins had to be close to eighty. He was also short and thin with slightly hollowed cheeks. His face was long and his eyes a watery blue behind his circular glasses. His dingy white T-shirt sported a faded yellow ring around the neck. A pair of white Adidas adorned his small feet.

"Afternoon. I was wondering if you could help me."

The old man was working on a carburetor that was held tightly between the teeth of a vice.

"Well, you came to the right place, sonny. Ain't many places like this left anymore. What's the matter? Car won't start?"

"No. Actually it's running fine. What I wanted to ask you was if you've ever heard of the Zimmermans."

"Are you talking about the Zimmermans who used to live over on Lake Head Drive?"

"I'm not sure of the address, but the husband was a lawyer. They had a daughter by the name of Rachel."

Jenkins hesitated before he answered. He stared at Fischer, who was dressed in blue jeans and a white T-shirt along with white sneakers.

"Yeah, I know them. They're dead, you know. Least the father and daughter are gone. Don't know about the missus, though."

"I was told she moved away. Do you happen to know where she may have moved to?"

The old man went back to working on the carburetor.

"I can't remember exactly, but I know she moved after she came out of the hospital. Why you interested? That happened over eight years ago." The old man shook his head. "Poor thing…lost her husband in a traffic accident just before Christmas. Drunk driver, you know," he said, glancing up. "Four months later, her and her daughter got attacked over at Grayson's filling station." He shook his head again. "Two guys over in Chester Junction did it. They murdered her daughter. Just about killed her, too. I wish I hadda known who they were." The old man looked at Miles, shaking a long screwdriver in his right fist. "I would have taken care of them myself. Why are you looking for her?"

Miles stepped over the air filter and an old muffler that was lying on the floor. He then leaned against the long bench, next to the old man.

"I'd like to talk to her. Do you know where I might find her?"

The old man turned and leaned against the bench and then wiped his forehead with his sleeve. A bell rang from somewhere inside the bay. A car pulled alongside the other pump.

"What's the interest? You her lawyer or something?"

"No," said Fischer with a straight face, "just a friend. Over the years we sort of lost touch. I was passing through, so I thought I'd pay her a visit."

"That's a mighty long time," he remarked, scratching his head. The old man turned and went back to his work. "I can't remember for sure, but I think she moved to the West Coast," he continued. "Something about starting over, wanting to be closer to her sister, better weather and all that. After her husband died in that traffic accident, she got a big settlement from the insurance company." The old man stopped tinkering and turned to Miles. "You know she was married, right?"

"Yeah, of course," he said offhandedly, and then without thinking he added, "went to the wedding and everything. That insurance policy—do you happen to know how much she got?"

"Sorry, sonny." The old man patted Miles on his back with his dirty hand. "Small towns talk, but they don't talk about everything." He was back working on the carburetor. "By the way, where was the wedding?"

The question caught him completely off guard. Fischer hesitated at first, trying to think of what to say, and then he pressed his lips firmly together.

"I've gotta be honest with you. I didn't go to her

117

wedding," he stated rather flatly, trying to sound somewhat remorseful. "I'm a reporter for the *Chicago Tribune*. I'm interested in her story."

The old man stopped tinkering.

"Why didn't you say so?" Jenkins mused. "*Tribune*, eh? No need to be ashamed about it. Just come right out and say who you are." The old man patted him on the shoulder. "It's the best policy, sonny."

Miles glanced over at his shoulder, looking for the spot where the old man touched him.

"So you don't mind if I ask you a few more questions?"

"Nope. Got nothing else to do around here other than work on this here carburetor—piece of junk, if you ask me. I told him he needs a new one, but he doesn't want to pay for it."

Miles reached over for one of the clean rags on the bench and gently rubbed the spot that the old man had left on his white shirt.

"Do you know exactly where she moved to?"

"Can't say for sure, but I believe it was to a big city. Seattle, I think. Said she needed a change." The old man stopped and looked up at Miles. "Shouldn't you be writing this down?"

Miles pointed in the direction of his head. "I keep it all up here."

The old man chortled. "I don't doubt it for a minute, sonny."

"Did she work?" Miles asked.

"Nope. She stayed home." Jenkins was leaning over his work, making adjustments with the screwdriver. "When her daughter got older, she started selling ladies' cosmetics to the locals."

"Do they have any relatives living in Eastbrook?"

"Not that I know of, but then I don't know everything that goes on around here."

"Did you ever meet her?"

"I met her a few times when she came in with her husband. Gas mostly. Fixed her vehicle the odd time, but that's about it. Carburetor problems, just like this one here." The old man hit it with his screwdriver. "Didn't keep it tuned up. Told him so, but it didn't seem to matter. Said she didn't drive it a lot. Other than that, I didn't see her much."

"Did they have any close friends?"

"I can't say for sure. All I know is what I read in the local newspaper."

"I read in the newspaper that on the night they were attacked they were on their way home from visiting with friends. You wouldn't happen to know where they were coming from, would you?"

He thought for a moment. "Nope."

"Did you happen to attend either of the funerals?"

"No time and no invite. From what I heard, it was mostly close friends, some corporate lawyers from his firm. Maybe some family, but I don't know for sure. Besides, I'm not interested in funerals, especially at my age. I don't want to get any closer to the Almighty than I have to," said the old man under his broken laughter. "There'll be plenty of time for that when my time comes."

A smile slid across Fischer's face. "Was she a slim woman?"

"What do you mean, was she slim?" he asked, now alert.

"You know—fit, athletic."

"I'm a bit too old to take notice of those things, but yeah, I guess you could say she was fit. She wasn't fat, if that's what you're driving at."

"How tall is she?"

"How the hell would I know? She never got out of the car."

"Do you know if she had any hobbies, any sport activities?"

"What did you have in mind?"

"Oh, I don't know," he said. "Tennis and golf are popular. Maybe she liked to hike. There's a lake close by. Maybe she liked canoeing?"

"Don't know."

"What about organizations? Did she belong to any clubs?"

"What kind of clubs?"

"Gun clubs. Archery maybe."

Jenkins stared at him through the top of his glasses. "You sure are a curious one. Next thing I know you'll be asking me if she owned a crossbow and killed those two boys over in Chester Junction."

Miles took this as a green light since the old man had mentioned it. He waded in.

"Did she?"

He stopped adjusting and spat where he stood. The old man looked upset.

"Now that's a hell of a question to be asking about someone who was raped and almost lost her life. If you're trying to infer that she had anything to do with those two boys from Chester Junction getting killed, then you're a bloody fool." Jenkins loosened the vise. "She wasn't in any condition, and besides, if she did, we would have all been behind her after what they did to her and her daughter. Does that answer your question?"

He stepped past him and stuck his head under the hood.

"Did anyone from the sheriff's office question her about their deaths?"

"Why would they?" he snarled. "Besides, she had already packed up and moved away."

For the moment the garage was quiet. Fischer scratched his ear and then said, "I wasn't trying to imply any association."

There was no reply from the old man.

"The garage is pretty warm. You must be thirsty. Can I get you a Coke or something?"

Jenkins poked his head from under the hood.

"Look, sonny. Don't you think I know what you're trying to do? Do I look like I just fell off the turnip truck? You don't have to go buying me no damn soda just because I don't like your questions."

Miles stared at him and then said, "Fair enough." He leaned back against the bench and folded his arms, crossing his legs at the ankles. "I was talking with the sheriff and his deputy earlier about the murder and rape, and man, I gotta tell you, they sure weren't very cooperative. When I asked them if they knew where Mrs. Zimmerman happened to moved to they kind of clammed up. Would you happen to know why?"

The old man looked up from under the hood.

"Didn't tell them you were a reporter, did ya?"

"No, it never got to that."

"Good thing," he said seriously, cleaning the area around the manifold. "They don't want any more publicity than what they already got."

"What do you mean?"

"Oh, hell. Those two boys have never wanted to talk about it much since it happened."

"Why not?"

"It seems they were madder than hell over the fact

that somebody else got to those two boys before they did. Made them look like fools. The townspeople here were talking amongst themselves about how incompetent they thought they were." The old man pointed to something behind him. "You wanna hand me that?"

Miles reached over and handed him the new gasket sitting on the bench.

"What do you mean?"

"The people here thought they should have been able to track them down and bring them back like dogs, especially since a stranger was able to do it. Trouble is, they didn't have anything to go on. They even asked us for our help in trying to trace the killer's steps—you know, in case we'd seen anything. But we didn't know a thing. We didn't even know they were from Chester Junction. If we had, we would have gotten to them before the sheriff did." He hesitated and then said, "Lucky them two boys were."

"How come they didn't fire the sheriff, if that's how they felt?"

The old man popped his head from under the hood and then reached for his shoulder.

"Look, sonny, let me tell you a little something. People in small towns tend to stick together. We take care of our own. When Mrs. Zimmerman left, it seemed to settle the town down to where it was before the murder. We tend to forgive, and might I add," he said, pointing to his head, "we also like to forget." He smiled as he said it.

"Did she leave a forwarding address?"

"Don't know, but you can check with the post office if you like."

"Can you tell me how to get there?

"Go back the way you came till you come to Jefferson, hang a right, and it'll be on your left, two blocks up. Brick building. You can't miss it—says 'post office' right on it. Just ask for Walt. He'll help ya."

"Thanks, you've been a great help." Miles started for the front of the open bay and then stopped. "You mentioned she had a sister. You wouldn't happen to know her name, would you?"

"Nope."

He turned and headed back toward the opening and the fresh air outside and then stopped again.

"Oh, yeah, just one more thing. Could you tell me how to get to the cemetery?"

"Why you wanna go there for?"

"Just curious, I guess."

The old man led Miles to the front of the garage, wiping his hands with a greasy rag as he walked. They stood just inside the open bay. Jenkins pointed in the direction Fischer had been headed before he turned in to the station.

"Just keep going until you reach Pineridge. Turn right and follow it along for about two miles. It'll be on your right."

"What do I owe you for the gas?"

The old man pointed in the direction of his young helper who was pumping gas into a brown delivery van.

"Pay the boy, sonny."

Miles flipped his sunglasses back over his eyes, leaving the old man standing by the open bay. He grabbed a Coke from the antiquated machine sitting in front of the small office and walked back to his vehicle, asking the attendant what he owed. He paid him and drove away.

Chapter 14

"Where have you been?" she asked tersely. "I've been trying to reach you all night. I thought something terrible had happened."

"Veronica?"

"Where the heck have you been? You were supposed to be back hours ago."

"Hold on a moment." Miles quickly dropped his suitcase next to the row of drawers below the kitchen counter, pressing the receiver closer to his ear. "Sorry, Veronica, but I got held up because of a mechanical problem with the plane. What's the problem?"

"What happened to your cell? I've been calling you since seven o'clock."

"The phone died. I forgot to take the charger with me. What's so important?"

"I found him, Miles. I found Malcolm Whitehead."

"Already?" he said, smiling. "I'm impressed."

"It isn't all good news, Miles."

"What do you mean?"

"He's dead."

Fischer quickly took a seat at the table, taking the phone with him.

"What do you mean, he's dead?" he asked, almost stunned, the smile completely wiped from his face.

"You know, dead, like in not breathing."

"Yeah, I know what it means, Veronica," he stated somewhat sarcastically, feeling his spirits sag as fast as a balloon could deflate. "When did this happen?"

"About two months ago." She heard him take in a deep breath and expel it forcefully from his lungs. "I'm sorry, Miles."

He leaned forward and placed his head in his hand

and rubbed his forehead. "How did he die?"

"They told me it was an accident. He was crossing the street against the light. The driver didn't see him until it was too late."

"Where, Veronica? Where did this happen?"

"Seattle."

"Seattle?"

"He had just left the ballpark. A delivery truck was pulling out of the stadium. The driver said he didn't see him because the sun was in his eyes. They rushed him to the hospital, but he died before they got there."

There was a pause as he tried to think of how this would impact his story, how it would affect his chance of finding out if Malcolm Whitehead had indeed leaked the story of Tiffany Ambro's death.

"Who were you talking to?"

"The people at the *Post-Intelligencer*. I tracked him like you asked. He originally worked for the *Bee* in Sacramento after leaving Whatley, but he left for the *P-I* six months later."

"When did he leave?"

"At the end of April of that year."

For a moment there was dead space. Nothing was said.

"Miles? Are you okay?"

"Yeah, I'm thinking." There was more dead space. "Sorry, Veronica, but I gotta go. I'll talk to you to-morrow."

Chapter 15

Miles did his best to avoid Veronica as he made his way towards his office on Friday morning. He was in a foul mood and didn't want to speak to anyone, especially her. Instead, he brushed by her and everyone else with hardly a word and purposely closed the door to his office. He tossed his briefcase in one of the chairs and went straight to the window. He stood with his hands spread-eagled across the glass and stewed quietly as he gazed out at the city below. His visit with Erin had been the worst one yet after his return home from Eastbrook. Surprisingly, the conversation had started off pleasant enough, but fifteen minutes into it, it started to get ugly. Things were said that couldn't be taken back, and he was sure that anyone within earshot heard every word of it. He wasn't proud of what had transpired, but there was nothing he could have done. Erin was like a woman possessed, angering him with her wild accusations about the Christmas party to the point where he could no longer defend himself. He gave up and left in a huff with no good-bye—nothing.

Behind him he heard the soft rap on the door but chose to ignore it, hoping whoever was there would take the hint and leave. Veronica stepped inside.

"Is there something wrong?"

He talked to the window.

"No. Nothing's wrong."

"I watched you come in this morning," she said, closing the door behind her. "You didn't look very happy. Does it have anything to do with what happened to Malcolm Whitehead?"

"No."

Veronica took a seat.

"Well, what is it then?"

"Nothing. It's personal."

"Is it something you want to talk about?"

"It wouldn't do any good."

"Sometimes it helps."

"I don't think so," he said, shaking his head slightly.

"Well, something had to make you act this way. This isn't like you to just ignore everyone. What is it? Is it Erin? Did something happen?"

All this incessant questioning suddenly pushed him over the edge. He spun around quickly and without thinking snapped at her.

"Quit asking questions about something that doesn't concern you. I told you I don't want to talk about it. I just want to be left alone. Don't you have some work to do?"

Veronica was momentarily stunned by his reaction and sat frozen in her seat. Miles watched in silence from his spot in front of the window.

"Yeah, okay, Miles," she said getting up. "I'll leave you alone."

He watched her leave and then went back to gazing out the window for the next twenty minutes and then left.

It wasn't often he would drink during lunch, only during special occasions or when the mood was right, but on this day he made an exception and ordered two martinis. He sat by himself in a booth at the back of the bar until he felt well enough to leave. He had little in the way of an appetite. He was more interested in his martinis, content to rehash his latest visit with Erin and his surprising confrontation with Veronica, so he picked at his food, a clubhouse with fries. He knew he had overreacted, but what the hell was he supposed to have said? That his name and Veronica's came up in the same sentence. That Erin had finally spilled her guts about what she had been told at the Christmas party. That someone had told her to watch out or her marriage could be in trouble.

Erin had phoned home when she hadn't heard from him, picking up the messages on the machine, when suddenly she heard Veronica's voice. She didn't like it. She didn't like it one damn bit, and she told him so in an aggressive tone. He tried to explain, but Erin wasn't listening. She kept at him, pressing him harder as to just what the hell was going on between them, dismissing his every attempt to defend himself because it all made sense to her. Someone was after her man, and she didn't like it. She didn't like it one damn bit.

She had a right to know, she told him. Miles was ready to tell her off when a nurse walked in, surprising them both. Rather than utter another word, he decided to leave. On his way back to the *Tribune*, he thought about who would have said such a thing. He had no enemies, at least none that he knew of. He thought he was well-liked, or at least he thought he was. Nothing that she had said was true. The problem wasn't Veronica. It was them.

Fischer took a deep breath and downed the last of his martini before waving at the waiter to bring him his bill. He decided to leave it alone for the moment. He only had a couple of days left before he had to meet up with Lynch back in his office. Sitting here drinking, whining about his marriage wasn't getting him anywhere. He was wasting time.

Veronica was nowhere to be seen when he made his way back to the *Tribune*, which was exactly what he was hoping for. He knew he would have to apologize sooner or later, but for the moment he preferred the latter.

He quickly closed the door and grabbed the receiver and started punching numbers. Malcolm Whitehead may be dead, but all was not lost. Veronica had told him that Malcolm Whitehead left the *Bee* on April, the thirtieth. Tiffany Ambro was murdered on the twelfth of June, giving Mr. Whitehead plenty of time to start his new position with the *P-I*, which meant if Malcolm leaked the story, it would have been with the *P-I* and not the *Bee*. From a business point of view, it made perfect sense. Why would he give it to his former employer? It had to be with the *P-I*.

In less than a minute, he was talking to Phyllis from their records division. He told her what he was looking for.

"I can't promise you anything," she barked, jotting down the information. "You know everyone is on vacation, don't you? They stuck me here with no help. Can you believe it?"

"I'd really appreciate anything you can do."

He thought Phyllis had been in her job too long. He gave her his fax number at work.

"Yeah, you and everyone else. I'll do what I can, but I can't make any promises." A second later, Phyllis was gone.

Without letting go of the receiver, Miles pulled a neatly folder slip of paper from his hip pocket. He hit the button and then punched another set of numbers and waited. Old Walt had dug up a forwarding address with no phone number after searching through a couple of dusty filing cabinets in one of the back rooms that was used to store old equipment and office furniture at the post office. Before leaving Eastbrook, Miles had asked Veronica to cross-reference the address to match it to a phone number and then call him back. Veronica called while he was driving back to Boston. It wasn't what he had expected. He had naturally assumed it would be a regular home number. Nothing had prepared him for the number of an upscale hotel.

He had no luck with the day clerk. The Alexis Hotel did not keep records that old, especially those dating back to 1991, he said. "No, we do not accept mail unless the patron is actually staying in the hotel. This isn't a post office. No, I don't know if she had her mail sent to this address. We have no record of her being here, but if she did, it would certainly have been returned from where it came." It was a hotel, for Christ's sake!

Fischer hung up the phone, and after a few minutes of pondering his next move, he quickly flicked his computer on and waited for the screen to come to life. He tried the Seattle directory first and then expanded it to the outlying areas and then expanded it again to include the whole of the state of Washington and cities and towns he had never heard of. After almost two hours of endless searching and endless phone calls to every M. Zimmerman he found, he finally quit. Maria Zimmerman was nowhere to be found in any of the directories.

Haskills, back from Tweeksbury, suddenly appeared from nowhere. He rapped on the glass and went inside without waiting to be asked. A newspaper was tucked under his arm.

"When did you get back?" Miles asked. He quickly pressed the button, and his computer screen went black.

"A couple of hours ago. I thought you might like to see this."

Haskills took a seat and then flipped a copy of the *Tweeksbury Herald* on his desk.

"What am I looking at?"

"Do you see anything strange about those two pictures on the front page?"

"It's a couple of arrows," he said, shrugging his shoulders. "So what?"

"They're the ones that killed Holt and Masalla," he said, pointing to the picture on the left. "Take another look and then tell me you don't see anything different about those two pictures."

Miles took another look. "I give up. What am I supposed to notice?"

"The picture of the arrow on the right is what you would call a stock item. It's the same kind of arrow you can buy at any shop that caters to hunters. You'll notice that the diameter of the ones that killed Holt and Masalla are smaller. They're about half the diameter of the other ones. That would probably account for the fact that they went through their bodies, not to mention the razor tip on each of them. I did some checking while I was there, but nobody I spoke to knows anything about them." He moved back in his chair. "I hope you don't mind, but I did some checking for you on my way in."

"Oh."

"Yeah. I visited a couple of shops here in the city. The arrows that killed Holt and Masalla aren't sold in any shop. At least that's what they told me. Every shop owner said these were one-of-a-kind, you know, a specialty item. Whoever this killer is, they had them specially made."

Miles was still scanning the pictures.

"I guess all you have to do is find out who made them."

"I suppose."

Haskills left his seat and went to the door.

"If you need any help in tracking these down, let me know," Haskills said.

"Yeah. Sure," Miles said without looking up.

After Haskills left, Miles leaned back in his chair and studied the pictures more closely but stopped when he noticed Veronica back at her desk. He tossed the paper over to the credenza and stepped outside.

"Can I talk to you for a minute?" he asked Veronica.

"Can it wait?"

"I'd prefer if we talked now. I think it's important."

Veronica followed him into his office and took a seat. Miles eased into his chair, thinking this was going to be easy. A little light conversation to loosen her up and then a few kind words, and they could get back on track. He grabbed a rubber band off his desk and started to play with it.

"So how's it going?" he asked.

"If you're asking about my job, its fine. Is there a problem?"

"No, not at all. I was just checking." He hesitated and then said, "How's the studying going?"

"Fine. Why are you asking me these questions?"

"No reason. Just wondering how you were."

"Miles, if you're trying to apologize for your earlier behavior by starting up a conversation, it's pretty feeble."

He folded his lips together but said nothing.

"Well?"

"Well what?"

"Is that it?"

Miles was thinking of something quirky to say.

"Well, if you have nothing to say, I might as well go back to my desk." She went to leave.

"Hold on." Miles expelled a deep breath. "I'm not very good at this."

"That's okay," she said. "I don't go home until five." She looked at her watch. "It's only three o'clock."

"You're not going to make this easy for me, are you?" He tried smiling.

"That all depends on how sincere it is." She folded her arms in front of her.

"This isn't exactly easy for me. It's a little embarrassing."

"A little humility is good for the soul, Miles."

"I'm just being honest with you."

"I know. Being honest is a good start. I like that." She purposely hesitated, looking into his beautiful blue eyes, holding her unruffled guise. "Look, Miles, I know what you're up to, but it's not going to work this time. You're going to have to earn this one."

"Okay, okay." He cleared his throat. "I guess I was a little rough on—"

"You guess?"

"Bad choice of words," he said, drawing in a deep breath. "I know I was a little rough on you earlier. What I said was uncalled for." He leaned forward. "I was totally out of line. I shouldn't have snapped at you and said what I said. I guess I wasn't in the best of moods when I came in. I should have been a little more understanding. I know you were only trying to help."

He finished his speech and waited for her critique on the finer points of delivering what he thought was a pretty good apology, considering it was unprepared. He stared into those gorgeous green eyes and studied her face.

"So?"

"Not bad."

"So I take it we're okay then."

"Yes, we're fine, Miles," she said, smiling. She left her seat and headed for the door. "Truth be known, I couldn't have stayed mad at you anyway."

"So what are you saying? That I apologized for

nothing?"

"I wouldn't say that. We're talking, aren't we?"

Chapter 16

Bruno Carboni stood on the flat, gravel roof of the hardware store overlooking the parking lot that it shared with the Foxhole. It was already midafternoon. It was also hot with a warm breeze that came up from the south. From the chimney he could see the side door leading from the Foxhole, noting how easy it would have been for the killer to pick them off without being seen. Other than the light hanging over the door, the parking lot would have been almost dark when Holt and Masalla exited the bar.

Bruno wasn't sure if the roof had been searched or not and neither was Jimbo after Bruno had lunch in the bar. The lay of the rocks appeared as if nothing had been touched. The surface was even and, for the most part, level. He had already done a preliminary search of his own and found nothing, but that didn't mean there was nothing there. His years as a cop had taught him that no killer was perfect. They made mistakes just like everybody else. The same could be said about those who may have searched the roof.

Bruno was once again on his hands and knees, a cigarette tucked in the corner of his mouth as he searched close to the old brick chimney, which was at the back of the building and not more than ten feet from the alleyway. He carefully moved the pebbles close to the surface and then checked every crack and corner he could find in the masonry. From there he checked the surface at the base of the metal racking that held an old air-conditioning unit directly behind it. Frustrated, he stood and removed his sunglasses and then wiped the sweat from his brow with his sleeve before squashing the butt against the metal rack. He checked to make sure it was out and then tossed it over the side. He placed his hands on his hips and stared at the roof, unsure if there was anything there or not. Maybe he was wasting his time when suddenly something occurred to him. It was as if a light went on inside that head of his. Buoyed by the possibility, he quickly retraced his steps and checked the metal frame again, only this time he looked under the angular iron that held it all together. In the rough fold of the metal on the underside of the angular iron, he noticed a black patch of ash with tiny bits of tobacco stuck to its rough surface. He quickly checked the gravel directly below the ash mark, slowly pushing the pebbles in every direction, careful not to disturb it any more than it already had been until the tar and the pebbles stuck in the base surface were revealed. Amongst the pebbles he found more tobacco and part of the paper that formed the cylinder of the cigarette stuck to the tar barrier that kept moisture from penetrating to the surface below. It was still white with hardly any discoloration, meaning it hadn't been there that long. There was small print on the paper, like that found on American cigarettes, only it wasn't American. Bruno smiled and quickly pulled out his wallet and stuck it in one of the plastic photo sleeves.

"What the hell are you doing up there?" barked a voice below.

Bruno peered over the side, into the parking lot. It was an old man. He had his hands on his hips and was staring up at Bruno. The old man was as thin as a rake. A transparent green visor was slung over his head of thinning, flaming red hair that flew freely in the face of the warm wind. His eyes looked like two black dots, and his nose was hooked like a beak, giving him a birdlike appearance.

"Just checking your chimney for cracks. The fire

marshal is conducting inspections of all commercial chimneys."

"Well, I didn't hear anything about no inspections. Damn inspectors! Get the hell down from there," he yelled, "till I make a phone call and find out what the hell is goin' on."

Bruno spat over the edge, away from the old man, and then he yelled down to him. "Yeah, you do that, pal. In the meantime, I'm going to continue with my inspection."

Bruno watched the old man disappear before quickly making his way to the back of the building. He grabbed hold of the ledge and then gently eased his large frame onto the stack of wooden crates he had stacked just before climbing on the roof. From there, he jumped to safety on the other side of the enclosed garbage container, almost tumbling into the alley. He grunted as he felt his ankle give way, and then he hobbled to his rental parked next to the Foxhole.

After talking with the fire marshal, the old man from the hardware store made a call to Sheriff Knibbs and complained about the thick man with the raspy voice.

Chapter 17

Walker Sutherland was a career cop with the Chicago Police Department, working for the Bureau of Investigation, Detective Division. His turf was the first district which included the financial district and an upscale shopping district they commonly referred to as the "Loop." They had known each other for close to nine years, almost as long as Fischer had been working for the *Tribune.* Walker was a patrolman with over eleven years under his belt, patrolling the eighteenth district, which included North Michigan Avenue and the *Chicago Tribune* until his sudden promotion and subsequent transfer back across the Chicago River a year later. The first district headquarters were on South State Street, where he occupied a desk with a phone where he could be reached on very short notice, which made him vitally important on urgent matters. Fischer hadn't seen or talked to him for months, but now in his hour of need he decided to call. He had not found Maria Zimmerman using the public directories and had no means of accessing the phone records of any of the telephone companies that she may happen to do business with. He had already tried the utility companies using the pretense of trying to locate a missing family member but because of privacy laws got nowhere. Walker was about to leave when his phone rang.

"It's Fischer," he said. "I need a favor from you. I need you locate a person for me."

Walker had come to expect these impromptu phone calls whenever Miles needed some assistance. He hadn't heard from him for a while.

"Did you try the morgue?"

"That's what I like about you, Walker, you're always

entertaining. Unlike your quick wit and ask-questions-later approach to law enforcement, this one's still alive."

"No need to get snippy, Miles. You called me, remember. Did you try filing a missing persons report?"

"No time. It'll take too long. And besides, she's not really what you would call missing."

"That would explain why you don't want to file a missing persons report. Why do you want to find her?"

"I can't tell you. It's rather complicated."

"Must be pretty important for you to call me since I haven't heard from you in a while. You broke our lunch date last time, remember? I waited in line for almost an hour."

"Sorry, but I couldn't help it. Something came up."

"So who am I supposed to be looking for?"

"Her name's Maria Zimmerman, but there's a catch."

"Coming from you, Miles, why does that not surprise me? I'm probably going to hate myself for asking, but what's the catch?"

"She doesn't reside here in Chicago. I was told she lives in Seattle. I checked the phone listings but found nothing. I was thinking that maybe you could check out the phone companies and get her—"

"Christ, Miles. Are you nuts?" Walker pressed the receiver closer to his ear, almost whispering over the phone. "I can't just walk in and ask to see a phone company's records. I have to have just cause, and in case you haven't looked at a map lately, Seattle isn't even in my jurisdiction."

"Yeah, I know, Walker. I took geography."

"Yeah, well if you took geography, then you know it's out of my jurisdiction."

"I know it's out of your jurisdiction, but I need this favor. Just tell them you're working on a case and you need some information."

"It a little more complicated than that, Miles. Companies have rights, in case you forgot, including the right to protect the privacy of their customers. We can't just walk in under false pretenses and ask them to open their books because I happen to have a friend who needs to find someone. We'd be breaking the law. And besides, do you have any idea how many companies we'd have to get access to in order to find your little friend?"

"Yeah, I understand, but I wouldn't be asking you if it wasn't important. I don't see the harm. It's just basic information that I could get off any petition, and nobody would be the wiser."

"Yeah, but in this case the information is unlisted, meaning it's unlisted for a reason. People who don't list their numbers do it because they don't want to be bothered by people they don't know. That's the difference, Miles."

"Who's going to know? If I walked into a store right now, there's a good chance before I walk out I would have given them my vital statistics, including my address and phone number."

"Maybe so, but you can't expect me to just walk in with no cause, involve another police department, which is on the other side of the country, I might add, and ask for information that quite frankly doesn't concern me or the Chicago Police Department. How do you think that's going to play to my superiors if they were to find out that I was using departmental resources illegally to help a reporter for the *Chicago Tribune* because you can't find someone?"

"I was hoping you could figure that out. You're the cop."

"That's pretty cold, Miles."

"Look, Walker, if I had something better to offer, I'd give it to you, but I don't. Right now I'm stuck in the middle of something really important. I've got a story that can't write itself without some outside help. I thought I could count on you."

"Isn't there someone else you can pick on?"

"No."

"If the phone company lodges a complaint, they can have my ass."

"You're my last hope, Walker. Help me out."

"Dammit, Miles. You're putting me in a hell of a spot."

"I wouldn't be asking, Walker, if it wasn't important."

There was a long silence like the phone had gone dead, and then the voice on the other line said, "I wish I could, Miles, but I can't. It's too risky. There are too many companies that we would have to access. If I get another police unit involved in something like this, there's no telling what will happen. There's no way to keep a lid on it. It's bound to get out. And it's not just me. I could be up for a possible promotion in a couple of months. I've got a wife and kids to think about. I can't risk it. Call me when you got something that doesn't involve me breaking the law and won't end up putting my ass in a sling."

Walker hung up.

Chapter 18

At precisely five, they started their mass exodus. Computer screens started going black. Chairs emptied. They quickly grabbed their belongings and then headed for the doors, herding themselves into the elevators like thirsty cattle on a long drive, headed to their favorite watering hole.

Veronica grabbed her purse and headed in the direction of his office before poking her head in the doorway.

"We're going over to Malone's for a couple of drinks. Care to join us?"

He almost frowned. "I could use a drink, but I don't think so."

"Come on. It'll be fun."

"There's Erin, and I've still got a lot of work to do."

"Just come by for a drink and then you can leave. You don't have to stay."

"I wish I could, but—"

"Come on, Miles. You've been working hard for over a month now. You could use a break. I can see it in your face. You can spare an hour. Come for a drink," she said, trying to coerce him into changing his mind. "Look. I'll make a deal with you. If you aren't gone in an hour, I'll get one of the bouncers to throw you out." She smiled at him. "What do you say?"

"When you put it that way, it almost makes it tempting."

"One hour?"

"I'll see," he said leaving his chair. "If I finish what I have to do, I'll meet you there."

He followed her out and stopped at the glass wall that separated him from the newsroom. He watched her leave through the doors along with the rest of the mob, lingering there till they were all gone, and then he slowly headed back behind his desk.

"You're not going?" asked Big Tony. He stood just outside Fischer's doorway.

"I thought you had already left," he said, slipping into his chair.

"Just leaving. And you?"

"I think I'm going to hang around for a while." Miles looked haggard, like he hadn't slept for days.

"What's the matta with you? Ya look like you've been kicked by a mule."

"I've had better days," he said softly. He hesitated and then said, "You got a minute?"

Big Tony checked his watch.

"Yeah, sure, kid. I ain't gotta be nowhere right now." He took a seat in front of Fischer's desk. "What's on your mind?"

"What would you do if you couldn't find someone?"

"That all depends who I'm looking for."

"Her name's Maria Zimmerman."

"Is this to do with that murder trial ya covered a couple of weeks ago?"

He nodded and then filled Tony in as to why he needed to find her. He told him about the post office in Eastbrook and the forwarding address to the Alexis Hotel. He told him about looking for her in the Seattle directory and every other directory in the whole of Washington and coming up empty.

"What about the realty company who sold her place?"

"Nothing," he said, shaking his head. "Her dead husband's law firm handled the sale as a courtesy. Everything went through them. You know how lawyers are. Everything is confidential."

"And the moving company?"

"Nothing. I guess the lawyers handled that, too."

"Why would somebody have their mail forwarded to a hotel?" asked Tony.

"I wish I knew."

"It doesn't make a lot of sense."

"It would if she did it on purpose."

"Why the hell would she do that?"

"I don't know," he said hesitantly. "Maybe she doesn't want to be found. Maybe the guilt is killing her because she survived and her daughter didn't. Maybe she can't cope with her loss because everything around her reminds her of her family. Maybe she just wants to be left alone, but she doesn't know how to do it. After being in the hospital for an extended period, maybe she finally figured it out. The best way to hide is to leave a bogus forwarding address such as the Alexis Hotel. Just make sure all the bills are paid first, and then you can disappear and nobody will miss you. Don't forget she has no family in Eastbrook anymore."

"She got any brothers or sisters?"

"No brothers that I know of. She has a sister in Seattle."

"What about her?" Tony asked.

"A dead end," he said, shaking his head. "I don't have a surname."

"So why a hotel? Why the Alexis?"

"The only thing I can gather is that it was a random choice. I checked with them, but they don't have any record of her being there. They said they don't keep records that old. It could have been just a ruse because she really had no reason to show up. If it is and she didn't show, then it's obvious she doesn't want to be found. There's nothing that would identify that address as that of the Alexis Hotel. It's just her name and an address on a form. For all I know, maybe she doesn't even live in Seattle. Maybe her sister doesn't live there either. In fact, maybe she has no sister at all. Maybe the whole damn thing is just a hoax."

"Ya sound a little frustrated, kid."

"What do you mean, a little?" he asked sardonically.

Big Tony clasped his hands behind his head. "So what are ya going to do?"

"I don't know. Keep plugging away, I guess. What else can I do?"

"Did ya check with the local governments? They should be able to help ya."

"Yeah. Nothing came up. It's like she's disappeared from the face of the earth."

"Maybe she's dead."

"Call it a hunch, but I don't think so."

"Well, kid, its looks like ya need some help, and I'm just the guy to help ya. When you've been around as long as I have, ya get to know a lot of people in the right places. I've got a friend who I think may be able to find her. I'll give him a call. Ya never know." He quickly glanced at his watch. "Sorry, kid, but I gotta go. The wife will kill me if I'm late. Sorry I couldn't be of more help," he said, sounding apologetic. Big Tony pushed his stubby frame from the chair but before he left, he stopped just short of the door. "While you're at it, ya might want to consider another possibility."

"What's that?"

"Let's say it happened to you. What would ya do if ya had no family left? What would ya do if ya really wanted to put the past behind ya and start over, ya know, wipe the slate clean so nobody could remind ya of your past life, or like ya said, hide from it?"

He thought for minute and then said, "I don't know."

"Christ, kid, for a reporter you're not very bright. That mule must have kicked ya harder than I thought. Try using that brain of yours."

Miles thought for another minute and then said, "I don't know. I guess I would consider changing my name."

Big Tony smiled at him rather awkwardly. "You're not a dumb as I thought. See ya Monday, kid."

Malone's was tucked away at the bottom of a large commercial building on Grand Avenue, not more than four blocks from the *Chicago Tribune*. It was beneath the street, some eighteen steps from the sidewalk, with large trees that grew out of colored planters next to the doors. From the sidewalk, Fischer could hear the music and the noise generated by the usual Friday night crowd of rabble-rousers and those just looking for a good time.

In the back, the gang from the *Tribune* had managed to sling a row of tables together much like lily pads on a pond. Pitchers of beer and shooters of all kinds along with platters of finger food were sprinkled haphazardly across the tables. Seeing an empty chair, Miles slowly made his way to the other side, waving to some, patting others on the shoulder, until he found the seat next to Laura. Much to his delight, Veronica was sitting next to her. Veronica noticed him and leaned over.

"I didn't think you were going to come," she said loudly.

"I finished earlier than I thought I would."

He turned to Laura.

"How are you, Laura?"

"I'm fine, Miles."

"I must be getting old. Is it just me, or is it unusually noisy in here."

"That's because you haven't been here for a while. You're going to have to learn to get used to it if you have a baby on the way," replied Laura, almost yelling in his ear.

"Don't remind me." He glanced at the food on the table, pointing to some, picking at others. "What are we eating?"

Laura moved her hand across the table, pointing out the various entrées. "Mahi-mahi, squid, octopus, humus, dried ribs, and you know the rest."

Miles ordered a drink and stole another glance towards Veronica, who was still engaged in a conversation. They would stay that way, talking to colleagues, until later, when they found themselves alone. In the meantime, Miles enjoyed the food, Laura, five more rum and Cokes, and the company around him.

By midnight, most of the gang from the *Tribune* had all but disappeared into the warm August night just beyond the doors at the front of the bar. The only remnants of the mob that had poured into Malone's some six hours ago were Veronica and Miles. They sat across from each other at a single table, amidst the company of perfect strangers who had slowly rearranged the tables.

They stayed for another hour and chatted and had a drink each. When the bill came, Miles paid using his credit card.

"Come on, I'll walk you to your car."

They made their way up the stairs and headed east on Grand Avenue. A bright yellow moon hovered in the darkness just above the tall buildings. She grabbed and held his upper arm and then pointed to it.

"Look, Miles. Isn't it beautiful?"

He looked up to where she was pointing. "It's very beautiful."

"Did you know that the Chinese celebrate Thanksgiving much like we do?" she said, still holding onto his arm as they walked along the sidewalk.

"No, I didn't know that."

"It's one of the most celebrated of the Chinese holidays. It's called the August Moon Festival. It's held on the fifteenth day of the eighth lunar month."

"But isn't today the twentieth?"

"Yes but I was referring to the Chinese calendar, not ours so that would make it the twenty fourth of next month."

"It sounds a little complicated."

"It is so I won't bore you with the details."

"Thanks. I appreciate it," he said. "You were saying."

"Chinese legend says that the moon is at its brightest and roundest on that day."

"It looks pretty bright right now, like a big piece of cheese."

"It's also called the Women's Festival because, according to Chinese mythology, it symbolizes beauty and elegance. The sun represents the *yang*, or man, whereas the moon represents the *yin*, or woman. According to them, Westerners worship the sun for its power, while people in the Far East admire the moon because it is a trusted friend. Chinese poets say that on that night long-lost lovers will find each other."

He smiled at her. "You're making this up."

"No. It's true," she said, almost laughing. "I'm studying Chinese culture. It's really fascinating. China is going to be the new economic power in the not too distant future, so we had better learn about them, or we're going to be left behind."

"Has this got anything to do with that future career you have planned?"

"I just want to be ready."

They walked arm in arm for the remainder of the four blocks, chatting till they reached the multilevel parking lot. Miles hit the button, and they rode the elevator to the third floor to where her car was parked.

"Are you sure you're okay to drive?" he asked.

"I'm fine, Miles. You needn't worry."

Always the gentleman, Miles held out his hand and asked for the keys to open the door to her vehicle. He opened and then held the door, holding the keys in front of him. She drew near, closing the door and bypassing the keys he was holding, and without thinking of the consequences, as if driven by an uncontrollable desire, she slowly kissed him on the lips. There was no resistance from Miles. She stepped back. The wetness from her kiss and her sweet fragrance clung to him. They stood there, staring at each other, eyes smoldering, saying nothing, waiting like two innocent high school teens who had just kissed for the first time behind the school bleachers, letting the sensation run for all it was worth.

Hesitating, they drew close and pressed their lips together a second time, only this time they explored the inside of each other's mouths. He moved his hands to her slender waist, partially exposing her smooth skin from under the thin gray blouse. His heart was racing, as was hers. She felt the warmth of the night air and his cool fingertips as they swept over her exposed warm skin, sending her into a soft shudder. She placed her hands against the door as he attacked her neck. Her head rocked backward while his tongue explored the tightness of her skin and then slowly caressed the muscles that begged for his attention.

They embraced yet again, exploring, touching, when suddenly it stopped. Veronica had changed her mind. If it was going to happen, it wasn't going to be in a parking lot.

"Not here," she cried in a soft, panting whisper. She placed her hands on his chest. "I'm sorry, Miles. Please don't be angry with me but this isn't the place."

In that fleeting moment, he stared silently at her still-smoldering green eyes. Slowly, she eased her slender torso into the black leather seat while Miles handed her the keys and held the door. He watched as her tall body gently slid down the smooth leather back until she was all the way in. Without a word, he slowly closed the door until he heard it click shut.

He stood close to one of the cement pillars, his hands by his sides, surrounded by the soft hum of her yellow sports car. Confused and shaken by what had just taken place, Fischer quietly watched the bright red taillights as they slowly disappeared down the ramp to the floor below.

Chapter 19

It was no great surprise that he hadn't slept all that well after what took place in the parking lot Friday night. A night of drinking had Miles confused, and at the moment he had not come to terms with how he was going to handle it. What he wanted most was time to sort it all out, and then he would be able to understand why it had happened, and then it would be easy to explain if it ever came to that. Right now he couldn't think straight because there were just too many things on his mind and he didn't work well under pressure, especially when his personal life was becoming such a mess. *Damn it! How the hell did this happen?*

He tried a couple of breathing exercises to try and relax. He was mad at himself and mad at Veronica and mad at his wife and mad at Walker and Lynch and just about anybody else he could think of. *This was not supposed to happen.* He was married, for Christ's sake. There was a child on the way. He was trying to write a story that for the moment couldn't write itself, and the pressure was mounting to come with up something before Tuesday or forget about who killed Holt and Masalla. He could feel his heart pounding from all the pressure and the events of last night, and he wished it hadn't happened. *Oh, for Christ's sake. Get a grip*, he told himself.

It was six thirty in the morning, and he was already dressed: shorts, runners, T-shirt. He was in the kitchen, sitting at the table, sipping coffee, something he rarely did at home, rubbing the ear of his dog and thinking about what to do. He had no headache, but his thinking was hazy. If Erin knew, she would kill him.

For the moment he believed he was safe. There had been nobody else in the parking lot, so who would know?

It was late at night. Everybody from the *Tribune* had already left. It was just him and Veronica and nobody else, and he hoped that what had happened in the parking lot would stay in the parking lot.

He was attracted to her and had been for a long time, but he was married, and married men didn't go after other women, especially when their wives were in a hospital expecting their first child. He had never done anything like this in his life, so what the hell happened?

It was common knowledge that this sort of thing happened every day to all kinds of families under all kinds of situations for all kinds of reasons, but damn it, not to him, and especially not to men in the Fischer family. Nobody in his family had ever had an affair. Was he to be the first? Sure, he had fantasized about her, but who hadn't? He was a man with normal urges, so why would he not fantasize? It was only natural. Was it the booze? Had he drank so much that he didn't know what the hell he was doing? He grunted at the feeble excuses he was making. He had kissed her back. How was he going to explain to Erin as to why he didn't make it to visit her at the hospital?

The fact that he had turned off his cell phone after this third rum and Coke could be easily explained. The battery had died. But maybe she had called the office. He would have to tell her something—something that would be believable as to why he didn't pick up. He should have called.

He had this bad feeling in the pit of his stomach. He was a terrible liar. He breathed hard and then quickly grabbed the leash off the counter and called Rocky to the door. He needed time to think.

Downstairs in the study, the phone rang four

times with no answer. The answering machine clicked on, followed by the prerecorded message and then the beep. It was seven forty-five in the morning.

"Mr. Fischer, you don't know me, but we share a mutual friend, Anthony Torricelli. He asked if I could help to find a person of interest, a person by the name of Maria Zimmerman. Needless to say, your subject no longer answers by that name. She changed it in November of 1991, taking her mother's maiden name as her own. Her new name is Anita Paletti. She emigrated here from Zikhron Ya'akov, Israel, in 1977 along with her husband and their daughter, who was one year old at the time. The husband's name is Joseph; the daughter's is Rachel. They were married in 1976 and achieved official citizenship in 1979. Mrs. Zimmerman, or Paletti, whichever you want to call her, was born to a Jewish father and an Italian mother. The father's last name was Leibovitz. The mother and father are no longer alive. I don't know the reason. None was given. Oh, yeah—she presently resides in Seattle."

Click.

Chapter 20

Miles called Lynch and asked him to meet him at the *Tribune*. He was headed there now. Yes, he knew it was his day off, but he would be there in fifteen minutes, and since he lived close by, he could meet him there at about the same time. No, it was better if they discussed it in his office. "Yeah, fifteen minutes."

Lynch was already there when Fischer arrived in his office. He was sitting in one of the chairs across from Fischer's desk, reading the morning paper.

"Couldn't Greenberg take care of this?"

Marshall Greenberg was in his midforties with thinning hair and no family. He was the assistant editor for the national desk—a real pain-in-the-ass, according to Fischer. He was also the chief editor, the go-to-guy when Patrick Lynch wasn't working, so on weekends he called the shots.

"He's on his way," he said, holding a fax he had taken from the machine.

"This better be good, Miles. I have a tennis match for this afternoon."

"This is better than good. This is going to knock your socks off."

Miles watched as Marshall Greenberg weaved his way down the aisle between the rows of mostly empty desks. Miles closed the door behind him and took his seat. Marshall took the one next to Pat.

"So why are we here?" asked Greenburg. He sounded a little annoyed.

"What if I told you that I can put the killer in the courtroom at the time of Holt's and Masalla's acquital?"

Both men's jaws stiffened but neither one said anything.

"What if I told you that the killer was sitting next to me in the courtroom?"

"What are you doing Fischer? Just get to the point," stated Greenberg.

"Remember that story you asked me to fill in on because Roger couldn't make it?" he asked, looking at Lynch.

"Yeah. What about it?"

"What if I told you that Anita Paletti is really Maria Zimmerman?"

Again, both men looked at each other.

"Are you sure?" asked Lynch.

"She changed her name after she left Eastbrook."

"Who told you?" asked Greenberg.

"It's confidential, but that's not the big news. She was there in the courtroom when the verdict came down on Holt and Masalla."

"You're telling us that you actually saw Maria Zimmerman in the courtroom?" asked Marshall.

"I didn't actually see her. She was in disguise. She was dressed as a potato farmer. She was sitting next to me."

"A potato farmer?" asked Greenburg. The voice was almost scornful.

"Okay, a vegetable farmer then. Who cares? What difference does it make?"

"And just how did she disguise herself as a farmer?" he asked.

"She was wearing a bodysuit."

"And how do you know it was a bodysuit and not a real farmer?"

"Why would a real farmer be dressed like he just came in from the fields? The courtroom was hotter than hell. Why wasn't he dressed like everyone else, or at least

155

in something a little more comfortable that didn't cover him from head to foot? Everyone in that courtroom was dressed casually except him."

"Maybe he did just come in from the fields," remarked Lynch.

"I don't think so," he said adamantly. "Just about everyone in that courtroom was sweating but I noticed there was no sweat coming from under his clothing, especially in the chest area like it was for the rest of us. There was sweat only under the armpits, and the only reason it showed was because that's where the bodysuit thins so that you can move your arms without looking like a robot. The only sweat I could see was along the front of his hairline—there and along the back of his collar, but that's it. Everything else was absorbed by the bodysuit. He had a mustache, so I couldn't see his lip, but there was nothing on his face—no sign of any sweat in his beard. He didn't smell, either, which means he wasn't working. If he had just come from the fields, he would have smelled like a farmer."

"Why would she be interested in their trial? Why would she care whether they got off or not?" Greenburg asked. "What's the connection?"

"Rachel was fifteen at the time of her murder."

"Yeah. So what?"

"So was Heather Burton."

"It could be just a coincidence."

"What if they both shared the same birth date?"

"It could still be just a coincidence."

"I don't think so."

"So you're saying that that's her motive?" Marshall asked contemptuously. "That her daughter happened to share the same birthday with some other unlucky girl, so she decided to kill them?"

"What about the Ambro girl?" Lynch asked.

Miles held up the fax and smiled.

"It's the same birth date as the other two. March nineteenth. The Seattle *P-I* sent it over."

"Let me see," asked Greenburg.

"Remember the meeting we had in your office last week?" he asked, looking at Lynch.

"I was there. Of course I remember it. Why?"

"The authorities back in Eastbrook couldn't come up with who killed Thornton and Patrick after it was discovered they were the ones who raped and killed Rachel Zimmerman and almost killed her mother. There were no witnesses, and yet months later both Thornton and Patrick were found dead. So who knew they were the ones who raped and killed Rachel if there were no witnesses?"

"The mother?" asked Greenberg.

"But the authorities said that she couldn't remember anything," added Lynch.

"What if she could? What if she finally could identify who raped and killed her daughter but decided instead to take care of it herself?"

"Why would she not go to the authorities?" asked Greenberg.

"She had just lost her husband because of a drunk driver four months prior to losing her daughter. What if she blamed them for his death because this drunk decided to get behind the wheel of his vehicle when he shouldn't have and nobody stopped him, which is exactly what happened? Maybe she doesn't trust them anymore. Maybe she wants to make sure that justice is served rather than risking them getting off on a technicality or not serving enough time or not getting the death penalty. What would you do?"

"Well, I certainly wouldn't take the law into my own hands, if that's what you're suggesting," stated Greenberg.

"But we're not talking about what you or I would do. We're not the ones who have suffered like she has. We're talking about a wife who had just lost her husband to a drunk driver. Four months later her daughter is raped and murdered, and she barely survives. Her world as she knows it just blew up. She's like a mother bear that couldn't protect her cub. She's furious and she wants revenge, but she wants it her way."

"That's all fine and dandy but how are you going prove it?" Greenberg asked without hesitating.

"When I first met Anita Paletti in her office, she was late by about four hours. According to Miss Joffe, the office had been closed for three weeks because her boss was on vacation. It sounded like it was a last-minute decision. When she finally came in, I thought she looked a little tired, which was strange considering she had just finished a three-week vacation in the Caribbean. She popped a couple of pills while I was there. She seemed excited about something. She stated that she had a hard time remembering from one moment to the next. When I asked her if it had anything to do with her business, she almost took my head off. You think she would have been a little more relaxed. Let me ask you guys something. Why do you go on vacation?"

"To relax," said Greenberg quickly.

"Good one, Greenberg. To relax, and if you went to someplace like the Caribbean, you'd be sitting in the sun, but there was a problem there, too. She didn't have a tan. Her skin was almost the same color as yours, Greenberg."

"Maybe she doesn't like to sit in the sun," Greenburg said sarcastically. "Some people don't."

"I would think that someone who was born in Israel would be pretty used to the sun wouldn't you?"

Greenburg didn't bother replying.

"I did a quick calculation on the time it would take to drive from Eastbrook to Seattle since I don't believe she took a flight there and back."

"How can you be so sure?"

"How would she get her crossbow along with the arrows past the detectors plus everything else she took with her? She used a bodysuit, remember. Besides, she was supposed to be on vacation in the Caribbean. How would she have explained that her name would have been on two separate passenger lists?"

Marshall made a face like he was impressed.

"I figure you could do it in about eleven hours if you did the speed limit. Some of the roads are narrow and wind through mountains, so the posted speed limits would be a lot lower than on a highway. Holt and Masalla were killed at around midnight, though nobody is sure of the exact time. Our meeting was for ten thirty in the morning. That would explain why she was late. Plus, she was probably tired since I doubt she had any sleep after she knocked them off, so she probably took her time getting back if she didn't want to end up killing herself by driving off the road or taking somebody else with her. Besides, why draw attention to yourself by speeding when you have a bodysuit and a crossbow in your trunk? It would be pretty incriminating. How would she explain it? Plus it would put her en route from the crime scene. She probably called from a pay phone when she knew she wasn't going to make it instead of using a cell phone. That way there would be no record of who made the call. She would have to go home and clean up. That's why Joffe asked me if it was okay if I came back at around two. When Paletti arrived, she was nicely dressed. If she was tired, which I think she would have been, there was no evidence of it. There were no bags under her eyes. Maybe that's what the pills were for."

"Why haven't the authorities been able to nail her if everything you've told us is true?"

"She obviously has an air-tight alibi. She wasn't counting on one thing, though."

"Oh, and what might that be?" asked Greenberg.

"She didn't expect to be sitting next to a reporter."

"So what are you proposing?" asked Lynch curiously.

"That we run the story linking all three murders."

"But you can't prove it," stated Greenburg.

"Anita Paletti has a scar that runs from ear to ear." he said. "What if I told you that I noticed the scar while I was sitting next to her?"

"But you already told us she was in disguise—a potato farmer, according to you," stated Greenburg with a hint of sarcasm.

"Yes," he said, glaring at Greenburg. "But what if the scar was noticeable?"

"How noticeable?" asked Lynch.

"It was just under her jaw, about an inch long. When she got up and left, I noticed the same thing on the other side. Some of the makeup must have worn off from the collar of the shirt rubbing against her neck. The temperature in the courtroom probably caused it to rub off."

"For a seasoned reporter, you seem a little anxious to get this in the paper," interrupted Greenburg. "It's like you want to bypass all the rules that are in place to protect this newspaper from a lawsuit. In case you forgot, we're not in the business of writing fiction. Everything has to be verified."

"Then you explain it Greenburg. If there were no witnesses then how is it that Thornton and Patrick are dead?"

"I don't have to Fischer."

"Then tell me this Greenburg," he said, glaring at him. "Why only these three involving a crossbow? Why is it the use of a crossbow never came into play until the Zimmerman case? Why is it that at least one of the victims in each of these cases just happens to share the same birth date as Anita's daughter? You think it's a coincidence? I guess it's just a coincidence then that the story of the Ambro girl is in the *Seattle P-I*, the very same place where Anita lives. Paletti's company does work for the film industry in case you forgot. It all fits Greenburg."

"But you can't prove it."

Miles bit the inside of his cheek to keep himself from lashing out at Greenburg.

"Look." he said. "If someone other than me was to walk in here and tell you what I just told you, what would you do?"

"I don't know," said Lynch, hesitantly.

"Don't give me that," Miles said. "You would investigate it and you damn well know it. You know damn well you would."

Miles didn't like the look on their faces.

"Look, just because I'm the one who can put her there and I just happen to be a reporter shouldn't matter. All I'm proposing is that we write what we have, linking the three different killings. We don't mention any names—at least not until I've had a chance to fly to Seattle and check everything out. That story about successful women in business is running in tomorrow's paper. I already checked. Anita was notified yesterday. In all probability, she will try and get a hold of a copy. Right now she thinks that she's gotten away with it. I say we print the story. At least that way she'll know that someone thinks otherwise."

"What about the passenger list?" asked Lynch.

"What about it? If the authorities suspect her and they've investigated as to whether or not she took that flight, then I think it's safe to assume that her name is on that list, which is exactly what I'm thinking. It would give her the perfect alibi. Why else do you think they haven't been able to pin her to the crimes? Up until now the authorities haven't been able to touch her. Why do you think that is?" Miles saw the grim look on their faces. "Look," he said, trying to convince them, "if we don't do this, then she's going to get away with it, and we will have missed out on one hell of a story."

"The motive seems a little weak, if you ask me," stated Greenburg.

"And why's that?" asked Fischer.

"Why would she bother killing Wilcox along with Holt and Masalla? It doesn't make a lot of sense."

"I know. I thought the same thing. She obviously has something else going on inside her."

With that, the room fell suddenly quiet. There were no more questions. Miles sat back in his chair and watched their faces for any telltale signs that he had convinced them to run the story. The editors looked rather grim with their lips pressed together. Lynch tapped Greenberg on the shoulder and motioned towards the door.

"We'll be right back."

Both men exited his office with Lynch closing the door to keep their conversation private. Fischer played with a paper clip and watched them through the glass wall. Two minutes later, they were back inside his office. Lynch sat in the first chair. Greenberg stood against the wall.

"I want you to know that I'm going out on a limb on this. How much time do you think you'll need before you have something ready?" Lynch asked.

Miles quickly checked his watch. "It shouldn't take me more than an hour."

"Okay. Write everything you can tying the Holt and Masalla killings to what happened in Eastbrook and the Wilcox case, but only write what you can verify. Leave the names Maria Zimmerman and Anita Paletti out of this for the time being until we can verify if she took that flight to the Caribbean or not. It may be a little thin, but that's the way I want it. I don't want to give anyone a reason to sue us. Give it to Greenberg when you're finished. Marshall, I want you to call me when it's done. If I don't like it," he said, looking at Miles, "you'll have to do a rewrite, so try and get it right the first time."

Lynch left his seat and headed towards the door.

"Before we go," said Greenberg, "I want to ask you something."

"Shoot," said Fischer.

"What about the others?"

"What others?"

"The other newspapers like the *Sun*. What if they get a hold of something that we don't have? Maybe we've missed something."

"What could they possibly have? Unless they were sitting there with me, I'm the only one who can expose Anita Paletti as the killer of Holt and Masalla along with the other three. You're the only two people who know that. They can snoop all they like, but they're not going to find anything. We control this story, nobody else. Not the *Sun*, not the *Herald*, nobody. It's just us."

Still slightly miffed, Greenberg hesitated by the door before leaving Miles's office. "So who went to the Caribbean then?"

"I don't know, but it wasn't Anita Paletti."

By two thirty, he had the final draft ready. Fischer gave it to Greenberg, who immediately phoned Lynch and provided him with the details. It was a go.

Chapter 21

She bought a *New York Times* and a copy of the *Chicago Tribune* at Newcastle's, a specialty store close to Pike Place Market, and then hiked the three blocks to the corner of Third and Pike and went inside the Starbucks. It was Sunday and it was early and it was part of the same ritual where every Sunday she would make the trek to Newcastle's, buy a couple of newspapers from out of state, and then sit in a Starbucks until she got tired and felt the need to do something else.

She paid for an espresso and a blueberry muffin and then sat at a table next to a window. She flipped through the pages of the *Times* first because if anything of interest had happened, it would have originated in New York City, and if it was of any importance it would be in the *Times*. She ordered another espresso and then started with the front page of the *Tribune*, knowing that sooner or later, she would find the article on successful women. She took her time browsing through the headlines and stories before flipping to the last page of the first section, and then she saw it. There in boldface was the story of what happened back in Eastbrook. It was old news, and she was familiar with all of it, but seeing it again after all these years suddenly made her feel sick. It was about a past life she thought she had put behind her, but some moron thought it was worth repeating. She quickly looked for the byline and then glared intently at the name. It was the same reporter who had interviewed her just over a week ago. It rehashed and regurgitated what had already been written years ago, but now there was a twist. There were others, it said, linking what happened in Eastbrook to an obscure little town called Tweeksbury, which she had never heard of. She had never heard of

Lionel Holt or David Masalla, either. The name Roger Wilcox also drew a blank. As she read through the story, she could feel her stomach tighten, and then she went pale. She wanted to scream when she saw the names of Thornton and Patrick. Angry, she put the paper down and then grabbed her wallet and left.

She wasn't supposed to be out, but Anita was in the midst of a crisis, and with nowhere else to turn, it was left up to Dina to take care of the problem.

Anita's blue BMW 540i was on the causeway connecting Mercer Island to the mainland. Dina was in the driver's seat, headed west, traveling at the posted speed limit because she didn't want to draw any attention to herself. The last she saw of Anita she was standing by the sink just before she took the card and keys from her purse, so technically she was a thief. But this was no joyride. She was headed to the downtown, to Two-Faced Productions.

Dina flipped a switch turning on the lights, and then pulled the blinds on all the windows before turning on the computer. She sat at Anita's desk and emptied part of the contents from the bag onto the desk. There would be no note, just a simple item to send a simple message. An investigative reporter of his caliber should be able to interpret exactly what it meant. After all, he was writing stories like he knew something. Said everything originated from Eastbrook. It shouldn't be all that hard to figure out for such a whiz kid.

Dina carefully snapped on a pair of latex gloves and then placed a thick layer of Styrofoam chips shaped like rounded Zs in the bottom of the box. The black aluminum shaft was wiped and cleaned again to make sure no prints could be brushed and then logged into a computer for identification later. "They would probably try it, the jerks." The item was then placed the length of the box before more Styrofoam was added until it was packed tight. "Don't want anybody hurting themselves, now do we?" she muttered to herself. The cardboard edges were then folded over and clear, three-inch tape applied to seal it tight. She put it aside and logged into the computer using Anita's code and searched for the address of the *Tribune*. Seconds later she had it. She hit the button, and within seconds she had a label with the address for the *Tribune*. It was addressed care of Mr. Miles Fischer. Finished, she admired it.

"Beautiful," she said.

Dina checked her watch and then grabbed the keys and headed for the door behind her. One key unlocked the dead bolt while another turned the lock in the doorknob. She flipped a switch and then went inside the small studio and locked the door. The small room had a single window. She reached over and pulled the blind. She was about to become a star.

Dina sat in the chair in front of the table and flicked another switch, turning on the twelve small bulbs that framed the large mirror. She cleaned her face and then started fitting the special rubber latex pieces into place with special glue to shape a thicker nose, a wrinkled forehead, fat cheeks with slight jowls hanging below a soft chin, and pieces of ear with tiny threads of white hair. She loved this part. They looked so real. Lastly, she applied a small piece along her jawline on either side. The makeup was next. With the aid of a brush, she used varying shades of makeup to blend all the pieces into one. The false contacts were blue to hide her brown eyes. There were special hairpieces to insert and a white mustache to hang over her upper lip. The lines would all be there to show his age, especially around the eyes. Probably add a mole here and there for effect. In just over an hour, she looked like a man of seventy, complete with a head of white hair. The hands were next. From a drawer she pulled out what appeared to be evening gloves, only they were masculine with veins showing and tiny threads of hair. The palms and fingers were soft and padded so that if anyone touched her, they would think they were real. She removed her watch and then pulled them on, first the right one and then the left. This took a little longer because they were made to fit tight to the skin and all the way up to the elbow. She taped her breasts and then slipped on a pair of light, tan-colored pants with the butt filled out along with the front to make her look heavy and a red shirt and a pair of black runners. She rolled up the sleeves just below the elbows. The forearms looked real. She finished the old man off with a Mariners baseball cap. From a tray inside one of the drawers, she took a man's fake wedding ring and slipped it on her fake finger. Her vision was perfect, but the old man was nearly blind, so she added a pair of fake glasses. For the final touch, she grabbed the cane next to the door and stared at herself in the mirror. Perfect.

In the garage, the old man put the sports bag in the trunk and then placed the tightly sealed box on the passenger seat next to him along with his cane. Fifteen minutes later he was on the other side of town, in the industrial area.

He parked his car in one of the alleys and then walked two blocks with the aid of his cane and then up half a block to the corner. Two doors down on the same side and he was standing close to the front door. The street was quiet, no traffic, and so was the sidewalk. He quickly checked the address on the slip of paper Dina had slipped into his pocket to make sure this was in fact the right place before peeking through the window.

There were other couriers she could have used but most were UPS stores that were in busier locations so she chose this one after finding it on the web. It advertised it was open from 10 a.m. to 4 p.m., as a courtesy, mostly for small business, accepting drop-offs only. It was almost four when he slipped the watch back into his pocket. Except for the person behind the counter, there was no one there. The old man went inside.

She had never done this before where the old man would be required to speak. On all the other occasions she had worked in the shadows, in anonymity, but this time she would have to interact with another person, so this was no time to be nervous, she told herself. She had practiced his voice while driving and after ten minutes believed she had it down pat. The old man wouldn't have to say much, anyway. The plan was to get in and get out. How long could it take? Two minutes? Five minutes, max? It would be better, she thought, if she could get her voice to go a little deeper, but she decided what she had was fine. He was old and frail, and sometimes their voices could be squeaky. *Just stay calm, and don't panic.*

"You just made it," Thelma said without smiling. She pointed to the clock on the wall. "Another five minutes and you would have been out of luck." She sounded unhappy that the old man had been able to make it through the door before she had a chance to lock it.

The old man stared at her but said nothing. *Remember, get in and get out.*

"Would you like to put a return address on this?" She pointed to the label that was already affixed with her fat finger. "Looks like you missed it," she said. "If not, it's okay by me." She shrugged her thick shoulders and

169

rechecked the clock as if to imply that he was holding her up. She took a step back and placed her hands on the counter behind her and waited for some kind of a response. The old man looked at her like he was deaf. There was no reply.

"Well, suit yourself. It's a lot easier to track it if there's a return address on it in case the waybill gets lost or the package gets wrongly delivered, but that's up to you." Thelma and her bad attitude quickly grabbed a shipping slip from a pile next to her. She took another quick glance at the old man and decided against making him fill out his own form. It would be much faster if she did it herself; otherwise, there was a chance she could be there another hour. It was already quitting time.

"Most people usually put a return address on their stuff," she continued, "in case it gets lost. No telling what might happen. Without a return address, we can't return it if it shows up. Are you still sure about not wanting to put a return address on it?"

There was no reply from the old man, who was looking the other way, towards the door.

"Ah, excuse me," Thelma said.

"Yeah, it's fine," he finally said, diverting his eyes back toward Thelma.

"You can't blame us, then. Sometimes these places can be hard to find."

The old man wanted to tell her what a twit he thought she was. Did she even bother looking at the label? *It's addressed to the Chicago Tribune, dumb-ass! The printed label is clearly marked. What's your problem? How could it get lost? Where's your supervisor?*

"It's fine," he said again, nodding slightly.

"Do you want insurance?"

"No."

"Suit yourself. When do you want it there?"

"Tomorrow, if possible."

"It'll cost you extra."

Thelma was getting on his nerves with all the pointless questions about a return address, whether or not he wanted insurance. *Doesn't she ever shut up!* The old man stared annoyingly at her through his thick glasses before saying, "Fine."

Thelma slapped a label on the box and then weighed it and checked the chart. "That'll be sixteen dollars and seventy-five cents." She pointed to a spot on the form. "I need your signature here."

The old man gave her a twenty and then signed the slip using his other hand, scribbling the name of Jackson Henshaw Dina had pulled from the phonebook. Thelma returned with his change and then gave him a copy of the shipping slip. Jackson Henshaw stayed long enough to see Thelma drop it into a bin, and then he disappeared back through the door, safe and undetected, like it never happened.

In the alley, the trunk was opened, the blue gym bag removed and then parked on the passenger seat next to the driver. He checked his mirrors before throwing the glasses in first and then the long, manly arms. He picked at his face, removing the fake chin, the small cheeks, the scraps of two ears, a layer of heavy latex skin from his forehead, plus the small pieces along the jawline before popping his blue eyes. Dina then washed what was left of the old man from her face with the aid of cold cream she took from a jar before wiping it away with a dry cloth. She washed her face again with a facecloth 'til her face was clean before tossing it in the bag. The clothes were removed and the black runners replaced with clean white sneakers. Dina started the engine before tossing the gym bag back in the trunk. Outside the car, she stood all in white: white T-shirt, white shorts, white socks, and white runners. The only thing missing was a tennis racket, which was in the trunk next to the blue bag and Anita's suitcase from the airport. They could pass for twins.

Dina lit a cigarette and leaned against the side of the car while she relived the moment. She was smiling. She was thinking about what the old man had done, and she was enjoying every minute of it. What she wouldn't do to see the look on his face. Tomorrow the smart-ass reporter who wrote wild stories for the *Tribune* was in for a real surprise, maybe the surprise of his life.

Dina took a final drag and then butted what remained of the cigarette against the sole of her runner, tossing what was left in the drain behind the back wheel. She was gloating and she knew Anita would be too if she decided to tell her. After all, she only did it to protect her. That's why she was there to begin with.

Chapter 22

Veronica had decided to arrive earlier than usual on Monday morning after thinking about it over the weekend. There was something she wanted to discuss about Friday night and she knew by arriving earlier than usual she would have a better chance at discussing it rather than trying to fit it in later when it might be too busy. At first, she had thought about calling him to clear the air since they worked together but thought it would be better to talk face to face. It was just past seven. She was in the lobby, standing in front of one of the elevators that would take her upstairs when she felt a gentle nudge behind her.

"You're early."

"Oh. Hi, Laura."

"So how was your weekend?"

"Oh, you know. The usual. Quiet," she replied in a soft tone. "How was yours?"

"The same as the last one. I haven't had a date in almost three weeks. I need to find myself a boyfriend, and quick. My best years are flying by, and I'm not getting anything, if you know what I mean. If things don't start to improve, I may have to pick up a stray," she said, glancing around at the men waiting for the elevator.

"It can't be that bad, is it?"

"What's wrong with the men in this city? It seems nobody wants to commit to a relationship anymore."

Veronica didn't reply. Instead, she shrugged her shoulders.

"How late did you stay on Friday night? I heard you and Miles were the last to leave."

"We were there till about one, and then we left."

The doors opened, and everyone piled in. Laura and

Veronica stood next to the doors.

"So?" Laura stared at her and waited.

"What?"

"The details. Tell me what happened."

"Nothing happened. We just sat around and talked for a while, and then we went home."

"Together?"

"No. He walked me to my car, and I left."

"Oh."

"You sound a little disappointed."

"I've seen you two together," she said, raising her eyebrows. "I just thought that maybe something happened."

"Sorry. Nothing happened. There's nothing to talk about," Veronica said calmly.

The elevator stopped on the fourth floor. Laura and Veronica were the only ones to depart.

"How about lunch?" Laura asked.

"Sure, but nothing happened."

"I know. I heard you. Nothing happened. How about Franco's? I feel like a little Italian."

"You don't look Italian, but sure. Why not?"

Laura smiled at her. "I have to use the girls' room. Care to join me?"

"I'll pass."

Veronica headed for the newsroom. Miles was already there, sitting at his desk. She placed her purse in one of the drawers and knocked on his door.

"Are you busy?"

"Not really," he said, pulling his nose from the paper.

"I think we should talk."

He looked at her, not surprised by her request. "I guess we should."

Veronica sat in one of the chairs in front of his desk,

but for some reason she didn't say anything. It was like she was stuck for words. Neither did Miles. They just sat and stared at each other for a long moment. It was Friday night all over again.

"This is awkward."

"What do you mean?" she asked.

"Usually one of us would be saying something by now. I guess considering what happened…"

"Yes, I know. We've always been able to talk about anything."

"I don't know about you, but this is hard for me. I know what you want to talk about. I just don't know if I can right now," he said, moving deeper into his chair.

"I think we should, Miles."

"I thought I had it all figured out this morning when I was driving to work. I was going to come in and say that it was all just a big mistake," he said with a sigh. "I was going to say that I loved my wife and we're expecting our first child and that what happened Friday night wasn't worth the risk of losing it all. That I should have known better. And now I don't know if I can say that."

"Miles, when I said maybe we should talk, I wasn't talking about making any life-changing decisions." She hesitated, trying to choose the right words. "That's not what this is about. That's not why I came in here. There's no rule that says we have to discuss this at all if you don't want to. I just think we should talk about what happened Friday night and how we're going to deal with it. We still have to work together. I'm not married, *but* I'm sure I have a sense of what you're going through right now."

Miles left his chair and stared out the window. He was obviously in some distress.

"I'm thirty-five years old. An adult, for Christ's sake!" he said in a low, angry tone. "These things aren't supposed to happen." He sounded naive. "At least, I didn't think it was going to happen to me. But isn't that what I'm expected to say? To say I didn't think it would happen to me and that somehow I'm the poor victim in all this, even though I know I'm not." He quickly turned and stared at her. "I'm sorry. I didn't mean to imply what it sounded like. I shouldn't have said it. I'm sorry. I'm thirty-five years old, not some kid who needs to run home for protection. I knew what I was doing. I'm just not proud of it."

"Nobody's a victim unless they want to be."

"Isn't that the whole purpose of being in our twenties and single? To explore what it is we want so this doesn't happen to us later on in life. Isn't that it? When you reach my age, aren't we supposed to be past all this high school stuff? Aren't we supposed to know what the hell it is we want and with whom?"

"I suppose, but life doesn't always work out that way. You know that."

"Yeah, I know," he said quietly, sitting back in his chair.

"If you're feeling guilty over what happened, don't be. Guilt will only tie you in knots and incapacitate you if you let it. I've learned that we do the things we do for a reason, and I'm sure you know that too. The thing is to be honest with yourself. We can't knowingly do something and then have our every emotion controlled by guilt. If we did, we would all be stuck somewhere where we don't want to be, unable to function. Guilt serves no purpose, Miles. Any good therapist will tell you that."

"I know," he said. "Life is just a little mixed up right now."

Veronica moved to where she was closer, sitting on the edge of her chair, being careful about what she wanted to say.

"I know you're unhappy," she said sadly. "I've been with you every day for the past year, eight to ten hours a day. I've seen you happy most times, but when you talk about life outside of this office, in particular your marriage, you change. You're not yourself. I know you haven't discussed it a lot and in detail, but I could tell. It was really noticeable when Erin got pregnant. I don't know what it means, and I don't want to know because it's none of my business. It's between you and Erin. And that's a true statement. Aside from the other day, I've never once asked you what was bothering you. I always left it up to you if you wanted to talk to me about things outside this office because you were married and I wasn't."

"Yes, I know."

"I never would, Miles. It was never my place to ask if you didn't want to talk about it. But I do know that Friday night didn't happen without a reason. If it weren't for Friday night, I wouldn't be sitting here right now and talking to you about it. I just thought we should talk to clear the air and make sure of the reason as to why it happened and where do we go from here."

Miles pulled himself forward.

"Veronica, it isn't easy for me to talk about what happened…I know I'm attracted to you. I have been since the day I first met you, but I should have known better. I should have left with the others. In retrospect, I probably shouldn't have gone at all. I should have gone to hospital like I had planned. I didn't know this was going to happen."

"I don't think either one of us did. Life doesn't come with a blueprint."

"This isn't the way I wanted things to happen between you and me. I'm not blaming you. If anybody is to blame for what happened, I am."

"Nobody is to blame, Miles."

"The way I feel right now..." he said, his voice trailing off. "I'm having trouble dealing with it. I'm frustrated right now at how life sometimes turns out, especially mine. I'm feeling sorry for myself, I know."

"That's okay," she said in a soft, soothing tone. "It's allowed, but we have to talk about this and how we're going to deal with it."

"Maybe you can cope with this better than I can. Maybe you're more mature than I am right now, which isn't surprising considering how I'm reacting to all of this. It can be somewhat intimidating, if you know what I mean." He shrugged his shoulders. "I just don't know what's going on anymore."

"It's not so much that I'm more mature," she said, staring at his beautiful face, "as it is that I'm honest with myself, and that's how I live my life. I won't apologize for it. I don't want to live life with my head in the sand, hoping that everything that is wrong with my life will eventually just go away if I don't deal with it. Anything that makes me unhappy I deal with, and then I go from there. I don't know—maybe you can't do that. But that's just the way I am, Miles. I'm sorry if you feel this situation is intimidating. I can't apologize for that, either. If I didn't come in here and say that I think we should talk about it, would you have approached me and told me the same?"

"I don't know."

Her look was serious, almost hurtful.

"I find that funny in a non-funny kind of way."

He furrowed his brow, letting his eyes cool. "What do you mean?"

"We've always been able to talk."

"I know. We do talk. We're talking now."

"But this is something way more serious."

He hesitated and then said, "I just don't like to hurt anyone."

"Nobody does," she replied calmly, "but that sounds more like an excuse, Miles."

If she required a response, he didn't give one.

"For the first time, I'm going to sound like I'm prying, but I hope you don't think that I am. I never told you this, but I grew up in a family where all my parents did was argue and call each other the cruelest of names. A week or two later, they would act like nothing ever happened, saying how much they loved each other. I know for a fact my father had two affairs, and my mother knew but did nothing about it. Once I witnessed my father striking my mother. I learned from it and promised myself I would never live like that, living a lie, and that I would always be truthful to myself and to those in my life about who I am, what I do, what I like, who I like, and why I like them. I kissed you. You could have told me no, but you didn't. You could have walked away, but you didn't."

Again she paused, quietly catching her breath.

"Things happen—that's what life is. And that's what happens when we choose to live life and not stand around watching it go by, trying to live for someone else, or in my parents' case, living in a lie. No regrets when life is over. If what you said was true, that that's how you deal with life and your feelings, then you should be asking yourself, who's living your life?"

She was at the door, holding the handle and looking straight at him.

"I'm not sorry for what happened. I'm attracted to

you, too. I admit that. I have been since I first laid eyes on you, but I'm not sorry for it. I say that not because I'm selfish, but because of what I see and what I feel. If I can't be honest with you, then I'm not being honest with myself."

She waited, looking at him intently.

"I'm only sorry if what happened causes you pain. To hurt you would be the last thing I would ever want for you. What happened Friday night didn't happen because I wanted to destroy someone else's marriage. Adultery is not part of my makeup, and I'm sure it's not part of yours. All I know is that it happened. It happened because one of us is unhappy and either doesn't know how to change their life to make it better or is too afraid of what that change might bring. I didn't come in here to change anything, if that is what's meant to be. You have to believe that. I only came in here to talk. I wanted to apologize for kissing you," she said ruefully. "I thought you were at least mature enough to want to talk about it."

She left.

Chapter 23

At precisely two thirty, two men exited the elevator on the fourth floor. The man with the hat, a cross between a fedora and porkpie, approached the desk while the other stood guard by the elevator as if this was now sacred ground and nobody was to trespass.

"Miles Fischer. Is he in?"

"And who may I say is calling?" Sally asked, ready to attack the console and punch in the numbers.

"That's okay," said Donlon, placing his hand gently over hers. He quickly flashed his badge. "We know where to find him." He nodded to his friend. "Let's go." Donlon and his buddy headed for the doors.

They found Fischer's office along the south wall after confirming with the small plaque attached to the door and went inside without knocking. Henley closed the door behind him.

Miles was on the phone.

"Yeah, it's okay, Sally," he said. He slowly placed the receiver back where it belonged and rose from his chair, a little puzzled at the unscheduled meet and greet.

"Are you Fischer?" Donlon asked, pulling his sunglasses from his eyes and tucking them in his shirt pocket.

"Yeah. What can I do for you?"

"Do you mind if I take a seat?" There was a hint of a southern drawl.

"You can if you want, but I don't know if you'll be staying that long." He glanced suspiciously at Henley, who stood next to the door like a Doberman.

"Nice office you have here."

"I like it."

"My name's Donlon." He flashed his badge and

quickly placed it back in his pocket. "This here is Agent Henley." He pointed to the man standing by the door still wearing his sunglasses. Henley was almost half Donlon's age and twice his size. "We want to ask you a couple of questions about the story you wrote in the Sunday paper on the crossbow killings."

Fischer settled back into his chair, a little wary as to what they wanted. He stared at the man across from him. He knew a lot of the agents out of South Dearborn, but he didn't know this guy, the one with the hat. He had never heard of Donlon or Agent Henley. They weren't from around here.

"That all depends on what kind of questions you intend to ask."

"Nothing too difficult, I hope." Donlon's head was cocked to one side with a smirk for a smile. His left leg was crossed at the knee. "Seems like you're one smart reporter."

"Oh." Fischer wanted to laugh. "It's not very often a reporter is told that he's smart—especially by the FBI."

"We've been trying for quite some time now to piece together the information on the three crossbow murders you just happened to report on in your story. I won't get into the specifics since your article explains it in a nutshell, albeit in a simple-minded manner, but we think you can help us."

"You're a little early, aren't you?"

Donlon's eyes narrowed. "What do you mean?"

"According to my calendar, Halloween's not until October."

Donlon glared at him. "You're a real funny guy, Fischer."

"Yeah, almost as funny as that crack you just made."

"I didn't know you newspaper guys were so sensitive."

"What do you want, Donlon?" Miles asked, glaring at him.

"I'm not one to beat a bush to death, so I'll just get right to the point." Donlon purposely hesitated and moved forward to where he was sitting on the edge of his seat, trying to size him up. "We would like you to work with us on this one by giving us what you have so we can nail this perpetrator. Kind of be like, oh I don't know..." he said, scratching the back of his neck. "Let's say, being the good corporate citizen, for lack of a better word."

"What makes you think I have something?"

"We read your story, Fischer. You tied everything back to what happened in Eastbrook. To do that, you would have to know something. Care to tell us what that is?"

"I don't know if you noticed, but this is a newspaper, not some public library where you can just walk in and get what you want. I don't know anything more than you do, Donlon. In fact, I probably know less."

Donlon chuckled lightly, taking a quick glance at Henley, who was still by the door. His expression had not changed.

"What did you do, Fischer? Eat a bad clam."

"No. I feel fine. Why?"

"You really expect us to believe that crap?"

"You can believe whatever you want, Donlon. This is a free country. It's protected in our constitution. You know—free speech, free thinking, and all that stuff."

"Look, Fischer," he said, staring at him. "I'm not some dumb-ass who just came into your office on some kind of a whim. You and I both know that if you printed something that wasn't true, you would be jeopardizing your reputation along with your career here at the

Tribune, not to mention the lawsuits that would follow. That would put your legal department and your employer in a very difficult position. I'm only guessing here, but they would probably be forced to let you go. Tell me something. Who would hire a journalist who fabricated the truth just to make some headlines? You'd be finished, so don't give me that bullshit you don't have anything." Donlon shook his head. "Like I said, you seem to be a pretty smart reporter. I know you got something, so why don't you make this easy on yourself and the newspaper and give us what we want?"

"Even if I had something, you know I couldn't do that."

Donlon stared at Fischer and thought for a moment. He snorted almost by instinct.

"This oughta be real good," he said with a smirk, easing back in his chair. "Go ahead, Fischer. Why don't you tell my pal Henley here why it is you can't or don't want to cooperate?"

"You ever heard of the first amendment?"

Donlon nodded his head and smiled at him. "Let me guess—freedom of the press. Am I right?"

Miles just stared at him but did not answer.

"That's a good one, Fischer. Mark that one down, Henley," he said, looking in his direction, "in case we come across it again. I want to be prepared for the next time a reporter tries to blindside me with the constitution. You surprise me, Fischer. I thought you were smarter than that. You newspaper guys are all the same, quoting the first whenever you find your backs against the wall. We both know damn well that it gives you the right to publish, but it doesn't give you the right to withhold information that is vital to the public interest by putting them at risk."

"The public isn't at risk, and you know it, Donlon. Whoever is doing this is only wreaking havoc on the perpetrators. When do vigilantes go after the innocent? If you ask me, the person or persons responsible for their deaths are doing the FBI a big favor, including the public, since you don't seem to be able to apprehend them."

"You're a real piece of work, Fischer, you know that? I thought you were smart. Now I find out you're just as dumb as the rest of them. What we're asking for is your cooperation, to see if you guys would play ball with us and help us nab those that are responsible for these killings, but all I get from you is your smart mouth. What's the public going to think when they find out that you and your newspaper don't want to cooperate? Somehow I don't think they're going to appreciate it very much."

"Yeah, well I don't appreciate you busting through my door without knocking, unannounced. This is a newspaper, in case you forgot, Donlon. We don't pander to the whims of the FBI. If you need help, I suggest you call 911."

"You and the *Tribune* have a civic duty to help when called upon."

"I think you have your facts wrong, Donlon. You're the law, the ones responsible for catching these guys. Not us. We're just a newspaper doing our job. We only report what we see or what the public doesn't know but has a right to know."

"Look, Fischer, why are you finding this so difficult? Why are you trying to butt heads with us? I'm assuming we're both on the same side. I'm only guessing here, but I think we both want the same thing—to nail these bastards. Unless I'm wrong, we should be working together on this, but maybe that's where the problem lies.

185

Maybe we don't want the same thing. Maybe you just want to keep your little secret so you can sell a few extra papers and to hell with the safety of the general public. Which one is it, Fischer?"

Suddenly the phone rang. Miles put the receiver to his ear.

"Fischer."

It was Lynch.

"I just got off the phone with Sally. She said that the FBI is in your office."

"That's right," he said, staring at Donlon.

"Do you want some company? I'm here with Kate. We can stop by if you like."

"I think that would be a good idea."

Lynch hung up the phone and looked over at Kathleen Finch, the sixty-one year old executive editor of the *Tribune*, who was sitting behind her desk.

"We've just been invited to a meeting. You coming?" he asked Kate.

"You go ahead. I'll be there in a minute."

"You might want to ask your pit bull to move away from the door," stated Fischer.

Donlon looked a little puzzled at the request. He left his seat and looked out into the newsroom through the glass wall in silence, his hands on his hips, waiting to see what was coming. Henley stayed where he was and watched through the door. Something was up. Miles watched as Lynch, dressed in a white shirt and purple tie, exited Katherine Finch's office at the front of the newsroom along the north wall. Donlon noticed the large man with the large stride making his way towards them. So did Henley.

"What have we here, Fischer, reinforcements?"

Donlon asked.

All three watched as Lynch weaved his large frame between the rows of desks. He entered without knocking.

"Pat." Miles pointed to both men. The doorman was standing next to Donlon. "I would like you to meet Agent Henley and Agent Donlon."

"Gentlemen."

They shook hands. Donlon took his seat while Henley went back to guarding the door. Lynch leaned against the wall to Miles's left. He smiled cautiously.

"So what brings two federal agents to the *Tribune* on such a nice, sunny day?"

"I was just telling your smart-ass reporter here that we're very interested in the story he wrote in the Sunday edition about the three crossbow killings, but he seems unwilling to cooperate."

Pat looked over at Miles. Miles shrugged his shoulders and almost rolled his eyes.

"Cooperate how?" asked Lynch.

"We believe your reporter here has some information vital to solving these cases. We came hoping the *Tribune* would want to cooperate with us."

"What information would that be?" Pat asked, slipping his hands behind his back.

"Your little friend here stated that everything originates out of Eastbrook. That's a hell of a bold statement coming from a newspaper for something that happened almost ten years ago. We've already checked everybody connected to these crossbow killings, and they're all clean, including those living in Eastbrook and Whatley. Maybe we've overlooked somebody, but I don't think so, which leads me to believe that Fischer here has something, something that could possibly close the book on these cases. All we want is the name." He looked over at Miles. "So tell me, Fischer, whose name is on your list now that your boss is here?"

"We have no list," replied Pat.

Donlon turned to the man leaning against the wall. "Everybody has a list, Lynch. We have one, and we know you have one. All we want is the name."

"What makes you think we're chasing anybody?"

Donlon held out a long, skinny finger and pointed it in the direction of Fischer. "In your little friend's story, he connected the dots that point in one direction."

Pat stiffened and then folded his arms across his thick chest. It was a ridiculous request. "You know we can't do that. Even if we had a name, we wouldn't divulge it."

"You newspaper guys all stick together, don't you, Lynch?"

"You're barking up the wrong tree, Donlon. This newspaper has rights, and we do what we can to protect them."

"You mentioned earlier that you investigated everyone that you thought might have had a hand in this. Care to divulge who it is you investigated?" asked Miles.

"You know we don't discuss our investigations with the media," Donlon quickly shot back.

"And we don't go around discussing our information that is outside the realm of the courts, which includes the FBI," replied Pat.

"Look." Donlon's smirk was gone. He decided to try it from a different angle. "Let's cut the bull. We're willing to make you guys a deal. You give us the name of your source, and we'll make sure you get firsthand information on as many of the details that we can give to the media." His tiny blue eyes shifted between the two. "We'll guarantee you first crack at the information before any of the other newspapers. What do you say?"

"What do you take us for, Donlon? A guarantee like that is worthless, and you know it."

"You sound desperate, Donlon," Fischer added.

Donlon quickly glared back in his direction.

"Look, gentlemen," said Pat, "I don't know how we got off to such a bad start, but this sniping isn't getting us anywhere. The *Tribune* would like nothing better than to help you with your investigation, Donlon, but we can't divulge what we don't have."

"Don't play coy with us," snapped Donlon, pointing at Pat. "Why else would you risk printing something when you would only be alerting your competitors? Isn't that what this is all about, selling more newspapers than your competitor? No, you guys have definitely got something, alright, and we want it. We want to know who your source is. In fact, I'll even go one better because I think you know who this person is."

"You're crazy, Donlon. If we knew who this person was, Fischer wouldn't be sitting on his tail right now. Instead, he would be out there pounding the pavement," he said, pointing to the window.

Donlon shook his head. "You're a terrible actor, Lynch. You see, I'm just as smart as you are, including Fischer over here. We're not leaving until we get that name."

"Sorry, Donlon. We can't give you what we don't have."

Donlon shook his head and bit his lip. "What do you want, Lynch? Everybody wants something."

"Look, Donlon. We're not gonna play this game with you. We're a newspaper, protected by the Constitution of the United States. We have freedom of the press, which makes this the great country that it is, and we're not about to be bullied into giving out information that we are not required to even if we had it, which we don't. We only deal in facts, and the fact is we don't know who this person is."

"Is that the best you got?" asked Donlon with a smirk.

"That's all you're gonna get."

"So that's it. That's all you have to say?"

"Not unless you've got something you want to add," Pat said, tucking his hands behind his back. "I think we're done."

Donlon stiffened up and turned his attention to Miles. He raised his voice, which flared his nostrils, widening his small, blue eyes.

"How would you like it if I took this before a grand jury?"

"You'd be wasting your time, Donlon," replied Lynch.

"It wouldn't be the first time," stated Miles.

"Don't be so sure, funny man. A grand jury has a way of dealing with tight lips like you. How would you like to be standing in front of a federal court judge right now?" He slapped the desk hard with his left hand. "Withholding evidence in a criminal investigation is a federal offense, in case you didn't know—aiding and abetting. Care to explain that to a judge?"

"What do you take us for, Donlon? Everybody in law enforcement knows that reporters have a right to their sources. It's called confidentiality, for Christ's sake, in case you didn't know." Miles stood up and placed both hands on his desk, leaning in the direction of Donlon. "You haven't got a leg to stand on. But go ahead. Serve me with a summons. In fact, I dare ya because you haven't got the proof that supports that pile of crap."

Donlon stood and glared at him, pointing a finger across the desk. "I'll promise you one thing, Fischer. If you print just one word that in any way leads to these killers, you'll be spending some hard time with some real shit that would just love to get their hands on a pretty boy like you. I can guarantee you that, funny man."

"Are you threatening my reporter?" asked Lynch.

Donlon did not answer. Instead, he quickly moved to the door and held the handle.

"I know you're hiding something, Fischer, and when I find out, I'm going to be back here with a big ol' southern smile, showing you just what real southern hospitality is all about. Let's go, Henley."

Donlon quickly yanked the door, leaving it open. Henley followed him out while Miles watched from his chair. Pat moved to the glass wall, watching the two black suits make their way back toward the elevators.

"That was quite the show," said Pat, relaxing a little.

"Can you believe him?" added Miles.

"How the hell did this meeting start out like this, anyway?"

"You know how they are."

Pat pulled up the chair in front of Miles and sat in it.

"No, Miles," he said, folding his arms in front of him. His voice was edgy. "Tell me how they are."

"What do you mean, tell you how they are?" Miles shrugged his shoulders. "You know damn well how they are. We do all the work, and then they stroll in here like we're Wal-Mart and they have a right to pick the shelves clean. I am not going to hand over what could be one hell of a story just because they can't figure it out. If they want it, they're going to have to push bamboo shoots up my ass before I even give them a sniff. This is my story, and it's going to stay that way. Like I told you and Greenberg, I'm the only one who can place her in that courtroom. What did you want me to do, cooperate and give them what we have?"

"No. I'm not suggesting that at all, but I think maybe you should have gone a little easier on them. We're supposed to try and keep them on our side, remember."

Kathleen Finch finally made it to Miles's office and peeked inside the door.

"So where are they?"

"They just left," replied Lynch.

Kate stepped inside without bothering to close the door and took a seat.

"What did they want?"

"They were here asking questions about the story we wrote on the crossbow killings."

Suddenly there was a rap on the door.

"Excuse me, Miles. Sorry to interrupt, but this package came for you." Laura entered the office and placed it on Miles's desk.

"Where's Veronica?" he asked, since usually it would be Veronica who would deliver his mail.

"She went home right after lunch. She wasn't feeling well."

Through the glass Miles could see her desk. It was uncluttered and unoccupied. He noticed there was no jacket hanging on the back of her chair as there was earlier.

"She never told me she was leaving."

"I guess she didn't want to bother you."

Miles watched her leave without commenting but thought it was strange that Veronica didn't tell him. He retrieved a letter opener from his desk.

"Whatever it is, it feels rather light," he said, placing it in front of him.

Miles broke the seal with the letter opener before peeling back the four folds. Without thinking, he aggressively dug inside with his right hand and took hold of the sharp, jagged tip by accident, but then he quickly released it, sending some of the white synthetic foam over the sides, where it spilled onto the desk and onto his lap.

"What the hell?" he said loudly.

"What is it?" asked Lynch.

"I don't know," he said, sucking his finger, "but I think I just cut myself."

Lynch reached over and grabbed the box. He looked it over before cautiously empting the contents of the box onto the desk. There, in the middle of the pile of white foam, he saw the black arrow with the black and yellow fletching. Kate and Pat stared at each other in quiet disbelief at the object resting in a pile of foam.

"What the hell's going on?" asked Kate.

Lynch checked the box before quickly grabbing the receiver and punching in a number. "Yeah, Sally. This is Pat. I want you to do something for me. I want you to do a trace on the package that just arrived for Miles. See if you can track down who sent it. No. There's nothing on the box. Thanks."

"I doubt that it will do any good," stated Miles as Lynch hung up the receiver.

"And why not?"

"Do you think she's that stupid?"

"Will somebody please tell me what the hell is going on?" asked Kate.

"Remember what we were talking about in your office?"

"Has this got something to do with it?"

"I didn't get to finish what we were talking about, but we believe the killer in these crossbow killings is the same person. We think it's Anita Paletti."

"And you think she might have sent this?" asked Kate, now studying the arrow more closely.

"I don't know," replied Lynch.

"Who else would have sent it?"

"I don't know, and neither do you, Miles, so let's not jump to any conclusions."

"So what are you going to do?" Kate asked, not wanting to interfere, preferring to stay on the perimeter.

"I don't know," Lynch said.

"What do you mean, you don't know?" asked Fischer.

"I mean exactly that Miles. I don't know what you're thinking, but this is serious. There's a real danger here." He glanced over at Finch, who was sitting quietly, taking it all in. "We're going to have to take a little time and figure out what to do on this." He nodded at Finch. "What do you think, Kate? You're the executive editor of this newspaper. What do you think?"

Kate crossed her leg at the knee. "Well, I agree with you. If you're right, this could be considered a death threat."

"This isn't a death threat," replied Miles. "It's a scare tactic."

"And you're not bothered by it?" asked Kate.

"No. Why should I be?"

"Christ, Miles!" said Lynch. "This isn't some joke. This is a goddamn threat against your life. Start taking this thing seriously," he stated, eyeballing him. "Or maybe you don't take things seriously."

"If it will make you happy, I'll wear a vest. How's that?"

"This isn't funny, Miles."

"I'm not trying to be funny, but we're a newspaper, or have you forgotten? We don't choose the stories that happen to come in here. We take everything that comes through those doors, and we run with it no matter what. This is what the hell we do. We can't pick and choose."

"Don't tell me what the hell we do here. I know what the hell we do!" he shouted. "I've been in this business a hell of a lot longer than you have. I know all about risks. Isn't that right, Kate?"

"Pat's right."

"I can't afford to send one of my reporters out there when I know he has a very good chance of getting himself killed."

"Why? Because you and Kate here wouldn't be able to sleep at night?"

"I can't speak for Kate, but you're damn right I wouldn't be able to sleep at night!" Lynch began pacing. "There's more at stake here than just you and this story."

Kate's lips were pressed tight, watching Lynch and Fischer argue their position. She missed the adrenaline rushes that she got from sparring with reporters. It was moments like this that she actually envied Lynch.

"What do you mean, more at stake?"

"There are other factors here."

"Christ! What the hell is going on here? You used to be a reporter once, or have you forgotten?" He looked at Finch. "Same thing for you, Kate. You were both reporters once. Since when do we back off on a story just because it has a little danger to it?"

"We haven't forgotten," interrupted Finch, "but we have different responsibilities now. Not just to you, but to everybody here and everybody who buys our paper, not to mention our advertisers. This is a death threat, Miles. If we were to send you out there and something happened to you that could have been prevented…"

"I can't believe what I'm hearing."

"I have the *Tribune* to worry about, not just you!"

Lynch said.

"And what is that supposed to mean?"

Pat's voice regained some semblance of calm.

"It's not as simple as you think, Miles. You're putting your life on the line and the credibility of the *Tribune* along with it. How do you think this is going to play with the public if you're dead, that we willfully sent you out there to get yourself killed, knowing full well the situation? They're going to want to know why we didn't let the FBI handle it." Pat pointed past the glass wall. "What this department does could affect the whole organization. If you don't believe me, ask Kate. She's sitting right there. I can't have one of my reporters from my department affecting the whole organization and everybody in it." Again his voice rose. "I'll have Kate here running up my ass. Is that what you want?"

"Of course it's not what I want, but this is a big story, a damn big story. Mine and the *Tribune's*, and if it comes to where..." Miles stopped short, letting his voice trail off.

Lynch looked at him rather funny.

"Go ahead. Finish what you were going to say."

Miles waved at them with his hand. "It's nothing. Forget it."

"Your wife is lying in the hospital, waiting to deliver a baby. What are we supposed to tell her?"

"You let me worry about my wife," Miles snapped back.

"Christ, Miles! You're not making this very easy for me or for Kate."

"Pat's got a point, Miles."

"So what do you want me to do?" he asked, looking at both of them. "Give up on this story now that we're this bloody close to exposing Paletti?" Miles eased out of his chair and stood by the window. "If I do that, I might as well kiss my career good-bye. Look, you both know as well as I do that every story worth having has a certain element of danger attached to it. Without taking those risks, we're pitching stories about little Bobby next door who opened a Kool-Aid stand down the street. Is that what you both want? Because if you do, I'll give you my resignation right now and walk across the street to the *Sun-Times* and give them the story instead."

"Hold on, Miles," interjected Kate quickly. "We don't want you to give up the story, but you have to agree, this is a different and dangerous situation."

"Reporters go into dangerous situations every day," he said flatly. "There's nothing different about it."

"This situation is different," replied Kate. "This Paletti, if that's who sent you this, seems to have you marked. Doesn't that mean anything to you, or are you just some crazy reporter who thinks that he can outsmart a person who hides in dark places before knocking people off?"

"Look, Kate, every person she's knocked off has been scum. She isn't going to be knocking off a reporter."

"You don't know that for sure," replied Kate. "You're a threat to her now—or maybe you don't see it that way. If it is this Paletti woman, why do you think she sent you this arrow?"

"I already told you. Look. Every reporter would give his or her right arm for a chance at a story like this. But according to Pat here, I should just back off and do nothing for fear that Paletti might put me in her sights. This is my opportunity, and I'm not going to give it up and walk away. Don't you see, or have you all forgotten what it's like to be a reporter? This is our story. It's just sitting there waiting to be written."

Lynch took a seat next to Finch, looking exhausted.

"For Christ's sake, Miles, I didn't say that. All I said was I wanted to think about it. There's a lot riding on this." He ran his hand through his mop of gray hair and looked at Kate. "It's days like today I wish I was on a bloody golf course and as far away from this place as possible."

Lynch looked at Miles.

"How's your finger?"

"It's fine."

"You might want to have that looked at," stated Kate.

"Maybe later."

Suddenly the phone rang. Miles quickly pulled the receiver from the phone and held it to his ear.

"Fischer. Yeah, hold on. It's Sally," he said, looking at Lynch.

"What did you find out?...Thanks." Lynch slowly handed the receiver back to Miles. He hesitated and then said, "It seems you were right. The package originated out of Seattle. It was dropped off there yesterday. An old man by the name of Jackson Henshaw delivered it. They pressed him to put a return address on it in case it got lost, but he declined their offer."

"I'm not surprised," said Miles with a faint smile. "She knows, but that doesn't matter," he said, shaking his head. "She's running scared." He looked at Kate and Pat, who were looking at him. "So what are we going to do?"

Pat and Kate both looked at each other. Kate halfheartedly hunched a shoulder and pursed her lips together.

"It's your call, Pat."

"Gee, thanks, Kate!"

"Well, you're the editor, and he's your responsibility. As long as we all know the risks involved and take every precaution to play it safe, then…We're a newspaper first, so I guess…"

"Don't worry, Kate. I'll stay out of dark places, and I promise to say my prayers before I go to sleep at night."

Finch narrowed her eyebrows and stared in his direction.

"For Christ's sake, Kate. Stop worrying. I know what I'm doing." He looked at Pat. "How about it?"

Lynch sucked in a deep breath before expelling it.

"It doesn't seem like there's any other choice for me to do otherwise."

Lynch got up to leave. Kate followed him.

"I want you to keep me in the loop as to what is happening," Lynch said. "I want to know your every move. That means you're to call me and let me know what the hell is going on if something comes up. I don't want to hear it secondhand. You got that?"

"No problem."

"You screw up just once, and I'll yank you off this story so fast you won't know what hit you."

"Don't worry."

Chapter 24

Donlon and Henley entered the moderately decorated field office of their superior on the ninth floor on South Dearborn and sat across from the fat man. Ruben Abrams was on the phone, issuing directives to whoever was listening on the other end. He unfastened the top two buttons of his blue shirt and then tugged on the blue silk tie as he spoke, releasing the restraints on his flabby neck, making his breathing a little less constricted. After a minute of discussion, he hung up the receiver. He stared at the two men across from him and then moved his rather large rump deeper into his seat.

"Well? How did it go?" asked Abrams in his husky voice.

"Not so well," replied Donlon, who looked less than relaxed.

"Give me the details."

"We went in there like you suggested and started talking with Fischer before his boss, Patrick Lynch, joined us—not that it mattered since things weren't going all that well to begin with."

"What did Fischer have to say?"

"He stated that he didn't know anything other than what was printed in the paper."

"And Lynch?"

"He basically said the same thing."

"Did they say anything else?"

"Nothing worth mentioning other than Fischer expressing his right to his source, which he claims there isn't one. I tried threatening him with a contempt of court, but I don't think he scares that easy. He knows his rights and that of the paper. The guy's a real smart-ass, if you know what I mean. Lynch tagged along, mimicking what Fischer had to say, so it's obvious the paper is okay with everything they said."

Abrams closed his eyes and thought for a moment.

"He's definitely hiding something," said Donlon.

Abrams rubbed his eyes and then placed his elbows on the desk.

"I agree, but he can't sit on it forever. My guess is he's going to make a move in the next day or so." He pointed a thick finger at Donlon. "I want you two boys to tail this guy. Sooner or later he's going to make a move, and when he does, I want you there. I want you two to check with the airlines. See if he's booked a flight. If he hasn't, then keep checking until you come up with something. I don't want him slipping through without us going along for the ride. If he's flying somewhere, I want you two on his tail. When he moves, he isn't going to be doing it from behind his desk."

"How long do you want us to tail him for?" Donlon asked.

"As long as it takes. He knows something, and eventually, he's going to lead us to whoever this person is. When he does, we'll be right there to escort them off to jail and a date with a grand jury. And Donlon?"

"Yeah."

"I don't want this Fischer guy to know you're tailing him."

Abrams watched as the two men headed to the door.

"Oh, and one more thing."

"Yeah."

"Don't lose him."

The small bar was on Wabash Avenue, not far from the Lincoln Building where he occupied space on the fifth floor. Bruno was somewhere inside after arriving just minutes earlier from O'Hare International Airport. It was Monday afternoon. His ass was parked on one of the stools that were closest to the doors. Except for Bruno and three others at the other end of the bar, O'Shea's was mostly deserted.

"So where 'ave ya been?" Shawn asked, making his drink. O'Shea was born with a rich Irish accent and was almost the same age as Bruno. He had a light brown to reddish beard, neatly trimmed on all sides, which made his emerald eyes stand out. A blue unicorn was tattooed on his right forearm. "Ya 'aven't been around for a wee while."

"I've been busy."

O'Shea returned and placed the double rye whisky straight up with ice on the side in front of Bruno.

"Workin' are ya? It's about bloody time! And what case is it that yer workin' on?"

"You wouldn't be interested."

"Try me."

"I'm working on that crossbow killing that took place in Idaho about a week ago."

Shawn thought for a minute.

"Idaho, ya say. Have ya read the newspaper lately?"

"How could I? I've been out of town. I haven't even been home yet."

"I love ya, Bruno. Ya come in 'ere straight from yer long trip. I should give ya a wee squeeze just for sayin' that." O'Shea with the green eyes motioned towards the rest of the bar. "I wish the rest of these sods felt like ya do. If they did, I'd be rich and somewheres else lying on a beach with sand up me arse." He laughed loud and short.

"Very funny, Shawn. Touch me and I'll have to pull out my .38 and do away with ya."

"In a foul mood, are we? Well there's no need gettin' nasty on me when all I'm tryin' to do is help ya. 'Ere. I've got somethin' to show ya." Shawn reached over and grabbed the paper. "There's somethin' in Sunday's paper that I think ya oughta look at. 'Ere," he said, sorting through the sections. "You kin read it yourself."

He flipped to the first section and then pointed to it. Bruno gulped part of his drink and butted out his cigarette.

"What is it?"

"Quit askin' questions, will ya? Just read the bloody thing."

Bruno finished his drink and lit another cigarette and began to read.

Shawn waited a bit, tugging on his black leather vest, which hung loosely over his white T-shirt before leaning his thin body against the side of the bar.

"Martino. He was in 'ere yesterday, ya know. 'Im and two of his boys were lookin' for ya. I told 'em I hadn't seen ya since last Tuesday. What da they want with a big weed like you?"

"I owe him some money," he said without looking up. "Horse races. He's looking for his money."

"Well, I don't like those boys coming in 'ere. Dirtballs, they are—every last one of 'em. They're nottin but dirtballs!"

"Don't worry about it, Shawn. I'll take care of it, and you won't have to see them in here anymore."

"Good, because I don't like their kind. They're bad for business. I run a respectable bar 'ere. They're nowt but trouble."

The arguing down at the end of the bar was getting heated. Their voices were getting louder. Bruno looked their way and said, "Yeah. Well. I think you got some trouble brewing at the other end of the bar." He nodded towards the two men who were starting to swing wildly at each other.

"Shite! Bloody rubes." Shawn headed towards the two men, yelling as he walked. "Okay, ya two. Grab yer scrawny girlfriend and beat it!" He grabbed a length of steel pipe from under the bar on his way to the other end.

Bruno dragged on his menthol and watched as the two thin men with missing teeth and the ugly woman with the ponytail continued to argue on their way out the swinging doors with O'Shea following from behind the bar, holding the pipe on his shoulders.

"Bloody drunks!" He looked at Bruno's empty glass. "Ya want a wee bit more?"

Bruno nodded, still reading.

"Nasty business, them crossbows," he said. "Ireland was fought and won with those things, ya know."

"Yeah, I know. I went to school, too."

"If ya ask me, they're better off dead," he said, pouring the whisky into the glass. "Scum like that wouldn't last a day back in Ireland!"

"Yeah, well, we're not in Ireland, now are we?" Bruno straightened the paper. Shawn's constant talking was annoying him. It was virtually impossible to read and get the gist of what he was reading and carry on a conversation at the same time. "We're here in good old America. You've been here long enough, Shawn. I think it's time you let it go. But thanks for your opinion. Now, if you don't mind. I'd like to finish reading?"

Shawn placed the drink in front of Bruno.

"There ya go ag'in, gettin' all nasty on me. I was just tryin' to make a point. All I said was they wouldn't last a day."

"Yeah, I know," Bruno said, still reading. "And

Ireland's got the IRA. Now there's a fun group," he remarked with sarcasm.

"That's in the north, ya dumb-weed. I thought ya told me ya went to yer fancy public schools?"

"Okay, wiseass. You got Irish fighting Irish. What's the difference?"

"At least they're not crooks like Martino."

"Yeah, I know. They're just cold-blooded murderers killing innocent people for what they believe in, whether the rest of them agree with them or not. To hell with what the rest of them think. Potato, potahto. Why don't you go do something," he said, gesturing with hand, "and let me finish reading?"

Bruno went back to reading the column, while O'Shea tended to the mess the three had left at the far end of the bar. When Bruno finished, he reached into his bag and pulled out the plastic sleeve holding the piece of paper from the cigarette that he had found on the roof. He called O'Shea over.

"What do you make of this?" Bruno asked.

O'Shea put on his reading glasses that hung from his neck.

"What am I lookin' at?" he asked. He stared at the tiny piece of paper, perplexed as to what he was holding.

"It's from a cigarette." Bruno took a drag of his menthol and then blew the smoke to his right, away from O'Shea. "Have you ever seen anything like that before?"

Shawn O'Shea pursed his lips together and shook his head.

"Can't say that I 'ave. The markins are a wee bit odd lookin'. It's nowt I've ever laid eyes on."

"You're a big help." Bruno chewed on an ice cube and then downed what was left of his drink.

O'Shea returned the tiny piece of paper back to Bruno

and took the empty glass and headed further down the bar to make him another drink. Bruno placed it back in the plastic sheath and placed the sheath back in black leather bag sitting on the stool next to him.

"Where'd ya find it?"

"I can't say."

"Oh, it's a clue, is it?"

"For an Irishman, you sure are a nosy one."

"Look who you're talkin' to. Look around ya, Bruno. I'm a bartender, for Christ's sake. It's what I do."

"You should fix this place up."

"Later. Right now I'm busy. So what are ya goin' to do?"

"About what?"

"'Bout this case yer on."

"I'm working on it. Why?"

"I've got an idea. Why don't ya go see this guy Fischer who's been writin' all this stuff? Maybe he can 'elp ya."

"I don't need any help. Besides, that wouldn't be such a good idea."

"And why not?"

"Do I have to give you a reason? It won't work, okay? Just mind your own business and fix me my drink."

"I've got anuther idea. Why don't ya take that piece o' paper to a tobacconist? They should be able ta help ya. There's one over on Monroe. It's probably the closest. And just so ya know, we 'ave those over in Ireland, too," he said with a chuckle.

"Just get me the damn drink."

"You may want ta think about layin' off this stuff. I think it's addlin' yer brain. Yer not thinkin' straight."

"If I stopped drinking, you'd be out of business."

"That's what I love about ya, Bruno. Yer my best customer. God love ya."

Chapter 25

It was almost seven thirty Monday evening when the black Jimmy exited off of Fifteenth Street and pulled into one of the stalls. It abruptly stopped before Miles locked the doors with the remote and passed through the doors of the multilevel parking lot on his way up to see Erin. The gnawing in his stomach had settled in like it was already winter. He was going to have to tell Erin that he was leaving for Seattle in the morning, and it wasn't going to be easy. The thought of rehashing it all over again had him dreading even going there. And how would Erin take the news? *If it was anything like the previous times...* The thought of another argument had him wishing he were somewhere else.

He tapped on the door and went inside.

She was sitting up, reading a magazine. She looked at her watch and then at him.

"You said you would be here around six thirty. It's now past seven thirty. What took you so long?"

"Just an hour," he said, glancing at his watch. "I was doing some research. Why?"

They gave each other the standard, abbreviated kiss. There was no feeling, like his lips were numb.

"I've been waiting for over an hour. I thought we could have dinner together." On the serving table next to her bed he noticed two large plates. "Why didn't you call?"

He took the chair next to the window.

"How did I know you wanted to have dinner? I didn't know I was going to be that late. If I had, I would have called you."

"How's Rocky?" she asked, changing the subject.

"Rocky's fine. Everything's fine," he said quickly.

"Is the house clean? You're not leaving your dirty dishes in the sink, are you?"

"I said everything is fine."

His snapping caught her attention. Erin sat up straighter, adjusting the pillows that propped up her back.

"You don't seem very talkative. Is there something bothering you?"

"No. Nothing. Why?"

"Because you're awfully short with me. Is it something I said?"

"No."

Miles left the chair and stood by the window, gazing through the clear glass at the beginning of what looked like the long shadows of night.

"I have something to say, and you're not going to like it." He turned and looked at her. "That story I'm working on—something has come up. I have to go to Seattle tomorrow."

There was a moment of silence as Erin processed what had been said.

"What time?" she asked.

"The plane leaves at eleven."

"Can't they get someone else?"

"No."

"Why do you have to go to Seattle?"

"I already told you."

"Can't you postpone it till later?"

"I can't. There's no time. I have to go."

"I don't understand why it is that you have to go when they know we're expecting our first child. I think they're being a little insensitive."

"It's not as simple as that. Something has come up, and waiting until later is not an option."

"You've been away for almost five weeks now."

"What do you want me to do, Erin?"

"I already told you."

"I don't understand why we keep going over this. You know this is my job. I can't change it."

"But we're expecting. I just think that at the very least they could get someone else this one time. I don't think that's asking for too much."

"It doesn't change a thing, Erin," he said, shaking his head. "If I could pass this off to someone else I would, but I can't."

"Maybe you're not trying hard enough."

"What is that supposed to mean?"

"Maybe you don't want to be here."

"That's a dumb statement."

"Did you ask him?"

"Ask him what?"

"Did you ask him to put someone else on this story?"

Miles went back to looking out the window but did not answer.

"Miles. I asked you a question."

"No."

"And why not?"

"Because this story is too important to give it to someone else."

Erin's jaw quickly stiffened. "I see." She took the magazine next to her and placed it on the night table. "So you're telling me this story is more important than me? More important than being here when the baby arrives?"

"You don't understand."

"Oh, I think I do."

"No, you don't."

"Tell me something—is your little friend going, too?"

"What friend?"

"Your little friend—is she going, too?"

"Veronica? Don't be ridiculous."

"Now I'm being ridiculous. A moment ago you said I was dumb."

Miles said nothing and shook his head.

"Will you please look at me when I'm talking to you?"

Miles turned from the window.

"I want you to tell me what's going on."

"Nothing is going on."

"I don't believe you."

"You can believe what you want."

"Then why won't you stay and be here with me? I'm not asking for much."

"Because I can't. I already told you. This story is too important. The *Tribune* is counting on me."

"Too important to you or the *Tribune*?"

"That's really unfair, Erin."

He sat down in the chair and set his blue eyes on his wife. Erin crossed her arms in front of her.

"How long are you going to be gone for?" she asked.

"I don't know."

Her voice was angry again.

"Why don't you know? It's a simple question."

"Because I don't know where this story is going. For Christ's sake, Erin! Ease up, will you? I don't have a crystal ball. If I did, I'd be able to tell you. I just told you that a minute ago."

He felt confined sitting in the chair and uncomfortable under her steady stare, so he stood at an angle by the window.

"Christ, Erin, why the pressure?"

Her eyes were hard like an owl. "She's going with you, isn't she?"

"Christ, Erin!"

"That slut. She's going with you, isn't she?"

"What did you just say?"

"You heard me."

"Are we talking about Veronica?"

"She's the only one who has come up in our conversations unless there's more that I should know about."

He snickered at the window. "It's hard to say. We get to know so many in the newspaper business."

"You know," she said, narrowing her eyes, "you can be such an ass at times."

"And you can ask the stupidest questions."

"I know. You already told me."

"If you're talking about Veronica, she's not a slut."

"Then why do you feel the need to defend her?"

Miles sucked in a deep breath. "We already discussed this. I told you it wasn't true."

"If it's not true, then how did it get started? People don't just make up rumors for no reason. There must be some truth to it."

"Well, you're wrong. Why the hell don't you believe me?"

"How do I know you weren't out with her on Friday night? Maybe that's why you couldn't make it, why you didn't call."

Miles was seething with anger. "Christ, Erin. What the hell is your problem?"

"Her! She's my problem, and she's the one causing this thing in our marriage."

He waited and then went on the attack.

"She's not the problem, Erin. You and your getting pregnant is the problem."

"Me? I'm the problem?" she asked sarcastically.

"That's right, and don't look so surprised. The

problem is you and the way you went about getting yourself pregnant without telling me." Miles moved towards the bed. "We never discussed you getting pregnant or us having kids," he stated. "What we discussed was how *not* to get pregnant. You decided this thing on your own. I've been trying to discuss this with you for the past three years, ever since you got pregnant the first time, but you never wanted to discuss it. You always turned away from it. You were the one always crying, remember? That was your way of dealing with it. Who always left the room? That's the problem with our relationship and our marriage—not her."

"You never told me this before," she stated defiantly, trying to backtrack, trying to deflect attention away.

"That's a bunch of bullshit, Erin, and you know it," he said sternly. "Where have you been all those times I tried talking to you about it? Where, Erin? What do you think we argue about half the time? How you went behind my back and got pregnant without telling me. How do you think that made me feel? You cut me out, Erin," he shouted. "The very things that are to bind two people together in a relationship, you cut me out of."

"We never discussed it?" she asked softly, trying to look innocent.

"Don't play stupid with me, Erin!" he shouted angrily. "Have a little more respect for me than that. No! We never discussed it, and you know damn well we didn't!"

"Lower your voice," she said, staring at him. "I thought it was what our marriage needed."

Agitated by her clouded perception, Miles paced at the foot of the bed.

"Christ, Erin," he said, almost laughing. "How can you sit there and logically tell me that it was what our marriage needed? This isn't what our marriage needed. What our marriage needed was a little honesty. We needed that same honesty when we were still living together, before you became pregnant the first time and we got married. Let's try it now and see if there is any honesty left in our marriage."

"What do you mean?"

Miles approached her. "Why don't you tell me how you got pregnant the first time?" Miles stopped and held his index finger to his lips. "No. Let me rephrase that," he stated in his mocking tone. "*Why* did you get pregnant the first time?"

She gave no answer.

"Okay then—if you won't tell me that," he said, glaring at her, "then tell me why you got pregnant the second time."

Again silence.

"You don't want to answer—fine. I'll tell you why you got pregnant."

"Why are you talking like this?"

"Because I'm tired of this, this mockery of an existence that has become our marriage. I'm tired of all this crap in our relationship. I'm tired of pretending. I'm tired of this thing that's between us, and I want to go home, but sometimes I don't know where that is anymore. Do you understand me?" he asked, shouting.

She looked at him and almost snickered.

"So you're blaming me for our problems? I'm the cause—I'm the one doing all of this?"

"Yes!"

"And you don't do anything wrong. You're the perfect husband. You're the victim in this marriage. Is that what you're saying?"

"Now who's acting like an ass?" he asked sharply,

214

moving back to the window.

She turned, gathering the sheets under her sweating palms. The strong language dug into her like a deep and infectious cut. Wounded and blinded by her own jealousy, out of control, she asked, "Have you slept with her?"

Miles stood motionless, dumbfounded by what he just heard.

"What?" he asked.

"Did you sleep with her?"

"So you think I'm unfaithful?"

"Just answer my question, damn it!"

"Why does everything revolve around you and your feelings? Why am I not the one considered here? Why is everything only about you?"

She gripped the sheets tighter with both hands.

"Did you sleep with her?" she shouted.

"No!"

"I don't believe you."

He turned to look out the window and shook his head.

"You can believe whatever you want, Erin," he replied. "What I told you is the truth."

"Then why don't you look at me?"

Miles turned and leaned against the window and folded his arms.

"Men can be such whores when it comes to another woman," she said sharply. "They would sell everything they have just for a taste of what it would be like."

"So now I'm a whore?" That was a new one.

Staring, she said, "Men are known to be liars. Every woman knows that."

"Not every woman," he retorted.

"You've had every opportunity to sleep around on me these past five weeks—all these late nights recently, trips here and there," she said, gesturing with her hands.

"Is that what you think? Is that what you want me to say? That I've slept around on you so that it would make it easier for you to cry to everyone how I hurt you?"

"And what is that supposed to mean?"

"If I wanted to sleep around on you, Erin, I would have done it long ago. But I've been faithful to you and our marriage. It's called trust, Erin. The kind of trust you should have shown me before you went and got yourself pregnant. It's obvious you have no respect for me or our marriage."

"How can you say that?"

Miles was standing by the door, facing the bed.

"If you respected me, you would have consulted me before you got pregnant the first time, never mind the second time. All these accusations of sleeping around— manipulating me like I was some kind of rag doll. Withholding sex to get your way and then just lying there like you wished I was someone else."

"How dare you!"

"You think I didn't notice?"

She was shaking.

"What? The truth hurts. What about the time you told me that your friends asked you how you hooked me just after we got married? I thought you were joking. Tell me, Erin. Did you plan it this way?"

She looked to the window and said nothing.

"Christ, Erin! Look at me!"

"What?" she screamed towards the figure standing by the door.

"Answer me," he exclaimed. "Did you plan it?"

"You bastard! You care more about her than you do me," she hollered back.

Miles squeezed the handle, his voice once again calm.

"I just finally realized what this marriage is all about." He stood silent for a moment, staring at four years of his life. "It's all about you. And now I understand it and why this marriage doesn't work." Miles held the open door. "As for Veronica, at least she respects me."

He glared at her with a sullen face and then disappeared through the opening.

"For now," Erin yelled back, watching the door slowly close behind him.

Miles stood quietly in the hallway, just outside Erin's door, the elevator only seconds away. He was breathing heavily. He could see the nurse, the few visitors who were there, and some of the patients leaning out of doorways and into the hall, staring at him from both ends. They were glaring in his direction, concerned with the intrusive commotion that had abruptly ended from behind the door. He felt deeply embarrassed and ashamed, having shared the most intimate details of his marriage with complete strangers. *Go back and apologize*, his conscience was telling him. Seconds passed as he paced back and forth, thinking feverishly as to what to do. *Do I apologize or should I just leave?* He paused and looked at the closed door, where, unbeknownst to him, Erin was experiencing the first signs of labor pain. *The hell with it!* He decided to leave and headed for the elevators and his black Jimmy waiting in the parking lot. He would not apologize. He had finally said what needed to be said.

Inside the room, the monitor was beeping stronger and faster. Erin clutched her abdomen again, only harder, and then she pressed the button.

Chapter 26

They were in the main terminal at O'Hare International Airport, inside the office of the assistant director for operations. Agent Donlon stood behind a black woman in her midforties and carefully watched the monitor. Henley, his partner, sat quietly on the other side of the desk and observed Mrs. Osbourne as she punched in a series of letters before hitting the enter button. It was just past eight on Monday night.

"If he made a reservation, he probably would have made it any time from Sunday on. That's Miles Fischer. F-i-s-c-h-e-r," said Donlon.

"I heard you the first time, Mr. Donlon. You don't have to scream it in my ear. I know what I'm doing," came her quick reply.

"I wasn't screaming, lady. I simply wanted to remind you how to spell his name since there are some variations."

"Well I don't need your help. I'm quite capable of doing this on my own. And please refer to me as Mrs. Osbourne. "

She pressed the mouse and highlighted the name: *Miles Fischer. Tuesday, August 24, American Airlines. Flight 945 for Seattle. Departure 11:05 a.m.*

"How's that, Mr. Donlon?"

"You did good, lady."

"Mrs. Osbourne."

"Yeah, right. Mrs. Osbourne. You did real good. Now what do we have to do to make sure we're on an earlier flight?"

Without responding, she quickly pressed a few buttons, changing the screens.

"You're in luck, Mr. Donlon." She pointed to the

door. "If you go back the way you came, one of the reservation clerks will be able to help you and your friend with your purchase."

Donlon signaled to Henley, and they were at the door.

"By the way, lady, what section is he sitting in?"

"Business!"

Chapter 27

The apartment was one of many high-rises that ran along Sheridan Road with a view to Lake Michigan. Miles parked his truck in a stall reserved for visitors and killed the lights before turning off the ignition. It was almost dark, and his cell phone was off. It was in the glove box and had been since he left the hospital. He had no intention of staying too long. Just long enough to see how she was and then he would leave. It was probably a feeble excuse for him being here at this time of night, but he didn't want to go home—at least not yet. He was feeling a little wounded and in need of some company but didn't want to hang out at a bar. The thought of drinking alone was depressing.

Miles scrolled through the names on the intercom, found hers, and then punched in the numbers and waited to hear her voice.

"It's Miles," he said. "I was in the neighborhood, and I was wondering if you would like some company?"

"Miles?"

"Yes. Is it too late?"

"No, I'm just surprised to hear your voice. I wasn't expecting you. Hold on and I'll buzz you in." She gleefully held the button on the receiver, allowing Miles to ease through the door.

The elevator opened to the sixteenth floor, and he quietly knocked on the door at the end of the hall. A bolt clicked not once, but twice, and when she opened the door, her white smile was there to greet him.

He felt nervous just being there. He was still undecided if this was the right thing to do. He raised his eyebrows and cleared his throat. "So, how are you doing?"

"I'm fine."

"This is little awkward," he said, "me standing outside your door."

She smiled at him. "Why do you say that?"

"I usually don't make house calls. I usually leave that up to the professionals, but since I was in the neighborhood, I thought I would drop by and see how you were doing. I hope you don't mind."

"Don't be silly," she said, almost chuckling. "You don't have to make excuses for being here. Come in."

Veronica waited until he was all the way in before closing the door, resetting the locks.

"I'm not intruding, am I?"

She shook her head. "No, so stop asking."

"If I am, I can leave."

"Miles." She shook her head ever so slightly. "Stop it. It's okay. Can I get you something? A drink maybe?"

"A drink sounds good," he said, letting out a heavy breath.

Miles took a seat on the cream-colored leather sofa while Veronica made her way to the central wall unit on the opposite wall which held a small bar.

"Nice place," he said, gazing around like he was in an art gallery.

"Thanks. I decorated it myself. So what will it be?"

"Is gin and tonic okay?"

"Sure." Veronica reached for a clean glass from the enclosed shelf just above her. "You took me by surprise," she said, looking over her shoulder. "I didn't expect you to be here." She turned from the bar. "But now that you are, I'm glad you came by."

Miles was holding an eight-by-ten picture in a gold frame.

"My parents," she explained without having been

asked. "And those are my two sisters," she stated, pointing to the two pictures at the other end of the couch.

He leaned over and looked but did not comment. Miles returned the picture to the end table and pushed the hair from his eyes.

"I hope you don't mind me barging in like this. When I heard you went home sick, I got concerned. I just wanted to know if you were okay."

She poured the gin and added the tonic. "Hold on. I'll be right back. I have to go get a lime."

He watched her leave and then said, "So how long have you lived here?"

"A couple of years now," she said with her head stuck in the fridge.

Miles waited for her return. "It's really nice. You've done a good job. I like the layout."

"Thanks but my parents own it."

"It still looks great," Miles said, heading for the window.

"I must look awful."

"No. You look fine," he replied back.

Seconds later she was behind him, holding his drink in one hand and a glass of wine in the other.

"So did I miss anything at work?"

"Funny you should ask. The FBI paid me a visit this afternoon. They seem to think I know who is responsible for the crossbow killings. One of them threatened me, telling me he was going to haul me in front of a grand jury."

"Can he do that?"

"No," he said, chuckling. "He was just blowing smoke." He shrugged his shoulders. "After him and his partner left, I got a surprise delivered to the office."

"A surprise? What kind of a surprise?"

"It was a box but that wasn't the surprise. The surprise was inside. It was an arrow. I actually cut my finger when I reached inside to grab it."

"Let me see," she said, sounding alarmed.

"It's nothing," he said, showing her his finger. "It's just a scratch."

"It's because of that story you wrote, isn't it?

"Probably."

There was silence for a moment.

"So what are you going to do?"

"I'm leaving for Seattle tomorrow."

"Oh."

"I have to be at the airport at around ten. The flight leaves at eleven."

"For how long?"

"I don't know. It all depends."

Veronica hesitated, thinking, knowing she was going to go back on her word. "I know I shouldn't ask this," she said, "because it's probably none of my business, but what did Erin say about all this?"

"It's not her decision so it doesn't really matter."

Miles moved to the doorway and then onto the balcony, gazing out onto the bright lights of Sheridan Road and the quiet of Lake Michigan. There was a hint of what was left of the rays from the sun hanging off the few clouds that were passing through. He leaned on the railing and sipped his drink.

"That's a hell of a view," Miles said.

"It's beautiful, isn't it?"

"It's gorgeous."

Veronica took a spot next to him to where they were almost touching.

"About what I said. I know you don't want to talk about it. I hope you don't think I was prying. I know it's none of my business. I'm sorry. I shouldn't have asked."

"I know, Veronica," he said, looking at her. "It's okay." He turned and looked out towards the lake. He was quiet for a moment and then said, "We had another big blowup this evening. It isn't the first time, but this time we said some things that weren't very pleasant." Miles quietly sipped his drink and stared out at the lights. Veronica stood next to him and watched the night with him.

"You look tired," she finally said, staring at him.

"It's more my brain than anything."

"Did you eat?"

"No. I went straight from work to the hospital."

"You must be hungry. Come in the kitchen and I'll make you something."

"No, I'm okay. I don't want to put you out."

She reached for his hand.

"You're not putting me out," she said. "I want to do it. Besides, I haven't eaten either. Come on. We'll eat together."

On the counter in the kitchen of the quaint home of Mr. and Mrs. Miles Fischer, the phone rang. Rocky was barking. It rang another three times, and then the message machine clicked on.

"Mr. Fischer, this is the hospital. We tried reaching you on your cell phone, but you didn't pick up. Your wife is being readied for surgery. Due to stress on the baby, Dr. Faraday has decided to perform a cesarean section. He is due to arrive within the hour. Please call maternity as soon as possible."

The machine clicked off, and the message was saved.

Chapter 28

Miles stayed another hour and then left. He had a flight to prepare for and a dog waiting to be taken for a walk. He purposely neglected the cell phone that was still in the glove box. *If Erin called, so what*, he thought. *Let her stew over it for a while. It might do her some good.* Besides, she was probably asleep already.

After arriving home, he grabbed the leash off the hook by the back door and then noticed the light flickering on the machine. A minute later, he vaulted from the house, cursing to himself as he headed for the hospital.

It was just after eleven when he burst out of the elevator leading to the maternity ward. He ran down the hall towards the nurses' station.

"How's my wife?" His heart was racing.

"Can I have your name, please?" she asked. She was young and pretty with blonde hair neatly tucked under her cap.

"Fischer. Miles Fischer," he said, trying to catch his breath. "My wife's Erin Fischer."

"Your wife is doing fine. They just wheeled her back to her room."

Miles headed in the direction of Erin's room.

"Excuse me, sir, but you can't go in there."

"Why not?"

"She left instructions that she didn't want to be disturbed."

"When did she tell you that?"

"Just before we took her back to her room."

"But I have a right to see my wife."

"I'm sorry, Mr. Fischer, but we have to abide by our patients' wishes."

Miles stared at her. "I don't care. I want to see my wife." He turned and started towards Erin's room.

"She said she didn't want to see you," she said rather loudly, but at the same time with a hint of sadness and regret. "I'm sorry, Mr. Fischer. I'm only following what she instructed me to say."

Miles stared at her with a raw look and then vaulted down the hall and pushed open the heavy door.

"What the hell is going on?" He stood at the foot of the bed and pointed to the door. "Why did you tell the nurse you didn't want to see me?"

Erin was lying on her back. She looked noticeably tired.

"Because I don't want to see you."

"I have every right..."

"You have no rights." She was screaming. "Now get out!"

She rolled onto her side and grabbed her abdomen where the stitches were and winced. The nurse and an attending physician were at the door.

"Mr. Fischer, I think it would be best if you stepped outside," the doctor said.

He stood glaring at Erin. He shook his head in frustration and then left. The physician went inside and quietly closed the door.

Fischer's hands rested on both his hips as he stood staring at the floor just outside the door with the nurse standing in front of him, watching and waiting. He felt embarrassed at what had just taken place. For some reason he felt this sudden urge to say something, to explain exactly what was going on between them in order to make himself look and feel better. Maybe she would understand. He sucked in a deep breath and then slowly exhaled it. He looked at the nurse.

"Can I at least see the baby?"

"I don't see why not," she said, trying to inject some cheer into an otherwise unpleasant scene.

She led him in the opposite direction, past the nurses' station, their footsteps barely audible as they made their way down the hall before standing in front of a large window not far from Erin's room.

"I'll be right back."

He watched as she disappeared behind the door. In seconds she wheeled a tiny baby girl, who was in an isolation unit, to the front of the window. He leaned on the glass with one hand and just stared, dismayed at what life had now become in so short a time. They had conceived and brought a baby girl into this world, not knowing now if they would ever be a family. For a moment he stared in the direction of Erin's room, his life flashing in front of him as if on a movie screen. He could feel the weight of the whole world as it slowly descended upon his thoughts.

Chapter 29

Laura was hovering next to Veronica's desk like a lost soul when Veronica arrived at the *Tribune* on Tuesday morning. She looked overly anxious.

"Good. You're here," she said. "I was worried you wouldn't show up today. Something really weird is going on." She quickly pointed to Miles's office.

"What are you talking about?"

"It's Miles."

"What's wrong with him?" Veronica peered over her shoulder towards his office. She could see the top of his head resting against the back of his chair through the panes of glass. He was facing the windows.

"He's acting kind of strange."

"What do you mean?"

"I got here at around seven thirty," she said, glancing at her watch. "He hasn't moved, and it's been almost hour. Don't you think that's kind of strange?"

Veronica peered again towards his office.

"Have you talked to him?"

"I said good morning to him when I got in, but he didn't respond."

"Are you sure he heard you?"

"Yeah. His door was open, so I poked my head in the door, but he didn't say anything. He hasn't moved an inch since I came in. I think something's wrong."

"Did you tell anybody about this?"

"No, because I didn't know what to do. I mean, I didn't know what to say, especially if nothing was wrong, but this isn't like him. That's why I waited for you. I heard his phone ring twice since I've been here, but he never picked up. He just let it ring. I've never seen him like this before. Should we tell someone?"

"No, it's okay," Veronica said, somewhat hesitantly, taking another look towards his office. "Don't say anything to anybody right now. I'll go and see if anything is wrong."

Veronica carefully hung her jacket behind her chair and placed her purse in one of the drawers before making her way to his office. She tapped lightly on the door.

"Miles."

There was no answer.

She went in and quietly closed the door. She moved towards the windows and looked at him.

"Miles."

Again there was no answer.

"Miles, can you hear me?"

She waited for a response, but he didn't answer. He just kept staring out the window.

"Miles—is something wrong? Is it Erin?"

"It's raining outside," he finally said in a low voice without moving.

"Yes, I know."

"It's been nearly a month, but its finally raining. We could use a good rain. I like the rain."

Veronica was puzzled by the way he was talking. He was too young and too fit to have suffered a stroke. He was coherent even though he wasn't making much sense. He looked a little tired and could use a shave, but aside from all that, he looked fine. Veronica grabbed one of the chairs and placed it close to where he was so she could face him.

"Is everything alright?"

"Yeah." His voice was low, barely audible.

"Is there something you want to talk about?"

"No," he said, continuing to stare out the window. He almost laughed. "Everything is fine."

"Are you sure?"

"Sure? We can never be sure."

"Why are you talking like this? If you're trying to scare me, it's working."

"Things can change just like that," he said, "with us never even knowing it. Sure? I don't even know what that means."

He shook his head, but it was barely noticeable.

"Stop it, Miles. Look at me. Something has happened. What is it?"

He ignored the request and continued to look out the window.

"It's okay," she said. She reached for his hand. "You can tell me."

Another pause, no response, and then finally in a muffled voice, like he was unsure, he said, "Erin had the baby last night."

The way he said what he said was rather peculiar, she thought. His reactions were contrary to what one would expect. There was no inflection in his voice—no excitement, no smile, nothing.

"That's a good thing, isn't it?" She waited for a response, something that would open him up, but she got nothing. "What's wrong, Miles? You don't sound very happy."

"What a shock."

"Something's happened. Is it the baby? Is the baby okay? Is it healthy?"

"Yeah."

"Well, that's good to hear. What was it—a boy or a girl?"

"A girl. A beautiful baby girl."

"I'm so happy for you. I take it Erin's okay?"

"Yeah." There was another pause, like his mind was

somewhere else. "She told me to get out," he finally confessed, his eyes still fixated to the window. "She said she didn't want to see me."

Veronica was shocked at what she just heard. It took her a moment to digest it, to take it all in. "I don't understand. What do you mean, she didn't want to see you?"

"She said she didn't want to see me."

"But it doesn't make any sense. Something must have happened. Tell me what happened."

"When I got home last night, there was a message waiting for me on the machine. They said they tried to reach me on my cell phone. They couldn't reach me because I had it turned off. When I got to the hospital, Erin had already had the baby. I went to see her, but she told me to get out."

"Didn't she let you explain what happened, why you weren't there?"

"I tried to, but she didn't want to listen."

Veronica leaned forward and gently squeezed his hand a second time.

"I'm sorry, Miles."

He sighed slightly and took in a shallow breath before expelling it quietly from his lungs.

"I missed the birth of my daughter," he said with a hint of remorse.

She watched his eyes. They were moist, like looking through water.

"I'm sorry, Miles. About last night—if I had..."

"It's okay," he said, finally looking at her. "It's not your fault. It had nothing to do with you. I should have been there, but I wasn't. It's my fault. I shouldn't have turned off my phone. If I had kept it on, none of this would have happened, but I didn't know."

"I don't understand. Why did you have your cell phone turned off?"

"I didn't want to talk to her. I got angry and turned my phone off when I left the hospital. I didn't want to hear from her in case she called. How was I supposed to know she was going to end up delivering the baby?"

"Did they say what kind of birth it was?"

"What do you mean?"

"Was it a natural birth or was it a cesarean?"

"A cesarean, I think."

"If it's any comfort, she probably didn't mean it. It was probably just a reaction to the drugs they gave her. We all react differently. Sometimes women react in a funny way after giving birth, especially if it's their first. Sometimes we say things we don't really mean. She's probably over it by now. Have you talked to her since then?"

"I went by the hospital this morning before I came in." He almost laughed. "They stopped me at the desk before I had a chance to see her."

"I'm sure this will pass. People make mistakes."

Miles left his chair and moved to the windows and looked out at the rain-soaked streets before speaking.

"It's a little more complicated than that. I didn't want to say anything," he said, "but I know about what happened in the bathroom at the Christmas party."

She paused, hesitating as she thought of her reply, and said, "Oh."

He turned and looked at her. "Why didn't you say something?"

"I'm sorry but I didn't think it was important. I thought it would just blow over. I thought maybe it had to do with drinking. People say things when they shouldn't. When did she tell you?"

"I don't remember exactly, but I think it was last week during one of our infamous arguments. I'm sure the hospital staff heard us. It wasn't pretty, if you know what I mean."

She pursed her lips together. "It's my fault this is happening to you."

"No, it isn't. It's Erin's and mine. You played no part in this."

"But it is my fault. If I hadn't kissed you…"

"I kissed you back, remember?" He pressed his lips together and folded his arms in front of him. "I hate to admit it, but this has been a long time coming. I'm just sorry for dragging you into it."

"You didn't drag me into it." She paused, thinking of what to say next, and then she said, "So what are you going to do?"

"Right now, there's not much I can do. Truth be told, there's probably nothing I want to do—at least not right now. I know that sounds a little cold. I'm just a little shaken by all of this. It was always in the back of my mind that we might split up because we've grown apart, especially in the last year. I guess I just didn't think it was going to end this way, in a hospital with a new baby."

"You look like you didn't get much sleep."

"We probably should have parted before we decided to have a child. It would have been better for everyone, especially for that little baby girl lying in that nursery."

"You don't have to go to Seattle if you don't want to. I'm sure Pat will understand if you decide to stay. He can always send someone else."

"No, it's okay. I have to go."

"If you stay, maybe you and Erin can work it out."

"I'm not so sure we can." He sucked in a deep breath

and expelled it from his lungs. "We've been at this over a year now, not getting along. I'm exhausted from it all. I'm pretty sure she is too. I don't think I can do it anymore," he said, shaking his head. "In a way, I feel totally responsible for what's happening. I could be the first one in our family who is divorced. I can just imagine what people are going to say now that a baby is involved."

Veronica left her chair and stood at an angle to the window to where they were almost touching.

"We've always been able to talk. It's one of the things we have between us. I hope I'm not saying the wrong thing. If I am, I want you to stop me. I know this is hard on you. Personally, I don't think you should make any snap decisions as to what you want to do about your marriage. I think you're right, though. You probably need some time by yourself, whether it's here or away somewhere else. I think you need to give yourself some breathing space. It could be what Erin needs, too. I know it's hard with a new baby, but maybe a little time away will help clear the air. You know, absence makes the heart grow fonder." She smiled at him. "My mother used to tell me that. She also told me it doesn't matter what other people think or say. The only thing that really matters is what you think. This is your life, Miles. Everybody has a right to be happy, including you, but only you know what that is. It takes two people to make a relationship work. A relationship is built on trust and honesty. The thing to remember is to be honest with yourself. If you're not honest with yourself, then you'll never be happy and you won't be able to make anyone else happy, either."

Miles checked his watch and let out a big breath.

"Are you okay?" she asked.

"Yeah. I think so." A small smile appeared. "Did I ever tell you how intimidating you can be at times?"

"Yes," she said, laughing lightly, "a few times, but I'm really not as intimidating as you think. I just try to look at things in a positive way. In life, things happen for a reason, and from every negative you can always grab onto a positive. You just have to reach for it."

There was a pause as he thought about what she said.

"Thanks—you know, for listening to me."

"For you—anytime." Veronica moved from the window and headed for the door. "I'll see you later."

Chapter 30

It was just past nine thirty in the morning, and Bruno was at the counter of the tobacconist on Monroe Street, waiting for an answer while the shopkeeper examined the piece of paper Bruno had lifted from the roof of the hardware store. The storekeeper held it under a bright light using tweezers and a magnifying glass.

"Yeah, it's just what I suspected. From these here markings on the paper, I'd say it's definitely from an Israeli cigarette." Next to him, a catalogue was open. He flipped through pages and then pointed to it. "There it is there."

Bruno leaned on the counter and looked at the page showing the brand.

"How would somebody go about buying these?"

"They'd have to have them brought in from overseas through a tobacconist like myself."

"You mean an importer?"

"That's right."

"Do you know how common these are here in the States? I mean, do you sell a lot of these?"

"I don't sell any, but that doesn't mean I can't get them."

"So they're pretty distinctive, then?"

"I'd say they're pretty uncommon, yeah. In fact, I'd never seen any until you showed me this here paper. You can try some of the other tobacconists in the city if you like, but I doubt if you would find any here in Chicago. We don't have a big Jewish community like New York City, but I could be wrong. Personally, I only bring in what I can sell. No point in bringing in something that nobody will buy. Are you looking to buy some?"

"No, no. I was just curious as to how common they

were."

"Too bad. I could have gotten them for you. I could have them here in about six weeks if you're interested. I could use the business, what with all this anti-smoking propaganda going on. Pretty soon we'll all be on welfare if the government has its way."

The shopkeeper handed him back the small piece of paper.

"That's okay," he said. "I'll just take another pack of these." Bruno pulled the last cigarette from his pack of Kools and stuffed it behind his ear. "If I change my mind, I'll be back."

Veronica slipped through the open door and sat in the chair in front of him. Miles was standing at an angle to the window, gazing out through the rain at nothing in particular. He caught a glimpse of her as she made her way in.

"It's almost time."

Miles checked his watch. "Yeah, I guess it is."

"Did you try calling her?"

"She's not taking calls, so I asked them to call me on my cell if there are any problems."

"Are you okay?"

"Yeah, I'm fine."

"So where are you staying?"

"You can reach me at the Hotel Sorrento. It's right downtown. I asked Sally to pull a few strings and get me one of the better hotels. I told her I would make up the difference if there was a problem."

"Have you got everything?"

"Bag is right there," he said, pointing to the side of his desk.

"What about your dog?"

"It's all taken care of."

"So I guess this is it then until you get back."

"I guess it is."

"How are you getting to the airport?"

"Taxi. Sally called and said they'll be here in five minutes."

Miles grabbed his bag and the case with his computer. Together they headed for the door.

"Hold on a minute." Miles went back to his desk and hit the button on his office computer to send the e-mail he had prewritten about the birth of their baby.

"Okay."

Veronica followed Miles out and stood at her desk and watched along with Laura as he made his way to the front desk and the elevators that would take him to the street where a taxi was already waiting. On the screen to her computer and every other computer in the newsroom, the message that Miles had prepared was already waiting to be read. It was short and sweet—two sentences.

"Thanks to all of you who were concerned about Erin. I'm happy to say that Erin and I are the proud parents of brand new baby girl."

Chapter 31

Just before boarding his plane, Miles took out his cell phone and called one of his buddies. They hadn't spoken for almost six months.

Clint Gladstone was an old school buddy. He and Miles had lived on the same block, chummed around together almost exclusively since childhood. They played on the same football team in high school. They played baseball with the same circle of friends. They even dated some of the same girls, believing all was fair in love and war. When they graduated, they went their separate ways. Miles went off to Europe while Clint went straight into the navy and then served overseas before making a career out of it.

Clint had finally settled in Honolulu, of all places, after working his way up the ranks, becoming a lieutenant and then landing a nice office job. Clint told him over the phone that he had found a new girlfriend after he and his former wife finalized the divorce back in April, and then he told Miles one more time how lucky he was to have waited for so long before tying the knot. Miles didn't say anything. They planned on getting married around Christmas, continued Clint, and he wanted him there along with Erin. They caught up on the rest of what was happening in each other's lives, and then Miles told him the real reason why he had called before he had to board his plane. He needed a favor from an old friend, he told him. He was working on a story, and he needed something.

"I don't know how long this is going to take," said Clint.

"Just do the best you can. Sorry buddy, but I've gotta go. My plane is just about ready to leave. Call me when you have something."

At precisely three in the afternoon, Bruno entered the lobby of the Tribune Tower and took the elevator to the fourth floor.

"Good afternoon and welcome to the *Tribune*. May I help you?"

"Yes. I'm here to see Miles Fischer."

"Do you have an appointment?"

"I was supposed to meet with him this afternoon at three o'clock."

"And your name is?"

He almost grimaced at the request. A name? He forgot that he may be asked to give his name, but he had no intention of giving it.

"Ah, Miller. Thomas Miller."

"I'm sorry, Mr. Miller, but there must be some kind of a mix-up. Are you sure your meeting was for today?"

"Yes. I'm positive."

"Well I'm sorry, but Mr. Fischer is not available at this time. Is there anybody else here who could possibly help you other than Mr. Fischer?" Sally asked.

"No. I need to talk to Mr. Fischer," he said with his raspy voice. "It's about that story he's working on. Can you tell me where I can get a hold of him? It's urgent."

"I'm sorry, but I can't tell you that. He left specific instructions before he left."

"Maybe I didn't make myself clear, miss," he said, leaning over the counter. "This is important. I need to talk to him."

"I'm sorry, but he's not here," she stated forcefully.

The badge was in his back pocket, a remnant from his days when he used to be a cop. Bruno had declared it lost when he handed in his gun and got his walking papers, but not before receiving a lecture on what would happen should it suddenly reappear and he decided to use it. The felony offense carried a sentence of up to one year, including a fine.

He had kept it solely for emergencies, emergencies like the one he was in now. He quickly flashed the badge at her and then slipped it back in his pocket.

"Now, do you know where I can reach him?"

"Well..." Sally ruffled papers to make it look like she was searching for something. "I don't know," she said, glancing towards the doors that led to the newsroom, hoping someone would make an appearance and help her out of this sticky mess. She looked at Mr. Miller, who was staring back before looking back over her shoulder at the doors that weren't opening. Hesitating, she looked at Mr. Miller. "Oh, I guess it'll be alright. Mr. Fischer left for the airport about five hours ago. He's on his way to Seattle."

"And do you know where can I reach him?"

Again she looked in the direction of the newsroom before saying rather reluctantly, "He's staying at the Sorrento Hotel."

"Would you happen to have the number?"

"I'm sorry but..."

"Ah, forget it then. Don't worry about it." He turned to leave and then turned back. "By the way, don't mention this to Mr. Fischer."

"What do you mean?"

"I may have gotten the dates wrong, after all," he said. "I'll get him when he gets back."

"No problem, Mr. Miller."

Bruno turned and took the stairs instead of the elevators. He thought it was best if he left as fast as he could in case somebody came through those doors and started asking questions. As far as showing the badge, it was her word against his. Besides, he never said he was a cop. He just showed her a badge, a badge that was still missing. One thing for sure, there was no way she could possibly remember the number. He had flashed it faster than she would have been able to read it.

Sally watched him leave by the side door and thought it odd that he took the stairs. Why not the elevator? Suddenly, this Mr. Miller was in a hurry to leave. The presence of Veronica coming through the doors almost startled her.

"Do you have the number handy to the hotel Miles is staying at? I forgot to ask him for it."

"Sure." Sally passed her the confirmation sheet. "I just had the oddest visitor."

"What do you mean?"

"Do you know of a Mr. Miller who was supposed to meet Miles?"

"No. Why do you ask?"

"This gentleman who just left said he had a meeting with Miles for three o'clock today. Said he was a cop. Said it had something to do with the story he's working on. Do you know if he had any meetings scheduled?"

"No. Why would he? He's known he was going to Seattle since yesterday, when he asked you to make the arrangements." She paused. "That's strange."

"Sure is."

"Did you tell this guy where Miles is staying?"

"Yes, I did. I didn't know if I should or not. I didn't see the harm in telling him, especially after he showed me his badge. Do you think I did the right thing?"

"It seems harmless enough. Why?"

"He smelled of alcohol."

Chapter 32

Carboni put his feet on his desk and punched in a set of numbers before settling deep in his chair. Under the agreement with Benjamin Holt, Carboni was to keep in contact every three or four days, whether he liked it or not. He was to call Holt at the number he provided and keep him abreast as to whether or not he was making any progress on finding who killed his son. A Dr. Pepper sat to his right on his cluttered desk next to the ashtray.

"Mr. Carboni."

Christ! There it was. That drone-like voice.

"How you doing, Ben?"

"Fine. And you, Mr. Carboni?"

"Thanks for asking, Ben. I couldn't be better."

"That's nice to hear, Mr. Carboni. I take it things are progressing?"

"Things are going not too bad."

"Care to explain, Mr. Carboni?"

"There's this reporter in Chicago who seems to know more than that there sheriff does in that little town of yours. His name's Fischer. He seems to have this notion that your son's murder in Tweeksbury is somehow connected to a couple of crossbow murders in Eastbrook and Whatley."

"Yes, I know, Mr. Carboni. I read the *Tribune*, too. Fascinating story."

"I just found out he's on his way to Seattle, so I'm going to tag him for a couple of days and see what he's up to."

"That's a good idea, Mr. Carboni."

"I thought you would like that, Ben."

"Anything else?"

"I found a small piece of paper from what looks like

an Israeli cigarette on the roof of the hardware store that overlooks the parking lot where your son was killed. It may have something to do with his murder."

"Very good, Mr. Carboni. I'm glad to hear my money is not being wasted. What else is there?"

"That's it, Ben."

"Where will you be staying?"

"I haven't quite figured that out yet. Why?"

"It's in case I have to reach you."

"I'll have to let you know when I get there."

"No problem, Mr. Carboni. I'll be expecting a call tomorrow then."

"Yeah—sure, Ben. Whatever you say."

Chapter 33

American Airlines Flight 945 with Fischer onboard landed at Seattle-Tacoma International Airport half an hour later than expected. In the parking lot across the street, Henley stood outside one of the rear doors of the small compact and watched through his binoculars as Fischer placed his leather bag along with his computer case in the backseat of the taxi.

"There he is," he said. "He's just getting into a taxi."

Donlon was up front, sitting in the passenger seat along with another member of the FBI on loan from the Washington bureau. He sat behind the wheel and kept the motor running.

Henley waited for the taxi to make a move away from the curb before tapping on the hood of the car.

"It's just pulling away from the curb," he said and hopped in.

In the backseat of the cab, Fischer sat with the window open and watched the changing scenery as the taxi made its way through the busy afternoon traffic towards Seattle. Twenty minutes later, it made its way off of the I-5 onto Seventh Avenue. It turned right onto Madison and then proceeded up the circular driveway just before Terry Avenue, past the wrought iron gate ringed by palm trees and around the Florentine fountain before easing to a stop by the front doors. Miles studied the grandeur of the old boutique-style hotel that stood on a hill that overlooked the city while the porter retrieved his leather bag from the backseat.

"How old is this place?" he asked the porter.

"It's almost a hundred years old. It first opened in 1909."

"It's impressive."

Miles followed the porter into the lobby made of rich wood and waited by the counter to check in.

"Can I help you?"

"Yes. I believe you have a room booked under the *Chicago Tribune* for Miles Fischer."

Miles admired the brightly decorated lobby while he waited for the clerk to check the registry.

"Yes. We've got you in room 606." The clerk grabbed the key while Miles signed the registry. "We also have a message for you."

The clerk handed Miles the folded message while another took the key and his bag. Together, they entered the elevator and rode it to the sixth floor before walking down the hall to room 606. Miles placed his computer on the desk while the porter placed his leather bag on the luggage rack close to the door.

"Is there anything else I can do for you?"

"No. That's fine."

Miles tipped him and closed the door and then headed to the phone on the desk after reading the note that Veronica had called. He punched in the numbers and waited.

"Good. You're still there," he said, checking his watch.

"Miles?"

"Yeah, it's me. What's up?"

"How was your flight?"

"It was good." He almost laughed. "Is that why you called?"

"No, silly, but I thought I should at least be polite and ask before I tell you the real reason why I called. Something happened after you left that I think you should know about. Sally had an interesting visitor today who said he had a meeting set up with you for three o'clock.

Do you know anything about this meeting?"

He thought for a minute.

"Not that I'm aware of. Did he leave his name?"

"He said his name was Thomas Miller. Sally said he was cop, so I checked with the Chicago PD just to make sure since you didn't have anything marked on your calendar. They said they didn't know any Thomas Miller, so they asked for a description. Sally gave it to them. It turns out Thomas Miller isn't his real name. His real name is Bruno Carboni. They said he was no longer with the department."

"Did they say why?"

"They wouldn't tell me. I did some checking, and there's a Carboni Investigations listed in the yellow pages. The office is on Wabash."

"Did you try calling the number?"

"Yes, but I got the answering machine. It was a man's voice. It had to be him because Sally said this Carboni fellow had a raspy voice, and the voice on the other end had the same thing."

Miles hesitated, thinking, and then he said, "I wonder who he's working for."

"I don't know. He didn't say."

"Did Sally mention that I was staying at the Sorrento?"

"Yes. She told him that you left at around ten."

"What does this Carboni guy look like?"

"According to Sally, he has a real raspy voice. It's the one thing that really stood out besides his bulky frame."

"What about the rest of him?"

"He's about six two and really thick in the chest with a bit of a stomach. I just missed him, but according to Sally, he has black hair, a big fat nose, large brown eyes, and she said he had a heavy growth like he hadn't shaved for a while. Oh, yes, there was something else. Sally said he smelled of booze. I guess he likes to drink."

Miles was already by the window, checking the street as if by instinct.

"You're not upset, are you?"

"Upset? Why would I be upset?"

"Because we told Carboni where you are?"

"No, it's okay," he said calmly.

"Promise me you'll be careful."

"Don't worry, Veronica. I'll be fine."

"Well, I do worry."

"I'll be fine. I'll call you tomorrow if I need anything," he said and hung up the phone. The thought that a private investigator might get involved had never crossed his mind.

Donlon stayed in the car along with the driver while they waited for Henley to return. They were across from the Sorrento on Terry Avenue with the engine running while Henley went inside the hotel and checked with the clerk. Five minutes later, Henley was back on the sidewalk in front of the hotel. He watched the street and waited for the traffic to clear and entered through the back door.

"What did the clerk say?"

"He's in room 606. They don't know when he's leaving."

"It looks like our little friend is definitely up to something."

"So what are we going to do?"

"It's almost four," Donlon said, looking at his watch. "He's probably not going to be doing much. Let's go back to the office and pick up a car, and then Bob here can go back to what he was doing. We can drive ourselves around. We'll come back later and see what he's up to."

Henley nodded in agreement.

Bob waited for a truck to pass before pulling away from the curb. They headed in the direction of the waterfront.

Chapter 34

Bruno's plane touched down just after three early Wednesday morning, and after going through the usual airport protocol, he hastily retreated for the exits. He was visibly shaken and in a foul mood after the plane barely made it over the Rockies due to an electrical storm, but at least he was alive. Bruno tossed his bag into the backseat of one of the waiting taxis and jumped in and slammed the door.

"Take me to a bloody hotel, and quick!" He cranked the window down and breathed deeply. "Do you know where the Sorrento Hotel is?"

The driver was a black woman with very dark skin; she watched him in the mirror and then turned and stared at him under the steady glare of the lights from outside.

"Are you feeling alright, mister? I don't want you throwing up in my taxi."

"Never mind how I look," snapped Carboni. "I'm fine, so just drive the damn vehicle. That's what you're paid for—not to give medical advice."

The cabbie continued to stare at him, almost gritting her teeth while the bright smile disappeared almost instantly. She turned back towards the wheel, her dreadlocks flying under a brightly colored knitted cap.

"Well, I don't want you throwing up in my cab. I just cleaned this here taxi yesterday."

She waited for a car to pass and then threw it in gear and pulled away from the curb.

"If you want to be helpful," he growled, "why don't you try finding me a hotel close to the Sorrento?" Bruno continued to breathe out the window, watching the airport disappear behind him before turning towards her. "So where are we headed?"

"To the Edgewater," she said, looking into the mirror. "It's only a couple of blocks from the Sorrento."

The Edgewater was in fact on the other side of town, along the waterfront, about twenty blocks from the Sorrento.

"Good. How long 'til we get there?"

"Just sit tight, mister, and relax. At three thirty in the morning, it won't take long."

Bruno pulled a menthol and lighter from his side pocket. He gazed uninterestedly through the dark windows at empty streets before lighting up, ignoring the sign in front of him stuck to the back of the seat.

"Hey, mister? I don't want you smoking in my cab."

Bruno ignored the request and continued smoking his cigarette.

The driver stared at him with a scowl through the mirror. Of all the people who were leaving the terminal, she had to end up with this one. She checked her watch and pushed hard on the gas and moved into another lane that was devoid of traffic. Fifteen more minutes and she'd be rid of this cantankerous fare.

From the backseat, Bruno sipped from a bottle of rye whisky stashed in his bag under the watchful eye of the driver as she wove through the quiet streets on their way to the hotel. Once there, Bruno paid the cabbie with barely a tip and then headed straight for the counter. He checked in and then took the elevator to his room, where he made the call to Holt.

"Yeah, Ben. Bruno here."

"Yes, Mr. Carboni. It's so nice of you to take the time to call so early in the morning. I take it you had a pleasant flight?"

"Yeah, peachy, Ben," he replied brusquely. "You know that letter you sent me?"

251

"Yes. What about it?"

"Something really strange happened to it. I can't read it. It seems the ink has disappeared from the letter. You mind telling me what the hell is going on?"

"There's nothing to explain, Mr. Carboni. It's just a precaution."

"What kind of a precaution are we talking about, Ben?" he asked.

"You're in a very dangerous occupation, Mr. Carboni. I'm a well-respected member of my community. They wouldn't understand if something was to happen to you and I was somehow involved. You see my point, do you not?"

"Don't screw with me, Ben. I'm not somebody you want to screw around with."

"I understand completely, Mr. Carboni."

"Make sure that you do, Ben. Otherwise, I'm out of here, and you can find yourself someone else."

"I assure you it's strictly precautionary, Mr. Carboni. No need to concern yourself. You're well paid for what you do. Let's not jeopardize it. So tell me, Mr. Carboni, where are you staying?"

"I'm at the Edgewater," he stated, still angry. "Room 310."

"Excellent, Mr. Carboni. It's late. I suggest you get some sleep. Call me when you have something to tell me."

Holt hung up the phone and then made another call.

It was early, and Donlon and Henley were parked just south of the entrance to the circular driveway leading to the front door of the Sorrento Hotel. They were sipping coffee and chewing on donuts. They had been there for close to an hour with no sight of Fischer. Henley was in the driver's seat. The engine was running. They were hiding behind their shiny, mirrored sunglasses and waiting for Fischer, who was still inside.

"Your car is ready, Mr. Fischer. It's parked just outside the front door."

"Thank you. I'll be right down."

Henley had a mouthful of donut when he noticed the small maroon import's sudden appearance at the entrance to the street. He quickly identified the driver. He swallowed hard to clear his throat as he watched it turn right.

"There he is," he said.

Henley waited for a couple of cars to get between him and the small compact before merging into the flow of traffic.

Fischer was headed for Lincoln Park in West Seattle and the Fauntleroy-Vashon Ferry Terminal. According to the map lying on the seat, Anita Paletti's sister lived somewhere just outside of the small coastal town of Ellisport on the east side of Vashon Island. Unlike Anita Paletti, who wasn't listed, Angelina Paletti was the first and only name that Miles found in the phone book. He had originally searched for the surname Leibovitz, their father's last name, the name both would have been given at birth, but he found none with a first name beginning with the letter A. He thought it was odd, if in fact this was her sister, that neither one had taken their father's surname as their own. It had him thinking as to what the reason was behind it. He made a mental note to check it out in the next day or so.

It was 8:49 a.m., and the ferry ran approximately every half hour. Fischer's rental was near the front of the line when the ferry pulled in to unload those coming from the other side. Donlon and Henley waited outside the tollbooths until it was safe to board before entering one of the lanes for those going to Vashon Island. At 9:05 a.m., Fischer and the Feds departed for Angelina Paletti's place just outside of Ellisport. Donlon and Henley stayed in their car and kept a low profile while Fischer leaned on one of the railings under the morning sun for the fifteen-minute ferry ride. Once docked, they took the narrow, two-lane Vashon Highway and then Ridge Road for Ellisport some eight miles away.

He found her house tucked in behind Ellisport. He did a slow U-turn and parked across the street from the crude metal gates that blocked the entrance to the long driveway and the large house at the end of it. Donlon and Henley stayed back a ways and watched from their position on the side of the road, hidden by tall trees and bushes that ran along the slight bend in the roadside, trying to figure out why he was there and who owned the house.

Miles's sole purpose for being there was not to meet Anita's sister. It was quite the contrary. The likelihood that Angelina would have anything to say that would be detrimental to her sister was almost nonexistent.

What he was interested in was talking to one of her neighbors. If Anita didn't take the flight to the Caribbean as he believed, then who did? It would have to be someone she trusted. His first inclination was to suspect Angelina. Since they were sisters, it was safe to presume that they looked alike. Both sisters had the same initials, which would make it easy to swap identification, including their passports. Anita had moved across the country to be closer to her sister, a sister she was now in business with, so it was obvious they were close. But just how close were they? Close enough for Angelina to take the trip in her place while Anita went to Tweeksbury to take out Holt and Masalla?

Outside the gates, Fischer stood looking at the house and the sprawling yard with his hands on his hips. It was bigger than he thought it would be. The fence itself stretched for a long distance along the road to his right before disappearing into the bend in the road. Along the side, next to the driveway, it ran for a good distance more before disappearing in some low-lying brush and another stand of tall trees. There was pasture in the back with horses, along with a barn. The house itself was old but well-kept. He was about to peek into her mailbox when he heard a male voice on the other side of the road.

"If you're looking for Angel, you're not going to find her."

On the opposite side of the street, an old man with thick glasses was standing next to a mailbox retrieving his mail.

"She's not home, if that's who you're looking for." He walked across the narrow road with the aid of his cane and held out his hand. "Hi. I'm, Ned."

Fischer shook his hand. "Miles. Do you happen to know where she is?"

"Oh, she's probably off somewhere working on another one of her movies. Are you a friend of hers?"

"Not really."

"That makes sense."

"What do you mean?"

"She's hardly ever home. The missus and I hardly ever see her. It's rare to see anybody on her property. We're both retired, so we kind of look after the place when she's not around." He pointed to Miles's car. "You're driving a rental, I see. Where you from?"

"Chicago."

"You're not an actor, are you?" he asked suspiciously.

"No," he said, almost laughing.

"You're not looking for a job, are you? Her sister does all the hiring."

"No. I've got one. When's the last time you saw her?"

"About two weeks ago, I'd say. She was here for almost a full month just prior to her leaving again. It's the longest we've seen her here for quite some time."

"So you saw her every day?"

"Well, I wouldn't say that," he said after thinking about it.

"But you talked to her?"

"Well, not really, on account she's so busy, but we saw her every now and then. I waved to her a couple of times, but that's about it."

"So what does she do when she's not working?"

"She spends a lot of time with her horses. You like horses?"

"Yeah, I guess, but I've never ridden one."

"Well, if you come back sometime when she's home, she might take you for a ride on one of them. She's pretty good. She should be able to have you up and riding in no time. Trouble is, I don't know when that will be. Angel never seems to be able to sit still for too long. She's always up to something."

"Maybe I'll take her up on it. Are you the one who takes care of the horses when she's not here?"

"No. She has someone who does that for her, if that's what you're looking for. He lives over in the Burton area," he said, pointing. "It's a little south of here. We only do it when he's on vacations and can't make it for some reason. It's mostly the wife, though, on account of my cane."

"How many horses does she have?"

"Right now eight, but that could change. She told me she would like to breed them someday, but she doesn't have the time right now because of her job."

"How often does he come by?"

"Just about every day when she's away. Usually in the morning to let the horses out and then again in the evening to lock them away, but if you're around here tomorrow, you should be able to catch him. He's also her groundskeeper, so he's here almost every second or third day during the summer besides the weekends when Angel's not around."

"How big is her property?" he asked, looking at the large spread in front of him.

"It's a lot bigger than ours. It's about five acres."

"It's a nice piece of property," he added. He checked his watch. "I guess I'll go then since she's not here. It was nice meeting you, Ned."

"Yeah. Nice meeting you, too."

Again they shook hands.

Miles headed for his car and then turned back towards Ned, who was retrieving the mail from Angelina's mailbox.

"This guy who lives over in the Burton—do you happen to know his name?"

"Jim Weaver."

He nodded. "Thanks again, Ned."

"If you want, I can tell her you came by."

"No, it's okay. I'll call her."

Just past Paletti's house, where the road bends to the left, Fischer eased off the gas after noticing a white car parked on the other side of the road which was not there when he pulled up to Paletti's gates just over half an hour ago. It was odd that it would be sitting there, he thought, with the front windows rolled down and nobody inside since there were no driveways within two hundred feet in either direction. It was also the only car he had seen parked on the side of the road between Ellisport and the ferry. He carefully scrutinized it as he drove by, noticing the plate that was vaguely familiar. He smiled faintly and stepped on the gas and headed for the ferry back to the mainland. It gave him an idea.

Back at the Sorrento, he approached the desk, looking for the concierge.

"Yes, I'd like to return the car."

"Is there something the matter with it?"

"It seems to be pulling to the left."

"Would you like a replacement?"

"No, that won't be necessary. It's a nice day. I've decided to take a taxi instead."

"It's no problem. I can have another one here in less than half an hour if you like."

"No, that's okay."

"Is there anything else I can help you with?"

"As a matter of fact, there is. Can you make sure that whoever comes and picks it up has black hair?" She looked at him rather strangely. "Maybe about my age, tall," he said, holding his hand above his head.

"Can I ask why?"

"Sorry. It's a matter of national security," said Miles, keeping a straight face.

Again she eyed him suspiciously. "Okay," she said slowly. "I'll see what I can do."

Miles took a seat in the lobby while he waited for the driver to come fetch the vehicle that had nothing wrong with it. It was running fine, but the white sedan that was parked along the side of the road close to Paletti's house was also on the ferry ride back to the mainland. Just to make sure he wasn't overreacting, he zigzagged through

258

traffic on his way back to the Sorrento, taking the odd wrong turn to see if indeed he was right about being followed. The white sedan followed him like it was tied to his bumper although it stayed well back so as not to be seen.

"Mr. Fischer." The concierge was standing in front of him. "They're just pulling into the driveway."

The driver was younger than himself, but his hair was long and black, combed directly back. He was a little shorter than Miles but it would be hardly noticeable once he was behind the wheel.

Miles watched both vehicles pull away, and then followed them to the front of the driveway where it met the street, hiding behind the bushes close to the gate. He watched with interest as the white sedan followed behind, being careful not to be seen until it disappeared around the corner at the end of the block. If he was surprised, he didn't show it, but Henley was driving. Donlon was there too, sitting next to him in the passenger seat. Miles smiled faintly before flipping his sunglasses back over his eyes, and then he went inside and ordered a taxi.

Chapter 35

The new production was stopped and the set closed until further notice. The script had to be reworked, and the producer along with the director gave everybody the remainder of the week off until the kinks could be worked out. Everybody was to be back on set the following Monday unless otherwise notified. Angelina Paletti first called her sister, and then she left immediately for the JFK airport and the long flight home. The crew had only been on set since Monday. On Wednesday, they had only been there for an hour when the order came down at around ten in the morning. Glancing at her watch, she figured she could be home on her five acres before seven that evening if everything went well.

Chapter 36

It was almost four, and Fischer was north of the city, making a last attempt to try and establish whether or not Anita Paletti, a woman of forty-three, was capable of climbing vertical heights. The private building was located in the Queen Anne district, just north of Seattle's main center. The three-story brick building was next to a park.

The lobby of the "Rockface" was a mix of stone and wood, what one would expect from an upscale club. Miles approached the lone attendant behind the counter.

"Sorry to bother you, but I'm looking for Anita Paletti. I was told to meet her here at around four o'clock."

"Are you a member?" asked the good-looking blonde behind the desk. She was around Miles's age, tall and slender and well-groomed. She wore tiny glasses that rested on the tip of her nose.

"No, but I believe she is."

"I'm sorry, but this is a private club. We're not allowed to give out any names."

"But I just gave it to you. She asked me to meet her here."

"I'm sorry, but we don't have anyone here by that name."

"How can you be so sure? You haven't checked your computer."

"I don't need to check the computer. I know just about everyone here. Now if you'll excuse me."

"If she's not a member, then why did she ask me to meet her here?"

"I don't know why," she said curtly. "Maybe you should take that up with her."

Miles held his ground and glared at her.

"Maybe you have us confused with another club," she suggested.

"No. She distinctly told me to meet her here."

"Well I'm sorry, but there's no one here by that name."

"Look, why don't you humor me and check your computer again? I'm sure the lady behind me won't mind waiting. It'll only take a second."

The attendant rolled her eyes and quickly clicked the mouse and brought up the general screen. "How do you spell that?"

Now why do you need me to spell it if you know everyone here? he thought. "Paletti—just as it sounds. P-a-l-e-t-t-i."

"Was that Anita?" she asked, making it sound like she was remotely interested.

"Yes."

Miles leaned on the counter and smiled faintly at the lady behind him. "It'll only take a minute," he said to her politely.

"I'm sorry. There is no one here by that name." She quickly clicked the mouse and cleared her screen.

"That was rather quick. Don't you have to strike the keys first?" he asked rather sarcastically.

"I'm sorry, sir, but you'll have to leave. You can wait for your friend outside."

Miles let out a deep breath and shook his head in disgust, all the while staring at the blonde. He slowly flipped his sunglasses back over his eyes without saying a word and then headed for the doors that led to the driveway and his waiting taxi.

"Excuse me. Did I hear you say that you were looking for Anita Paletti?"

Miles quickly turned when he felt the tap on his shoulder. It seemed strange that this person would know her. She looked like something out of a comic book though a little on the thin side. She wore black tights and large, boxer-like shorts that were a mix of purple stripes. The makeup was definitely gothic. *What an oddball*, he thought. She wore a black cape.

"You know Anita Paletti?" he asked inquisitively, flipping his glasses back onto his head.

She chewed with her mouth open. Her jaw moved up and down incessantly, and she smelled of peppermint. "Maybe. Why are you asking about Anita?"

She held a water bottle to her lips and squeezed it hard.

Miles pointed to the clump of chairs across the lobby. "How about we talk over there?"

She followed Miles and took a seat across from him.

"How is it you know Anita?"

"Because she's a member here, and I'm a friend of hers, so I would know that," she said, popping her gum. She sounded cocky.

"You're a friend of hers?"

"Yeah, does that surprise you?"

"Well…" He held out his hands.

"Don't let the costume fool you. I only dress like this to piss them off."

"Why's that?"

"Isn't it noticeable? They're all a bunch of snobs."

"So why do you come here, then? Why not go somewhere else?"

"Because my dad owns the place."

"Your dad doesn't mind?"

"What? This?" she said, holding her arms out to her sides. "My parents are divorced. I'm the only child, so he puts up with it. My mother told me this is his way of buying my affection. It's kind of cool, don't you think? I can get what I want when I want it."

"I guess that makes you a lucky girl. So what's your name?"

"What are you, a cop?"

"No, I'm not a cop."

"What are you then, a reporter?"

"What makes you think that?"

"Because you look like one."

"How's that?"

"You look a little too preppy to be a cop."

"Not your taste?"

"Not really. So why are you asking about Anita?"

"It's a long story."

"Is she in some sort of trouble?"

"No."

"Then why are you asking about her?"

"It's for a story I'm working on."

"What kind of a story?"

"You wouldn't be interested." Miles paused. "So do you have a name?"

"You're not going to use it are you?"

"Not if you don't want me to."

"It's Brooke," she said, after hesitating. "Brooke Whitney."

"Whitney. That's an English name?"

"Yeah. My great-grandparents settled here back in the eighteen hundreds. They're originally from Sheffield."

"Brooke. That's a nice name."

"It's okay."

"How old are you?"

"Twenty-two. I'll be twenty-three in a couple of weeks. Why?"

"You're in college, then?"

"UW."

"What's your major?"

"Is that important?"

"Not really. Just curious, I guess."

"First year law."

That's about right, Miles thought, considering how she was dressed. You had to be a little crazy to want to study law.

"How about you? You must have gone to college," she said. "Where did you study?"

"Northwestern."

"That's in Chicago."

"Yeah."

"So you're from there?"

"Born and raised." Miles pulled out his notepad. "You don't mind, do you?"

"No. Be my guest."

"So how long have you known her?"

"Almost a year."

"Was she a member before you joined?"

"I think so."

"So how is it you know each other?"

"We're in the same aerobics class."

"You take aerobics?"

"Don't look so surprised. A girl has to stay in shape, you know."

Miles tried not to laugh. "Do you share in any other classes around here?"

"Like what?"

"Oh, I don't know. How about that wall in there?" Miles could see part of it through one of the doors on the other side of the lobby.

"You mean rappelling?"

"Yeah."

"She teaches some of the classes."

"Why do you take it?"

"I like to try different things."

"I guess that explains your costume, then."

She smiled at him. "You're catching on."

Miles glanced toward the counter. The attendant watched them through her glasses and then turned away and went back to what she was doing.

"How often does she teach?"

"I can't say. I don't go to every class."

"Is she any good?"

"I haven't heard anybody complain."

"What do you think?"

"She knows her stuff, if that's what you're getting at."

"Do you weight train?"

"What do you think?"

"Sorry. Bad question. How about Anita?"

"From what she's told me, she does the odd time, but not a lot."

"When's the last time you saw her?"

"Why? Is that important?"

"Just curious."

"She is in trouble, isn't she?"

"No."

"Are you sure? You're not just saying that?"

"I wouldn't lie to you."

"Last week," she said after thinking it over. "Thursday, I think."

"And before that?"

"About a month ago."

"You never saw her in between that time?"

"No, but I wasn't here every day, either."

"Do you and Anita talk a lot?"

"No more than I would with anyone else around here."

"What do you talk about?"

"Girlie things—why?"

"You said you hadn't seen her in a month. Did she say anything to you about where she was?"

"No. Why would she? It's none of my business. Why would I ask?"

"I don't know. I was just curious if you knew."

"Well, I don't."

Miles quickly changed the subject to get her mind off the direct questions he was asking.

"So what's with your receptionist? I asked her if Anita was a member here, and all I got was a lot of attitude. What gives?"

"Oh, her," she said in a disgusted tone that wrinkled her face. "Don't worry about her. She's nothing but a snobby bitch." She stopped and leaned in towards Miles. "She's my dad's girlfriend."

"How old is your dad?"

"Old enough to know better."

"I take it you don't approve?"

"Let's just say I'm working on it. I told my dad he should kick her ass out of here. She's bad for business. She treats everybody, including my friends, like she's somehow better than everybody else."

"Your friends come here?"

"Yeah, but only to meet up with me. She makes them wait outside when she's on duty. They can't afford memberships." She smiled. "It's too bad."

"What do you say that?"

"We could really turn this place upside down. It would be a hoot. This place could use it."

Miles put his pad away.

"Is that it?" she asked.

"Almost. I just have one more question I want to ask. It's been bothering me since we sat down. You and Paletti. You say you're friends, but—and don't take this the wrong way—but I don't see the connection. I mean, you're two different people. How is it you two are friends?"

"Again with the way I'm dressed?"

"It's a logical question."

"I don't know. We just seemed to hit it off. I guess she likes me."

"I like you. So what gives?"

"I don't know. Maybe because neither one of us had the best of childhood's."

"Care to elaborate?"

"My parents divorced when I was young. That's my father's fourth girlfriend. They seem to get younger every time he trades them in."

"Did her parents divorce?"

"I don't know. She never said."

"Does she talk about her childhood much?"

"It seems to be a sore spot, so I don't press her. I leave it alone. Maybe that's why she likes me. I don't go poking my nose around where it doesn't belong. No offense."

Miles laughed. "Touché."

"Are we finished?"

He nodded. "Yeah, I think so unless you have something else you want to say."

She hesitated like she wanted to add something, like there was something on her mind, and then she decided against it and finished the last of her water instead.

"Is there?"

"No."

"Are you sure because you look like you wanted to say something?"

"No. Everything is cool."

"Well, I guess I'll go then. Thanks for your time. I appreciate it."

They shook hands.

"What's your name?" she asked. "You never told me."

"Miles."

She smiled. "It was nice meeting you, Miles."

Miles left her sitting and headed for the door. Outside by the taxi he heard someone call his name. It was Brooke.

"This story you're working on—it doesn't have to do with the murders in…" She hesitated. "Damn it. I can't remember the name."

"Tweeksbury?"

"Yeah, Tweeksbury."

"You know about it?"

"I read the paper. Is that the story you're working on?"

"What makes you think that?"

"Because you asked me if I had seen her around the same time it happened."

Miles didn't say anything. He just looked at her.

Suddenly her demeanor changed. She was no longer the gum-chewing smart-ass he had just finished talking with. The brassiness was gone, replaced with a certain level of maturity.

"Look, I'm a law student, not an idiot. Your questions were more than a little pointed—a fifth grader would be able to see through it. Back there," she said, nodding towards the building, "when you were asking me all those questions, when I put it all together, everything you asked me seemed to point to what happened there even though you didn't come right out and say it. I can read between the lines, in case you didn't know, so don't bullshit me. In there you said you wouldn't lie to me, but you did. I want you to level with me. Is that the story you're working on?"

"Yes, it is."

"And you think that she is somehow involved?"

"I can't say."

"You don't have to."

"So what is it you want to tell me?"

"Do you know that Anita has a sister?"

"I'm aware of it. Why?"

"I don't know if this is important, so I'll just come out and say it. I've never seen her sister, but Anita brings her here the odd time as a guest."

"How do you know?"

"Sometimes I do work for my dad. I saw her name on the guest list."

"Do you remember the last time she was here?"

"I can't remember exactly, but I think it was before what happened in Tweeksbury."

"How much before?"

"I don't know—maybe a couple of weeks."

"Thanks," he said. "I appreciate it." Miles reached for the handle and then stopped. "You wouldn't happen to have Anita's home address, would you?"

At first she didn't say anything; she just stared at him. Then she said, "Hold on a minute."

Two minutes later she was back and handed him a piece of paper.

"I have to ask you something. Why did you come out here just a minute ago and tell me what you told me?

Why help me by giving me her address? Why do you care, if she's a friend of yours like you say?"

"I guess it's because I'm a law student. I figure we're on the same side, right? We're both searching for the same thing—the truth. In spite of what you see, don't let this costume fool you. Not everything is what it seems. Besides, I still want my father to be proud of me."

"So this act is nothing but a charade to get your father's attention?"

"You're the reporter. You should be able to figure it out."

Brooke smiled halfheartedly and headed back towards the building.

Chapter 37

Bruno slept later than he probably should have, due to the fact that he got in late and needed to sleep. It was also due to the fact that he had no idea what this Miles Fischer looked like. What he needed to do first was to concoct some sort of a plan so he could see what Fischer looked like without being seen before worrying about whether or not he had slept too late. The only question was how?

After showering, Bruno had it all figured out. He quickly phoned downstairs, requesting one item in particular, and then waited for one of the attendants to bring it to him. Fifteen minutes later he was dressed and ready to look for Fischer.

Bruno placed the envelope on the counter and waited for the clerk, who was just hanging up the phone.

"I would like to have this envelope couriered over to the Sorrento Hotel, today if possible."

She checked her watch. "It's almost two, but I think we can make it. We can probably have it there by five, if that's okay with you?"

"That's fine."

"Is there anything else I can do for you?" she asked.

"Yes. I would also like to send some flowers."

"What kind of flowers did you have in mind?"

It had to be something big—something bulky that couldn't be left at the desk.

"Oh, I don't know. I'm not really sure." In all the years Bruno was married, he never once thought of sending flowers to his wife. "What about some sort of an arrangement in a vase. I was thinking of something big and yellow. Do you have any suggestions?"

"Sunflowers might be nice."

He nodded his approval.

"And how much did you want to spend?"

"It doesn't matter. Just make sure that it looks nice."

"And will that be on your credit card?"

"Yeah, just add it to my bill."

"And where would you like them sent?"

"Send them to the same address."

"And whose name should I have them put on the card?"

"You can use this one here," he said, pointing to Fischer's. "It's supposed to be a surprise, so I prefer they be sent separately and at different times, if possible."

"No problem."

"I also need some help with directions to the Sorrento Hotel."

"Are you walking, sir, or do you want a cab? The Sorrento Hotel is at least twenty blocks from here."

"Excuse me!"

"The Sorrento Hotel—it's up on Madison. That's almost twenty blocks from here."

Bruno suddenly stiffened; his face grew angry as he stared scathingly at the clerk.

"Are you sure?" barked Bruno. "I was told it was only a few blocks away," he said loudly.

"Whoever told you that wasn't telling you the truth."

The female clerk took a half step back after watching Carboni's face change to a light crimson.

"That bitch!" He slammed the counter and looked at the startled clerk.

"I beg your pardon!" The clerk looked unnerved.

"No. Sorry. It's not directed at you," he explained. "It was that damn taxi driver who brought me here last night."

Cautious, the clerk asked, "Sir, would you still like

that cab?"

"Do I have any other choice?" he asked sarcastically.

Bruno took a seat in the lobby and waited for the clerk to signal that his taxi had arrived. Five minutes later he stepped into the taxi waiting just outside the front door.

It was just past two thirty, and the streets were busy when Bruno's taxi pulled into the circular driveway of the Sorrento Hotel. Bruno paid the cabbie from the backseat and exited quickly, purposely leaving the passenger door open.

"Take that, ya bastard," he mumbled under his breath.

"Hey, close the door," cried the driver, watching him leave.

Bruno ignored him and walked through the doors into the lobby. The counter was opposite him.

Because it was an older hotel, they still used slots to hold mail, keys, and whatever else they put in there. He smiled to himself. He couldn't have asked for anything better. He would be able to watch the envelope until Fischer picked it up with no problem. As for the flowers, there was limited space as to where they could place them. They would have to take them upstairs to his room if they didn't want them to get damaged. It was all working just like he had planned, only better. He almost laughed. Fischer couldn't have picked a better hotel.

Donlon and Henley spent the entire afternoon waiting just outside the Sorrento, parked alongside the curb in the hot sun, and neither one was in a particularly good mood. Fischer had pulled a fast one on them by retracing his route instead of driving through Ellisport like they thought he might, leaving them stranded in the bushes like idiots. They called Abrams after Fischer ditched them by using a decoy to return the rental and requested another background check on Angelina Paletti. Abrams told them they were looking at a minimum of at least a couple of days before anything concrete would surface. There was nothing in the files.

Bruno was outside, sitting at one of the tables of the Porte Cochere, one of two in-house restaurants at the Sorrento, under an open umbrella on the other side of the driveway when the flowers finally arrived just before five. He had already decided this was the best vantage point to wait for the flowers without being noticed. To anyone there, he looked like just another patron having a late lunch, enjoying the fresh air.

The arrangement of flowers was big and yellow, just as he had ordered. Bruno flagged a server, telling him he would be back in a few minutes to finish his meal before following the driver inside, stopping next to the small alcove some fifteen feet from the doors, pretending to read the menu that was posted outside the Hunt Club just off the lobby. From there, he watched a clerk take the flowers and head for the elevators. Bruno followed him. He was about to discover Fischer's room number.

It was almost six when Fischer's cab turned right onto Terry Avenue from Spring Street. He asked the cabbie to go slowly. He wanted to check if Donlon and Henley were there waiting. He had a trick he wanted to play.

The taxi driver did as Fischer asked before pulling into the circular driveway leading to the Sorrento. Fischer paid the fare and quickly exited through to the lobby and then to the restaurant inside, where he ordered dinner for two. He wanted it delivered to the white sedan parked on

Terry Avenue. Fischer remembered seeing it in *Beverly Hills Cop* with Eddie Murphy back in the eighties. The scene was priceless. He waited, signing his name to the tab, and then headed for the check-in counter.

In the lobby between the front doors and the passage way leading to the bar and the restaurant, Bruno hid behind a newspaper and waited for Fischer to approach the desk and retrieve the envelope. He had been doing this peeping-tom act for nearly an hour, and he was getting a little tired of it. His back was starting to ache and so were his feet from standing so long.

He already had Fischer's room number, thanks to the clerk who delivered the flowers without his knowing he was being followed. Bruno had followed him down the hall but kept walking, using the exit door and then the stairs. He walked back outside to the sidewalk and then to his table, where he finished his dinner, but not before checking to see if the envelope that had arrived twenty minutes earlier was still there.

Bruno left his spot by the wall when a small busload of tourists entered the lobby and swarmed the counter. Bruno could barely see the slot that held the envelope, so he moved to the left of the doors that gave him a better view of the envelope while the clerks worked feverishly to thin the small herd. Seconds later, Bruno noticed a man enter from the passage way. He headed straight for the counter. Bruno watched from behind his newspaper and smiled when he saw the clerk hand him the red envelope. It was him. It was Fischer. He waited and watched as Fischer headed for the elevators. He smiled once more and then slipped into the lounge to use the restroom.

Chapter 38

Miles placed the opened envelope on the desk and headed for the window to check on the white sedan that was now parked close to the entrance leading to the Sorrento.

Much to his surprise, the envelope was empty. His first thought was that whoever sent it had forgotten to insert whatever it was they intended to give him, but then he remembered Veronica's phone call and the private investigator and his sudden visit to the *Tribune*, and suddenly it all fit. Bruno Carboni had arrived in Seattle. He must have been hiding in the lobby somewhere when he picked up the envelope. That would account for why it was red instead of white and why there was nothing in it. It was a signal, like shooting a flare into the night sky. The color red could be easily seen from a distance.

From the window he noticed the vase over on the table by the couch, and found the card with his name on it. Miles had been in enough hotels to know that flowers courtesy of the hotel didn't come with cards attached to them. Curious, Miles grabbed the phone off the desk and rang the desk downstairs. It was just as he thought. The flowers weren't courtesy of the hotel at all. They were from someone else—someone who wanted to remain anonymous. Miles hung up the phone and let out a faint grunt under his breath. *Clever*, he thought. *In fact, it was brilliant*, thought Fischer. It was now plainly obvious that not only did this Mr. Carboni fellow know what he looked like, but he also knew what room he occupied.

Miles had been putting off calling Erin since Tuesday morning, when he made an attempt to visit her before he had to leave for Seattle. Maybe she was ready to finally take his call and they could talk. Maybe she was ready to listen to what he had to say rather than jump to her own conclusions.

Miles punched in the numbers for the hospital and waited for someone to pick up. A couple of minutes later, he was placing the receiver back on the phone. There was no change in the mood coming from Erin's room. She still didn't want to talk him. But there was also some good news, which lightened his mood. The baby was doing fine. She had also gained half a pound.

Miles checked the window again to see what Donlon and Henley were up too. Their dinner hadn't arrived yet so he punched in another set of numbers, and after the sixth ring, he heard Veronica's voice.

"Hello." Her voice was much deeper than he expected.

"Veronica. It's Miles."

"What time is it?" She sounded a little groggy.

"Your time or mine?" he asked.

"It doesn't matter."

"Almost eight thirty your time." He heard a yawn come over the line. "You sound tired."

"I must be. I fell asleep on the couch."

"How's everything at the *Tribune*?"

"It's not the same without you there. Before I forget," she said, "I heard Pat and Kate talking about you today."

"What about?"

"Something about the fact that they're not too comfortable with you being in Seattle. After Sally told them about Carboni, they're a little less than pleased by the attention you're drawing. They're worried about you."

"Well, tell them not to worry. I've got the FBI looking out for me."

"What do you mean?"

"Those two agents who were in my office are here in Seattle."

"What about that private investigator?"

"He's here too. It seems I'm drawing quite the crowd."

"You can add me to list," she said. "I'm worried about you too."

"It's okay, Veronica. There's really nothing to worry about."

"Pat and Kate don't think so."

"Tell them I think they're really sweet."

"You shouldn't make light of it, Miles. They're really concerned about your safety, and so am I."

"Tell them everything is fine," he said, staring at the empty envelope.

"I hope so." There was a pause. "So how much longer do you think you'll be there?"

"I can't say, but there's a reason why I called. I need you to do something for me. You may want to write this down. I need you to find out what you can on Anita Paletti and her sister, Angelina. Neither of the sisters was born here, so it's going to take a little work on your part."

"Where exactly were they born?"

"In Israel, of all places."

"Where? What city?"

He gave it a shot. "Zikhron Ya'akov."

"What?"

"I know. My Hebrew isn't very good." He spelled it for her. "It's close to Haifa. You might want to look it up on a map to give you an idea of where it is."

"What exactly am I looking for?"

"I don't really know, but there's something strange going on that doesn't make a hell of a lot of sense."

"Like what?"

"Neither of the Paletti girls uses their father's surname. Paletti is their mother's maiden name. That makes me think that something happened, but I don't know what it could be. I would start with the police chief. This town or hamlet isn't very big. Maybe he can shed some light on the family. Maybe there's something there that can tell us why it is that neither one of them uses the surname 'Leibovitz.'"

"What do I tell him?"

"Tell him you're working on a story and you're looking for some background on the family. Maybe he can put you in touch with any relatives who may still be living there; then start digging. Just see what you can find out for me. If you have to, see if Tony will help you. He seems to know a lot of people."

"You're going to owe me."

"Yeah, I know," he said, almost laughing. "Call me on my cell when you have something."

Chapter 39

Bruno was back in the lobby. He sat by himself at the only table that was close to the elevators, which were just behind him and to his left, and patiently waited for Fischer to reappear. *What could be better than this?* he thought. The high, wingback chairs offered the perfect place to hide his large frame. It would be virtually impossible for Fischer to see him when he reentered the lobby from the elevators—unless, of course, he went looking for him, but that was highly unlikely. Instead, Fischer would probably go to his right after he glanced over at the table and realized that it was unoccupied. Bruno naturally assumed that Sally had told someone about his visit to the *Tribune* the day before and that they in turn had alerted Fischer. If Fischer was as smart as he thought he was, he would be able to put it all together: the flowers that were addressed to him but gave no hint as to who may have sent them, the red envelope that had nothing in it. It was now safe to assume that Fischer knew that he might have a private investigator on his tail.

Fischer would have been given a description of what he looked like, but it hardly mattered. Fischer hadn't seen him. The description of what Bruno looked like could fit a lot of men his age. Half of the men in America were overweight. As far as his facial features—so what? A lot of men fit that description too. It was his voice that would give him away, but he had no plans to meet and talk to him. What he wanted most was to get inside his room and see what he could find. To do that, all he had to do was stay out of sight, and the table tucked in the corner offered the perfect place from which to do it.

Bruno stayed low in the chair and kept the newspaper close to his face, pretending to read. Then every now and then, when he heard one of the elevators open, he would time how long it would take for someone to enter the lobby, and then he would peek from behind his chair and see how accurate he was. He had done this for twenty minutes and had it down to a science. It was almost six thirty, a time when most people who lived out of hotel rooms would eat, and if Fischer had been out all day, there was a good chance he was hungry and head for the restaurant.

He started to count off seven seconds when he heard the elevator, and then he peeked from behind the chair. Sure enough, it was Fischer. Bruno watched as Fischer made his way to the counter, where he talked to a clerk, before walking past the doors to the restaurant. Bruno immediately left the newspaper in the chair and casually walked to the elevators and pushed the button, hitching a ride to the sixth floor.

"What the hell is this?" asked Donlon.

"It's your dinner, sir."

"What do you mean? We didn't order any dinner."

"It's compliments of the *Chicago Tribune*."

"Well we didn't order it, so take it back."

"But it's already paid for."

"I don't care if Mother Theresa paid for it herself. Take it back!"

Donlon thrust open the door, nearly hitting the waiter, and headed for the lobby, leaving Henley to fend for himself. Inside, Donlon abruptly pushed past a couple and leaned on the counter.

"I'm looking for Miles Fischer of the *Chicago Tribune*!"

"He's in the Hunt Club."

The surprised clerk pointed in the direction of the

282

restaurant. Donlon quickly stormed towards the entrance and past the maître d', headed in the direction of Fischer, who was sitting in a corner. Donlon placed his thin frame in front of Fischer so he could get the full picture and removed his sunglasses.

"What the hell do you think you're doing?"

"Donlon! What a surprise." Fischer consumed what was on his fork and then slowly placed it on the plate. "What brings you to Seattle?"

"You know very well why we're here."

Miles nodded at him. "You might want to remove your hat. It's impolite to have it on when you're in a restaurant."

"Still the smart-ass, eh, Fischer? One of these days that big mouth of yours is going to get you into a lot of trouble."

Miles smiled back coolly. "So you've told me."

Fischer watched as the waiter placed his drink in front of him. As he left, the maître d' approached the table.

"Is there a problem?" he asked.

Without looking, Donlon nonchalantly flashed him his badge, forcing the maître d' back towards his station by the front door.

"That's very good, Donlon." Miles sipped his rum and Coke and then smiled. "Do you suppose I could borrow that? I could use it when the in-laws come over."

Donlon ignored the comment and took the seat opposite Fischer. He quickly glanced around the room and leaned forward.

"Look, Fischer, let's cut the crap. Why don't you just cooperate and forgo all this hide-and-seek bullshit? That way, you can save yourself a lot of time so you can get back to that pretty little wife of yours. Just give us the damn name, and we can all go home!"

Miles paused—noticing the strain he was putting Donlon through, which delighted him to a certain degree—before pushing back in his chair and balancing it on two legs.

"And what name would that be, Donlon?"

"Don't play dumb, Fischer. We've already been through this. Just give us the damn name."

"I can't do that."

"And why not?"

"Because I have a job to do just like you."

"You've got a real lousy attitude, Fischer, you know that?"

"Yeah, well maybe I'd have a better one if I wasn't being followed."

"Well I've got a newsflash for you. You better get used to it because we're going to be on your tail every second you're here until we find out who it is you're looking for. That's what happens when people like you don't want to cooperate. What were you doing at the Paletti house?"

"I needed some fresh air, so I thought I would take a ride. Unlike you, Donlon, I like to enjoy myself. You got a problem with that?"

"That's real amusing, Fischer."

"Not as amusing as you and Henley hiding in the bushes. What were you two doing in there, anyway? I thought you FBI agents were smarter than that. Now if I was you, I would have parked in a driveway so I didn't look so conspicuous."

"Don't tell me how to do my job."

Fischer eased the chair to the floor.

"Then don't tell me how to do mine." They glared at each other. Finally, Fischer said, "Look, Donlon, we keep knocking heads, and it isn't getting us anywhere. Why don't you let me do my job, and then you can do yours?"

"Because unlike you I'm a professional, and you're just a smart-ass reporter who thinks he can play cop," said Donlon with contempt. "Need any other reasons?"

"Nicely put. I see they don't spend a lot of time teaching you agents about the finer points of etiquette." He leaned on the table. "Didn't they teach you anything at that academy? They say you get more bees with honey than you do vinegar."

"That's very funny, Fischer, but do you want to know what's really funny?"

"What's that, Donlon?"

"You're in over your head, Fischer, and you're too stupid to see it. This isn't some game where everyone gets to go home once it's over. It doesn't work that way. This is a dangerous game you're playing, and if you're not careful, you're gonna get hurt. Whoever is doing these killings is playing for keeps. What do you think is going to happen to you if you get in the way? How do you think your wife is going to take it when she finds out her husband is dead because he got involved in something that he couldn't handle? What do you want us to tell her? That we gave you an opportunity to cooperate with us but you were too dumb to take it? Is that what you want us to tell her? You can save yourself a lot of grief, Fischer, by giving us the name, and then you can go home. Or maybe you want to go home in a body bag?"

"If you think your scare tactics are going to work, you're wasting your time, Donlon. I think I know what I'm doing."

"Do you, Fischer? Do you?"

"You know, Donlon," Miles said before sipping from his glass, "I don't know why it is, but you don't look like you're having a lot of fun here in Seattle. You should learn to relax, loosen up a little. I would think that with all that free time I gave you and Henley that the two of you would have had a pretty good day to do some sightseeing. Have you been to the top of the Space Needle?"

Donlon pulled himself to the edge of the chair. A less than affable smile glided across his face. He glared through his small blue eyes, nodding.

"Okay, smart-ass! Have it your way. You want to play by the rules? We'll play by the rules." Donlon stood and then moved behind the chair, still glaring at Fischer. "You so much as make a wrong turn or cross in the middle of a street, and I'll slap the handcuffs on you so fast you'll wish you were back in Chicago behind your desk writing little stories on prep schools."

Miles picked up his fork and stabbed a piece of meat and moved it to his mouth, amused at another of the thin man's idle threats.

"Donlon, you know I'd never do that," he said, chewing. "I'm a law-abiding citizen." His eyes glowed, sparkled almost; the sarcastic smile was back on his face. "By the way, how were the dinners I sent you? Did you notice I left out the oysters? I didn't think it was a good idea to include them after I saw you and Henley in the bushes."

Donlon glowered at Fischer and then strode past the maître d' for Terry Avenue and the white sedan. Fischer watched, sipping his drink as Donlon disappeared out of the restaurant.

Bruno smiled when he saw what Fischer had placed on the doorknob to his suite. He found it quite amusing that Fischer would take the time to hang a Do Not Disturb sign on his door, thinking that a simple sign would keep anyone from entering his room, especially someone who didn't have a key. *What a dumb-ass idea,* he thought. Bruno already knew he wasn't in his room. At this very moment, he was downstairs, sitting in the restaurant.

Because of the sign, Bruno became suspicious about what else Fischer may have done before he left for the restaurant. Bruno was now alerted to the possibility that Miles may have done something else to warn him if anyone entered his room while he was out. Not wanting to be outsmarted by Fischer, Bruno checked the space between the jamb and the door. He started at the top and quickly worked his way down the door, and then he stopped. There, at about the same height as his knee, he noticed a black hair spanning the gap between the jamb and the door. Bruno smiled as he took it and placed it in his pocket. Fischer had obviously seen one too many murder mysteries.

Bruno turned the handle out of habit, found it locked, and then pulled a set of small tools from inside his jacket. Carefully watching the hall, he picked at the lock like a precision jeweler until the lock finally clicked. Once inside, he locked the door and checked his watch. It would take him no more than a couple of minutes. It was a hotel suite, not a house.

On the bed he noticed a notepad along with a pencil. In seconds, he was in the bathroom, holding the pad to the light, the pencil firmly clenched between his lips. Heavy indents from previous markings were clearly visible, so he sat on the toilet and vigorously shaded the area around the markings. Anita Paletti was the first name recovered, and then he found the name of Two-Faced Productions, whatever that was. Vashon Island was next and then Angelina Paletti's name along with her address and something called the Rockface, another name that he had no clue what it meant. When he was finished, Bruno stuffed the single page in his pocket and then placed the pad along with the pencil back on the bed exactly where he found them.

He quickly checked the rest of the suite and then replaced Fischer's hair with one of his own just above his knee. He rode the elevator to the lobby before walking unnoticed through the front doors.

Holt's men got in late and immediately went to their room at the Edgewater Hotel. On the bed lay two Ruger 9 mm handguns, their identification numbers filed clean. They came complete with short silencers and enough ammunition to take out two hundred men. Ali Hamza, the Fijian, had retrieved the package containing the guns from the clerk behind the counter while Mospoli took the key from the porter and headed for the elevator. They didn't need any help. They could find the room themselves.

The Fijian closed the drapes while the tall Moroccan turned on the television. They sat one to a bed and quietly dismantled each one, taking care to carefully clean every part before reassembling each gun, saying very little if anything between them. At just past six, while Carboni was at the Sorrento trying to invade Fischer's room, Ali Hamza and Mospoli Katayoon slipped into the hall and stood in front of the door next to theirs. Ali pressed his ear to the door and then jostled the lock while Katayoon watched the hall before shoving a flat-edged instrument between the door and the jamb until the bolt gave way. Ali stood just inside the door while Mospoli planted a highly sensitive wireless bug complete with transmitter under the bed, and then they quietly closed the door and sauntered back to their room.

They took room service instead of eating in the restaurant and studied the picture of Bruno Carboni that had been given to them by Holt. At ten they turned off the television and the lights and fell into a deep sleep. They would be up before daybreak and well before Carboni.

Angelina Paletti arrived home safely just after seven. She was looking forward to the four days' rest before she had to return to New York. Before entering the house, she checked the horses in the barn and released Bolt, a three-year-old Appaloosa, into the corral, and then she made a call to the man in Burton, telling him he did not have to come back until Sunday morning when she would again be flying back to New York on an early flight.

After she unpacked, Angelina stepped from the back door past the bright flowers and proceeded to the open corral. Bolt was near the back fence. She called out to him and then whistled and waited for him to come towards her. It was still warm, and the sun would be up at least another hour. She slipped the bit into his mouth, and then she saddled him, took hold of the reins, and walked him to the front.

"Angel!"

Angelina could see Ned across the street. He was almost to the edge of his driveway.

"Hi, Ned."

"Evening, Angel. I thought you would like your mail," he said, handing her a small pile of envelopes along with a magazine.

Angel had no place to put them, so she tucked them back inside the mailbox.

"My wife noticed your truck in the driveway. We didn't expect to see you home so soon. You weren't gone very long."

"Something came up," she said without elaborating. "I have to be back this coming Monday. I'll be leaving Sunday, so if you can get my mail, I would appreciate it."

"I think we can do that. You had a gentleman caller earlier today—a good-looking fellow," he said without being asked. "Said his name was Miles."

"Oh. Did he say what he wanted?" she asked curiously.

Bolt was by the near fence, just behind her left shoulder. She pulled three half-size carrots from just inside her jeans pocket and fed him while she listened to Ned.

"Said he wanted to speak to you."

"Did he say why?"

"He didn't say. I asked him if he was looking for work in the film industry because of his good looks, but he said he wasn't. I hope you don't mind, but I told him your sister did all the hiring if he was. I noticed he was driving a rental, so I asked him where he was from. He said he was from Chicago."

"Did he give you his last name?"

"Sorry. I didn't ask, and he didn't say."

"Did he ask you anything about me?"

"Just when you were expected back. He said he was going to call you."

"Did he say when?"

"Sorry."

"Did he say anything else?"

"Nope. That was about it."

"Well thanks, Ned."

"You're welcome, Angel." He moved behind her. "I

see you're taking Bolt here for a ride," he said, petting the horse. "Nice evening for it."

"I thought I would before the sun goes down. Say hi to your wife for me."

"I will. I'll talk to you later."

Angelina Paletti watched Ned make his way back across the street before mounting Bolt. She headed down the road towards what was left of the sun. She planned to ride until it got dark and then head for home.

Bruno sat at the bar in the Edgewater Hotel. He had been there since eight, after eating dinner at one of the restaurants not far from the hotel. It was his third drink in just over two hours. A half-burned menthol with a long ash smoldered slowly in the ashtray to his right. The paper that he had lifted from Fischer's room lay on the bar next to him alongside an open phonebook. Bruno was making notes for Wednesday's itinerary.

Just past ten he inserted the key to his door. He sat on the bed and yawned loudly before setting the alarm for five. Bruno decided he would tail Fischer first before using the names and addresses he had taken from Fischer's room and the ones he had lifted from the phonebook. He would be at the Sorrento Hotel sitting in the lobby hiding behind a brand new paper, waiting for Fischer.

Tired, he stripped to his shorts then fell between the sheets and slept hard.

After three drinks, Miles left the Fireside Lounge at around ten thirty and rode the elevator to his room. He stood outside and checked for the single hair pasted across the crack between the door and the jamb. Seeing it was still there, he turned the key and disappeared through the door.

Chapter 40

Bruno swung his thick arm towards the radio, violently slapping the button like he would a fly, abruptly stopping the alarm that was piercing his ears. It was precisely five, and he would need a couple of minutes to orient himself before he found the floor and headed for the shower. Thirty minutes later, he was dressed. Downstairs, three cabs were already waiting. Bruno headed for the closest one and got in.

"Sorrento Hotel."

Seconds later, Hamza and Katayoon followed suit and grabbed one of the remaining taxis. Ali gave the driver instructions to follow the cab that had just pulled away from the curb. They would follow Carboni all day if necessary.

It was just past seven, and Miles was peering through the window from his sixth-floor suite. The white sedan with Donlon and Henley was back at the curb. Donlon was outside, leaning against the passenger door, his tinted eyes keenly trained on the circular driveway leading to the hotel. He looked for Henley but couldn't find him; then he went to the phone and punched in a number.

"Yes, could you send someone up to help me? I seem to have hurt my back."

Miles hung up the phone and left the door ajar, and then he stood by the window, watching the thin man. Two minutes later, a young lad pushed the door open and eased into the room.

"Are you the one who hurt his back?" he asked. He looked like he was just out of high school.

"Yeah, but forget about that right now. I need to get

out of here, but I'm being watched by some thug on the sidewalk." Miles pulled him to the window and pointed to him. "That guy right there."

"What does he want with you?"

Miles looked at the nametag pinned to his vest.

"You got any sisters there, Peter?"

"No, sir."

"Good." He smiled and looked out the window. "He thinks I was fooling around with his sister, and now he and his brother want to take it out of my hide." Miles put his arm around the lad's slender shoulders and pulled him close. "You're a good-looking guy, so you know how it is with us young guys and pretty women."

The young man, who had a mild case of acne, smiled from the compliment though he nowhere near fitted the description. Peter took a second look through the curtains and then looked strangely at Miles.

"He's looks kind of thin." The clerk did a quick study of Miles's physique. "You should be able take him with no problem."

"Looks can be deceiving, kid. His brother is probably waiting in the lobby right now. He's the guy I'm really worried about. He's the size of a gorilla." Miles pulled him away from the window. "Think you can help me?"

Peter looked a little puzzled at the request. He shrugged his shoulders.

"I don't know. It all depends what you want me to do."

"I need you to give me your clothes."

The lad stood back and then jerked his head forward, his eyes wide from the suggestion. He almost stuttered.

"Did I hear you just ask me for my clothes?"

"That's right," Miles said, gesturing with his hands for him to hurry up. "Give me your clothes."

"Why do you want my clothes?"

"Do you like the sight of blood, Petey? Because if you do, you're going to see a lot of it. Is that what you want to see, Petey? You want to see my blood spilled all over the lobby?"

"No, sir."

"Good, because you know who would be cleaning it up, don't you?"

Peter pointed to himself.

"That's right, Petey. So can you help me or not?"

"I guess, but why do you want my clothes?"

"Because I need them so I can get the hell out of here without them coming after me."

"If I give you my clothes, what am I going to wear?"

"You can wear mine. Take anything you want. I'll leave yours in the back alley just outside the kitchen door. I'll give you fifty bucks for your troubles."

"My boss will have my hide if I do that. I need this job. It pays for part of my college tuition. Besides, we're not even the same size."

Miles stared at him, thinking. He sucked in some air and then released it.

"Good point. Glad to see you're paying attention. Okay then." He quickly turned and looked out the window. "We gotta think of something else. Is there a spare uniform around?"

"Yeah. Downstairs."

"Think you can get it for me?"

"Do I still get the fifty bucks?"

"Get back here in five minutes and the money is yours. And while you're at it, bring me back a bag. Paper, if you got it."

"What do you want a bag for?"

"You want the uniform back, don't you?"

Miles watched the young clerk scoot past the open door before picking up the phone and punching in the numbers. He ordered a taxi with instructions to wait for him in the alley and then stood by the window, smiling at the thin man.

Miles's intention was to leave Donlon and Henley by the curbside, which would really tick them off, but he didn't care. He had no intention of allowing Donlon and Henley to follow him at will, whenever they felt like it. Wasn't it Donlon who stated that he was the professional and that he, Fischer, was nothing more than some smart-ass reporter?

Miles watched Donlon walk to the edge of the driveway and then back towards the car. "Well, we'll see," he said, muttering to himself. "We'll see who out-foxes who."

Miles turned away and checked his watch.

"What's keeping that kid?"

He had been gone ten minutes already. Suddenly there was a rap on the door. It was Peter. Miles pulled him in and closed the door.

"Did anybody see you?" he asked.

"I don't think so."

"Good."

Miles gave him the money in exchange for the clothes and the paper bag.

"I'll have them back to you this afternoon. Thanks."

In the bathroom he pulled the pants over his jeans and then slipped the vest over his white cotton shirt. In the mirror, he looked like Jerry Lewis from one of his comedy skits where everything was either too tight or too small. The cuffs of the pants were just above his ankles. When he finally zipped up the zipper and snapped the tab, he could barely breathe. And that was without the belt. The vest, without being buttoned, was tight across his back and snug to his armpits.

Miles locked the door and took the elevator to the basement. Peter told him how to get to the alley through the kitchen. In the kitchen, he moved quickly to where the food was being prepared and grabbed a serving tray. Before anyone noticed, he quickly grabbed some fresh fruit along with a plate of bacon and eggs and headed for the door. Outside, he saw Henley to his right, about twenty feet away. He was against the wall, sitting on a chair, picking at his teeth with a toothpick. The taxi was by the loading dock, about forty feet in the other direction. Miles quickly dropped his head, shielding his face from Henley by tilting the tray at an angle towards his shoulder, all the while making sure nothing slid off. Henley stared at him and noticed something rather odd about the way he was dressed. The outfit looked a little tight. Then he saw the jeans protruding from under the brown pants. Henley quickly stood up.

"Hey, hold it!"

Fischer quickly dropped the tray and took off towards the taxi. He yanked open the back door and got in before sinking deep into the seat.

"Go! Go!" he yelled.

The startled driver did what he was told and shifted it into drive, turning the wheels feverishly, laying a patch of rubber ten feet long down the alley. Henley rushed the taxi, sidestepping the tray, but he gave up when he wasn't able to outrun it. He watched in disgust as the taxi scooted down the alley and then onto Marion Street without stopping. Fischer watched Henley fade from the back window before instructing the driver to drop him off somewhere on Union Street.

Hamza and Katayoon were outside the Sorrento, waiting in the taxi and eating figs to help pass the time. Every fifteen minutes they would take turns and check on Carboni and see what he was up to.

Inside, Bruno sat at the same table as the day before and checked his watch. It was already eight, and he was getting tired of playing this little game of listening for the elevators and then looking to see if it was Fischer or not. He had no idea when Fischer planned on leaving or where he was headed, but he was bound and determined to follow him no matter what, but the wait was beginning to test his patience. He had been waiting for over two hours. Patience was one thing, but this mindless waiting was hell. Carboni glanced at his watch a second time and then headed for the desk.

"I'm looking for Miles Fischer. Do you know if he's still in his room?"

"If you want, I can check for you. I'll just be a moment."

Bruno leaned on the counter while he waited for the clerk. Hamza had already left the taxi and entered the lobby. Halfway across the room, he took notice of the large man at the counter. Hamza headed back, circling Bruno like a fox would circle its prey, and took a position at the end of the counter to Bruno's left, but not before picking up a brochure. From here, he would be able to hear everything that was said.

"There doesn't seem to be any answer. If you want, I can send someone up to check his room."

"Just make sure whoever you send up doesn't mention that I'm here. I want it to be a surprise."

"No problem, sir."

Bruno turned and faced the lobby while he waited, taking little notice of Hamza, who had his back to him.

Two minutes later the clerk was back with an answer.

"Excuse me, sir. I'm sorry, but Mr. Fischer isn't in his room. He must have left the hotel."

"Damn it! Did anyone see him leave?"

"I'm sorry, sir," he said, shaking his head. "If you like, you can leave him a note."

"What the hell good would that do? If he's not here, he's not here."

Bruno stared at him, disgusted that he had somehow missed his chance to follow Fischer. He grunted his disapproval and asked the clerk to order him a cab, telling him he would wait for it outside.

Hamza, having heard all this, quickly jumped ahead of Carboni and exited the hotel, headed for Katayoon, who was waiting in the taxi.

Donlon and the white sedan were no longer at the curb.

Before exiting the taxi, Miles left the clothes with the driver and instructed him to return them to the Sorrento. He rented a car from the building across the street on Union before having breakfast in a little diner next door. After breakfast, he started visiting the first archery club marked on the list inside his pocket attached to the rest of the notepad.

Mercedes Browne parked her little blue compact next to the curb on Denny Way, close to the reservoir, and sat there quietly, undecided as to what to do. Even though it was just a phone call, and nobody would be able to identify her, she was, nonetheless, extremely nervous. Unsure if she was doing the right thing, she rolled down the window and lit a cigarette in order to calm her nerves. Five minutes later, she was in the booth asking assistance for the number to the *Chicago Tribune*. After dropping in her change, she dialed the number and waited.

"*Chicago Tribune*. May I help you?"

The voice startled her, and Browne panicked. "I'm sorry. I must have the wrong number."

She quickly hung up the phone and left the booth.

Chapter 41

Bruno took the taxi back to the Edgewater to have breakfast and ponder what to do next. Since Fischer had eluded him, he decided over his eggs and bacon to use the notes that he had taken from Fischer's room the day before. He decided he would start with the Rockface first, since it was the closest.

After breakfast, Bruno ordered a rental car and headed north. The Fijian and the tall Moroccan followed in another taxi.

Donlon made the call from the white sedan, placing a local agent at the Fauntleroy Ferry Terminal in case Fischer happened to take another ride to Vashon Island without their presence. Henley was at the wheel, and they were stuck in downtown traffic, a couple of blocks from Two-Faced Productions.

"So, why are we going to see her?" Henley asked, still stinging after Fischer had eluded him in the alley.

"How else are we going to find out where he is?" snapped Donlon. "He's been to her sister's, so there's a good chance he'll end up here."

"What do you think he's up to?" Henley asked, waiting for the signal to turn green.

"That's the million-dollar question, isn't it?"

"Do you think he suspects one of the Paletti sisters?"

"I don't know. It's hard to say."

"She's not going to like it, seeing us show up on her doorstep again. What's it been, six years?"

"Something like that."

Henley proceeded to the curb and parked in a tow-away zone and then killed the engine. They exited and entered the elevator and rode it to the sixteenth floor before pushing through the glass door of Two-Faced Productions. Donlon flashed his badge at Ms. Joffe. It was just past nine.

"We'd like to see Anita Paletti."

"I'm sorry, but she's not in yet," replied Ms. Joffe.

"When do you expect her?"

Ms. Joffe looked at her watch and then at Donlon.

"She should be here any minute. Would you like to wait for her?"

Donlon nodded, and along with Henley, they took a seat close to the door.

"Can I get you anything?"

"No, we're fine," stated Donlon.

Just then Anita appeared on the other side of the door with a briefcase in hand.

"Good morning, Abigail."

"These two gentlemen just arrived," she said. "They're waiting to see you."

Anita turned to where Abigail was pointing. Suddenly she felt a chill. Donlon was the last person she expected to see sitting in her office. If Anita was in shock, she didn't show it. She concocted a halfhearted smile towards Donlon but did not offer her hand.

"Mr. Donlon," she said almost hesitantly. "This is a surprise." She noticed Henley sitting next to him. "What are you doing here?"

Donlon removed his sunglasses but not his hat. "We're sorry to bother you, but we need to talk to you for a moment."

"What about?"

Anita was highly suspicious at seeing Donlon and Henley in her office.

"Can we talk somewhere private?"

She hesitated and then said, "Sure. Come into my

office." Anita grabbed her mail from Ms. Joffe's desk. "Hold my calls," she said. Paletti led the way, with Donlon and Henley in tow. "Have a seat."

"Thanks, but we'll stand," Donlon replied. "This won't take long."

Anita took her seat behind her desk and waited for Donlon to explain exactly why he and Henley were there.

"Have you ever heard of a reporter by the name of Miles Fischer?"

When she heard Fischer's name, a sense of anger swelled inside her although she didn't show it. Her brain quickly recounted the article she had read Sunday morning, when all she had wanted to do was relax and enjoy the day before Fischer's story had her rushing from the coffee shop. Her response was slow but direct.

"Yes. He works for the *Chicago Tribune*. We did an interview here in my office about two weeks ago. Why do you ask?"

"He's here in Seattle, and we're trying to locate him."

It took her a moment before she responded.

"Why is he in Seattle?" she asked.

"We don't know."

"Then why are you here? What does this have to do with me?" she asked him.

"My partner and I would like to know if you've had any contact with him in the last couple of days."

"Not since our interview."

Paletti slowly leaned back in her chair with her eyes fixed on the thin man.

"What interview?" asked Henley.

"The *Tribune* was doing a series of articles on women in business. He said he was filling in for one of his colleagues who couldn't make it. Something to do with appendicitis. What does all of this have to do with me?"

303

she asked again.

"We don't know, other than he's been poking around your sister's place," stated Donlon.

"What was he doing there?"

"We're not sure. We thought maybe you could tell us."

She shook her head slightly.

"How should I know?"

Henley glanced over at his partner.

"What's this all about?"

"Do you read the newspaper?" asked Donlon.

Anita looked at him like it was a dumb question.

"Yes. Why do you ask?"

"Do you read the *Tribune*?"

"Only the one time because of the interview. Why?"

"Have our ever heard of a little town called Tweeksbury?"

"No," she said, shaking her head. "Should I?"

"There was a murder there about two weeks ago. Two guys by the name of Lionel Holt and David Masalla were killed with a crossbow after being found not guilty in the rape and murder of two teenage girls. It has a lot of similarities to your own case."

"And that's why you're here Mr. Donlon—to dig up old wounds?"

"That isn't our intent," stated Henley. "That's not why we're here."

"Then why are you here, Mr. Henley? Haven't I already gone through enough?"

"We're just doing our job, ma'am."

"Well you're not doing it very well. We've already been over all of this," she said, opening one of the drawers to her desk. "I have a new life for myself now, and I wish to be left alone." Anita pulled a tissue from the drawer and dabbed at her eyes. "You have no idea how upsetting this is to see you here."

"We're sorry," said Donlon. "This isn't intentional. We're not here trying to upset you."

"Well, you're doing damn good job of it, Mr. Donlon. I feel for those parents to have to go through what I've been through."

"We're sorry," Donlon said again. "We know how difficult this is for you."

"How the hell would you know what it's like to lose a child?" she snapped back. "If my memory serves me correctly, you've never been married, Mr. Donlon, unless that's all changed since the last time you were here. So don't come in here and pretend you know how it feels. How do you know what it feels like?"

Donlon stood there, speechless.

"It must be just awful for them," she said, dabbing at her eyes.

"Yes, I'm sure it is."

"But what does all of this have to do with me and my sister?"

"Our friend seems to think that what happened in Tweeksbury is somehow tied to what happened in Eastbrook eight years ago."

Suddenly Anita flushed. She could feel her heart thump in her chest. All this conjuring up of a past that was supposedly behind her was making her ill. She pulled in a deep breath and then quietly expelled it from her lungs.

"There are some striking similarities. The girls that these two were accused of killing were the same age as your daughter."

Anita stared blankly at Donlon, but she said nothing.

"Your daughter's birth date was March nineteenth.

Am I right?"

"You know very well when her birthday was. Why are you asking?"

"It seems one of them shared the same birth date as your daughter, just like the Ambro girl."

"Just what are you implying?"

"Nothing," Donlon replied, nodding slightly. "Nothing at all."

"Well it sounds to me like you are. It must be a coincidence."

"Yes, I'm sure it is."

"Then why are you here telling me all this?"

"We just thought you should know in case Fischer shows up on your doorstep."

Anita sat there and said nothing. She had heard enough. She wished they would leave.

"Well, that's all we came for." Donlon pulled one of his cards from his pocket. "If he shows up, call this number. We'd like to talk to him."

"Do I have anything to worry about if he does?" she asked.

"No. We just want to talk to him."

Donlon moved towards the door, followed by Henley. "Sorry to have troubled you."

Donlon moved his shades back over his eyes, and they both left.

Anita waited until she was sure they were gone before picking up the phone.

"Abigail, I need you to call the hotels in town and see if you can find out where a Mr. Miles Fischer is staying."

Anita slowly placed the receiver back on the phone and sat quietly, thinking about the man with the cobalt blue eyes.

Donlon and Henley returned to the curb and sat in

their car.

"Why did you tell her he was poking around her sister's house?"

"I wanted to see what her reaction would be. Telling her that Fischer was at her sister's house doesn't hurt us in the least. If anything, it might help."

"In what way?"

"Let's just wait and see what she does."

"So you suspect she could have something to do with these latest murders?"

"Let's just say everybody is still a suspect, even Anita Paletti."

"But she's already been cleared after the Ambro case. What do you hope to achieve?"

"That was six years ago. A lot has happened since then."

"Why do you think Fischer was at Paletti's house?"

Donlon looked out the passenger window. "If we knew that, we wouldn't be sitting here."

"So what are we going to do now?"

"Let's go back to the hotel. We can grab a coffee there while we wait for Fischer."

Bruno Carboni was a lucky man. He had fared better than Fischer when he parked his car and entered the Rockface at around ten o'clock that morning. Unlike Fischer's visit the previous day, the young lady behind the counter, not the same one Miles had locked horns with, was more than cooperative. She pulled up Anita Paletti's name in a matter of seconds, along with her sister's.

In the parking lot, Bruno sat in his car and lit a cigarette, mulling over what he was going to do next. The fact that Anita or Angelina Paletti could scale a wall at least put them on the roof of the hardware store if that's what Fischer had in mind, but the question of whether or not they were capable of shooting an arrow some fifty feet with dead-point accuracy under the cover of darkness still remained to be answered. He had originally planned to take the ferry over to Vashon Island and check out Angelina Paletti's place, but he decided to put it on hold for now. Thanks to Fischer's notes that he had lifted from the notepad and the lady at the counter, he decided to stay put and continue on with his investigation here, but first he had to find a coffee shop where he could make use of a phonebook. He planned to jot down the names and addresses of every shooting range and archery club he could find and then spend the rest of the day checking them out. Maybe Anita and her sister were members at one of these clubs.

Chapter 42

Angelina Paletti pushed the right buttons and waited for the connection to take place.

"Hi, sis. It's me, Angel. Do you remember that reporter you told me about who you did the interview with?"

"Yes. Miles Fischer, but I already know Angel," Anita said matter-of-factly.

"How did you find out?"

"Through the FBI. Donlon just left my office an hour ago."

"So that was him," Angel said.

"Who told you?"

"My neighbor, Ned. He said he saw him peeking in my mailbox."

"When did you get in?" Anita asked, changing subjects.

"Last night about seven. I was going to call you, but I decided to go for a ride instead. Why?"

"No reason. We can talk about it later. Did Fischer say anything to Ned as to why he was there?"

"No. Ned asked him if he was an actor or if he was just looking for a job, but he said no. What's going on, sis? Why was he here?" Angel asked.

"I don't know, but I think it has something to do with what happened back in Eastbrook," replied Anita.

"You have to be kidding me."

"I wish I was, but it's happening all over again."

"Jesus Christ! Why don't they leave you alone? You've been through enough already. What's wrong with these guys? Don't they have anything else better to do? Who are they after now?"

There was a pause, and Anita said, "I don't know."

"You don't sound very happy. Are you alright? You sound tired," said Angel.

"I've got a headache, that's all."

"I'm going to be in town later. Do you want to do a late lunch? It may help to take your mind off of it."

"Not today. I'm not up to it. How about tomorrow? We can talk then," said Anita.

"Is one o'clock okay?" asked Angel.

"Sounds good. How about we meet at Carmine's?"

"Splendid. I'll meet you in front. And don't worry, sis. Everything will work out."

"I'm not worried, Angel. I can take care of myself. I just wish they would leave me alone."

"I know, sis. Us Palettis always could. It's probably because we've been through so much. I'll see you tomorrow at Carmine's then. Hang in there, sis. I'm sure you'll feel better in the morning."

Anita hung up the phone.

Miles had been at it since nine that morning, but so far he had nothing to show for it. He had racked up nearly two hundred miles on the odometer from driving through most of Seattle and its closest suburbs, one time narrowly missing an oncoming car. After nearly five hours of endless inquiries, he had nothing he could use that would prove that Anita Paletti had indeed fired the crossbow that killed Lionel Holt and David Masalla. Anita Paletti's name was simply not there on any of the lists. The Paletti name had not shown up on any of the rosters from any of the archery or gun clubs that he had visited from his long list that were now crossed off in frustration. He had been so positive, so cocksure after his visit to the Rockface that it would simply be a matter of time before her name would surface on a membership list at one of the clubs, but that hadn't been the case. So far Anita Paletti's name was missing.

Miles did not reach the Down Range Shoot and Archery Club until just before two. It was his last stop from a long list of archery and gun clubs that meandered wildly through the neighborhoods of Seattle, and he had yet to find her. There were enough clubs around to train an army, and yet somehow her name had not appeared on any of the lists. Frustration had already set in when he parked his rental in the parking lot adjacent to the Down Range Shoot and Archery Club in Medina. *Maybe it would be this one*, he thought. *It had better be. It's the last one on my list.*

"Good afternoon," he said.

The man behind the counter repeated the same salutation, his voice having a rich twang to it which suited his fiftyish rugged exterior. The oversized black buckle attached to his thick belt which looped through his wide denim pants had the initials NRA raised on it in bright silver like it was a badge of honor. The nametag said his name was Luke.

"What can I do for ya?"

Miles hastily cleared his throat.

"Yeah. I'm looking for someone. I was supposed to meet her here at one o'clock, but I'm running a little late." Miles checked his watch to ensure the request sounded real. "Do you know anybody here who goes by the last name of Paletti? I'm supposed to be meeting her here."

"Let's see."

Miles waited while he checked the roster.

"What's the first name?"

"Anita."

It took him a second. "Nope," he said quickly. "She's

not here. Are you sure you got the name right? All I've got here is an Angelina Paletti."

At first it didn't register. Miles looked at him kind of awkwardly. Did Luke just say Angelina Paletti?

"Is that her?" Luke asked him.

"Yeah, that's her," he quickly replied without much thinking. He smiled warmly at Luke.

"I thought you said her name was Anita?"

"I did, but it's obviously a mistake. I meant to say Angelina, but for some reason I was thinking of her sister, Anita." Miles gestured with his hands and offered some halfhearted laughter supporting the fact that it had indeed been an honest mistake and would he please forgive him. "I make that mistake all the time what with both their names starting with an A. I don't know why I was thinking of her sister, but yeah, that's her."

Miles was pleased with his answer. It sounded about right.

"Well, I don't know any Anita. She's not listed."

"No, it's Angelina I'm looking for. Her friends call her Angel for short. Is she still here?"

Luke didn't react to that little tidbit. Instead, he put his large, thick hands on the counter and stared at Miles.

"Funny, but you're not the first person to ask for her today."

"Oh." Miles actually looked surprised.

"No. Someone else was in here asking the same thing."

"Popular girl, I guess."

"Sure is."

"What did they want?"

"Same thing as you. He wanted to know if Angelina was here."

"I guess one of us got our signals crossed or something like that. The problem is that I'm late. Do you know if she's still here?" he asked again.

"I haven't seen her. Maybe you got your signals mixed up, too?"

"I don't think so. She was going to show me around."

"I see," he said, slightly hesitating. "So you're thinking of joining?"

"I was thinking about it."

"Well, I can do that for you."

"Do what?"

"Show you around."

"I think I should wait for Angel. She kind of had her heart set on showing me the place. You know how women are."

"It'll only take about five minutes."

"I think I should wait."

"Well, suit yourself. You could save yourself some time if you let me do it."

"She's a friend, and besides, you and me," he said, gesturing with his hands. "Don't take this the wrong way, but it wouldn't be the same, if you know what I mean."

"Yeah, I getcha. You'd rather have your girl show you around."

Miles pulled out his phone.

"I think I'll give her a call and see where she is," he said to Luke.

Miles stepped over to a corner where he would have some privacy. He dialed the Sorrento Hotel and started talking like it was Angelina Paletti on the other end.

"Excuse me," he said to Luke. "This other guy. Angel is curious as to what he looked like."

"I'd say he was about my age," said Luke. "I guess he was about your height but stockier, especially around the chest. He had a real strange voice, like he had gravel in his throat."

"Did he give his name?"

"Nope."

"Thanks." Miles continued on with his fake phone call, and then thirty seconds later he slapped the phone shut. He headed for the door. "Thanks for your help, Luke. Angel said to say hi."

In the parking lot, Miles placed the key into the ignition but didn't bother starting the engine. The fact that Angelina's name showed on the registry and not Anita's was not what was bothering him. What had him upset was the fact that the private investigator had shown up at the club. He had been extra careful after he received the envelope and the flowers. So how is it Carboni ended up showing up at the club?

He had checked the door before entering his room. The hair was still there, stuck between the door and the jamb just like he left it. He had checked the carpet just to make sure nobody had found the hair and then replaced it with one of their own. If they had, he should have found his on the floor, but there was nothing there. He checked.

So how did this Bruno Carboni know to show up here and ask for the Paletti sisters? It had to come from him. Miles was positive. The story that was published in the Sunday Edition never mentioned either of the sisters. Bruno Carboni only showed up *after* the story appeared in the newspaper and *after* he paid a visit to the *Tribune*. Miles could have added the FBI into the mix because Donlon was just as eager to learn what he knew if it wasn't for the envelope and the flowers. Donlon already knew what he looked like and where he was staying.

Bruno must have never left the hotel. He must have hung around and waited and then saw him enter the restaurant. That's when he made his move because he was in the lobby somewhere, but where? He had checked the lobby when he came out of the elevator. A moment of contemplation and then it hit him. The bastard was probably sitting in one of those wingback chairs that he didn't bother to check to closely because he didn't see the point because he couldn't see anybody in them to begin with.

Bruno must have found the hair he had placed between the door and the jamb. That would explain how he got into the room but where did he get the information from?

The computer was under the bed and hadn't been touched. If he had, there was nothing he could have gleaned from it anyway without the password. In the suite, he had left nothing in the open. The desk was clean. So were the two wastebaskets Then he remembered the notepad. He had a habit of pressing hard when he wrote. It had to come from the notepad. It was the only thing he had written anything on.

That bloody bastard. That meant he had the name of the other club, the Rockface, along with Angelina's address.

"Bloody hell."

Miles started the engine and pulled quickly from the parking lot. He made a mental note to check his room when he got back. There was no telling what else Carboni may have walked away with.

She found an empty bench behind the buildings where the grass hadn't been uprooted and replaced with more concrete. There were trees and a path that meandered from one end of the park to the other before ending at the parking lot, which was almost empty. She peeled a banana and watched the public phone some fifty feet away. It was deserted and had been since the time she got there. Along the path, a group of people passed by but kept going. She finished the banana and made her move towards the booth. Somewhat apprehensive, she picked up the receiver and punched a number, and when the operator came on, she asked to be connected to the *Chicago Tribune*.

"Good afternoon, *Chicago Tribune*. How may I help you?"

Hearing the voice and the name of the paper had her shaking. Her heart pounded wildly, and it echoed in her voice.

"I want to speak to Mr. Miles Fischer."

"I'm sorry, he's not available right now. Could someone else help you?"

"No! It has to be Miles Fischer."

"Hold on and I'll see what I can do."

Sally quickly pressed the button sending music over the line before garnering the attention of a staff member who had just come through the door. "Go get Veronica, quickly!" Sally watched him leave, and then she pressed the button, retrieving the caller. "We're trying to locate him; hold on."

"I can't hold on. Either I speak to him right now, or I'm hanging up."

Just then, one of the elevators opened and Tony exited.

"Hold on. He's just getting off the elevator."

Sally quickly hit the button and pulled the headset from her head.

"Tony. I need you quick. This lady is asking for Miles. Pretend that you're him. I don't know what she wants, but she sounds nervous and she'll only speak with Miles. See what you can do."

"Why do I have to pretend I'm Miles?" he asked reluctantly.

"I'll explain it to you later. Just do it!"

Sally quickly thrust the headset in his hand. He placed the headset over his ears, pulling the microphone close to his mouth. Sally pressed the button.

"Miles Fischer. Sally said you wanted to speak to me."

"Are you still working on that story?"

"You need to speak up—I can barely hear you."

Mercedes's eyes became brighter against her Hershey skin as if she was awakening from a deep sleep.

"Are you still working on that story?"

"The crossbow murders?"

"Yes, if that's what you call them."

"Yeah, why?"

Tony listened and watched as Veronica approached and stood next to Sally. They began to speak, and he quickly held his index finger to his lips and silently shushed them. He could barely hear the caller. Sally pulled Veronica to the side, away from Tony so they could continue talking out of earshot.

"I have some information that may be of interest to you."

"What sort of information?"

Tony quickly motioned for a pen and paper before cupping his hand over the microphone, pushing it away from his face. "Sally," he whispered cautiously. "Get me Miles's cell number."

"It has something to do with those two guys who were killed in Tweeksbury."

"Where are you calling from?"

"That's not important. Are you interested?"

"We're a newspaper, lady. Of course we're interested,

317

but why aren't you going to the authorities with this?"

"Because they ask too many questions—just like you are right now."

"Sorry. Go ahead—I'm listening."

"You're on the right track, but you're missing some information that might be of some help."

"What kind of information?"

"I thought you were just going to listen?"

Tony quickly gestured with his hands as if to say, "What's with you, lady?"

"You're not dealing with a normal person."

"What do you mean?"

No reply

"Sorry."

"This person is suffering from a mental disorder. Have you ever heard of DID?"

"No. What's DID?" Tony asked, writing down the three letters.

"Dissociative identity disorder."

"So, what does it mean?"

"In simple terms, it means multiple personalities."

"How do you know all this?"

"I saw something I wasn't supposed to. I was in his office, and the file was open. I didn't mean to look at it. He usually keeps the special ones under lock and key."

"And where was he?"

"He stepped out for a while. I guess he forgot to lock it away."

"What did you see exactly?"

"I can't tell you everything, but I saw the newspaper clippings about the trial in Tweeksbury. That's how I got your number."

"What else did you see?"

"More newspaper clippings," she said, breathing

hard.

"I need you to be more specific. What clippings?"

"They date back to Eastbrook. There were also clippings of what happened in Whatley. There were a lot of pages with notes from their sessions, but I didn't get a chance to read them all." There was a pause. "Hold on. Someone's coming." Browne lowered her head and watched until the couple passed and were at least fifty feet from the booth. "Did you get that?"

Tony ignored the question. "Do you have a pen?" he asked.

"Why do I need a pen?"

"I need you to write down this number," Tony said. "It's important."

"I don't have time to jot down no bloody number!"

"Look, lady, just do it!" Tony ordered. "I don't have time to explain. This is important in case we get cut off. You can call me back on my cell phone."

Browne quickly found a pen deep in her purse and wrote the number on the palm of her hand. Sally and Veronica continued to stand just off to the side, huddled together, listening.

"Have you got it?"

"Yes, I've got it!"

"Good. Go on."

"Are all you reporters like this?"

"What do you mean?"

"Are all you reporters such assholes?"

"No. Just me. I come by it honestly. You were saying."

Mercedes Browne hesitated before saying, "This person is being treated, but off and on but they never stick with it. They're here and then they're gone."

"How long does this person stay?"

"I'm not sure. I'm only guessing. Maybe four sessions at any one time."

"Why don't they stick with it?"

"I think they panic."

"How did this person get this DID condition?"

"Something happened during their childhood."

"Can you be more specific?"

"No."

"How many personalities are we talking about?"

"Too many."

"How long does it take to cure them?"

"Depends on the person and how bad the experiences."

"Give me an idea."

"It could take years—it depends. I thought you were going to listen?"

"Sorry. You said this person doesn't stay with it. How long are the breaks in treatment?"

"Months. Sometimes as much as six, and then he has to start all over. It's hard for them to deal with." Mercedes paused and checked her watch. "If you persist in interrupting and asking questions, I'm going to hang up. I don't have a lot of time."

"Sorry."

"Do you believe in God, Mr. Fischer?"

"Yes, why?"

"Do you believe that God punishes those who don't do the right thing?"

"I suppose so."

"He knew."

"Who knew?"

"The doctor. He knew before it happened, and he did nothing about it."

"Knew what?"

"That's the only reason I'm calling. He broke his ethics as a doctor. He's supposed to save lives, not let people die. He could have saved them, but instead, he let them die. He crossed the line. He should have warned the authorities. He had a duty to inform them, but he didn't. I lost all respect for him when he did that."

"Why do you think he didn't?"

"I don't know."

"So is the patient aware of this DID thing?"

"Yes, but it's still in the preliminary stage."

"How long has the patient known?"

"What do you mean?"

"When was the person told about having DID?"

"I'm not sure. Maybe four years ago. I didn't have time to read the whole file. Damn it! Will you stop asking so many questions!"

"Can the person control these personalities?"

"No."

"Why not?"

"Because they haven't learned how to integrate them. They don't stick with it long enough. I told you, this person panics and leaves, and doesn't come back until they want the doctor's help again."

"So you mean this patient isn't aware of what these other personalities are doing or what they're capable of?"

"I already told you," she snapped back. "This patient doesn't know anything other than the diagnosis of DID. Only the doctor knows about her other personalities and what they're capable of."

"You said you saw the file, so you must know what they're capable of even if the patient doesn't know."

"I can't answer that."

"But you said you saw the file."

"I did, but not everything."

"Is she taking anything for this?"

Suddenly, there was a long pause.

"Why did you just say 'she'?" Mercedes asked anxiously.

"Because you said 'her' in one of your previous statements."

Browne panicked.

"No. No, I didn't," said the unnerved voice. "You heard me wrong. I never said that."

She quickly hung up and left the booth. Tony stared at Sally and Veronica and then handed the headset back to Sally.

"She just hung up."

Chapter 43

Bruno was close to Ellisport, driving along Ridge Road on the water's edge just before the pier, headed for Angelina Paletti's house. He parked in front and then exited the vehicle and walked the driveway to the front door. Hamza and Katayoon drove by in a taxi and ordered the driver to turn left at the corner, up a ways from Paletti's house. The cabbie did as he was asked and did a U-turn and parked on the side of the road, just before the stop sign. From there, they could see part of the house and Carboni's rental parked next to the entrance to the driveway.

Carboni knocked on the door. If she was home, he planned to ask for a fictitious person and then leave. At night, armed with a flashlight, he would come back and search the grounds. He knocked again. He peered through the window and then strode to the back.

Bruno immediately grunted his disapproval when he stepped behind the house. The place was huge. Everything beyond the house and the lawn was separated by a white picket fence. The barn, painted red, was to his right and a hundred feet in the distance. A large corral was adjacent to it. There were horses inside. Beyond that, there were open fields spotted with patches of trees and then more fences and more trees. *This isn't going to be easy*, he thought.

He checked the barn first and found nothing that interested him. Next, he checked the corral, making sure he closed the gate behind him so none of the horses could escape. The horses circled around him and kept their distance as Bruno scuffed and kicked at the dirt. He made one complete sweep before exiting. He stared at what lay in front of him, the endless pasture. He grunted as he removed his tweed jacket and then headed for the pasture.

After fifteen minutes of searching, he changed his mind. It was too big, and the grass was too tall. He decided to walk to the end of the property, through the line of trees ahead of him, and see what was there.

Even though the ground was more hilly than flat, the grass was much shorter like it had just been cut. There in the distance, standing back a ways, some two hundred feet on a diagonal to his left, he saw an object that looked like it had legs. There was another one to his right. He started to walk towards the one to his left and then tried jogging but gave up.

As he approached, he noticed the object had three legs and not two. It wasn't a scarecrow, either, as he had imagined. It was a tripod with big, flat circular bales of hay attached to the top of the legs. When he approached it from the front, he noticed it was more than just a bale of hay. It was a target.

Bruno immediately dropped his jacket and went to work. He stooped from the waist and slowly circled it and then looped around again, expanding his search out further until he was ten feet or more from the tripod. He cursed under his breath, looking at the ground after he found nothing. He looked at the other tripod sixty feet away and shook his head before reluctantly grabbing his jacket and trudging towards it.

There, he repeated the process, only this time he crawled on all fours. He pulled and clawed at the strands of grass as he worked his way from the tripod, hell-bent and determined to find what he was looking for. Breathing heavily from the exertion and the heat, he was about to give up when he caught a glimpse of something close to his knee. It was buried deeply into the grass. He pulled away the blades of grass and reached for it. It was the discolored butt from a cigarette. There was another one behind him and another one three feet away. He checked them against the one in his wallet. The printing on the paper was a match.

"Bellissimo!"

Bruno hastened to his feet, slipping the matching papers back into the photo sleeve of his wallet. He threw his jacket over his shoulder and walked quickly through the open field, past the thicket of heavy trees and the corral to his vehicle parked at the side of the road, just beyond the gates blocking the driveway. He lit one of his menthols and then did a wild U-turn and headed down the roadway towards the ferry. Ned, her neighbor, was outside, standing on the shoulder in front of his house. He was retrieving his mail and watching Bruno leave. Ten seconds later, he watched the taxi with Hamza in front and Katayoon in the backseat pass by. He watched until they disappeared around the curve, and then he walked back down the dirt driveway towards his house.

At three in the afternoon, Anita Paletti dismissed Abigail Joffe for the rest of the day. Anita waited until she disappeared past the turn in the hall before locking the doors and secluding herself in her office. Anita punched in a set of numbers and waited for the connection to the Sorrento Hotel.

"Mr. Miles Fischer."

"I'm sorry, Mr. Fischer is not in. Can I take a message?"

"No. That won't be necessary."

Anita pressed and held the button and then hung up the receiver.

He was parked along the curb in Discovery Park

overlooking the bay when his cell phone rang. He had gone there instead of to the hotel to give himself sometime to think without Donlon harassing him about being ditched a second time. He had gotten over the initial shock of Carboni being in his room and was now dealing with the fact that Angelina's name had shown up on the registry of the archery club and not Anita's as he had hoped and thought it would be. He was now curious as to how she fit into all of this.

"You're not going to believe this," Veronica said. She sounded a little excited. "A woman called. She said she saw something. It has to do with the crossbow murders."

"What woman?" he asked.

"She didn't leave her name. She said she saw your name on one of the stories about Tweeksbury sitting in the file along with what happened in Eastbrook and Whatley. You weren't here, so Sally asked Tony to talk to her on your behalf."

"What file are we talking about?"

"The file that she mistakenly read. She saw something in one of the files that the doctor keeps under lock and key. Have you ever heard of DID?" Veronica asked.

"No."

"Me neither, but it stands for dissociative identity disorder. Multiple personalities, Miles. Whoever is doing these killings is suffering from multiple personalities."

"Did she give you a name or any kind of a hint as to who she was talking about?"

"No, but just before the end of the conversation, she let the word 'her' slip, so Tony asked her what she was taking for this condition. When Tony referred to the patient as female, the caller called him on it. She denied using the word 'her' when she was telling Tony that the patient didn't know about her other personalities and what they were capable of. That's when she hung up."

Miles sat there momentarily stunned. He was almost speechless.

"Miles? Are you still there?" Veronica asked.

"Yeah, I'm just thinking. This is unbelievable." His mind racing, Miles paused a moment to gather his thoughts. "So is she aware she has this condition?" he asked.

"Yes, but its more complicated than that."

"What do you mean?"

"She knows, but it doesn't help the way you or I would think. These personalities have to be integrated."

"What do you mean, integrated?"

"I'm not really sure."

"Can she still function like you or I while she has this DID?"

"From what I can understand, yes, but she has no control of these other personalities. That's why they have to be integrated. I think it's based on which personality is the strongest. Something sets her off, and then one of her personalities appears to suit the situation. I think that's the way it works, but I'm not sure. She said it takes time to integrate all of the personalities so that she can function as a normal human being again."

"How long does it take to integrate them?"

"She told Tony it could take years. It all depends on the person and how bad the experiences were that brought it on."

"How long has she been seeing this doctor?"

"Approximately four years."

"How long does it take before she's cured?"

"I don't know. According to the caller, she doesn't stay in treatment."

"Why not?"

"She thinks it's because she panics, but she also told Tony she didn't see the whole file. She only read parts of it."

"How many personalities are we talking about?"

"According to her, too many."

"And this person is aware that she has these multiple personalities, but she can't control them?"

"That's what she told Tony."

"So how did she get this DID thing?"

"She said that something happened in her childhood, but she didn't elaborate."

"Is that the main cause?"

"I don't know," she said. "So what are you going to do?"

"I don't know," he replied rather flatly.

"You don't sound very positive. What's wrong? I thought this would make you happy."

"It does, but I just came back from visiting a slew of archery and gun clubs. Angelina's name popped up on the registry at one of the archery clubs. I wasn't expecting it. I was expecting to see Anita's. Now I don't know what to think. Is there anything else that you haven't told me?"

Veronica checked her notes again.

"After the caller hung up and I talked to Tony, I researched what I could on DID, multiple personalities. I thought you might need it, so I sent it to you via fax to the hotel."

"Thanks. I'll read it when I get back."

"Oh, and there's one more thing—Tony gave her your cell number."

"Why did he do that?"

"It was in case he lost her. He was afraid she might

hang up. She seemed awfully nervous. Maybe she'll call back."

"Let's hope she does. It would go a long way to simplifying things. I just hope she doesn't notice the difference in our voices."

Chapter 44

Donlon phoned Abrams, and Abrams phoned the Washington State office, and after explaining the problems of containing their elusive prey, two more agents were added to the team. One was posted in the lobby after management turned down Donlon's request to have an agent positioned just outside Fischer's door. The second agent was posted in the back alley—which wasn't official hotel property—just in case Fischer had any more ideas like the one earlier.

Donlon was sitting in the passenger seat when Fischer finally drove up and parked across the street. Donlon watched as Miles stood at the corner and waited for the signal. Fischer crossed the street with the light and met Donlon, who was now outside the vehicle, leaning against the passenger door.

"Hey, hotshot. I just thought I would let you know that you won't be doing anymore sightseeing without one of my agents tagging along with you. I've got men posted all around the hotel in case you start wandering off on your own. I hope you enjoyed yourself today because it's your last. You'll have to have lady luck by your side if you plan anymore shenanigans like this morning."

"Don't flatter yourself, Donlon," he said, stopping just in front of him. "You're like one of those old boxers who thinks he can still fight—a lot of bobbing and weaving, but not a lot of quickness."

"Still with the mouth, I see. You're wasting your time, Fischer. If I was you, I'd give up and go home to my wife."

"You'd like that, wouldn't you, Donlon? You know, I'll bet your mamma could outfox you. Didn't they teach you anything at that academy?"

"Don't kid yourself, smart-ass."

"We'll see," he said, pulling away.

Miles chuckled to himself. He was actually enjoying sparing with Donlon.

Miles left the thin man at the curb and went directly into the lobby, where he picked up the faxed sheets, four in all, before taking the elevator to the sixth floor.

Miles grabbed the phone sitting on the desk and took it with him to the window. He punched in numbers while he watched the white sedan that was parked next to the curb. Donlon was sitting in the passenger seat with the door open. Henley was outside on the curb, leaning against the right fender and smoking a cigarette.

"Veronica. It's Miles."

"Did you get the fax?"

"Yeah, but I'll read it later. I hate to do this to you, but I need you to find out when Paletti's parents died. I need to know how they died and if the sisters were present when this happened. See if you can get names of any of their neighbors or relatives. Ask for their numbers and call them. They may not speak English, so find someone in the office who speaks Hebrew if you have to. Check with Welch. I think he told me he comes from a Jewish background. There's also that new guy, Weiss. He started at the city desk a couple of months ago. See if they can help you. Try and find out what kind of an upbringing the Paletti sisters had—if there were any problems in the family."

"Tell me exactly what it is you're looking for so I don't go asking the wrong questions and one of them hangs up on me."

"I want to know if the sisters were abused in anyway. If they were, we need to know by whom, and if they can tell you, ask them what exactly went on. Give them any excuse you have to, to get the information."

"What do you think it was?"

"I don't know but something happened back in Israel while they were growing up. We need to find out what it is. It could hold the key to how this all plays out and what happens to this story."

Anita Paletti parked her BMW 540i on Madison, next to a meter, and walked the short distance under an early night sky to the lobby of the Sorrento. An FBI agent, one of the ones Donlon had asked for, was outside, close to where the driveway met the street. He watched her until she disappeared through the front doors before calling Donlon on his cell phone. Inside, Anita stood by the counter. She looked edgy, eagerly waiting for the female clerk to finish with her current customer.

"May I help you?" she asked.

"Yes. I'm looking for Miles Fischer. He's a guest here at the hotel."

A male clerk sitting behind the counter overheard the request and pointed in the direction of the lounge.

"I just saw him go into the Fireside Room about five minutes ago."

Anita hastily excused herself and walked into the lounge, in the direction of Fischer. Miles was alone, sitting at one of the tables in the far corner. There was no one within ten feet of him. He was drinking a rum and Coke and reading the faxes. It was at that moment that he looked up and spotted Anita approaching him. He quickly folded the fax sheets and slipped them into his pants pocket.

"Mr. Fischer, I think it's time you and I had a little talk."

Anita pulled out one of the chairs and sat down.

"Ms. Paletti! This is a surprise. What brings you here?"

"You do, Mr. Fischer. And there's no need to stare. I'm quite aware it's there."

"My apologies, but I wasn't staring at your scar. It's just strange seeing you here sitting at my table."

"That's funny, Mr. Fischer. I was thinking the same thing about you being here in Seattle."

"I'd prefer it if you called me Miles."

"No. Mr. Fischer will do. This meeting isn't under the same circumstances as our previous meeting, Mr. Fischer. Contrary to what you might be thinking, this isn't what you would call a social visit."

"Why am I not surprised?" he said, sipping his drink.

"Good. Then we're on the same page."

"Can I get you drink?" he asked.

"No, thank you. I prefer to order my own."

"Suit yourself."

"My sources tell me you've been a very busy man, Mr. Fischer. I was told you were at my sister's place the other day. Do you want to tell me what exactly you were doing there?"

"It was a nice day. I thought I would go for a ride."

"I hardly expect your newspaper to fly you all the way out here from Chicago just so you could go for a ride, Mr. Fischer. My sister's neighbor said he saw you looking in my sister's mailbox."

"Ned?"

"Yes, Ned. Why were you at my sister's place? What were you doing snooping in her mailbox?

"That's rather a harsh term, don't you think?"

"Where I come from, looking into someone's mailbox is snooping, Mr. Fischer. It's invading one's privacy—or maybe you don't think so?"

"I wouldn't call it snooping, Ms. Paletti. In the newspaper business, we like to call it investigating." He took a gulp of his rum and Coke.

"Call it what you want, Mr. Fischer. What I want to know is why you were at my sister's house."

A waitress hovered nearby and then made her way to the table.

"Bourbon, straight up," she ordered.

"Bourbon is a pretty strong drink for a woman."

"Don't get cute with me, Mr. Fischer. It won't work. I've handled stronger and harder things in my life than bourbon and a reporter who has a hard time with the truth. What were you doing there?" she asked again.

"Well, since you asked—I'm working on a story, but I don't think you would be interested."

"Why don't you let me be the judge of that?"

Miles took a slow sip of his drink.

"Have you ever heard of a town called Tweeksbury?"

"No. Should I?"

"There was a double murder there about two weeks ago." Miles watched closely for any change in her expression, any change in her facial features that could possibly give him a hint that she knew what he was talking about. "A couple of guys by the name of Lionel Holt and David Masalla were found dead in the parking lot of one of the bars there. They were killed with a crossbow."

"So what does that have to do with my sister?"

"About a year ago, two teenage girls were found in the forest not far from Tweeksbury by some hikers out for a day of hiking. They were strung up on some trees like you would find bats in a cave. They were raped, and then their throats were slashed. Before the killers left, they doused their bodies in bleach to hide any evidence.

Holt and Masalla were later charged and tried for their deaths. After a three-week trial, they were acquitted of all charges. Five days later, they were found in the parking lot."

"That's awful," she said. "For the girls, I mean."

"Yes, it is."

"But that doesn't explain what you were doing at my sister's house."

The waitress reappeared with Anita's drink. Miles sipped from his while Anita paid for hers. They both waited for the waitress to leave.

"You haven't answered my question."

"I'm investigating those two murders. I believe they're part of a bigger story."

"And what story would that be, Mr. Fischer?"

"When I got back to Chicago after covering their trial, I had my assistant do some digging. She found what happened to you and your daughter in the archives— yours and another one with similar circumstances that happened in a place called Whatley."

"What do you mean, similar circumstances?"

"I'm not at liberty to say, but the similarities are compelling, to say the least."

"And you think my sister is involved?"

"They're all unsolved, Ms. Paletti, sitting cold in some file somewhere, so that makes anyone who is remotely related a suspect. All I know is that these killings involved the use of a crossbow in the commission of these murders, which is highly unusual since Americans prefer guns over arrows. The last time a crossbow was used to kill someone took place just over six years ago. That was in Whatley. And the time before that, it was in Chester Junction. The use of a crossbow never came into play until what happened in Eastbrook.

Do you see my point? Everything originates from the first."

"That's quite a theory, Mr. Fischer."

"Facts don't lie, Ms. Paletti."

Anita glared at him after reading between the lines.

"You're not interested in my sister, are you, Mr. Fischer? You think I did it," she stated with a steely look. "That's why you're here in Seattle and why you were snooping around my sister's place. You were hoping to ask my sister some questions about me, but instead, you got her neighbor, Ned. You must have been awfully disappointed that my sister wasn't home."

Fischer offered no response.

"So is that it? You suspect me?"

"Like I said, everyone remotely connected to these killings is a suspect."

"So I guess you want me to tell you I didn't do it. That way I could walk away from this table reassured that I'm no longer on your list of suspects, which would only make you suspect me more since that's what all killers would say, that they didn't do it—isn't that so? Isn't that right, Mr. Fischer? Or that somehow I should feel sorry for what happened to those two pigs in Chester Junction. That would give me that human touch you reporters so desperately look for, that vulnerable, soft, warm and fuzzy feeling necessary to sell your stories to the highest bidder, to exclude myself as the killer. Is that what you want? Is that it?" she asked, almost taunting him.

"You can tell me whatever it is you want to tell me, Ms. Paletti," he said calmly. "I'm investigating multiple murders, so I'm interested in what anybody has to say."

Miles noticed Donlon standing stationary in the doorway. He watched with interest as Donlon made his way to an empty stool at the corner of the bar, not far from where he and Anita were sitting.

"Well, then write this, Mr. Reporter. I didn't kill those two lowlifes. Oh, I thought about it, all right," she said, her eyes glowing. "I thought about it from the moment it happened even though I couldn't remember what they looked like. I dreamed it. I must have killed them a thousand times in my sleep, and not once did I ever regret how it felt. They took everything of what I had left. They should burn in hell for what they did to me and my daughter," she growled angrily. "Did I kill them? No! But I sure wish I had because I had it all planned, and never would I have felt anything for it. If you want something to write, Mr. Know-it-all Reporter, you can write that."

The bourbon sat untouched, and the chair was empty, still warm from where she sat just a moment ago. Miles watched as she strode briskly past Donlon and the bar and then disappeared into the lobby. From his seat, Donlon had watched it all, hearing snippets of their conversation, including Anita's outburst at being considered a suspect and her subsequent reaction and denial. He watched her leave and then looked back at Miles, who hadn't moved. Donlon placed his hat back on his head and then left his stool and walked out.

Hamza and Katayoon stayed close but watched from a distance in different clothes as Bruno enjoyed the feelings of the rye whiskey as it washed over him. He had been a good boy by not drinking and doing a good day's work. He was owed, and he was now drinking his reward The Fijian and the tall Moroccan sipped club soda in a corner deep inside the lounge of the Edgewater and played cards while Carboni sat at the corner of the bar, close to the door, and ordered one after another. Bruno had one more errand to run before he would call Holt with the good news. He needed to see Angelina Paletti smoking, and she had to be smoking the same brand of cigarette as the ones sitting in his wallet. When she did, he would make the call.

It was almost one when he finally left his stool for the elevator and his room on the third floor. He had plans. He would be back on Vashon Island at first sailing. He would tail her all day if he had to.

Chapter 45

He had only slept for an hour when the phone rang. When it rang, every muscle in his body twitched in unison like he had been hit by a bolt of lightning. It rang again, and he cracked open one of his eyes, sneaking a peek to determine whether it was still night or day, whether he had actually heard the phone ring, or if it had all been a dream. The room was dark, no light except what crept through the window. *I must have been dreaming*, he thought, but it rang again. Fischer grudgingly reached for the cell phone and put it to his ear.

"Hello," he said groggily.

"Miles. It's Clint. Did I wake you?"

"What time is it?" Miles asked. His brain was still half-asleep.

"Nine o'clock. Why?"

Miles flicked on the light sitting on the night table and sat at the side of the bed in his boxer shorts while checking his watch, which said it was midnight.

"No reason."

"I've got that information you were looking for."

Information? Suddenly Miles's ears perked up. *Oh yeah, Clint. Clint Gladstone.* The fog was lifting.

"It wasn't easy, but I got it."

"What did you find out?" he asked, rubbing his eyes.

"They were in the army just like you thought, but that shouldn't come as a surprise since its mandatory anyway."

"They could have gotten an exemption," he said, almost from memory.

"They could have, but they didn't. It's kind of frowned on if you don't serve, whether you're a woman or not."

"When did they enlist?"

"It was in 1973. After their basic training, they both ended up doing administrative duties since women can't serve in a combat role—at least not yet."

Miles was standing and now fully alert.

"Hold it, Clint. Did you just say that both sisters enlisted at the same time?"

"Yeah, in 1973. Why?"

"Are you sure you got your facts right?"

"That's what they told me."

"How is that possible?"

"What do you mean?"

"They have to be at least a year apart. One of them would have had to enlist at least a year before or a year after the other one."

"Usually that would be the case, Miles, but they're twins."

There was a long pause, a slight hesitation in Miles's speech as his mind went into shock.

"What do you mean, they're twins?" he asked.

"They're twins, Miles. In fact, they're identical twins, born five minutes apart. The real term is monozygotic twins, which means they're identical. I take it you didn't know. You sound a little surprised."

"Are you sure?"

It had never occurred to him. From all the people he had talked to, not once had anybody ever mentioned the fact that the Paletti sisters were twins, never mind identical twins.

"Positive."

Clint's quick affirmation was like being hit over the head with a rubber mallet. *Identical twins? Son-of-a-bitch!* Miles sucked in a deep breath and held it.

"Miles?"

No reply.

"Miles. Are you still there?"

"Yeah, I'm still here," he replied softly, letting the air drift from his lungs. "So that's how she did it," he said, letting the thought reach the receiver.

"What are you talking about?"

"Nothing—forget it. What else did they tell you?"

"I thought this was kind of strange, but one of the sisters enlisted using her mother's maiden name."

"Which one?"

"Angelina."

"Did they tell you why?"

"Sorry, I didn't bother to ask. Is it important?"

Miles didn't answer.

"Sorry, buddy. Whatever it is you're working on, it must be one hell of a story."

"Let's just say it's rather complicated."

"Well, I hope it works out for you. I guess I should let you go so you can get back to sleep. Sorry to have awakened you. I'll talk to you later. And don't forget about the wedding. I want you there with me."

"I won't forget," he said, rubbing his forehead. "Before you go, which of the two sisters is the eldest?"

"Anita."

"Thanks, Clint. I'll talk to you soon."

Miles slapped his cell phone shut and then tossed it on the bed and immediately headed for the minibar. *Might as well have a drink*, he thought. He was going to be up for a while anyway after this latest bombshell.

Chapter 46

Even though he stayed up late and slept little, Bruno made good on his promise to be on the first ferry destined for Vashon Island. It was important he be there as early as possible if he was going to have any chance of following Angelina Paletti. If he wasn't there at daybreak, he might as well forget about it. She could be gone, doing whatever, so being late was not an option.

Today of all days, he felt luckier than usual. In his gut, he felt this would be the day that he would be able to tie it all together and then call Holt with the good news. Bruno was all too familiar with addiction and the urges that went with it. He had been drinking and smoking for most of his life. He smoked two packs a day, and one day it would kill him if the booze didn't get him first. With addiction came urges, and sooner or later she would have no choice but to light up. When she did, he would be there to see it and scoop up the evidence. But the trick was to catch her at it first.

The plan was simple. All he had to do was tail her without being seen and catch her in the act, stalk her like some jilted lover until the urge hit and then wait until she was finished. When she was, he would be there waiting in the shadows to scoop up the butt and match it to what was in his wallet, and then he would call Holt and hightail it back to Chicago.

Bruno sat in his rental car just up an adjoining street from Angelina Paletti's house. He was far enough away not to draw attention to himself should she happen to look out from behind her front window. Through his binoculars, he could see the driveway and most of the house. A shiny, bright red truck was parked in the driveway just beyond the gates. Bruno settled in for what could be a long wait. He notched his seat back a degree or two and then turned on the radio to help pass the time, but he kept it low. One block away, up another adjoining street, Holt's two men sat patiently and quietly in a white sedan, having ditched the use of a taxi for the freedom of a rental.

It was almost eleven when Angelina Paletti closed the front door and pulled out of the driveway in her shiny Ford pickup. Bruno waited, taking one last drink before flicking the menthol past the open window. Wiping away the booze from his lips, he stuffed the bottle back into the brown paper bag and pushed it under the seat, next to the binocular case. A reflex camera with a telephoto lens lay on the seat next to him. Keeping his large brown eyes fixed to the bumper of the shiny red truck, he eased down the road in slow pursuit. Behind, the Fijian Hamza pulled away from the shoulder of the road while Katayoon sat in the passenger seat. They would ride in back of the three-vehicle procession as Paletti made her way to the ferry and her luncheon date with her sister. On the ferry, Ali Hamza and Mospoli Katayoon stayed in their car while Angelina, with Carboni stalking her from behind, strode the upper deck of the ferry.

Miles was up but still at the hotel by the time ten o'clock rolled around. He had been awake most of the night, plotting the pros and cons of each sister's possible involvement in the crossbow killings, trying to figure out how being identical twins figured in all of this or whether it really mattered before he finally fell asleep. He still believed that Anita was the one who had been sitting next to him in the courtroom when Holt and Masalla were acquitted in the rape and murder of Michelle King and Heather Burton. It was Anita who after months of suffering a case of amnesia finally began to recapture her memory even though she denied knowing what they looked like and then plotted to do away with the two men who had raped and killed her daughter and left her to bleed to death behind Grayson's gas station. It was Anita who went to Tweeksbury instead of the Caribbean to take out Lionel Holt and David Masalla. Why else did she not exhibit any hint of a tan when he did the interview? It was Anita who had the motive. It was the brutal rape and murder of her daughter, the shared birth dates of the other victims, and the manner in which the girls were slaughtered that for some reason sent her off the edge of a cliff to commit these killings of revenge. The business of Two-Faced Productions gave her the means by which she could go about the business of killing without being noticed. It was Anita who had used that very means to disguise herself as someone else and send the arrow, the same type of arrow as the two that killed Holt and Masalla, in order to persuade him to drop his investigation into who was committing these acts of revenge. It was Anita who had lost the most. Didn't the caller tell Tony he was on the right track? How did the killer know it was Thornton and Patrick who raped and murdered Rachel and left her mother for dead if there were no witnesses? The only person who had witnessed the brutal rape was Anita. There was no one else.

By morning, Miles had it all figured out as to how she could have done it—he had plotted out a theory as to how she could have killed Holt and Masalla without being detected. It was Angelina and not Anita who went to the Caribbean. After reading or hearing about it, Anita had watched the court case of Lionel Holt and David Masalla as it unfolded and proceeded through the court system. As it got closer to the trial date, she planned and then booked the vacation to the Caribbean, but instead of going, she offered it to her sister at the last minute as some sort of a gift after giving her some lame excuse as to why she couldn't go. Her name would show up on the passenger list, but her sister would take her place. It would give her the perfect alibi if she was ever questioned as to where she was when Holt and Masalla were killed. When her sister questioned her about the difference in the names, she brushed it aside and offered to swap her ID with hers. They were identical twins, so it wouldn't matter. Nobody was able to tell them apart. It was the perfect solution to an unfeasible trip to the Caribbean. Since Angelina was doing Anita a favor by going on the trip, Anita offered to stay at the house and take care of the horses while she was gone. Anita probably drove her to the airport using Angelina's vehicle and then drove back to Angelina's place, which meant Anita would have left her own vehicle at the airport the day before Angelina was scheduled to leave. If Angelina questioned her as to where her vehicle was, she could have given the excuse that it was at the shop being worked on. When the court went into deliberation, she left Angelina's vehicle at the airport before she left for Tweeksbury with her own vehicle and then called the hotel where her sister was staying and left a message telling her that her vehicle was parked at the airport. And in all that time, neither Ned nor any other neighbor would know a thing. They would have seen the red truck parked in the driveway and presume the rest. Anita only had a small window of opportunity to take out Holt and Masalla because she had to be back in Seattle on or before the day her sister got back. Anita had to be incredibly lucky. If Holt and Masalla had stayed off the streets a little longer, she would have had to abandon her plans of taking Holt and Masalla out and save it for another time.

It was a wonderful hypothesis. It even sounded good, especially to him, but it came with its problems. He couldn't prove any of it. There was no way he could prove if everything he knew and assumed had actually taken place. If Anita's name was on the passenger list, then he couldn't prove that it was Anita sitting next to him in the courtroom. It would be his word against Anita's. Then there was Ned, the neighbor. He said he had seen Angelina at home during the time of the trial even though he never actually talked to her. For all he knew, it was Angelina he had waved to. Anita never delivered the arrow to the courier company, either, according to whomever Sally talked to. Jackson Henshaw did.

By noon, Miles was finally dressed. He had a few places to visit, but he didn't expect anything major to come of them. Anita Paletti had insulated herself well from the onslaught of any investigation. With no clues and no witnesses, there was simply no trail, just a lot of assumption as to how she could have done it. There was some fact but no hard evidence to back it up. Even if her name wasn't on the passenger list, it still didn't prove that she was actually there, sitting next to him, though she might have a hard time explaining exactly where she was when Holt and Masalla were killed.

He was running out of options, and he knew it. For the first time since he arrived, he was starting to feel lost as to how to go about putting her in the spotlight, maybe even forcing her into a corner where she couldn't escape if the anonymous caller never called back or if Veronica's search produced no results.

Miles locked the door to his room and headed for the

fresh air outside, where he knew Donlon would be waiting. He was about to do something by involving the thin man, figuring he had no choice. He needed something—something he couldn't get on his own. He only hoped he wouldn't regret it later.

"Christ, Fischer! I thought you'd be gone by now and we'd be tailing you from behind. What's your problem? No good news today?"

"Nah, just taking a break," he replied, stretching. "I thought I would come outside and hang with you boys for a while." Miles leaned on the car next to Donlon. Henley was off to the side. "So tell me," he said, "what have you and Henley got planned for the day?"

"That all depends on what you do. Where you go, we go."

"I thought as much. I noticed you were in the bar last night," he said, nodding.

"Yeah, but what I don't understand is why you're bothering her, Fischer? We already checked her out. She's clean. There's nothing there."

He crossed his arms. "What makes you so sure?"

"What's this, Fischer? Am I detecting a change in your attitude?"

"Not really. It's a logical question. After all, I am a reporter."

"Yeah, but not a very good one."

"See, Donlon, there's your problem."

"What problem is that, Fischer?"

"You have to learn to be a little more sociable. I came out here thinking that maybe we could exchange a little information."

Donlon removed the wrapper from a piece of gum and stuck it in his mouth. He was skeptical as to Fischer's motive, this sudden change in his demeanor.

"Information, huh? Just what do you have in mind?"

"What if someone could place her in the courtroom at the time of Holt and Masalla's acquittal?"

"That's a mighty big 'if,' Fischer."

"What about it?"

"This person of yours—do they have a name?"

"That's not important right now."

"Could this person identify her in a lineup?"

"Yeah, but it's a little more complicated than that."

"How complicated?"

"When this person saw her, she was in disguise."

"Disguise, huh? What kind of a disguise?"

"She was dressed up as a farmer."

"Hmm. If this mysterious person of yours saw her and she was in a disguise, then how do you know it was her?"

"From the scar on her neck."

"But you said she was in disguise."

"Yeah, but what if she didn't completely conceal her scar?"

"What are you getting at, Fischer?"

"It just so happens that I did an interview with her about two weeks ago because the guy who was supposed to do the interview couldn't make it."

"Yeah, we know. She told us something about you being there to conduct an interview about the business," said Henley.

"When I turned up to do the interview, she wasn't there because she was running late. It turns out she was on vacation. According to her assistant, the office had been closed for three weeks."

"So what? Everybody goes on vacation."

"Yeah, I know, but she wasn't in the Caribbean. If I were you," he said, not wanting to divulge everything at this moment, "I'd check the passenger list on that flight to the Caribbean. When you do, give me a call and we'll talk."

Miles started to head up the street.

"Hold on, Fischer. Something isn't right. I thought you had this all figured out?"

"I do," he said, turning around. "I just can't prove anything. At least not yet."

"So I take it you're looking for our help?"

"Check the passenger list, and then we'll talk," he stated, walking backwards.

"What's the…"

"Just check the list, Donlon. You'll get your chance to quiz me later." He turned and headed towards his car.

"Where are you headed?"

"South, I think. There are a couple of places I want to check out." He stopped and looked back at Donlon and Henley, who were still leaning against the car. "I take it you and Henley are still coming along for the ride?"

"We'll check it out, but yeah, we're still going to tail ya."

Anita and Angelina Paletti were at the Il Terrazzo Carmine restaurant, sitting on the patio outside. When Carboni saw them together for the first time, his jaw nearly dropped along with the binoculars. They were the same height with the same curves, the same cheek bones, and the same brown eyes. Even their hair was the same. Bruno quickly snapped off two pictures of the twins and then placed the camera back on the seat. He was lucky, he thought. Without knowing ahead of time what Angelina was wearing, there was no way he would have been able to tell them apart.

They had been there for almost two hours, and Angelina had yet to draw a cigarette from her purse and

349

put it to her lips. How could she? The two sisters were deeply involved in a conversation that seemed to never stop from the moment they sat down. They barely made time to eat.

The topic of their conversation started with Miles Fischer. They had already touched on his being at Angelina's house when she called Anita the day before, but now it was a full-blown discussion into how they were going to deal with him. Fischer was prying into their lives, lives they liked to keep private. They knew nothing about Tweeksbury or Whatley and what had happened there other than what they had read in the newspapers, or in Anita's case, what Fischer had told her in the bar, but even then it was sketchy. Eastbrook and what happened in Chester Junction was barely mentioned. After eight years it was still painful and difficult to talk about, especially for Anita, so why bring it up? Angelina mentioned something about going to the police, but Anita nixed the idea. They could handle Fischer themselves, she said. He was nothing more than a minor nuisance, and sooner or later he would get tired and go back to Chicago, but in the meantime, they should keep their eyes and ears open. If he stepped foot on Angelina's or Anita's property, they would go straight to the authorities and get a restraining order.

Anita told her sister about her visit with Miles Fischer at the Sorrento Hotel, which brought a barrage of negative remarks from both sisters before Angelina told Anita what her neighbor had witnessed earlier that day. There had been another intruder on her property, only it wasn't Fischer this time. Ned had watched him lumber up the driveway and then crawl through the gate before taking off in a blue compact. Another rental, he said. He mentioned the two characters in the taxi who followed Carboni's car past her house soon after. They weren't African Americans as far as he could tell. They looked more Middle Eastern. Angel had been watching the road through her rearview mirror ever since she left the house to come to the restaurant. The fact that this character had invaded her privacy—that he may have combed the grounds of her property without her being there—made her feel violated and angry. Although she hadn't seen him, he was probably out there now, him and the other two, watching.

Bruno was there, all right, sitting in his car just down the street with the binoculars up to his face. He was far enough away that it would be hard for Angelina to see him, let alone catch him. He had been watching the sisters for over an hour and a half, and yet nothing had happened. It was becoming painfully clear to Bruno that Angelina Paletti was nothing more than a social smoker, a part-timer who smoked only when she felt like it and not because of a deepening urge that could send the strongest-willed person scurrying for a cigarette. She seemed too busy talking with her sister to light up, which caused him considerable consternation. The odd time she did stop, it was to look out onto the street as if she was looking for something or someone, but then she would go back to talking with Anita. Never once did she reach into her purse to pull out a cigarette. The sisters had barely touched their food. Whatever it was they were discussing, it seemed more important than what was on their plates.

Impatient, Bruno ditched his vehicle and his binoculars and jaywalked to the other side of the street, under the observing eyes of Hamza and Katayoon, careful not to be seen before hiding behind a building close to the terrace. When he peeked around the corner, a waiter was at their table. He left them the bill and then carted himself off inside the restaurant somewhere. Minutes later, both sisters finished what wine remained in their glasses and casually walked back into the restaurant.

Bruno watched the entrance. Ten minutes later, they still hadn't emerged. His immediate thought was that there was another way out of the restaurant or that they may have gone to the ladies room first, but they should have been out by now. Curious, Bruno headed towards the restaurant. When he was just past the building, the Paletti sisters finally stepped into the sunlight.

"*Merda!*" he cursed.

Bruno suddenly felt naked. He quickly turned to his right and then bent down to tie his shoelaces, which were already tied. That's when the skateboarder hit him, sending the kid head over heels in front of him and leaving Bruno flat on his stomach. The kid was facedown but moving. A small crowd formed around them. A lady attended to the youth, who was already sitting and rubbing his knee, while another stared at Bruno and asked him if he was okay. Bruno quickly picked himself up and then briskly helped the teen to his feet before giving him a short lecture to watch where the hell he was going. The young teen cursed him loudly and then took off down the sidewalk, his skateboard back under his feet. The crowd dispersed, and that's when Bruno noticed Angel some forty feet away. She and her sister were talking as if they hadn't noticed the minor mishap, saying their good-byes. They hugged each other, and when Angel turned to leave, that's when he saw it. It was lit and hanging from her hand. He quickly retreated and then hastened back towards his car, keeping his eye on Angel, who was headed in the other direction towards her truck.

From his car he watched Anita Paletti drive back in the direction of downtown while Angelina Paletti pulled away from the curb, tossing her cigarette past the open window before heading in the direction of Lincoln Park and the Fauntleroy Ferry. Bruno waited until he could no longer see the bright red truck before crossing the street and scooping the butt from the pavement amidst the traffic. He stood on the sidewalk and turned it to where he could see the fine print. A broad smile etched itself across his thick face, spreading the deep lines on either side of his heavy cheeks. Home was just a phone call away.

Chapter 47

Fischer had little choice but to involve the FBI. He didn't know if he had made the right decision or not when he confided in Donlon, but he was near a dead end. At the moment, he couldn't prove anything. Anita Paletti had insulated herself from the law and the scrutiny of suspicion and committed what she thought was the perfect crime. Much like Houdini himself, who had perfected the art of illusion, Anita had unwittingly crafted the art of killing without being detected simply by having an identical twin. Anita had skillfully used the art of illusion by exchanging IDs with her sister, giving her the perfect cover so she could go about administering her form of vigilante justice without being discovered. Miles fully expected that once Donlon checked the passenger list, Anita's name would be there even though he knew she never went to the Caribbean.

Searching the passenger list was just a formality, one more piece to a complex puzzle that had to be checked out if he was ever going to write the complete story on how she did it. Donlon was just another source, an unwitting one, but a source just the same. There was no way Miles could get a look at the passenger list, but Donlon and the FBI could.

He had already factored in what the caller had told Big Tony. Whether Anita had DID or not, it played no major role in his decision to talk to Donlon. If anything, it only proved that Anita had a problem, presuming that the caller was talking about Anita, but it didn't tie her to any of the scenes where the crimes were committed. The only one who could do that was the person who had called the *Tribune* after looking at her file. She had told Big Tony that the file contained the stories on what happened in

Eastbrook and Whatley along with pages of notes taken during the discussions. If one of the sister's wasn't involved then why was that information in the file, especially about what happened in Whatley and Tweeksbury? What was the connection? What was the point of making the phone call if neither of the Paletti sisters was involved? But that was the point. They were— at least one of them anyway. He didn't know for sure but there was probably a good chance that the caller knew more than what she had told Big Tony. Just like he had done to Donlon, the caller had only given what was needed in order for Miles to continue on with his investigation as to who killed Holt and Masalla before hanging up. As for her calling back, he wasn't holding his breath because she would have called back by now. He could talk to Anita's sister if he wanted, but there was little chance that Angelina would be forthright with any information that would incriminate her sister, especially about who took the flight to the Caribbean. After all, they were twins, identical twins, and blood was thicker than water.

At the moment, there was little choice but to try and stay positive and keep digging if he wanted any chance of connecting Anita with the crimes and being the first to expose the truth of what really happened in Tweeksbury and all that happened before it. All he needed was a little luck—the same kind of luck that Anita had.

Telling Donlon everything was not in his best interests, at least not yet. Telling him everything would have meant giving up control of a story he so desperately wanted to write. If he told Donlon everything, the roles would be reversed, and Miles would be following the FBI and not the other way around. If and when he ran out of options, he would make a deal and tell Donlon everything, but only if they had a deal.

Miles found the courier company on Findlay Street next to a hydraulic lift shop and a small blasting company. Donlon and Henley had followed him, just like they said they would. Fischer parked his vehicle in the parking lot in front of the building and then went inside. Donlon and Henley parked across the street and waited.

"Excuse me. I'm looking for the person who may have handled a package that was delivered to the *Chicago Tribune*," he said.

"Is there something wrong?" asked the clerk behind the counter.

"No, everything is fine. I just want to talk to the person who handled the placement."

"What day did you receive it?"

"Last Monday."

The clerk checked the monitor. After tapping the keys a few times, he said, "That would be Thelma. Hold on." Miles watched as the clerk headed to a door. "Thelma, there's somebody here to see you."

Miles watched as a rather tall and bulky woman approached him. There was no smile, and her body language said she didn't want to be here.

"You Thelma?" he asked.

With her thick finger, she pointed to the plate bearing her name high on her left breast.

"Are you the one who handled a request to ship a package to the *Chicago Tribune*?"

She thought about it for a moment and then said, "Yeah. What about it?"

"Do you remember the person who brought it in?"

"Yeah. Some old guy with a cane. Why? Did he have a coronary and die?" She said this with a straight face.

"No, nothing like that," he said, barely cracking a

smile.

"Then why are you here? I asked him if he wanted to put a return address on it, but he declined. It was too much of a bother, I guess. Why you asking? Did they not get it? Because nothing has come back saying they didn't," she said defensively.

"No, no. They got it. In fact, *I* got it. It was sent to me. I was just curious as to who sent it. You said an old man brought it in. Do you remember what he looked like?"

"He was old with a lot of wrinkles. What else can I tell ya? Old people look the same to me."

"Can you describe him a little better than that?"

"I ain't promising you anything, but sure. What do you want to know?"

"How tall was he?"

"If he was to stand straight, I guess he would come up to about here on me," she said, pointing to the space between her large breasts.

"Weight?"

"He couldn't have weighed more than a hundred and ten pounds."

"What about the face?"

"I already told you—it was wrinkled."

"Did you happen to notice anything unusual, like a scar?"

"What's unusual about a scar? Lots of people have them."

"Yes, they do, but this one runs from one side of the neck to the other. Did you happen to see it?"

"Should I have?"

"Well, that all depends. It would be pretty hard not to notice it."

"Well, I wasn't looking at him that hard." She

shrugged her shoulders.

"Just yes or no will do."

"Then the answer is no. Look, mister, I don't know who you are or anything. You could be a company inspector, for all I know. For me, I just want to come in here, do my job, and go home. Is that okay with you?"

"Yeah, that's fine, but I'm not who you think I am." Miles slipped her one of his cards to put her at ease, thinking it may help her memory. "Does that help you?"

Thelma glanced at it and gave it back to him. "My answer is still no. Now, anything else I can help you with?"

"I can't think of anything. Thanks for your help."

"No problem."

Thelma left and headed back towards the door. Miles watched her leave, a little disappointed in her attitude, and then he did the same and headed for his car.

Donlon and Henley were still following him as he headed for the Lake Washington Bridge that connected Mercer Island with the rest of Seattle. There was something he had to do before Donlon came back at him and told him that Anita's name was on the passenger list. He needed to tie up a loose end. He needed to talk to some of her neighbors—see if she was home during the trial and the aftermath that followed. She may have her name on that list, but she also may have come home during that time, if only for a minute.

He was on the island, on Eighty-fourth Avenue, headed south just past Pioneer Park when his cell phone rang. He opened it like you would a clam and pressed it to his ear. It was Veronica.

"Where are you?" she asked. She was excited. He could tell from the tone in her voice, which brought on an excitement of his own.

"I'm on the road. Why?"

"You're not going to believe what I have to tell you. It seems you were right," she said. "The sisters didn't have a very good home life when they were growing up. According to the authorities in Zikhron Ya'akov, their father sexually abused them up until his death. Get this. He was poisoned, and they suspected the two sisters. They questioned them about the poisoning, but no charges were filed. When I asked them why, they said they didn't know for sure because they only suspected them, and besides, they were too young to be prosecuted. That's how they found out about the sexual abuse. When they were questioning them, it all came out."

Miles's heart was thumping wildly. He was hardly breathing as he listened.

"Hold on a minute."

Miles quickly glanced in the mirror and then pulled over to the curb. He put the car in park but left the motor running. He noticed the white sedan pull to the side, about a hundred feet back.

"How old were the two sisters when this happened?"

"Nine."

"Where was the mother when all of this took place?"

"She died from an illness two years earlier, but the sexual abuse started when they were five. It seems the mother either didn't know or did nothing about it. Mr. Leibovitz was a prominent storekeeper in his neighborhood and was held in high regard, but from what I was told, he could be a real mean son-of-a-bitch at times, especially towards women, which brings me back to the mother. I talked to the aunt who raised the two girls after the death of their father, and she told me that he used to beat her sister. I guess she was too afraid of him to say anything to the authorities about the sexual abuse that went on while she was alive. Christ! How many times have we heard that one?"

"Too many times. Did they say which daughter may have actually killed Mr. Leibovitz?"

"I asked the Zikhron Ya'akov police who they thought had the capacity to kill the father, and they said it was too hard to tell. They talked to both girls, together and separately, but nothing came of it."

"What about other suspects?"

"They didn't have anybody other than the girls. The sexual abuse was their prime motive for suspecting them. Mr. Leibovitz didn't have any enemies, according to what they told me."

"What was he poisoned with?"

"Sleeping pills and antidepressants. They found traces of them in his food. It seems Mr. Leibovitz suffered from major depression and a sleeping disorder. It's no wonder since he was beating his wife and molesting his daughters. I wouldn't be able to sleep, either."

"Was anyone else present when they were questioning them?"

"Yes. The aunt they were living with."

"And they didn't give you any inclination as to who they thought might have done it?"

"They couldn't tell because, according to them, the girls said they didn't know anything. I got the impression that they thought the girls may have been in on it together since they were both being molested, but they couldn't tell."

"That's kind of strange, don't you think? The father's dead, and yet neither of the girls knows anything."

"Yes, but what can you do? The girls were being molested, and there was nobody to help them. You know what they say about identical twins. They both feel the same things. I guess they were sticking up for each other. After their mother was gone, they only had each other to rely on. They certainly couldn't go to their father. If it was me, I would have done the same thing rather than put up with my father abusing me."

"What about a child psychologist? Was there one involved?"

"Yes, but those records are sealed."

"That's too bad. I would love to get my hands on them. Do you know if they got any professional help afterwards?"

"I was told that it was suggested to the aunt that she get them some help, but I don't know if she did because she hung up on me when I asked her if she knew which of the daughters poisoned their father. Other than that, I don't know. I couldn't find anyone who would tell me."

"It doesn't sound like it. If they had, then this DID thing wouldn't be an issue."

"Sorry, Miles. Was I too blunt? Isn't that how you reporters ask the tough questions? Just come right out and ask them?"

"As harsh as it may seem, yeah, that's how we do it."

"I never want to be a reporter," she said with a yawn.

"You sound tired."

"I am. I've been up most of the night talking to all these people, trying to get this information like you wanted. I didn't go in to work. I phoned and told them I was going to bed."

"Sorry, Veronica. I'll make it up to you. I promise."

"I'm too tired to think about it right now. But if I remember tomorrow I'm going to hold you to it."

"If you don't, I'll remind you," he said almost laughing. "Before the aunt hung up, did she say anything else?"

"She really didn't want to talk to me at first, so I had to be careful about what I asked her. When I was talking to her, I asked her if either of the girls ever talked about their father, and she told me that his name rarely came up. She didn't push it because of what happened to them."

"What about their neighbors?"

"I got to talk to an old neighbor who has since moved to Natanya, and he confirmed everything I just told you about the poisoning and the husband beating Mrs. Leibovitz. He was shocked when I mentioned the sexual abuse. It seems nobody knew about it. He made a comment that I thought was interesting. He told me that Anita was the one who always took care of her little sister. You know how big brothers always look out for their younger siblings. Well, Anita was her protector, if that's what you want to call it. Also, before the aunt hung up on me, I asked her if there were any marked changes in the girls since the death of both parents, and she said that when the mother died, both girls withdrew."

"What do you mean, they withdrew?"

"They became more closed in their ability to show their feelings. They didn't express them very well. After their mother died, when the aunt and uncle would visit, the girls were very quiet. She said the girls really relied on each other more than anybody in the family after their mother's death."

"Sounds like they're pretty close."

"That's what it sounded like to me too."

"It also sounds like the mother was their only source of protection, for what it was worth, even though it sounds like she didn't do a very good job."

"Yes. It's sad, isn't it?"

"Did the aunt and uncle know that the girls were being sexually abused?"

"Not until the death of the father. That's when it all came out. She said something that was a little strange. She said that the girls had always hugged their uncle when they saw him, but after the abuse started, they no longer would go up to him and hug him unless the aunt coaxed them into giving him a hug. She said this really hurt her husband. She could never figure out why until she and her husband found out about the sexual abuse. Until the day she left her aunt's house, Anita never hugged her uncle again whereas Angelina did."

"Every child acts differently."

"I guess, but I thought that children that young who fall into a cycle of sexual abuse wouldn't know what's right or wrong, considering how young they were when it first started. I thought they would hug their uncle, regardless. I don't know; I could be wrong."

"I don't know either, Veronica. I wish I did. I guess Anita was the most traumatized of the two."

"Actually, no. The aunt told me that Angelina seemed to be the most traumatized by the death of her father. Of the two, she said Anita was the one who was most in control of her emotions—too much control for her liking. She said Angelina at least cried when her mother and father passed away. Anita never did."

Angelina Paletti parked her truck behind the gated driveway before saddling Bolt for a ride along the quiet streets behind Ellisport. The presence of an investigator prying into her life left her uncomfortable and angry. The long discussion over lunch with her sister and seeing the thick man who fit the description that Ned gave her crouched on the sidewalk pretending to tie his shoelaces before being knocked over by a skateboarder brought it to the forefront in front of the restaurant. Angel had told Anita she would take care of the intruder and his two shadows herself, and so she rode, thinking what she would do if they turned up at her doorstep a second time.

Fischer was on his bed, thinking about the two Paletti sisters. He had arrived back at the hotel at around seven after talking to some of Anita's neighbors. Donlon and Henley had stayed in their car and watched from the sidelines as Fischer worked the neighborhood like a door-to-door salesman.

Two of her neighbors confirmed what he had already concluded. They hadn't seen Anita in three weeks. Her sister came and drove her to the airport. Anita had taken a vacation, and yes, it was to the Caribbean. One said she collected her mail while another had their son cutting her lawn.

While on the landing of another house, he noticed Anita roll up the street in her blue Beamer. She slowed it to a crawl when she saw Fischer and glared at him. The steely stare didn't go unnoticed by Fischer or the neighbor, who was already closing the door. He watched as she eased the BMW into the driveway before disappearing inside the house. That's when he decided to call it quits and left.

He was staring at the ceiling, trying to make sense out of what Veronica had told him over the phone. It was now conceivable to think that maybe—and this was only a maybe—that perhaps Angelina was somehow the one responsible for the murders of Holt and Masalla, especially after Veronica told him that either of the girls could have poisoned their father. It was now reasonable to assume that it could easily have been Angelina who was sitting next to him in the courtroom instead of Anita. The only problem with that belief was the scar. Had Angelina put it there intentionally in the event she was ever questioned as to who killed Holt and Masalla? Showing the scar would absolve her but implicate Anita should anybody have witnessed her sitting there, someone like Fischer. The thought then occurred to him that maybe it was meant to create mass confusion should anyone finger either of the Paletti sisters, much the same way that the police in Zikhron Ya'akov couldn't prove which of the sisters poisoned their father. Anita had an alibi. She was in the Caribbean. Her name would be on the passenger list even though he had yet to hear back from Donlon. So did Angelina. She had a witness in Ned, who said he saw her. Anita had the motive, but it was Angelina's name that popped up on the registry at the Down Range Shoot and Archery Club. Anita was the only witness to who killed Rachel and left her for dead. So did that mean that Anita had told her sister? If she did, then that meant she either didn't know when the police questioned her and remembered it all later as her memory regained its capacity to recall events, or she outright lied when they questioned her. That would partially explain her sister's involvement in the murder of Thornton and Patrick, but not the others. Angelina would have to have a motive, but there wasn't one—at least none that he could possibly think of. *Was that who the caller was talking about when she called and talked to Big Tony? Is Angelina the one who is suffering from DID?*

Miles closed his eyes and rubbed his temples to try and ward off the headache he could feel coming from all the possibilities that were starting to cloud his judgment as to who actually killed Holt and Masalla when the phone rang. It was Donlon.

"We checked the list like you suggested. She's on the list, Fischer. She left on the thirtieth of July and arrived back here on the twelfth."

"So you checked them both?"

"Yeah. I think we should get together and talk. What do you say?"

Miles checked his watch. It was seven forty-five.

"How about we meet in the lounge at around ten?"

"We'll be there," he said and hung up.

Miles pressed the button and then made a quick two-minute phone call to Clint.

From what he had been told, he said, both Paletti sisters' military records were clear of any damaging medical history. There was nothing in either of their files to suggest that there was anything wrong medically. Everything checked out, both their psychological and physical tests when they originally enlisted. If there was anything there, then in all probability they would never have been admitted to begin with. Angelina hadn't been treated for so much as a cold and neither had her sister.

Fischer hung up the phone and immediately headed for the bathroom to change. He decided he held what he thought was a trump card. He had a couple of hours to kill before he was supposed to meet with Donlon back at the hotel. He decided to play his hand and see what transpired without the thin man around. It was his last chance to nail the killer, or the story was dead and Anita was free. He had nothing to lose.

Chapter 48

Bruno Carboni stood by the edge of the bed in his room at the Edgewater with the phone in his ear, admiring the photos.

"Mr. Holt, its Bruno."

Benjamin Holt stood in his silk robe; his eyes were partially shut from the deep sleep the sudden call had awakened him from. His bodyguard, Gilles Stracker, stood by the door just off the hall.

"Yes, Mr. Carboni. I didn't expect to hear from you so soon."

"Yeah, well I didn't think I would be calling you this soon either, Ben, but everything fell into place, so here I am," he answered proudly.

"Yes, Mr. Carboni. Here you are," he replied derisively. "So what do you have to report?"

"It's done, Ben."

Holt slowly lowered his small frame into a thickly padded couch.

"Are you sure, Mr. Carboni?" He motioned to Gilles to fetch him a cigar.

"I'm sure, Ben."

"Well then, let's have it, Mr. Carboni."

"There's just one problem, Ben."

"What kind of a problem, Mr. Carboni?"

"I can't explain it, Ben. I can't figure out why they would want to kill your son. There has to be a reason."

"That's not our problem, Mr. Carboni. That's for the authorities to figure out. That's what they're paid for. Let's let them worry about it, shall we?"

"But there has to be motive, Ben. Do you see what I'm getting at?"

"I do, Mr. Carboni, but let's not make this any more

difficult than it is. This person obviously has no respect for the law. My son was falsely accused and then acquitted, proving his innocence. Whoever did this to my son is obviously deranged in some way. Let's let the authorities handle it, shall we? What I want from you is the name of this person so that they can get the proper justice they deserve."

There was a slight hesitation on Bruno's part before saying, "You're not going to do anything stupid, are you, Ben?"

"No. Why do you ask?"

"Good, because I wouldn't want anything to happen that shouldn't."

"I sense some doubt in your tone, but you don't have to worry, Mr. Carboni. I plan on going to the authorities, to bring it to the attention of the district attorney. I want this person prosecuted to the full extent of the law. Does that sound about right, Mr. Carboni? Isn't that what all good cops want? I'm sure once I have spoken to them they will be in touch with you, and you can provide them with all the details once this person is apprehended. But if it would make you feel any better, you can do it yourself. I have no objection, if that's what you're implying."

For Bruno, the thought of approaching the authorities with what he knew was less than appealing. He had no intention of getting involved in something that could affect him directly. There was the issue of him flashing a badge that was still supposedly lost. The name of Angelina Paletti meant nothing to him other than a paycheck. Besides, there was still of the issue of Holt making good on his promise to pay off Bruno's debts. Why ruffle his feathers?

"See that you do, Ben, otherwise I'll be going to the authorities myself."

"I give you my word, Mr. Carboni. A man is nothing if he doesn't keep his word. Are you a man of yours, Mr. Carboni?"

"Yeah, I am, Ben."

"Good, Mr. Carboni. The name—I want the name."

"It's Paletti—Angelina Paletti."

There was a slight hesitation, and then Holt said, "Excellent, Mr. Carboni! Excellent!" Holt moved to the edge of the plush cushion, ready to hang up the receiver. "This then concludes our business arrangement, Mr. Carboni."

"Hold on there, Ben," he ordered with noticeable indignation. "Not so fast. Aren't you forgetting something?"

"And what would that be, Mr. Carboni?"

Holt bit the end of the cigar, spitting it across the room before lighting it.

"You said you take care of those that do as you ask— or did you forget?" he asked with an utterance of annoyance.

"No, Mr. Carboni. I haven't forgotten. I take it this is about your debts?"

"That's right, Ben. You just said you were a man of your word."

"I am, Mr. Carboni. I will take care of you and your debts as promised. Is that what you wanted to hear, Mr. Carboni?"

"Yeah, Ben, that's exactly what I wanted to hear," he stated, his muscles beginning to relax.

"How much are we talking about, Mr. Carboni?"

"Fifty thousand, Ben."

"Fifty-two thousand to be exact, Mr. Carboni. That's a lot of money. You should learn to handle your money more wisely."

"Forget about how I handle my money," Carboni shot back. "Isn't your son worth it?"

"Yes, Mr. Carboni. My son is worth it. You'll get your money. It's a small price to pay. I will make the arrangements to have everything taken care of. I will have the proper authorities contact you with regards to the evidence you found. Keep it well. I'll take care of it from here. Rest assured, Mr. Carboni, I plan to bring this person to justice. This concludes our business, Mr. Carboni. Good-bye."

"It's been a pleasure doing business with you, Ben," said Carboni, letting his voice trail off. He heard the click of the receiver and the dead air before he could finish. Bruno paused, looking at the receiver, and then he placed it back on the phone.

Bruno was in the clear. He had done his job. His conscience was clear. If Holt crossed him, if anything happened to Angelina Paletti without going through the proper channels, he would sing like a bird.

Benjamin Holt checked his watch. He chewed on his cigar and quickly punched in the numbers for the Edgewater Hotel. He waited for Hamza to answer.

"Did you get all that?"

He spoke with a British accent. "Yes."

"Then you know what to do."

Holt ended the call and puffed on his cigar. He looked at his bodyguard, Gilles Stracker, who was standing by the window, listening.

"That should take care of Mr. Carboni and his debts. Make the arrangements to leave before noon. Our business is done here."

Stracker nodded and disappeared into his bedroom.

Holt poured himself a double scotch and sat on the

balcony overlooking the city of Lisbon, its grandeur still shrouded in darkness. In a matter of hours they would leave the hotel and their assumed names and the dirty business of killing behind his villa in the small Portuguese town of Lagos in the Algarve to the south. Once there, they would wait for Hamza and Katayoon to return.

Ali Hamza locked the door and then met his accomplice in the lounge of the Edgewater, where Katayoon was keeping a close eye on the man with the raspy voice. They drank ginger ale and waited deep in the lounge until the thick man could drink no more.

Chapter 49

Miles pulled the arrow from the drawer, the one he had bought from one of the archery clubs. He had waited while they replaced the feathers to replicate the one he had been sent since he couldn't bring the original with him without it being detected when he went through airport security. He then grabbed the phone and placed a call for a taxi to meet him in the alley behind the Mayflower Park Hotel on Olive Way. He would be there in fifteen minutes. He hated to do this to Donlon for the third time since they might end up being partners if this didn't work out, but he wanted one more crack at Anita, one last chance to expose her as the killer before he gave up the story.

When Miles reached the street, he expected to see Donlon waiting for him, but he wasn't there. Neither was Henley. Instead, the agent who was posted in the lobby was leaning against another white sedan. Fischer glanced at him through his sunglasses, watching as the agent pulled a cell phone from his pocket and stuck it to his ear. He was probably calling Donlon, he thought, looking for instructions on what to do now that he was on the sidewalk and heading towards his car. No matter. He had a taxi waiting.

There were no long shadows when Miles pulled up to the front of the Mayflower Park Hotel. It was almost dark from the thick, heavy clouds and a low-lying sun that was hidden and barely there. Fischer quickly exited the vehicle with the arrow cautiously tucked between his armpit and his jacket. He caught a glimpse of the white sedan as it pulled in behind his rental as he entered the lobby. Miles walked briskly and then jogged straight ahead through the lobby, headed for the exit to the alley.

After meandering through hallways, he flung open the back door and hustled into the backseat of the awaiting taxi. He told the driver where to go and then called the rental company from his cell to complain about the rental. They could find the keys under the mat.

Twenty minutes and he was on Mercer Island. Anita Paletti lived on Ninety-fourth Avenue, not far from the water. The taxi pulled around the last corner and stopped. Miles paid and exited through the back door. Up on the left-hand side, three doors down, was Anita Paletti's house. The lights were on. He was bound and determined to go after her and try to pull her out of that warm, fuzzy cocoon of hers. He was going to tell her everything that he knew in the hope of pinning her down and getting her to confess. If she got mad enough, she might just lose control and say something she might regret but wouldn't be able to take back. If he was lucky, he might even get to witness one of her other personalities. As for his safety, he wasn't too concerned. She only killed rapists and murderers. Besides, what could she do? *Shoot him on the steps of her house with a crossbow.*

Fischer walked past an array of well-kept grounds and expensive homes and then up the long driveway before pushing the doorbell by the front door. Anita flicked the switch to the outside light and looked through the peephole before opening the door.

"What are you doing here?"

"I think we should talk."

"I have nothing to say to you." She tried closing the door but was impeded by his left foot wedged between the door and the threshold. She glared at him. "If you don't take your foot away from my door, I'm going to call the cops."

"Before you do, I have something I want to give

you."

Curious as to what it could be, Anita waited and then slowly relented, releasing the pressure before partially opening the door. Miles removed his foot and pulled something from under his jacket.

Miles held the black arrow with the yellow and black fletching in front of him.

"I thought you might like this back."

"What's this?" She stared at it but did not take it.

"It's the arrow you sent me."

"I don't know what you're trying to pull here, Mr. Fischer, but I don't know anything about this arrow or who sent it to you. I'm not involved in this crazy story of yours. I've told you that before. Now, please..."

"I can put you there."

"Put me where, Mr. Fischer?"

"In the courtroom in Tweeksbury when the final verdict was read to Holt and Masalla," he said harshly. "You were sitting next to me. You were dressed as a farmer. Your scar was visible just as it is now."

"You're delusional, Mr. Fischer," she said, opening the door wider. "Where the hell do you get these crazy ideas from?"

"Your company—it likes to dress people up in disguises using false noses and makeup to look like someone else, isn't that right? Just like your employees, Ms. Paletti, you have the perfect means of making yourself into somebody other than who you really are. What's behind the door in your office? I take it it's a studio. Is that why you keep it locked?"

"You're getting to be one hell of a pain in the ass, Mr. Fischer!"

"Isn't that how you delivered the package to the courier company? Isn't that where you made yourself up to look like an old man so you could deliver this arrow without being detected?"

"What are you talking about?"

"The package you sent me. That's how I got this arrow. You took it to the courier company. The lady who served you noticed your scar. She can put you there."

It was a lie made to frighten her.

"I told you, I never sent you this arrow."

"Didn't the FBI question you in the killing of Thornton and Patrick?" he asked, pressing her.

"Yes, but they didn't find anything because I'm innocent. I told you that in the bar, for Christ's sake! If you don't believe me, why don't you ask them yourself?"

"You told me that you thought about it."

"I told you I thought about it, but I also told you I didn't do it. Don't you listen, or do you just believe what you want to believe?"

"You also told me that you dreamed about taking them out," he added. "You then took that dream and made into a reality, Ms. Paletti. Isn't that right?"

"Yes, I dreamt about it, but I didn't do it. How could I? I couldn't remember anything because of the beating they gave me. I lost my daughter, Mr. Fischer. I spent three months in that hospital until I was able to go home. I barely escaped with my own life—or maybe that doesn't concern you. Whoever did do it did me a favor. They got what they deserved."

Fischer ignored her answers. He kept it up, pressing her, hoping she would crack. He came at her again. He was like a shark feeding on a carcass.

"Is that how you killed Thornton and Patrick?" he asked abrasively. "You put on one of your faces and then killed them?"

"I wasn't even in the business when they were

killed," Anita replied. "I was still learning the business in class. I couldn't have made myself up if I tried."

"Isn't it true that you own a crossbow?"

"Yes, but that doesn't make me a killer."

"Did you kill Holt and Masalla?" he asked loudly.

"Why would I kill two people from a town I knew nothing about until you brought it up in the lounge the other night? You want to tell me that, Mr. Reporter?"

"Revenge!"

"Revenge? Is that the best you can do?" she asked, almost laughing.

"It's a hell of a motive, don't you think?"

"How could it be based on revenge when I didn't even know who these people were? These people would have to have done something to me for it to be revenge," she said smartly. She was glaring at him. "You know, you're one hell of a reporter with one hell of problem when it comes to dealing with reality, Mr. Fischer. Did you know that?"

"Isn't it true you're seeing a psychiatrist? Isn't it true you suffer from DID? Isn't it true you're living with more than one personality?"

"Why? Do I look insane to you? If anyone has a problem with reality, it's you, Mr. Fischer," she said, shaking her head.

He ignored the sardonic tone and her disdainful look and decided to keep on her, to pound her with question after question. Sooner or later she would crack, say something that she couldn't retract, and then he would have her. The questions spewed from his open lips, full of contempt, ignorant of how they made her feel. He stuck his foot back between the door and the threshold and continued with his barrage of questions.

"Is it because of what happened to your daughter—

that the rape and murders in Whatley and Tweeksbury mirrored your own daughter's nightmare?" he asked, his eyes now flaming, his tone challenging. "Isn't that it?" he asked. "That the girls were the same age as your daughter?" His face was becoming flushed from his barrage. Large veins stuck out from his neck. "That they shared the very same birth date as Rachel? Isn't that the real reason you took them out? When you read about them, it made you relive it all over again. Isn't that why you snapped? Isn't that why you killed them?"

"Get out, Fischer," she exclaimed, screaming. "You have no right..."

"Is it because of what your father did to you and your sister? Is that where all these different personalities originated? Did you poison your father?"

"Go to hell!" Her hands started to tremble openly. Fischer took notice.

"Is your sister involved in this with you? Are you covering up for your sister?"

"Fuck you, Fischer! I'm warning you for the last time. If you don't leave my property, I swear I'm going to call the police."

Suddenly, the small riot just outside her door stopped, the churning waters calmed to the point where they were still. No more insulting and insinuating questions flowed with the openness and cruelty of a defiant prosecutor. Fischer was done. The feeding was over—the carcass of Anita Paletti, though battered, was still intact.

"You do that. I'll just sit over there on the curb and wait," he said, pointing towards the street. "They might be very interested in hearing what I have to say."

Anita Paletti did not reply. Instead, seething with anger, she waited for Fischer to remove his foot pressing against the door. When he did, she slammed the door, barely missing his foot, and shut off the light.

Miles stood looking at the door and then slowly made his way down the driveway towards the street, stopping and looking back before sitting by the curb, waiting for the police to arrive. If they came, he would have a hell of a lot of explaining to do. After that, who knows—he could be spending some quality time in jail for what had just transpired on the doorstep to Anita Paletti's house. Trespassing. Harassment. Libelous claims. *While they're at it, might as well throw in withholding information crucial to a criminal investigation and refusing to cooperate with law enforcement.* With everything that had just transpired, it was probably worth something. After all, if he didn't want to go to jail, everything would have to come out after he explained what he was doing there and why he was lambasting Anita.

He decided to call her bluff. If she knew anything and if it struck a nerve, she might be willing to talk before the cops got there. He lit a cigarette and crossed his fingers and waited under the dark clouds with the arrow lying next to him.

Chapter 50

Bruno was drunk, but he was a happy drunk. Benjamin Holt was out of his life for good, and he was going home to Chicago in the morning. Over fifty thousand of easy-made American dollars would be there to greet him. *What could be better*, he thought? There was no need to hold back, to stay sober, so he drank like a fish. After all, it was his short-lived acquaintance with a man he had never met who was buying the drinks on what was left of the original twenty thousand, so he drank and chatted with the bartender until he could no longer see straight and barely stand on his two good legs.

He sat in his all too familiar spot at the end of the bar on the stool closest to the door and quickly downed what was left in his glass and then asked the bartender for the time. It was just past eight, he told him. It was a little early to be leaving for a man of his great capacity, but he could hold no more. He laid a hundred-dollar bill on the bar to cover the bill including tip, and then he left with great difficulty for the elevator and his room on the third floor.

In the bathroom, Carboni leaned against the sink, using his weakened legs, before pulling the knob hard to seal the drain so no water could escape. He slowly turned the tap to where it was partially open, waiting until the sink was half-full before sloppily sprinkling his face and his bare chest by accident from the water that was pooling below him. He dried his face with the facecloth along with his chest and then placed it over the edge of the sink, accidentally covering the small hole whose sole purpose was to prevent the sink from overflowing. He braced himself, using his arms for support, and stared into the mirror. He smiled, thinking of the notoriety his company would receive. His stalled private investigator business would soon be thriving under the publicity once it hit the newspapers about who was responsible for finding the killer of the string of crossbow killings, and he owed it all to that annoying little drone, Benjamin Holt.

Bruno fumbled for the switch to turn off the light but forgot to flick off the switch to the fan before standing next to the bed, where he took off the remainder of his clothes until he was only dressed in his boxers. He pulled back the covers and then fell into bed and faded into a hard sleep.

Hamza and Katayoon were in their room, listening as Carboni snored. It had been two minutes since Bruno let out his last grunt. He was dead to the world and wouldn't feel a thing. Ali Hamza slapped Katayoon on the shoulder and then nodded towards the door. Hamza checked the hall and then he and Katayoon slipped into the long corridor. Hamza worked the lock, careful not to make too much noise—not that it would matter. Carboni was comatose and wouldn't awaken for at least twelve hours.

Hamza watched the door while Mospoli moved quickly toward the bed, both men oblivious to the sound of dripping water, which was muffled by the bathroom fan. Katayoon stood in the pale light that filtered through the curtains, pointing it at the back of Carboni's head six feet away, and then he gently pulled the trigger twice.

"That should hold him 'til the morning," remarked Hamza with a wide grin.

Ali grabbed the keys to the rental off the table and held the door before quickly easing past the opening behind Mospoli. They entered their room and gathered their bags and then took the stairs. Outside, they headed across the street for Carboni's rental.

In the bathroom of Bruno's room, the water was steadily spilling over the sink. It covered the floor and was now just seeping past the door into the bedroom. It was only a matter of time before it started seeping into the suite below.

Chapter 51

Miles had been sitting on the curb for almost twenty minutes, and yet nobody had shown up. The sun had already set. It was dark except for the light emanating from the houses and the streetlights that lined the street. He had come to the conclusion that there were no police because she hadn't made the call. If she had, they would have been there by now and possibly hauling him off to jail for a whole litany of reasons. But they weren't there.

Miles took a deep breath and then slowly picked himself up from the sidewalk, taking the arrow with him. He was visibly frustrated. He dragged on his cigarette and then thumped it to the concrete, hard, before crushing it with his foot. To make matters worse, there was a light drizzle that was now just beginning to fall. Fischer placed the arrow under his armpit and pulled out his cell phone to call for a taxi when the light behind him caught his eye. He looked back towards Paletti's house. Though not on before, the outside lights to the garage were now on. He watched as one of the garage doors lifted. He waited, fully expecting to see Anita rush to get into her car and then drive away and leave him there. A couple of minutes passed, and there was still no sign of Anita. His eyes shifted back to the house. There in the front window he noticed her staring back at him, and then a moment later she disappeared into another room. He casually stuffed his cell phone back into his pocket and waited another minute, wondering as to what was going on before his curiosity got the best of him. He hesitated and then started to make his way back up the driveway towards the garage, leaving the arrow by the door that led into the house. He saw this as an opportunity—a last chance to find the truth and perhaps nail Anita. The worst that could happen was she could kick him out.

He found Anita in the living room. She was sitting on the couch with her legs close to her chin, hugging a pillow. On the doorstep he had acted like a bull in a china shop. *How ironic*, he thought, *that he would now be standing in her living room, watching her dab at her eyes after what took place on the doorstep.* Miles took a chair next to the couch. A television could be heard in the background from somewhere in the house.

"You're a real bastard, Fischer! Why couldn't you just leave us alone?"

There was no reply from Miles. It was better if he kept his mouth shut if Anita was going to talk. Say the wrong thing and whatever she was about to say could be over in an instant. Instead, he pulled the tape recorder from his jacket and placed it on the table in front of him and waited. There was no objection, so he pushed the button to start the recorder.

"I thought that was the end of it when that guy Wilcox died. I thought my pleading had gotten through to her. I begged her to let it go. We had no immediate family left other than each other. I asked her not to jeopardize it. What we had left was still worth holding onto." She hugged the pillow tighter. "I begged her not to destroy it." Anita grabbed another tissue from the box beside her and blew her nose. "Do you have any children, Mr. Fischer?"

"Yes, a brand-new baby girl." He did the math. "She's four days old today, as a matter of fact."

Anita looked solemnly at him, puzzled by his reply. "Then what are you doing here?" she asked. "You should be with your wife and your new daughter."

"I would if I could."

"It sounds more like an excuse than a choice. You

should have done us all a favor and stayed in Chicago instead of coming here and destroying other people's lives."

Paletti threw the pillow aside and pulled a picture from the table.

"My sister couldn't have children of her own. She never married because of it. She loved Rachel. When Rachel was young, she used to take her every summer for a month when she could. Rachel could hardly wait. Rachel would always tell me how much fun they had. Sometimes it made me jealous just to hear my daughter say that. My sister would do whatever Rachel wanted to do while she had her. She probably spoiled her, from what she told me, but I guess that's what aunts do."

Paletti smiled faintly and placed the picture back on the small end table.

"Yeah, I guess" he said, blurting something out. "Kids are great, aren't they?"

"After what happened to Rachel, she just lost it. I don't know who suffered more, her or me. When she heard about what happened, she took a leave of absence from her job and stayed with me for almost two months before returning to Seattle. She visited me every day while I was in the hospital. She practically lived there with me. When I was well enough to be on my own, she traveled back to Eastbrook. I had another funeral for Rachel so I could be a part of it since I couldn't attend the first one. She was the only family I had at the original funeral."

"What do you mean, she lost it?"

"She kept asking me about what happened while I was in the hospital. She wouldn't let up. It was like she was obsessed with it. I almost wished she would go back to Seattle and leave me alone. I just couldn't handle the pressure she was putting on me to try and remember, but I couldn't. I feel guilty for the way I felt at the time. She's a good sister. She was only trying to help."

"Did you ever tell her?"

"About what happened?"

"Yeah."

"Yes. When it all came back to me, I told her."

"Did you tell her who attacked you and your daughter?"

"Yes. There isn't a day I don't look back on it and wish I hadn't. It was the worst thing I could have done. It's my fault. I did this to her!"

"How did you know it was Thornton and Patrick?"

"I saw their faces. They were helping me with my car after it broke down. I saw their faces under the hood. I prayed I would someday remember what they looked like. Months later, after I had left the hospital, it all started to come back to me, and when it did, I looked them up."

"But how did you know where they lived if all you could remember was what they looked like?"

"From the license plate on their truck. The only thing I could remember at first was this set of numbers and letters, but I didn't know what they meant. Everything else was gone. Months later, after I had left the hospital and I had it all together, I had it traced."

"Why didn't you tell the authorities?"

"I don't know. I guess because I wanted to take care of them myself. Remember, I told you I had it all planned. I wanted them dead. I wanted to kill them myself. I wanted to make them suffer like no human being had ever suffered before. I was going to make them pay for what they did."

"So what stopped you?"

"I don't know. I guess I just couldn't do it. It probably has something to do with my Jewish upbringing."

"Did your sister ever say she was going to kill Thornton and Patrick?"

Anita glared at him. "No. She just said she would take care of it. I wasn't supposed to get involved. She would do it for me like a sister would stand up for another sister."

"When she said she would take care it, what did you think she meant by that?"

"I thought she was going to talk to the authorities for me. I was still too angry to say anything to them. I still wanted to kill them. I thought she was trying to protect me—to save me from myself."

"Did your sister know how you felt?"

"Yes. We talked about it."

"When your sister said she would take care of it, did she mention anyone else, by chance?"

"Yes. She mentioned someone by the name of Dina."

"Who is she?"

"Someone she invented, I guess."

"Is it a result of her being DID?"

"Yes."

"Did you ever meet this Dina?"

She swallowed hard. "Yes."

"How many times have you met her?"

"I don't know."

"When did you first meet her?"

"When I was seven."

"Did the cops ever question your sister on any of these murders?"

"To my knowledge, no, and if they did, she never told me."

"When would Dina appear?"

"When Angel would be reading the newspaper. Isn't that where you reporters do your best work? Reporting on all the dirt that's happening out there instead of reporting on the good things that happen. Isn't that how you get your kicks? Isn't that what sells your newspapers?"

Miles ignored the questions.

"How many personalities does your sister have?"

"I won't answer that, so don't go there."

"Does she know she's DID?"

"That's almost impossible to answer."

"Why?"

"Because."

"Because why?"

"Why are you pushing? You got what you came for."

"Because it's important for people to understand so they can make their own judgment as to why this happened."

"No, she doesn't! She doesn't believe what they're saying. There! Does that make it better for you?" Paletti left the couch angrily.

"Why doesn't she believe it?"

"I don't know. She just doesn't," she said, returning to the couch. "It's a difficult illness to understand. It's almost like sleepwalking. Something sets them off and they transform into another personality that controls their every thought. I can't explain it any better than that. When their mood changes, so does the personality."

"What about professional help?"

"I tried to get her some help, but the doctors misdiagnosed her from being a manic depressive to having schizophrenia."

"How did she get into the army?"

"There was no problem. There were no medical

records because my aunt didn't know, and since the death of my father, everything seemed okay."

"Why the lapse in time between Wilcox and Holt and Masalla?"

"I can't answer that."

"So you're saying you never saw or heard from Dina for six years?"

"Never. I thought Angel had gotten rid of her. I never asked her because I was so delighted after not hearing from her for over a year. I thought if I asked her, it might bring Dina back."

"What about after the death of your father?"

"Like I told you, I never heard from Dina until Eastbrook."

"What about her other personalities?"

"I told you not to go there! Dina is all that concerns you."

"Who knew that Dina existed?"

"Only me that I know of."

"Is she being treated now?"

"I tried telling her, but she denied the existence of any personalities other than herself. She said I was talking like a crazy person. She called me crazy. Me," she said, pointing to her chest, "her sister—who's only trying to help her. I told her. I even took her to see my psychiatrist, the one she's seeing now, to try and get over the loss of Rachel only because she was suffering as much as I had. He helped me deal with the loss of my daughter, but she wouldn't stay—one appointment here, one appointment there. Then she would be gone until I talked to her again. She said she was only doing it for me. I didn't want her to do it for me. I wanted her to do for herself. I blame all the other doctors who misdiagnosed her—years of damage that this psychiatrist is trying to undo."

"How long has she been seeing this psychiatrist?"

"Almost four years."

"You said you hadn't seen Dina for six years, so why was she seeing a psychiatrist?"

"I already told you. This isn't cured overnight. It takes time."

"When's the last time you saw Dina?"

"This afternoon. I had lunch with my sister. She told me about this guy who's following her. When we left the restaurant, he was standing on the sidewalk. It made my sister angry. That's when Dina appeared." Paletti studied his expression. "You look like you know him."

"He's a private investigator."

Anita was up again, walking away but not going far.

"Who is he working for?" she asked.

"I haven't been able to find out." Miles turned and faced her. "I can't help but notice you protect your sister Angelina, but you don't protect Dina. Aren't they one and the same to you?"

"I love my sister, and I'll do anything to help her, but I can't help Dina. It sounds crazy, doesn't it? My sister needs help, and I know that. But it's Dina who is making her sick. It's not my sister's fault."

"I have to ask you something that's been bugging me since I came in here. Why did you decide to talk to me?"

"The arrow. I know the markings. When I saw it, I knew it was my sister's. She told me that Dina made them for her."

"Did Dina say anything to you after she saw this guy on the sidewalk?"

"Yes. She said she would take care of him."

Anita headed to the small bar in the corner and started to make herself a drink. "I guess it would be rude of me not to offer you one, or are you on the clock?"

"I'll pass, but if it isn't too much of an imposition, I wouldn't mind a glass of water."

She stared at him and said, "Yeah, sure. Come in the kitchen."

In the kitchen, Miles leaned against the counter while Anita pulled a glass from the cupboard, the news bulletin already flashing across the screen on the television in the room off to the right. He gazed at Anita by the sink and then turned his attention to the television. The anchorman was giving way to a reporter standing just outside the Edgewater Hotel. He heard the faint words of "Carboni" and "murder."

"Where's your remote?" Fischer asked.

"Over there on the table. Why?"

Fischer went into the other room and grabbed it and increased the volume. Anita stood by the fridge with the door open and watched. Fischer stood closer, glued to the picture of the Edgewater Hotel in the background. A photo of Bruno Carboni was on the screen.

"That's him," she exclaimed. "That's the man who was following Angelina. He's the guy on the sidewalk." Paletti passed Miles his glass of water and then sat in the chair, her eyes fixed to the screen. Miles took a long drink and pumped up the volume so he wouldn't miss anything.

"*...shot twice in the back of the head. Staff found the body when people below the room occupied by the deceased complained about water seeping through the ceiling. The deceased had apparently forgotten to turn the water off in the bathroom before going to bed. Police have no motive established at this time but would like to question two men who occupied a room on the same floor. One is described as a dark-skinned male, balding, with black hair, standing five feet ten inches tall, and* *speaks with an English accent. The other male is described as light-skinned with black, wavy hair standing six feet six inches tall. Anybody who sees these individuals is asked to contact their local police. They are…"*

"That's probably the two guys who went by my sister's place," stated Anita.

Miles decreased the volume to a background noise.

"What two guys?"

"Those could be the two guys Ned told her about. He saw them the day this Carboni fellow was at her place. They were in a taxi. Ned thought they were following the other guy."

"Christ!" Miles searched for his cell phone.

"Who are you calling?"

"Donlon!" Miles punched one number and then waited for the operator. "Get me the FBI." Again he waited and then asked for the number to Agent Donlon. He hit a button and then quickly punched in the numbers. "Call your sister."

"Why?"

"Because those two guys your sister's neighbor saw are probably headed there right now. They're obviously professionals, and your sister is probably the next one on their list. Tell her to get out of the house and to meet us at the ferry terminal."

"Donlon. It's Miles." He talked while watching the TV. "Did you hear?"

"Yeah! We're at the Edgewater right now. Where are you? You were supposed to meet me and Henley half an hour ago."

"Never mind where I am—hold on a minute." He turned to Anita. "What time do the ferries run 'til?"

"I don't know," she replied.

"Donlon. Call the ferries and find out how long they run 'til. If they're close to shutting down, tell them to keep it running. I don't have a schedule."

"Don't give me orders, Fischer!"

"Christ, Donlon! Just do it!"

"What do you want with the ferries?"

"Carboni was investigating the murders of—Christ, Donlon! I don't have time to explain it to you right now. Just call the ferries and tell them to keep them running if you have to. I'll meet you at the Fauntleroy Ferry Terminal in half an hour."

"This better be good, Fischer."

"Just meet me there." Miles hung up the phone. "Where are your keys?" Paletti was still holding the receiver, waiting for an answer.

"In my purse," she replied.

"Where's your purse?"

"On top of the fridge. She's not there."

"Try her cell."

"She doesn't have one."

"What do you mean, she doesn't have one?"

"She doesn't have one. She doesn't like them. She thinks they're an invasion of her privacy."

"Christ! Did she tell you she was going anywhere tonight?"

"No, but my sister doesn't tell me everything. Christ, Fischer! We're not each other's keeper."

"Get your keys and let's go! I'll drive."

"I'll drive. You don't know where you're going. You've already wrecked my life. I'm not going to let you wreck my car, too."

Miles gave a short smile and then fetched the recorder from the living room before heading for Anita's Beamer sitting in the driveway.

Chapter 52

Ali and Mospoli escaped just minutes before the water started seeping into the room below. Had they waited much longer to take care of Bruno, there was a minute chance they would be in the back of a police cruiser by now, if not dead from a hail of gunfire after a botched attempt trying to flee the police. Instead, they were in the parking deck, commandeering Bruno's rental for their trip to Vashon Island and Angel Paletti's place. Ali took the wheel while Mospoli sat next to him and quietly wiped his gun. The blue compact eased slowly through the parking lot and then into the rain and the slick traffic and headed west along Elliott Avenue.

Ali found the marina just beyond the park on West Marina Place not far from Pier 91. The parking lot was a series of three short streets between the park and the water. Mospoli checked the building while Ali circled the perimeter before parking Bruno's car in one of the stalls. After retrieving their bags from the trunk, Ali tossed the keys back through the open window, before they headed for the office not far from the pier.

Hamza stepped inside while Katayoon waited by the door and watched for intruders. Ali found the lone attendant over by a rack of clothes. He approached him, inquiring about the possibly of organizing a charter, and then he ended the conversation by calmly placing the steel barrel of his Ruger up against the side of the young man's head. He demanded the keys to a boat that could make it to Vashon Island but in the quickest time possible. He wanted something just off the pier, close to the shore so they wouldn't have to walk too far. There was no telling how many boats were still out there, making their way back in because of the nasty weather.

The less people they saw, the less likelihood that anybody could alert the authorities about a tall Moroccan and a shorter Fijian who just happened to be seen walking on the pier, looking for a boat.

Ali escorted him to the dock with Katayoon watching their back. Because it was such a big marina, it would be hours before one of their precious boats were reported missing. Katayoon cast the rope from the pier, and the three of them headed across Elliott Bay for the pier at Ellisport on Vashon Island. Halfway across, the boat slowed. Katayoon quickly checked the horizon for any boats and then fired a single shot in the back of the attendant's head before pushing his body over the side. By the time he was reported missing, they would be off the island and somewhere else. Hamza checked his watch and booted the engine. They would be at the pier in Ellisport no later than ten thirty.

Anita Paletti and Miles Fischer were on the I-90 in less than eight minutes, making their way across the Lake Washington Bridge. Six minutes later they were making their way onto the I-5, and five minutes after that, the Seattle Freeway, heading west for the Fauntleroy Ferry Terminal. They talked little as Anita concentrated on driving through the pelting rain and the heavy Friday night traffic, doing speeds in excess of the posted limits. Fischer tried repeatedly to get a hold of Angelina using his cell phone, but he got no answer. Twenty-five minutes later the blue BMW pulled into the terminal. Donlon was already there, along with Henley and Agent Teno Kostopoulos, who had replaced Agent Teresa Pang in the late afternoon.

The ferry was small, no bigger than a barge that could fit fifty vehicles of varying lengths on its open deck. It had an overhead bridge and public toilets, but it offered little in the way of seating capacity, so most people stayed in their cars for the short ride across the bay. There were seven lanes open to traffic, but only three were occupied.

Anita's blue Beamer parked behind a yellow Volkswagen and was the last to board, the almost empty ferry waiting until Donlon gave the captain the signal to pull away from the pier. It was 10:16 p.m., and a minute behind schedule. It would be another twenty minutes before the ferry docked on the other side.

Miles handed her the phone.

"See if you can reach your sister. I'll be back in a minute."

Fischer shut the door and headed towards the car near the front of the line where Henley was holding the wheel. Teno was in the backseat. He tapped on the glass. Henley rolled the window down.

"Where's Donlon?"

Henley nodded with his head. "Up there."

Miles watched as Donlon made his way down the stairs towards the white sedan.

"Get in," he said. Donlon opened the door and sat up front. Miles took the backseat behind Henley. "So what's this all about?"

"The dead guy at the hotel is a private investigator," said Miles, running his hands through his rain-soaked hair and then wiping his forehead with his sleeve.

"We already know that, Fischer. The name of the company he works for is Carboni Investigations. He's an ex-cop out of Chicago. We found one of his business cards in his wallet. We also found this."

Donlon pulled out a plastic sleeve and showed it to Fischer.

"What is it?"

"From what we can tell, it's the remnants of a cigarette."

Miles opened the sleeve and sniffed the contents and then handed it back to Donlon.

"Why would he have these in his wallet?"

"We don't know, but it probably has something to do with why he was murdered." Donlon nodded behind him with his head. "Is that Anita Paletti's car back there?"

"Yeah."

"What's she doing here? After what happened in the bar the other night, I thought she wanted nothing more to do with you."

"It's a long story."

"The ferry doesn't dock for another fifteen minutes," Donlon said without looking at his watch.

Miles proceeded to fill Donlon in, starting with the trial in Tweeksbury and who he believed was sitting next to him. He told him about the package containing the arrow and who he suspected had it courier to the *Tribune* the day after.

"That's why you were at the courier company today," remarked Henley.

After Henley's interruption, he continued on, telling Donlon about the mystery caller and what she had told Big Tony, which brought him to why he was at Anita's place.

Donlon shook his head. A smirk slid across his face. "You reporters are all the same, Fischer. You're always worrying that somebody else is going to get the story before you do. That's all that matters to you guys. It's all about who can be the biggest. You guys think you can just play cop whenever you want to. Well it's not that easy, Fischer. If you had cooperated with us when we came to your office, there's a good chance this Carboni fellow wouldn't be lying dead in his hotel room right now. So what about this Carboni fellow? What do you know about him?"

"There's not much to tell. You probably know about as much as I do. The other day he showed up at the newspaper, asking for me, giving the receptionist some phony name. When the receptionist wouldn't tell him, he pulled out a badge. Of course when she saw the badge, she caved and told him where I was staying. Next day he breaks into my room."

"How do you know he was in your room?" asked Henley.

"Let's just say I know. I believe he lifted a page from a pad I writing on. From the paper he lifted the name of Anita and Angelina Paletti along with Angelina's address. The next day he shows up at her place."

"That would explain why we found this in one of his pockets." Donlon handed Miles a slip of paper. "It's been shaded with a pencil. It has both Palettis' names on it along with Angelina's address and a couple of other names."

Miles studied it. It was the information Bruno had gleaned from the slip of paper while he ransacked his room.

"Who's he working for?" asked Donlon.

"I don't know. Anita told me that her sister's neighbor saw Carboni on her property. Right after he left, the neighbor noticed these two guys following behind him in a taxi. They're probably the same ones who knocked him off," said Miles.

"Did she give you a description?"

"She said that her sister told her they looked like they might be from the Middle East."

"That would fit the two men who were in the hotel," said Henley.

"So you know about them?"

"There were two men staying at the same hotel as this Carboni character," said Donlon. "They were in the room next to his. We found a computer when we searched their room. Henley here found the bug they planted in Carboni's room under his bed. We're assuming Carboni called someone before he went to sleep. Whoever it was, it probably got him killed. We're having the security cameras checked so we can get a positive description of what they looked like. They paid with cash, so there's a good chance the names on the registry are fake. We're also checking the hotel phone records. We want to see who they and this Carboni person may have been talking to."

Miles looked out onto the water, towards Seattle. The terminal was all but gone, the lights barely visible through the rain-soaked window.

"You might want to think about posting one of your agents at the terminal in case they show up."

"Relax, Fischer. We've got it covered. There are two ferries running between the two points," he stated, motioning with his hand. "I've got one guy on the mainland watching for them. Teno here has been watching the terminal since we found the body in case they were headed this way, but they haven't surfaced. Teno's going to stay on this side and keep a watch."

Suddenly Donlon's phone rang. He pulled it from his pocket and put it to his ear. After about a minute he pushed a button, which ended the call.

"Carboni made a call at about five thirty this afternoon to a hotel in Lisbon to a Mr. Pitt," he said, slipping the phone back in his pocket.

"Lisbon? But that's in Portugal," stated Henley.

"One of our agents found the number on the hotel bill after we left, so he called the number. It belongs to the Trafaria Hotel. It seems this Mr. Pitt was in a hurry to leave. He and his friend checked out about two hours ago."

"How did they pay?" asked Henley.

"With cash, just like our friends at the Edgewater. Lisbon is eight hours ahead, so that would have made it at about four thirty in the morning Lisbon time. Right after Carboni made his call, Mr. Pitt placed a call back to the Edgewater, to the same room occupied by our suspects. The numbers match. It's probably not his real name, but it's not going to help him much. The hotel in Lisbon has a security system. Everyone who checks in or out is caught on camera. We'll have to wait and see until we can get a photo of what this Mr. Pitt looks like. We'll go to Lisbon if we have to."

Fischer had an inquisitive look on his face.

"What's wrong with you?" Donlon asked.

"David Masalla had no parents. He was an orphan."

"So?"

"So lawyers don't come cheap, Donlon. David Masalla had no money. Lionel Holt's father paid for both his son's and Masalla's lawyers."

"So you think this Mr. Pitt could be Lionel Holt's father?"

"That would be my guess. He had no other kids except for Lionel. He's what you call a mining baron. He owns a bunch of them in South America and Africa. He's got pretty deep pockets."

"Thanks for the heads-up. We'll check it out."

"So what about these two guys? Do you think they're going to show?" asked Fischer.

"I don't know. We'll have to wait and see how this all plays out. What about her sister?"

Miles looked out the window to his left. The terminal was coming into view. The lights were visible and so was the ramp.

"So far she hasn't been able to reach her. I guess I'll go and check to see if she got a hold of her."

"Do me a favor, Fischer. When you go back to the car, don't say anything. I don't want to raise any alarms until we've had a chance to talk to both of them."

"You can talk to her now if you like."

"No need. She can't go anywhere," he stated, looking in the side mirror. "We'll do it at the house. Hopefully her sister will be there by then." He looked suspiciously at the reporter from the *Tribune*. "So do us all a favor and keep your mouth shut."

Miles reached for the handle.

"And one more thing, Fischer," said Donlon, twisting his frame to where he faced the reporter. "For once in your life, help the side that's trying to do the right thing."

The cruiser carrying the Fijian and the Moroccan could barely see the lights of the ferry headed to Vashon Island through the taunting rain from the stern of their sleek boat as it eased past the small jetty towards the pier in Ellisport. Ali was at the wheel with Katayoon seated next to him. They watched the shoreline in silence and the dim lights from the houses that dotted the landscape as the boat eased quietly through the rough water. Ali slowed the boat as it approached the pier, before cutting the engines and steering it next to the dock. They would need it later to escape from the island, so Katayoon tied it to the pier rather than let it drift from the shore. The blue rain jackets were found in a locker in the cabin below. Ali pulled the hood over his head, as did Katayoon, and then Hamza stepped onto the pier first with Katayoon close to his back. They looked like maritime boaters in their slick gear and white runners. They headed up the ramp to the small parking lot and through the quiet, rain-swept streets of Ellisport, towards Angel Paletti's house.

Angelina Paletti was in the barn tending to her horses when her sister called for the last time, but she wasn't there now. She was in the house. The light on the message machine was no longer blinking. There was no time to waste, the message told her. They were coming, Anita said, the two men Ned saw in the taxi. They had just killed the man they saw on the sidewalk outside the restaurant. "Get out now! I'll explain it all to you later. Head for the ferry. I'll meet you there," said Anita's voice on the answering machine.

Angel wasted little time. She quickly grabbed her keys from the counter and shut the front door without bothering to lock it. Anita said they had killed the man on the sidewalk, so they would probably blow the lock anyway. She ran for the gate and caught a glimpse of two black silhouettes under the streetlight, but then she lost them in the rain. She quickly wiped the wind-driven rain from her eyes and then found them again, only this time they were headed up the street, towards her house. They were walking quickly, and then they began to jog towards her. One was noticeably taller than the other. Angel hesitated and then quickly left the gate and headed back down the driveway. She left the lights off and locked the door this time to buy her some time in case they got to the house before she had a chance to leave. Seconds later, she was in her bedroom upstairs, water dripping from her hair, reaching for her black pants and her black T-shirt when they reached the gate. She left through the back door and headed for the barn and her crossbow inside. She could change there. There would be enough time while they searched the house.

Chapter 53

"When's the last time you charged the battery?" Anita asked, watching Fischer climb into the passenger seat.

"I don't know. Why?"

"Because your phone is dead. Give me your charger."

"It's back at the hotel."

"How am I supposed to get a hold of my sister?"

"Didn't you get a hold of her?"

"No. I only got a chance to leave her a message. I want to keep calling. Maybe I can reach her."

"Where's yours?"

"I don't have one for the same reason my sister doesn't. Christ, Fischer! You're making my life a living hell."

"Don't worry. We're going to be there in a couple of minutes."

"That's easy for you to say, Fischer. It's not your sister who's being hunted like a prized deer."

"If you want, I can go ask Donlon and see if we can borrow one of theirs."

"It's too late. The cars are starting to unload."

Miles watched as the first lane of traffic started to leave the ferry. The white sedan with Henley at the wheel was the third one off.

"If anything happens to my sister, I'm going to hold you personally responsible," she said without looking at him.

"Nothing's going to happen. They haven't even shown up. We'll be there in a couple of minutes."

"You better hope you're right." Anita put the Beamer in gear and followed the yellow Volkswagen off the ferry.

Miles tried his seat belt.

"What's wrong?" she asked.

"It's the seat belt. It doesn't seem to want to work. I think there's something wrong with the buckling mechanism." Miles tried it again, trying to jam it in with a few short stabs and applying as much force as he could before giving up.

Anita took a quick glance. "That's funny, it was working before."

"I thought Germans made quality cars?"

"Just relax, Fischer. You probably won't need it." Anita watched the white sedan just ahead of her. Somewhere up ahead there would be a fork in the road. Fischer was fumbling through his pockets. "What are you looking for," she asked.

"A cigarette." Miles pulled the pack from his jacket pocket. "Damn it."

"What's wrong?"

"It's empty."

"Look in the console. I think there are some in there."

Miles flipped the lid and pulled a cigarette from the pack. "I didn't know you smoked."

"I don't. Somebody left them there."

Miles lit his cigarette and studied the package. Suddenly he felt the car veer to the right and pick up speed. "Shouldn't we be following Donlon?"

"That's the slow way. This way is faster." She paused for a moment and then said, "God, I hope they get there before we do."

"I thought you said this was faster?"

"It is, but they have the guns—remember?" she said, smiling, her eyes gleaming. "How's the cigarette?"

"It tastes different." Miles hit the button to lower the window to let the smoke out. "Where did you get these?"

"I told you somebody left them in my car. Why?"

"Just asking." Miles flipped on the overhead light and stared at it. The markings on the paper were the same as what Donlon had found in Carboni's wallet. Suddenly his old suspicions were coming back. Alarm bells were starting to go off.

"Why are you looking at it like that? It's just a cigarette."

At the moment he had no intention of telling her that the cigarette he was smoking matched the paper found in Carboni's wallet. He was already at a disadvantage. He had no seat belt, which was now playing in his head as to why it didn't work. Anita had taken the fork in the road, isolating them from the FBI. He was on a road that he wasn't familiar with. Outside it was almost as black as the interior of the Beamer; the only light was what came from the headlights and the dashboard. It was pouring, and the pavement was slick. If he didn't know better, he thought he felt his heart skip a beat.

Miles flicked the light off.

"I think you should watch the road. Either that or slow it down a bit."

"Why does my driving scare you?"

"It wouldn't be so bad if you would stay between the lines."

"You want to drive?"

"Maybe I should."

"Forget it, Fischer."

"I still think you should slow it down a bit," he offered without being asked. "It's pretty slick out." With no seat belt to hold him in place, Miles's hands were now on the dashboard to steady his body as the Beamer wound through the tight curves, his eyes locked to the rain-swept road ahead. The small bushes and thin trees along the shoulder approached head-on and then quickly cut to the right and then to the left as the headlights caught a glimpse of each before they disappeared into the solid black night behind him, the yellow lines darting in and out of sight under the approaching glare of the Beamer's headlights. It was like a dream, where everything comes and goes so fast.

"Relax, Fischer. I drive this road all the time when I go to my sister's. I know it like the back of my hand." Anita turned the radio up. "Do you like Bob Dylan?"

"Shouldn't you be watching the road?" he asked, looking out the side window for the edge of the asphalt.

He never got a reply.

Suddenly, for no reason, the car pulled to the right, careening off the highway in a quick burst, just past the bluff where the highway declines to a quarter of a mile of straight road. It shot past the initial set of low bushes and thin trees lining the shoulder, their bent and buckling branches scraping and swatting the side of the blue BMW as it thrust forward. Miles could hear the loud thrashing of the branches, the swooshing sound around him as the Beamer forced its way through what looked like a trail big enough to accommodate a vehicle. In the dark he tried to brace himself as Anita steered the Beamer through the surrounding trees and into the solid cedar less than a few hundred feet from the edge of the cliff and the quick falloff to the water below.

Fischer was thrown forcefully to his left against the wheel and then thrust back towards the center from the centrifugal force and the pull of the vehicle as it squirmed and skimmed the slick forest floor. His head hit the corner support beam hard, breaking the skin, creating a deep gash. The Beamer came to an abrupt stop from the right front impact with the large tree. There was a loud pop and then the sudden and quick rush of air as the bags deployed, catching him in midflight, which slammed Fischer back hard like a rag doll into his seat. His neck curled, and his head snapped over the headrest, finalizing his journey into unconsciousness from the force of the explosion. The seat rocked hard, shuddered, and then stopped. His head was spewing blood from the side, spraying a corner of the dashboard and the airbag. From his nose, blood began to trickle, which meandered down and over his lip and into his mouth. The whiplash had forced his head up, wedging the bag under his chin for the briefest of moments before retreating, deflating almost as quickly as it had sprung to life, his body slowly slithering back down into the seat. It was the perfect scene, choreographed to perfection, through to every fine detail. To his left, Paletti was locked safely in her seat, cushioned and protected by the airbag, her eyes frozen open, her brain numb but intact.

At the top of the bluff where the road came to a crest, the road lay silent, wrapped and smothered in a dripping darkness. In the stillness beyond the jagged edge of the curb, the blue BMW sat nestled amongst the trees, the radiator hissing and spewing green coolant, which first pooled on the forest floor and then slowly seeped past the rocks and the foliage around it before forging itself into the soil below. The rain continued in its deluge as it danced on the rooftop and dripped off the branches of the trees to the ground below. In the quiet just before the hill, Dylan sang in the background to an unappreciative and stunned audience, his voice fading eerily through the trees.

"What's wrong?" asked Donlon.

Henley was looking in his rearview mirror, looking a

little perplexed.

"That's strange," he said. "Paletti's Beamer just went to the right."

"Maybe she knows another way to her sister's house."

"Maybe. Do you have his cell number?"

"No."

"Too bad."

"Don't worry about it. They'll probably meet us there."

Katayoon stood at the corner of the house, his gun drawn, while Hamza tried the front door. They had seen their prey when they turned the corner under the streetlight—a dark figure with a slightly glowing silhouette standing by the gate, motionless, staring down the darkened road. That's when they quickened their pace and decided to jog, just before she bolted from the gate and headed back towards the house.

Mospoli wiped the water from his rain-soaked eyes as Ali broke one of the panes of glass in the door with the butt of his gun and turned the lock. He nodded to Katayoon and then eased past the opening. Mospoli watched Ali disappear into the house and then proceeded to the back, checking as he went. Minutes later, they met by the back door. The house was empty, and so was the yard. The barn was straight ahead, about a hundred feet back and off to the right. Hamza could see the solid thicket of tall cedars like a thin line on a carbon drawing far beyond the white fence that formed the corral. The horses were in the barn. They stepped cautiously around the flowerbeds and through the rain-soaked grass, watching each other's back. Hamza signaled for Katayoon to circle to the rear of the barn. He would go in through the side door, which was off to their right.

Angel was in the loft, dressed in black, with the crossbow loaded, ready to pierce the flesh of those who now threatened her life. She breathed heavily, and her heart thumped hard in her chest. The doors leading into the barn from the front and the side door could be easily illuminated with four large spotlights that were suspended from the rafters. They could be rotated and controlled from the loft above. When activated by the foot pedal, they could illuminate and blind any figure standing just inside either of the doors. She waited in the dark, poised and ready for the unlocked side door to open and for the figure to step inside. Then she would kill.

Henley killed the lights on Donlon's orders at the bend in the road and then drove to the gate. They waited and watched the house. There were no lights on, which didn't mean a hell of a lot. Then they noticed the door. They quickly exited and drew their guns.

The front door was open, left that way by Ali when he entered the house. If he had found her, he would have pumped her with lead from his 9 mm. Then he and Mospoli would have escaped in the cruiser off the pier in Ellisport.

Both Donlon and Henley entered the house through the front door and quietly checked the rooms.

Outside in back, along the side of the barn, Hamza slowly pushed the door open after finding it unlocked. It creaked ever so slightly. Ali smiled when it drew no response, thinking he would have to hunt her in the dark. Rather than give up easily, his prey was going to make a game of it. He wiped his eyes with his sleeve and then placed his right foot over the threshold. Nothing. He took a deep breath and held it and then quietly pulled his left leg over. He was inside. Ali slowly raised himself using the strength in his knees. The whites of his eyes shifted from side to side and then up towards the loft and then down again before looking straight ahead. He rotated the Ruger towards the stalls and the horses that were eerily quiet, which made him uneasy. If she was hiding among the horses, he would kill everything and then look for her body after. He wet his lips.

Suddenly, the lights came on, blinding him. Instinctively, he tried to shield his eyes from the lights. He shot wildly at the stalls, up towards the loft amid the noise from the horses, and then at the lights before the arrow struck. Ali dropped in a second, his body frozen and still—utterly still.

Angel watched him die and then quickly killed the lights, grabbing another loaded crossbow to her right, before jumping to the ground below. The horses were twirling wildly from the gunshots, snorting and grinding their teeth. Ignoring the dead body to her left, she moved swiftly to the large doors and flung them open. She then moved to the stalls and quickly released the horses into the corral.

Mospoli was on the other side of the barn when the stray bullets pierced the siding. It wasn't like Hamza to have so many misses, but he knew Ali better than anyone. He was good at his craft. One of them must have got her for sure. Katayoon moved rapidly from the corner towards the front of the barn before his shoes sunk in the soft mud, just narrowly escaping being hit by one of the flying doors. He pointed the Ruger towards the open door, the pelting rain soaking through to his light beige skin. He felt a chill. His heart pounded. He wiped his face with his shoulder.

The sound of gunfire and splitting cedar drew them

out. From just inside the house, Henley exited through the back door first. The horses were just now escaping their stalls and heading for the open corral. Donlon stood just inside the open back door before bolting past the porch and his partner, diving for any refuge he could find. He lay on the ground, having slid to a stop while Henley made it past the porch and stooped by a white post that formed part of the corral. They watched the swinging doors and the large opening to the barn and waited in the dark. Katayoon carefully eased past the corner, oblivious to the presence of the two FBI agents just beyond the white fencing. He called to his accomplice in a hushed voice.

"Ali." He could hear nothing over the heightened anxiety of the horses. He called again. "Ali."

Henley heard the voice and saw the silhouette and what he thought was a gun. He spoke first.

"FBI!"

Katayoon quickly fired off the first shot towards the voice, splitting a corner of the post just above Henley's head, narrowly missing him, forcing him to the ground. Donlon quickly moved to the corner of the barn. He crouched and looked through the crack between the door and the barn. Katayoon was not there. The thin man motioned for Henley to hold the front; he would move to the rear and take him from behind.

Donlon found the body of Ali Hamza by the side door. He quickly checked for a pulse and then moved back, past the door and down the long side while Katayoon moved back towards the corner from where he came and then backwards, heels first, toward the open field, his eyes oscillating from side to side. Katayoon hastily looked behind him. He believed he could move into the clump of trees that were just behind him and then take out Angelina Paletti and the FBI agents. If not, he would do it there, in the open. Henley moved from post to post and then to the corner of the barn using the door as a shield.

Angel was already by the barn door after the shot from Katayoon. She stooped and then crawled on her belly through the mixture of mud past the open door to the corner where she could see the tall Moroccan. With the aid of the night scope, she fired the bolt. Katayoon took it on the right side, just past the last rib, where it lodged itself behind his left shoulder blade. He staggered on his heels, trying to pull the trigger as the energy quickly drained from his body before he released his Ruger and fell backwards into the grass. Katayoon lay there with his eyes fixed towards the sky and the rain as it pelted his face. He was dead on impact. From the corner of the barn, Donlon saw him fall.

Henley moved past the doors and caught her lying in the mud.

"FBI! Don't move."

He moved towards her and pulled the crossbow from between her shoulders.

Donlon glanced back towards Henley, who had Angel up against the barn, and then he checked Katayoon for a pulse before walking over to where Henley and Paletti stood.

"You okay?"

"Yeah, I'm fine."

Henley cuffed her, and then they escorted her back into the house. Donlon went to the front door to look for Fischer. He turned on the light but saw no sign of Anita's blue BMW.

"Sit tight," he said and headed down the front stairs.

"Where you going?" shouted Henley.

"To look for Fischer."

The car could be replaced. She was fine except for a slight headache, a pounding heart, and a sprained left wrist, which was good. It would look more like a real accident. The two paper clips inside the buckle mechanism had worked their magic.

Dina sat numb in the driver's seat. She could feel something inside her but at the moment, she had no way of stopping it. She wasn't and hadn't prepared herself for what was about to happen, the oncoming shock as it swept over her after the car hit the tree. The sensation took over in seconds, freezing her body cold. Her heart raced and her breathing stopped, held in check by fear, fear of what was happening. The infusing shock washed over her in a single intense wave, like when a junkie injects and then feels the oncoming rush of the cocktail; then it ebbed slowly. She sat suspended for close to a minute. Her panic-stricken eyes stared into nothing and then closed tightly as she experienced the unnerving effects of the mild trauma. She waited uneasily for the experience to subside into something manageable. A minute later, only a faint tremor remained inside her. Mildly relieved, Dina felt something trickle just above her lips. Anxious, almost fearful, she wiped her nose with the back of her right hand, smearing her olive skin red from the wrist to the knuckles. She let out a deep breath, comforted that it was only a nosebleed. Slipping out from the shock, she turned the radio down and stared at the quiet reporter. She eased to her right, wincing as she moved, and she quickly felt his jugular with her right hand. He was still alive. The force of the airbag had not ripped his head off like she had envisioned, which was a shame. Dina pounded the steering wheel hard with her right hand.

"Damn it!"

She grabbed his bloodied hair, pushing his head hard against the side window, cursing him.

"You stupid fuck! You should never have told me you saw me there."

Her voice was smoky, but it wasn't the seductive or provocative type of a Lauren Bacall. It was the sinister type: vile, vulgar, demeaning, and full of rage.

"You malignant son-of-a-bitch!" Her anger seethed.

She looked for fresh blood, but there was none. She did it again, and then a couple of more times, cursing him each time until she could see his blood running down the glass. It looked like a psychiatrist's inkblot, the kind that had been jammed in front of her face over the years as they tried to find out what the hell was wrong with her. Satisfied, she unbuckled her seat belt and then crossed her right hand over her torso, her fingertips blindly scratching the leather until she found the door handle. She pulled and then pushed the door with her shoulder. She winced—it was her collarbone. The force of the impact had yanked the strap hard against her shoulder, wrenching the socket. Grabbing a quick breath, she exited the disabled BMW.

"Son-of-a-bitch!"

Now her knee hurt. *Even better*, she thought. The night air was pitch-black, the color of ink, and the roadway behind her was quiet. She limped slowly to the front of the Beamer, past the glowing left headlight and around the large tree, holding her left arm to inspect the damage, which caused her to smile. She then stood by the passenger door, staring past the crimson smudge that looked like a blurry watercolor at the slumped reporter. Something wasn't right. Something was missing.

Hurriedly, she searched wildly in the downpour and the bush, grabbing a short, thick log just off to the right of the car. Her left wrist hurt like hell. Grimacing from the pain and cradling the log with her left arm, Dina started smashing the side window until it cracked. *Not good enough.* She hit it again and again, muttering through her labored breathing as she smashed the window until it finally broke into pieces inside the car and over his slumped torso.

"If only you had left us alone, Fischer."

She pulled hard on the door with her good hand, grunting in the process, until finally it opened. Her wrist along with her sore knee had wasted precious minutes. Dina pushed back her wet hair, wiping the rain from her eyes.

"Now you're going to pay, you useless, festering, pustule. If only you had left us alone, none of this would be necessary."

She lit a cigarette with her gold lighter and held it between her lips, and then she leaned in, turning his body towards the driver's seat so she could carry it onto the forest floor. She talked while she labored under the weight that felt like a corpse. Her voice was strained.

"That Anita can be such a wuss. I'm thinking of getting rid of her. She's kind of useless, just like you, Fischer. I told her not to go see you at the hotel. I told her I was going to take care of you myself, just like I took care of our papa and all the others. But she wouldn't listen," she said sarcastically, grunting as she pulled on his body. "Now you have to pay for her stupidity. I know, Fischer. It doesn't seem fair, but what can I do?"

Dina placed her arms under his armpits and dragged him out, pulling him towards the front of the vehicle and away from the road. She stood over him, wincing from the pain. *Christ, it hurt!*

Teno Kostopoulos collapsed his cell and then flashed his badge to commandeer one of the vehicles from the deck of the ferry just before it was ready to leave after Donlon told him to take the road to the right. He would cut across using the side streets and then head back towards the terminal using the Westside Highway. One of them should be able to find Fischer and the blue Beamer.

Dina frantically paced the wet ground in a limp, smoking what was left of her cigarette, thinking of what to do with the comatose reporter. The FBI was on the island, which meant they could reappear at any time. Who knew what was going on at the house. If the assassins had shown up, they could be dead. So could the two agents. The flights of fantasy brought a sickly smile to her face, which then disappeared. Her sister could be dead too.

Dina stood over him and spat at him.

"You're such a fucking idiot, Fischer," she said in disgust, shaking her head, the cigarette tucked in the corner of her mouth. "Did you honestly think I was going to let you just leave?" she asked, reaching for the inside pocket of his jacket. "Did you honestly believe what I told you back at the house?" She laughed and then pulled the recorder from his pocket and removed the cassette before tossing the recorder toward the cliff. "You're so gullible," she said, stripping the tape from the cassette. "You're just as stupid as the rest of them. You actually believed I would finger my sister? You're a real dumb-ass. Some reporter you turned out to be. Where's the challenge, Fischer? Where?" she yelled, taunting him, smiling a scornful glance before stepping over him. She pulled the lighter from her pocket and arched her back to keep the tape from getting wet and then held the flame over it and watched it shrivel and burn before tossing it aside. "You stupid fuck." Dina kicked him hard in the ribs with her good leg, cracking four of them on his left side. She almost lost her balance from swinging her leg but steadied herself by grabbing a branch. "What did you think of my impersonation?" she asked with a sinister smirk. "Did you like the tears?" she asked again, smiling, pulling the rain from her face and then jerking her head back to flip the rain from her hair. "Pretty convincing, huh? I cried for you, and I don't cry," she yelled angrily, shaking her head. Her yelling turned to laughter, only this time it was in defiance. It was deep and throaty, from the belly of her soul. "But maybe that was Anita." Again she laughed.

Dina threw her cigarette towards the bush and then went back to the passenger seat for a piece of glass. She would cut his jugular and watch him die.

Teno drove slowly along the Westside Highway, checking the road and the bushes for the reporter and Anita Paletti. He was almost at the top of the bluff when he noticed light coming from somewhere inside the trees to his right. He noticed the tire tracks in his headlights just off the road leading into the bushes beyond the shoulder. He pulled to the side of the road and flicked on his high beams so he could see the entrance created through the trees and the low brush. It looked like the opening to a cave. Teno left the car running on the shoulder and quickly headed for the blue Beamer. He noticed the back of Anita Paletti, a soft outline just to the right, kneeling in front of the car by the large tree. He rushed towards her.

"Jesus Christ! Are you okay?" he asked, touching her shoulder.

Caught off guard, Dina shuddered and then quickly pushed the shard of glass between herself and Fischer with her right hand, hiding it from Teno's view. Teno noticed Fischer's torso, propped up against Paletti. He felt Paletti's quake.

"Sorry if I scared you."

"He's unconscious," said a startled Dina. She was looking up with water dripping into her eyes. "We need to get him to a hospital."

"What about you?"

"I'm okay. Here. Take his head. I'll go see if I have a blanket in the car."

"Let's get him out of this rain first. We can put him in my car," said Teno.

"I don't think we should move him. He's hurt really bad. My cell phone is in the car. I can call for help."

"Here," he said, reaching into his pocket. "You can use mine."

"It's okay. I have to get the blanket anyway."

Dina pulled the latch just inside the door and then limped to the back, her anger seething to the surface under her quick breaths. She opened the trunk and pulled out the crossbow, expanding and locking its wings, and then she inserted the bolt, all the while shrouded under the protection of the open trunk. After a quick glance and with some difficulty, she stepped to the side, just past the trunk. In the open, she cradled it gently across her left forearm and then aimed it at the back of Kostopoulos who was checking on Fischer. The tip drooped slightly from the pain in her shoulder, and her long, quiet shadow extended to the base of his shoes, which were folded under his buttocks. If she could manage it, Teno wouldn't feel a thing.

"Drop it, Paletti! FBI."

Donlon stood some twenty feet off the shoulder with the Beamer straight ahead. Teno was slightly to his right, his eyes fixed through the slight glare of the headlights. The thin man's arms were raised and extended, holding his service revolver. His vehicle was parked at the top of the bluff, facing Teno's with the lights off, its arrival muffled by the steady torrent.

"Don't make me kill you, Paletti. Drop the bow, or I swear I'll drop you where you stand."

Dina looked at Teno, who was still cradling Fischer's head. Dina stood uncommitted, pulling ever so slowly on the stock until it was tight against her torso to where her muscles were hard as bone. Then quickly, as best she could, she turned towards Donlon, her index finger set hard against the trigger that could send the bolt to lightning speed in a flash; she tried to raise the bow and support her weight on a forming crouch and a sore knee all at the same time.

Donlon fired rapidly three times. The exploding gunpowder immediately ripped the night air, echoing hard through the trees and beyond.

The first bullet struck Dina in the side of the shoulder, forcing her arm limp along with an instant cry, her burning shoulder rendered useless. Instantly, the crossbow sprung from her hand, sending it outward, slamming against the side of the car from the spinning crouch that was now disintegrating, but not before the bolt was released, sending it somewhere into the bushes to Donlon's left. The second bullet penetrated the lower portion of her right forearm and then her stomach. The third hit her in the middle of her chest, just to the left, sending her slim frame backwards.

Donlon walked over to where she was, approaching her from the left. Dina was on her back. She stared at him through the downpour, coughing and gurgling as her blood started to ooze slowly from her mouth and over her lips. Anita's dark eyes were wide and confused like a child's, her mind and body in a state of shock. Donlon stood over her, the gun at his side, and watched as she slowly closed her eyes.

Chapter 54

She sat in the only chair, reading a book, and if it wasn't for how she felt about him, she would not be there. She was in the hall just outside his room after being asked to leave while they checked him over. She had been there for almost an hour.

Miles was finally awake after being in a coma for almost five days, falling in and out of consciousness for brief moments of life; before he finally opened his eyes and left them there. Veronica was sitting next to him when the first real signs of life began to appear. She noticed his eyes twitching, and when he let out a few groans, she hastily retreated from the room and called the nurse.

"You can go in now."

"How is he?" Veronica asked.

"He's going to be fine, but don't overtax him. If he gets tired, then maybe you might want to let him rest. Other than that, you can go talk to him."

"Thank you."

Veronica hesitated, watching as the doctor made his way down the hall along with rest of the entourage, before pushing the door open. She approached the bed.

"How are you feeling?" she asked. She touched his hand and gently squeezed it.

Instead of lying flat, Miles was partly elevated on the bed. The tubes and machines that were put in place to keep him alive until they got inside and repaired the damage that Anita had done were still there. The tubes were hooked up to monitors that beeped and blipped and shot blue and green lines across their screens. His right leg was in a cast and suspended over the bed with the aid of pulleys. The tube that they had stuck in the left side of his rib cage was still there, draining his left lung of fluid so he could breathe. It connected to a box that was tethered to the side of the bed by a strap. It would be out in another day or so. His neck was in a brace and would be for another month, if not longer, while the vertebrae healed. His head was partially bandaged with white gauze from the surgery to relieve the pressure that had built up inside his brain. An oxygen mask covered his mouth to help him breathe. When he saw her, his eyes lit up. He quickly pulled the mask away from his face.

"Fine, I guess."

He smiled at her and then winced. His ribs were still healing, which made it difficult to breathe without experiencing some sort of discomfort. He kept his breaths short to minimize the pain.

"You're looking good."

"Gee, thanks." He almost laughed, but the pain in his ribs stopped him.

"You had us all scared," she said.

"It wasn't on purpose."

"I know." She hesitated and said, "Pat calls every day to see how you are. The *Tribune* is picking up the tab for your room and anything else you need that isn't already covered. They all send their best wishes."

"That's nice." He grabbed a breath. "I didn't expect to see you here."

"Do you want me to go?"

"I could die if you did."

She smiled and squeezed his hand a little tighter.

"I guess I better stay then."

There was a pause in the conversation as they searched for words.

"You got lots of flowers," Veronica finally said, taking her hand away.

"I can see that," he said as his eyes spanned the room as best they could. "It looks like a flower shop in here."

"Your mother and sister are here."

"I don't see them. Where are they?"

"They'll be back a little later. They went to get something to eat."

"How are they holding up?"

"They're worried, but they'll be fine once they see you're awake."

"I guess I put everyone through hell," he said between breaths.

"It's okay. It's not your fault. The doctor said you're going to be fine once everything heals."

The reassurance was soothing, but Miles fell suddenly quiet. Erin's name hadn't been mentioned in the same sentence as that of his mother and sister. He was sad to think that maybe she hadn't shown up, but that would be just like her not to show. She had a stubborn streak a mile long. In his heart he knew the relationship was over, but to not show up at his bedside punctuated what he had known for a long time.

"What's wrong?"

"I was going to say something…"

Veronica knew what was coming. This was going to be awkward, especially coming from her.

"She didn't come, Miles, if that's what you were going to ask."

For the moment, both could hear a pin drop.

"Oh."

"I didn't want to be the one to tell you. I was hoping your mother and sister would be here so that they could tell you themselves. The *Tribune* offered to fly her out here, but she declined. She said she couldn't make it because of the baby being premature and all. She said she had to be there because she was breastfeeding. I'm sorry, Miles."

Miles went silent for a moment while he collected his thoughts.

"I know it hurts," she said, placing her hand on top of his. She could see the disappointment in his eyes.

"It's okay," he said, grabbing a short breath. "I guess it says a lot about our relationship. I shouldn't be so surprised." He took another breath. "I thought she would at least show up."

"Do you want me to leave?"

Miles hesitated before he answered and then said, "No. I'd rather you stay. I'll be fine."

"Are you sure?"

Slowly. "Maybe not now, but I will be." He reached for her hand and quickly changed subjects. "So tell me, how long have you been here?"

"Since Saturday afternoon. Donlon called Lynch, and Pat called me. I grabbed the earliest flight I could."

"What about work?"

"I told Pat I was taking the rest of my vacation time. I told him I'd see him in a couple of weeks."

"Do you think that's a good idea?" he asked, wincing. "I don't know when I'm going to be getting out of here. You don't have to stay, you know."

"I know, but I heard Seattle is lovely this time of year."

"So where are you staying?"

"Over at the Sorrento. I took over your room."

"Nice."

"Your mother and sister are staying there, too, courtesy of the *Tribune*. Pat made the arrangements."

"It's a nice place," he said.

"It'll do. Can I get you anything? A glass of water? I

can even get you a Coke if you like. It's just down the hall."

"No. I'm fine."

"Do you remember anything about Friday night? The doctor said you might suffer some memory loss."

There was no reply from Miles.

"It's okay. We don't have to if you don't want to. We can talk about something else."

"No, its fine. It's just that everything seems a little foggy. I remember we had just left the ferry, and...we were headed for Angelina Paletti's house. I remember Anita was driving...Donlon and Henley were in front of us." He paused and then said, "The last thing I remember was the car going off the road...but I'm not sure. By the way, how is she?"

"She's dead, Miles. Anita tried to kill you. If Donlon hadn't shown up when he did, she would have killed both you and agent Kostopoulos. Donlon had to shoot her. She died at the scene. Do you remember hitting the tree at all?"

"We hit a tree?"

"You and Anita went off the road in the downpour and struck a tree. The impact of the airbag knocked you unconscious. They believe she deliberately tried to kill you. Donlon said he thinks she purposely broke the side window because the glass was found inside the vehicle instead of on the outside. If you had hit your head hard enough, the force of the blow would have sent the glass outwards, not inwards. They found two paper clips in the buckle mechanism, which is probably why your seat belt didn't work. She was hoping the airbag would kill you. That's why they think she intentionally ran her vehicle off the road. Do you remember Agent Teno Kostopoulos?"

"Vaguely."

"Well, he said that he found a piece of glass just behind you when Paletti asked him to care for you while she went to get you a blanket. He believes she was going to cut your throat. If he hadn't come along, she would have cut you and you would have bled to death. Donlon said the only way the piece of glass could have gotten there was if she put it there herself."

"So you talked to Donlon?"

"He checks in every day to see how you are. He called me while I was waiting out in the hall."

"I guess Donlon's pissed at me?" Again he winced, grimacing from the pointed pain that filled his left lung.

She laughed softly. "Kind of. Donlon said he and Teno saved your ass. He said hopefully you'll have a little more respect for him and the FBI the next time you screw around on your own."

"What did Pat do about the story?"

"He let Haskills take it over."

"Haskills?"

"Yes, but not without some help from Tony and me. The full story didn't get into the paper until Tuesday. The *Tribune* ran what they could until then. They saved you a copy back at the office."

"Have you seen it?" Miles asked.

"Not yet, but I had Laura read it to me. That anonymous caller called back after she heard about the car accident on the Saturday morning news. She said she tried your cell phone, and when you didn't answer it, she called the *Tribune*."

"Who did she talk to?"

"One of the guys from the morning staff. They called Pat, and Pat called Haskills. Haskills flew out to meet with her. Tony filled him in before he left. Haskills met up with me at the hotel, and I helped with what I knew before he went to meet with her. Mercedes Browne filled in the gaps."

"So that's the lady's name," Miles said.

"It's kind of a cool name, don't you think?" Veronica asked.

"I guess. So what did this Mercedes Brown...have to say?"

"It seems she knew more than what she told Tony over the phone. She acknowledged it was Anita Paletti who was the person with the multiple personalities."

"Why didn't...this Mercedes Browne tell us everything from the beginning?"

"According to her, she didn't want to get involved. She was thinking about her children and the impact it would have on them if she became the center of attention in a murder investigation. She didn't want to lose her job."

"It makes sense, I guess," Miles said. "So where is she now?"

"She decided to quit her job for Dr. Jacob Van Veen on Monday rather than wait and be fired. Eventually it was going to get out anyway, so she quit, but that was after she decided to talk to us. Pat said she felt morally obligated, feeling she owed the reporter who almost lost his life."

"What about the tape?" he asked, taking in a short breath. "I made a tape when I went to see Anita. What happened to it?"

"Donlon found the tape next to you, but Anita had already gotten to it. She destroyed the tape, but from what you told Donlon on the ferry, they were able to piece most of it together. Donlon believes it was Dina Paletti who was talking to you that night. We assumed Dina made up that stuff about Angel because she knew her sister was a safe out. Donlon figured she was only buying time until she could figure out how to get rid of you. When Carboni was killed in his hotel room, it gave her the opportunity to kill you without arousing suspicion."

"So Donlon's talked to this Browne woman?"

"Yes."

"What about Anita's sister?"

"She called us, if you can believe it. She wanted to talk to whoever was going to write the story because she wanted to make sure the facts were correct. She verified everything we had on the family history, but that was all—nothing about the circumstances involving the death of her father. Haskills asked her, but she offered the usual no comment."

"But she's under suspicion?"

"For the crossbow killings? Seems like it but we'll have to wait and see. They seem to think she may have been involved in some way. Donlon told me to tell you to give him a call when you feel better."

She was smiling sweetly.

"What's that smile for?"

"It seems he's grown quite fond of you. He said he would help you out if there were any new developments that linked Angel to her sister's killing spree. But he also told me to tell you to stay out of their business. Just a warning."

"The man has a chip on his shoulder."

"He also told me to tell you that they figured out what the cigarette paper was doing in Carboni's wallet. Carboni must have found one of the pieces on the roof of the hardware store in Tweeksbury. They checked the airlines and found out that Carboni was in Tweeksbury just before he showed up at the *Tribune*. They called the hardware store and found out that he'd been snooping around on the roof. When the FBI searched Angel's grounds, they found butts in one of the pastures. Ned, Angel's neighbor, confirmed what you told Donlon, that he saw Carboni leaving Angel's property. When he broke into your room and found the notepad, that's what led him to Angelina Paletti. That's the theory behind the story."

"But how does Donlon know…that it was Angel that Carboni suspected as the killer?"

"Do you remember Donlon telling you about the phone call Carboni made just before he was killed?"

He closed his eyes. "Vaguely."

"Donlon believes that phone call got him killed. Whoever he was talking to made a return call to the room next to Carboni's. Donlon believes they're the ones who killed him in his sleep. While you were taking the ferry, they had taken Bruno's rental car and hijacked a boat from one of the marinas close by, killing the attendant. They found his body in the bay along with the boat. When Henley and Donlon got to Angelina's place, they found the front door open. While Anita was taking care of you, they were searching the house. That's when they heard gunshots coming from the back. It was the same two men that Angelina's neighbor saw following Carboni when he left her property. A skirmish ensued, and they were both killed, but not by the FBI."

"Who killed them then?" Miles asked.

"Angelina."

"Wow."

"I know," replied Veronica.

"So that's why Donlon thinks Angel might be involved."

"He didn't really say why, but I guess that has something to do with it."

"Did Browne mention Anita's sister at all?"

"Not that I know of."

Miles was silent for a moment, thinking as best he could as to what it all meant.

"Is something wrong?" Veronica asked.

"I was just thinking. If it wasn't for that lady…"

"Mercedes Browne?"

"Yeah, Mercedes Browne," he repeated. "If it wasn't for her making that initial phone call, Anita would have gotten away with it." He hesitated, looking at her. "Christ! She just about pulled it off. She was in the clear. She almost committed the perfect murder."

"True, but it really wasn't her."

"What do you mean?"

"She was sick, Miles. It's too bad nobody could help her."

"I guess that's it then. It's all over." He took a slow, deep breath before adding, "I guess I owe you?"

"Well," she said, "I do remember you mentioning something about a dinner."

"When did I say that?"

"About a week ago."

He tried to look serious. "Are you sure?"

Her face smiled instantly. "I'm positive."

"Do you have a place in mind?"

"There's this nice, cozy restaurant in the south of Spain I'd like…"

"Spain. You couldn't pick someplace closer?"

"After you get better, of course."

He smiled. The thought of going to Europe was intriguing.

"Perfect."

Epilogue

THREE MONTHS LATER...

Veronica was sitting at her desk when she saw Donlon walking through the newsroom, past the rows of desks, headed in her direction. Henley was with him, walking just behind him as usual. Veronica quickly left her chair and leaned through the doorway of Miles's office.

"I think you have a visitor."

Miles was at his desk, his nose glued to the computer screen, working on the Avery Croft file that had been ignored for the past three months. Miles was back to being himself. The injuries that he had suffered at the hands of Anita were all healed. Erin had filed for a divorce, with Miles's blessing. They had been to the courthouse three times since they could not agree on what to do about their assets. Their relationship was now one of acrimony, with Erin pushing to get as much as she could. The trip to Spain was on hold until everything was over, but not their relationship. It was growing stronger, but they were keeping it low-key, especially around the office.

"Who is it?"

Before she could answer, Donlon was already beside her.

"Ms. Hughes. It's nice to see you again. How's our boy doing?"

Veronica stepped away from the door and gestured towards Miles.

"See for yourself."

Miles got up to greet him.

"Donlon."

"You busy?"

"No. Come on in. Have a seat."

"We heard you just got back, so we thought we'd drop by, but we can't stay. We have to be in New Orleans before tomorrow. We just came by to bring you up to speed on what's happening with Angelina Paletti."

Miles sat on the edge of his desk and folded his arms in front of him.

"We've decided to let it go. We don't have enough to prove she had anything to do with any of the murders. The DA turned it down."

"I guess you can't win them all."

"We figure Anita acted on her own. We couldn't get her sister to acknowledge that she took the flight to the Caribbean instead of Anita, but I believe you had it right."

"I heard about our Mr. Pitt."

"Yeah, he wasn't so lucky. We're trying to get him extradited back to the U.S."

"How's that going?"

"It takes time, but we'll get him. How about you? How are you doing?"

Miles held his hands up. "Fine, I guess. Everything still works."

"Good." He nodded towards Henley. "I guess we should get going then."

Miles watched the thin man turn and head towards the door.

"Before you go, I have to ask you something that's been bugging me since we've never had the chance to talk."

"What's that?"

"When these murders started happening, did you ever once interview Angelina?"

"Yeah. A couple of times."

"So you knew they were identical twins?"

"Yeah. Why?"

"No reason."

Donlon looked at him suspiciously. "You didn't know, did you, Fischer?"

"No. Not until later."

"You should have listened to us," he said, shaking his head.

"What about Anita? Did you ever interview her?"

"Yeah, but we couldn't pin anything on her. She had an air-tight alibi each time."

"Let me guess—her sister, right?"

Donlon kind of nodded his way. "You could say that."

Donlon turned and headed for the door. Henley followed and nudged him gently.

"Aren't you going to tell him?"

"Tell me what?" asked Miles.

Donlon glared at Henley and then turned and faced Fischer.

"We found out that Rachel wasn't really Anita's daughter."

Miles grunted. "What do you mean?"

"We did some checking around and discovered that Anita was never pregnant. According to her doctor, she wasn't able to conceive."

"But if Rachael wasn't Anita's, then whose was she?"

"Angelina's."

"How do you know?"

"The DNA of identical twins is the same. You can't tell them apart, much like the twins themselves. Rachel's DNA matches both of the sisters. We found out that Angelina was pregnant soon after she left the army.

Because Anita couldn't have children, we suspect that when she delivered the baby, she signed off as Anita. That way Anita could have a family."

"But when Angel signed the birth papers, she would have had to sign as Maria Zimmerman."

"That's right, but she wasn't married yet. Anita was only engaged. She was still going under the name of Paletti."

"But Anita entered the army using his father's name."

"Yes, but documents show that Anita changed her name while in the army. I guess Angel told her what she had done and Anita did the same."

"But somebody would have known that it wasn't hers. What about the families?"

"After the sisters left the army, they went to live in Tel Aviv where nobody knew them. As for family, I don't know. If she was engaged and depending on when they saw them, it could have easily been Anita's."

Miles let out a deep breath. "Hmm. I guess it's true what they say then."

"What's that, Fischer?"

"That blood is thicker than water."

"In this case, yes."

Donlon turned and headed out the door.

"I'll see ya, Donlon."

Donlon, with Henley in tow, had this to offer: "Christ, I hope not!"

"There you go again, Donlon," said Miles, moving towards the door, watching him leave. "You have that chip on your shoulder again. You gotta get rid of it."

"See ya, Miles."

AUTHOR'S NOTE

All characters herein are purely fictional. Any similarity to a real person is purely coincidental. There is no Tweeksbury in Idaho, no Eastbrook in Massachusetts. Nor, for that matter, is there a place by the name of Chester Junction in Massachusetts or Whatley in Missouri. Some of the other cities can be found on a map.

In creating this work of fiction, some names were used that represent real businesses to provide a sense of realism, but the reality goes no further than the use of their names. There is and was no intention on the part of the creator to impinge or imply anything that would cast doubt as to their professionalism or their standing in their community. Their use is solely for the purposes of entertaining the reader.

ABOUT THE AUTHOR

This is the author's first novel. The author lives in New Westminster, BC.